Goldenhand

Goldenhand

GARTH
NIX

HOT
KEY
BOOKS

To Anna, Thomas and Edward,
and to all my family and friends

First published in Great Britain in 2016 by HOT KEY BOOKS
80–81 Wimpole St, London W1G 9RE
www.hotkeybooks.com

This paperback edition published 2017

A CIP catalogue record for this book
is available from the British Library.

ISBN: 978-1-4714-0446-7
also available as an ebook
1

Typeset in Obelisk ITC by
Palimpsest Book Production Ltd, Falkirk, Stirlingshire

Printed and bound by Clays Ltd, St Ives Plc

Hot Key Books is an imprint of Bonnier Zaffre Ltd,
a Bonnier Publishing company
www.bonnierpublishing.com

The Great Rift
High Steppe
Athask Mountains
High Steppe
Seasonal Flood
Low Steppe
Field Market
Ferry
Greenwash Bridge
River Greenwash
Red Oasis
Yellowsands
Elbin
Northwest Desert
Mrule Oasis
Lospoth
Navis
The Nailway
Clayr's Glacier
Boom Hook
Mt. Shulle
Estwael
Sindle
Belisaere
Belis Mouth
Sea of Saere
Ilgard
Metal Canal
Upper Ratterlin
Winding Post
Orchyre
Ponstayn
Great Forest
Yanyl
Port Nidlyn
Mt. Aunden
R. Yanyl
Aunden
Hafmet
High Bridge
Olmond
Ridmoor
Gardil
The Westway
Grynhold
The Old Kingdom
Chasel
Onceet Pass
Beardy Point
The Crumbs
Great Sickle Wood
Callibe
N
W
E
S
Ganel
Bay of Mountains
Qyrre
Uppside
Roble's Town
Nestowe
Holehallow
Red Lake
Edge
Long Cliffs
Abhorsen's House
R. Ratterlin
Ratterlin Delta
The Steps
Cloven Crest
Western Light
Old North Rd
The Wall
Line of the Lost (No Southern Passage)
The Perimeter
Crossing Point
Eastern Light
Forvale
Prohibited Zone
Bain
Wyverly
Wyverly College
Forwin Mill
To Ancelstierre proper
Ancelstierre
Bain High Rd.
0 50 100 200 400
miles

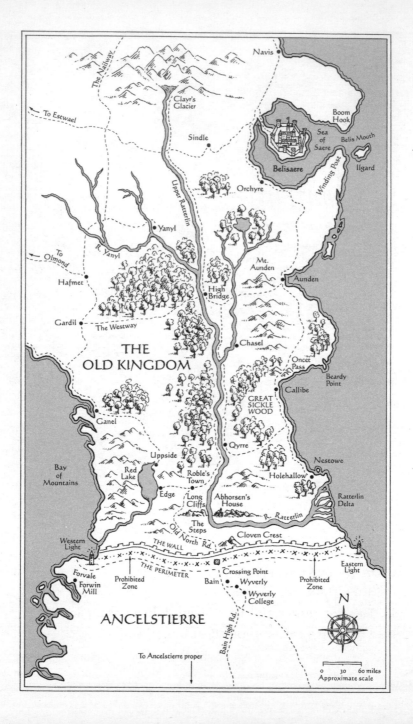

contents

prologue

In the Sixth Precinct, the inexorable current of the river that flowed through Death slowed almost to a stop. It was a natural gathering place for the Dead who hoped to go no further, and for those who strived to claw their way back through five gates and precincts and out into the living world again.

Amid the myriad Dead who waited, and hungered, and fought against the compulsion to go deeper into Death, there were two *living* people. Necromancers, of course, for no others could be here while still alive. At least alive for the moment, for unwary necromancers going deeper into Death than their knowledge and their strength allowed were the particular prey of the Greater Dead who prowled the precinct, ever eager to consume any scrap of Life that would aid them in their desperate desire to live again.

But in this case the Greater Dead stayed well away, knowing the two women were most uncommon necromancers. Both wore bandoliers containing the seven bells, necromantic tools of power infused with Free Magic, but their bells had mahogany handles rather than ebony, and the silver bell-metal crawled with bright Charter marks.

That alone declared their identity, but it was confirmed by their apparel: armoured coats made from many overlapping plates of a material called gethre, with surcoats over the armour. One wore deep blue, sprinkled with many silver keys, the other a coat also with silver keys upon the blue, but quartered with golden stars on a field of green.

The silver keys were the blazon of the Abhorsen, foe and nemesis of all things Dead, and this was the Abhorsen Sabriel, fifty-third of the line. With her was her apprentice Lirael, the Abhorsen-in-Waiting, who also bore the stars of the Clayr to show her own unique heritage: she was not only an Abhorsen, but also a Remembrancer, who could See deep into the past, just as the Clayr could See the future.

'She has evaded us,' said Sabriel, looking out over the grey and dismal river. She could feel the presence of the Dead, many of whom were lurking under the water, hoping to avoid her attention. But they were all lesser things than the one she and Lirael had hunted a long and weary way. The desperately scrabbling small things about would weaken in time, and go on, without the need for interference.

'You're sure it was Chlorr of the Mask?' asked Lirael. She looked around more warily than Sabriel. This was only the eleventh time she had come into Death, and only the second time she had come so far, though once she had been very far indeed, to the border of the Ninth Gate. She was very grateful that Sabriel was by her side, while still not being quite able to quell a feeling of great loss. The last time Lirael had passed through the Sixth Precinct, her great friend the Disreputable Dog had accompanied her, lending the young woman great comfort and strength.

But the Dog was gone forever.

Lirael still felt the pain of that loss, and the dread, dismal days that had followed the binding of Orannis were never far from her thoughts. The only slight note of cheer from that time had come from Nicholas Sayre, who had told her how the Dog had sent him back from this same cold river, albeit on the very fringe of Life. Lirael would have liked to talk to Nicholas more about this, particularly if he had seen which way the Dog went, grasping at the hope the wily hound had not gone towards the final gate.

In fact Lirael would have liked to see more of Nick in general, for he was one of the very few people she had ever met who she had immediately liked and had felt some unspoken connection with, or at least the potential for something of the sort.

But Nick was gone too. Not dead, thank the Charter. But returned to the Ancelstierran regions far south of the Wall, to get him away from the pernicious magics of the Old Kingdom. He needed to escape the legacy of both Free Magic and the Charter, to live a normal life, Lirael told herself.

She must forget him.

'It was definitely Chlorr,' said Sabriel, recapturing Lirael's momentarily wandering attention. The older woman wrinkled her nose. 'Over time, you'll learn to differentiate the various types of the Dead, and individuals strong enough to earn the description of Greater Dead. You sense it now, I suspect.'

'Yes . . .' said Lirael.

It was true she could feel the Dead all around, with that strange sense she had not known she possessed for much of her life. She narrowed her eyes and tried to sort through the different sensations, for that sense was something beyond sight and hearing, touch and smell, but it drew upon them all. There was the hint of something more powerful amid all the Dead about them, but it was a fading trace, like the scent of smoke from a fire extinguished some time before.

'Has Chlorr gone deeper into Death?' asked Lirael. She hoped the slight quaver in her voice was not apparent. She was quite prepared to go on if it was necessary. She only hoped it wasn't.

'No,' said Sabriel. 'I think she was too fast for us, and went sideways and then *back* towards Life. But to do that . . .'

She stopped talking and looked around again, intent upon the placid though still treacherous river. Lirael watched her, once again marvelling that the famous Abhorsen, Queen of the Old Kingdom and the subject of so many stories that were already becoming legends, was also her relatively newly discovered half-sister. A twenty-years-older half-sister, though Lirael felt that after the events of the summer past, she was no longer so young herself.

'To do that,' repeated Sabriel, 'Chlorr must be anchored in Life.'

'Anchored in Life?' asked Lirael, startled. Chlorr of the Mask had been an ancient necromancer until she was physically slain by Sabriel. But she had not gone beyond the Ninth Gate, instead becoming a very powerful Greater Dead creature, a thing of fire and shadow that needed no flesh to inhabit out in the living world.

'I destroyed the shape she wore,' said Sabriel. 'But even at that time I wondered. She was very old, hundreds of years old. I could feel that age, a leaden weight within the far younger skin . . .'

She stopped talking and turned about in a circle, sniffing, her eyes narrowed. Lirael looked around too, listening to the faint sounds of movement in the river, sounds that would normally be obscured by the rush of the current.

'There are various ways to extend a life,' continued Sabriel, after a moment. 'I was too busy to consider which she had used, and became busier still, as you know. But now I think she must be connected to some anchor in Life. That is why she did not fully obey my bells, and did not die the final death.'

'B-but how . . .' stammered Lirael. 'How could she do that?'

'There are a number of methods, all of them foul,' mused Sabriel. 'Perhaps . . . I must tell you how Kerrigor did so, and there are passages from *The Book of the Dead* which speak to the point, though it may not show those pages to you. As always, it has its own ideas of when the reader is ready . . .'

'It certainly does,' said Lirael, who, despite considerable

familiarity with sorcerous texts from her time as a librarian, was still unsettled by the way the contents of that strange tome were never quite the same and how, reading it, she often felt the same bone-deep chill she felt in the river now.

Lirael spoke slowly, half her mind still focused on her sense of Death, and the Dead. There were things going on, small movements, like flotsam on the tide . . . it took her a few seconds to work out that the dozens and dozens of lesser Dead were gathering together, massing to form a host.

'We shall have to find out, in due course, but Chlorr by herself is not of primary importance,' said Sabriel. 'Not now Orannis is bound again, and provided she stays in the North. There are other, more immediate problems. Some at hand, I would say.'

Sabriel unfastened the strap that held her favourite bell quiet on her bandolier, her fingers closing on the clapper, bright Charter marks swarming from the silver bell to her hand. She smiled a slight, quirking smile. 'I think Chlorr has left us something of a surprise, even an ambush. It is interesting that these lesser things are more afraid of her than they are of us. We must correct that view.'

Lirael barely had time to draw her sword and a bell of her own before the Dead attacked, particularly as her right hand moved slowly. It was still being perfected, the new hand that had been made for her by Sameth of clever metalwork and considerable Charter Magic.

There were more than seventy Dead creatures reluctantly moving to attack. Most were warped and misshapen from too long in Death, their original shapes long lost, spirit flesh unable to maintain even a vaguely human shape. Some were squat, as if compressed to fit some awful container; some were stretched long. They had too many teeth, and shifted jaws, and talons or teeth in place of fingernails. Red fire burned in sockets where their eyes once were, and came dripping from their gaping, overstretched mouths.

Lurching and hopping, darting and zigzagging, they came, building courage as they approached, taking hope from the sheer numbers of their companions. They began to growl and slobber and shriek, thinking perhaps this time they would feast on Life!

But as the throng of Dead finally charged, Sabriel rang Saraneth in a continuous figure-of-eight motion above her head. The pure, commanding tone of the bell cut through all the foul noises of the Dead, and at the same time the Abhorsen spoke. Not shouting, just speaking firmly, perhaps as she might to a child, or to a horse. Her words were backed by an implacable will, and the strength of the bell.

'Be still.'

The charge faltered and came to a stop, Dead creatures stumbling over one another as those closer came first under the compulsion of the bell. Their cries faded, voices quailed. Even their fiery eyes grew dimmer, quenched by the power of Saraneth in the hand of the Abhorsen.

Sabriel flipped Saraneth and caught it by its clapper, silencing the bell. But its voice remained, a long-sustained echo, and the Dead did not move.

'Good,' said Sabriel, noting the bell the younger woman held. 'Kibeth. The right bell will often come to your hand, unsought. Send them on, on to the final death.'

Lirael nodded, and rang Kibeth the Walker, a lively, leaping bell, so eager to sound that she had to exert herself to ring it true and not be carried away herself. And as always now she had to steel herself, for in every peal she also heard the memory of a joyful dog's bark, pleased at the prospect of going for a walk.

The Dead began to sob and groan under Kibeth's spell, and then as one they turned and began to shuffle. Lirael kept the bell ringing, and the Dead started to run and hop and skip, slowly moving into a great circle, a horrible parody of some village dance as performed by monsters.

Twice this long parade of Dead trod around in an ever-closing circle, compelled by Kibeth; the third time the Sixth Gate opened under them with a great roar, drawing them down and onwards, never to return.

chapter one

an unlikely messenger at the gate

Greenwash Bridge, North Castle, the Old Kingdom

Winter was hard in the North, beyond the borders of the Old Kingdom. The nomadic clans who lived on the steppe would seek the lower reaches before the snow began to fall, leaving the high plateau. But there was one tribe that did not roam so far, whatever the season. They lived in the mountains in the northwest, beyond the steppe, and did not ride or revere horses, though they would eat them if the opportunity presented itself.

These mountain-folk were easily distinguished from the other clans because they did not wear the long slit tunics and silk sashes of their nomadic cousins. Instead they favoured jerkins and breeches made of patchwork goatskin stitched with thick red thread, and rich cloaks from the fur of the athask, the huge cats that roamed their peaks and gave the clan its name. For weddings, feasts and their own funerary pyres, they donned heavy bracelets and earrings made of alluvial gold from their mountain rivers.

It was unusual to see any of these folk outside their mountains at all, let alone hundreds of leagues to the south and east, so the guards on the gate tower of the Greenwash Bridge Company's North Castle were understandably both curious and cautious when one such fur-wrapped, red-thread goatskin-patched nomad appeared as if from nowhere out of a swirling wet snowfall on a spring afternoon and shouted up at them, asking permission to cross the bridge into the Old Kingdom.

'You're no merchant,' called down the younger guard, who'd set his crossbow on the merlon, ready to snatch up and fire. 'So you have no business to cross the bridge.'

'I'm a messenger!' bawled the nomad. She was even younger than the young guard, perhaps having seen only sixteen or seventeen of the harsh winters of her homeland. Her lustrous skin was acorn brown, her hair black, worn in a plaited queue that was wound several times around her head like a crown, and her dark eyes appealing. 'I claim the message right!'

'What's that, Haral?' the younger guard asked his elder quietly. He'd only been with the Bridge Company eleven months, but Haral was an old-timer. She'd served twenty-six years, back into the bad old times before King Touchstone and the Abhorsen Sabriel restored order to the Old Kingdom. Before that restoration, the bridge and its castles on the northern and southern banks and the fort in the middle of the river had essentially been a fortress constantly under siege. It had been much more peaceful since, though there had been great trouble in the south during the last summer.

'The tribes give messengers immunity from challenges and feuds and the like,' said Haral. She looked down at this unusual – and unusually attractive – messenger, and thought it was just as well the younger guard wasn't here by himself. People who wanted to cross the bridge were not always what they seemed. Or were not actually people at all, apart from their outward form. 'But I didn't know the mountain-folk followed that custom. I've only ever seen them a couple of times before, and they were traders, going northwards to home.'

'Who's the message for?' called out the young guard. His name was Aronsin, but everyone just called him Aron.

'Must I tell you?' asked the young nomad. It was an odd question, said as if she was uncertain of the etiquette involved, or unfamiliar with dealing with other people in general.

'It would be a start,' said Aron. He glanced at Haral, sensing her suddenly straighten up. She was peering out into the falling snow, looking into the distance, not at the nomad below.

'Thought I saw movement,' said Haral. She took a perspective glass from her belt, extended it, and held it to her eye. Having one nomad pop up almost at the gate could be blamed on the snow and the fading light, but to have any more get so close would be a dereliction of duty.

'So who's the message for?' asked Aron. He smiled down at the mountain girl, because he liked the look of her and he couldn't help himself. 'And what's your name?'

'The message is for the witches who live in the ice and see what is to be,' replied the mountain nomad reluctantly. 'My name . . . I don't really have a name.'

'People must call you something,' said Aron. He glanced over at Haral again, who had lowered the perspective glass but was still looking out, her eyes narrowed. With the snow beginning to fall more heavily, and the light fading with it, visibility was ebbing.

'Some call me Ferin,' said the nomad, the faintest hint of a smile quirking in the corner of her mouth, sign of a fond memory. 'Now, can you let me in?'

'I guess –' Aron started to say, but he stopped as Haral laid a hand on his shoulder, and pointed with the perspective glass.

Three figures were coming into sight out of the swirling snow and the lowering darkness. Two of them were on horseback, nomads clad in the typical long woollen tunics of black and grey, slit at the sides for riding, and wound about the waist with multicoloured silk sashes. Those who knew could tell the tribe from the pattern of colours in a sash.

But they were not common nomads. One was a shaman, with a silver ring around his neck, and from that ring a chain of silvered iron ran to the hand of the second nomad, the shaman's keeper.

Even without seeing the neck-ring and silver chain, Haral and Aron knew immediately who . . . or what . . . the nomads must be, because the third of their number was neither on horseback, nor was it human.

It was a wood-weird, a creature of roughly carved and articulated ironwood, twice as tall as the horses, its big misshapen eyes beginning to glow with a hot red fire, evidence that the shaman was goading the Free Magic creature he'd imprisoned inside the loosely joined pieces of timber fully into motion. Wood-weirds were not so terrible a foe as some other Free Magic constructs, such as spirit-walkers, whose bodies were crafted from stone, for wood-weirds were not so entirely impervious to normal weapons. Nevertheless, they were greatly feared. And who knew what other servants or powers the shaman might have?

'The Guard! Alarm! Alarm!' roared Haral, cupping her hands around her mouth and looking up to the central tower. She was answered only a few seconds later by the blast of a horn from high above, echoed four or five seconds later from the mid-river fort, out of sight in the snow, and then again more distantly from the castle on the southern bank.

'Let me in!' shouted the mountain nomad urgently, even as she looked back over her shoulder. The wood-weird was striding ahead of the two nomads now, its long, root-like legs stretching out, grasping limbs reaching forward for balance, strange fire streaming from its eyes and mouth like burning tears and spit.

The shaman sat absolutely still on his horse, deep in concentration. It took great effort of will to keep a Free Magic spirit of any kind from turning on its master – a master who was himself kept in check by the cunningly hinged asphyxiating ring of bright silver, which his keeper could pull tight should he try to turn his creatures upon his own people, or seek to carry out his own plans.

Though this particular keeper seemed to have little fear her sorcerer would turn, for she fixed the chain to the horn of her saddle and readied her bow, even though she was still well out of bowshot, particularly with the snow falling wet and steady. Once she got within range, she would get only two or three good shots before her string grew sodden. Perhaps only a single shot at that.

'We can't let you in now!' called down Aron. He had picked up his crossbow. 'Enemies in sight!'

'But they're after *me*!'

'We don't know that,' shouted Haral. 'This could be a trick to get us to open the gate. You said you were a messenger; they'll leave you alone.'

'No, they won't!' cried Ferin. She took her own bow from the case on her back, and drew a strange arrow from the case at her waist. The arrow's point was hooded with leather, tied fast. Holding bow and arrow with her left hand, she undid the cords of the hood and pulled it free, revealing an arrow-head of dark glass that sparkled with hidden fire, a faint tendril of white smoke rising from the point.

With it came an unpleasant, acrid taint, so strong it came almost instantly to the noses of the guards atop the wall.

'Free Magic!' shouted Aron. Raising his crossbow in one swift motion, he fired it straight down. Only Haral's sudden downwards slap on the crossbow made the quarrel miss the nomad woman's gut, but even so it went clear through her leg just above the ankle, and there was suddenly blood spattered on the snow.

Ferin looked over her shoulder quickly, saw Haral restraining Aron so he couldn't ready another quarrel. Setting her teeth hard together against the pain in her leg, she turned back to face the wood-weird. It had risen up on its rough-hewn legs and was bounding forward, a good hundred paces ahead of the shaman, and it was still accelerating. Its eyes were bright as pitch-soaked torches newly lit, and great long flames roared from the widening gash in its head that served as a mouth.

Ferin drew her bow and released in one fluid motion. The shining glass arrow flew like a spark from a summer bonfire, striking the wood-weird square in the trunk. At first it seemed it had done no scathe, but then the creature faltered, took three staggering steps, and froze in place, suddenly more a strangely carved tree and less a terrifying creature. The flames in its eyes ebbed back, there was a flash of white inside the red, then its entire body burst into flame. A vast roil of dark smoke rose from the fire, gobbling up the falling snow.

In the distance the shaman screamed, a scream filled with equal parts anger and fear.

'Free Magic!' gasped Aron. He struggled with Haral. She had difficulty in restraining him, before she got him in an armlock and wrestled him down behind the battlements. 'She's a sorcerer!'

'No, no, lad,' said Haral easily. 'That was a spirit-glass arrow. It's Free Magic, sure enough, but contained, and can be used only once. They're very rare, and the nomads treasure them, because they are the only weapons they have which can kill a shaman or one of their creatures.'

'But she could still be –'

'I don't think so,' said Haral. The full watch was pounding up the stairs now; in a minute there would be two dozen guards spread out on the wall. 'But one of the Bridgemaster's Seconds can test her with Charter Magic. If she really is from the mountains, and has a message for the Clayr, we need to know.'

'The Clayr?' asked Aron. 'Oh, the witches in the ice, who see –'

'More than you do,' interrupted Haral. 'Can I let you go?'

Aron nodded and relaxed. Haral released her hold and quickly stood up, looking out over the wall.

Ferin was not in sight. The wood-weird was burning fiercely, sending up a great billowing column of choking black smoke. The shaman and his keeper lay sprawled on the snowy ground, both dead with quite ordinary arrows in their eyes, evidence of peerless shooting at that range in the dying light. Their horses were running free, spooked by blood and sudden death.

'Where did she go?' asked Aron.

'Probably not very far,' said Haral grimly, gazing intently at the ground. There was a patch of blood on the snow there as big as the guard's hand, and blotches like dropped coins of bright scarlet continued for some distance, in the direction of the river shore.

chapter two

two hawks bring messages

Belisaere, the Old Kingdom

The hawk came down through the clouds, dodging raindrops for the sheer fun of it, despite having already flown more than two hundred leagues. Born from a Charter-spelled egg and trained for its work since it was a fledgling, the hawk carried a message imprinted in its mind, and with it the burning desire to fly as swiftly as possible to the tower mews in the royal city of Belisaere.

The rain-dodging hawk from the south beat another bird flying in from the north by half a minute, so it was first to get to Mistress Finney, the chief falconer, while the later hawk had to be content going to the fist of an apprentice.

As a matter of procedure, Mistress Finney checked the anklet on the bird, to see where it had come from, though she already recognised him. She knew all the message hawks of the Old Kingdom, having raised them herself, even if they were later assigned elsewhere, and became only occasional visitors to the capital.

'From Wyverley College, my lovely,' she said softly, making

her own peculiar tongue-clicking sound, one all the hawks knew from the egg. 'What a long way, and over the Wall too, my brave one. What's your message, dear?'

The hawk opened its beak and spoke with a woman's voice, that of Magistrix Coelle, who taught Charter Magic at Wyverley College, in that strange land beyond the Wall, where magic waned and then disappeared entirely, once too far south.

'Telegram from Nicholas Sayre for the Abhorsen. Extremely urgent,' said the hawk.

'Ah, for the Abhorsen,' said Mistress Finney. 'Messenger!'

A seven-year-old page who hoped to become one of the falconer's apprentices leaped up from the bench where she sat with three others, waiting to take the messages the hawks brought in on the next part of their journey.

'Yes, Mistress!'

'Find out where the Abhorsen-in-Waiting Lirael is. Tell her I am transcribing an urgent message from Ancelstierre calling for the Abhorsen, and ask her to either come here for it, or to stay wherever she is and you come back and let me know and we will send it on.'

'Yes, Mistress,' said the girl, with a slight hesitation that suggested she didn't know where to look for Lirael, or why she was looking for Lirael instead of the Abhorsen herself.

'Try Prince Sameth's workshop first,' said Mistress Finney, after a moment's thought. 'I believe she is often there, for he is making her new hand.'

The girl bent her head in acknowledgment, spun on one foot, and dashed to the stairs.

'Slow down!' called out Mistress Finney after her. 'You'll do no good if you fall to the bottom!'

The clatter of footsteps slowed a little. The falconer smiled and lifted the hawk to the perch that sat on her writing desk. The bird stepped off onto it, watching the woman as she took up her quill, dipped it in the inkwell, and made ready to write.

'Now, my dear, give me the message,' said Mistress Finney to the hawk, who once again spoke, clear and loud in the voice of Magistrix Coelle. Wyverley College, though it lay across the Wall, was close enough that Charter Magic could be wielded there. Though its location meant Ancelstierran technology could not always be relied upon, a telegraph boy's bicycle would not fail. So it had become the de facto place for Ancelstierran telegrams to be transferred to Old Kingdom message-hawks for onward delivery to authorities in the north.

'Abhorsen, I've just received a telegram. It reads "TO MAGISTRIX WYVERLEY COLLEGE NICK FOUND BAD KINGDOM CREATURE DORRANCE HALL TELL ABHORSEN HELP STOP THIS FROM NICHOLAS SAYRE STOP VIA DANJERS VALET APPLETHWICK END." Now, Dorrance Hall is several hundred miles south, so this seems very unlikely. But I have heard it is some sort of secret government place, so perhaps should be investigated. I have sent telegrams to the Bain consulate and the embassy in Corvere, but have not yet had an answer –'

The message ended suddenly. The message-hawks were

19

invaluable, but their minds were small and could not hold very long communications, and their capacity also varied from bird to bird. Unless you knew the particular hawk in question and counted out your words beforehand, it was easy to be cut off in mid-flow. Senders often forgot this in their eagerness to pass on important information. Nor, once a message was impressed, was it an easy matter to start again.

'Well done, my dear,' said Mistress Finney softly to the hawk, carefully drawing a line below the message she had just transcribed and initialling it 'MF'. She gestured to one of her apprentices, who came and took the hawk over to its own perch, to be fed some fresh rabbit and to have a drink.

The apprentice who had heard the message from the northern hawk approached her, passing over the paper where he'd written down that bird's missive.

'This one's for the King,' he said. 'From the Greenwash Bridge Company, at the bridge. Not marked urgent. Follow-up to their earlier report.'

'Spike it for Princess Ellimere,' said Mistress Finney, gesturing at a table adorned with numerous spikes, most of them already impaling message sheets. 'She's coming up this morning; I saw her at breakfast.'

'Not taken to the King immediately?'

'Does no one here pay attention to what is happening in the court we serve?' asked Mistress Finney. It was a rhetorical question, and no one in the mews dared to treat it any other way, remaining silent while hoping they looked suitably attentive. 'The King and the Abhorsen left for their holiday this morning. A well-deserved one. Their first holiday! Ever! You could all learn from their example. Hard work –'

She broke off as another hawk flew in, briefly settling on the landing perch before spying Mistress Finney. Upon seeing her, it immediately flew to her fist.

'Hello, my beauty,' said the falconer, forgetting her rant. 'Come in from High Bridge, have you?'

Lirael hurried up the steps to the mews. She flexed her replacement hand as she did so, marvelling at how well it worked. When her own hand had been bitten off by the Disreputable Dog almost seven months before in order to save her life from the ravening power of Orannis, Sameth had promised to make her a replacement. He had lived up to that promise, and shown he was indeed a true inheritor of the Wallmakers' engineering ingenuity and magical craft, though it had taken him a long time to get it right, with much tinkering and adjustment. It was only in the last few days that it felt entirely normal to Lirael, really just like her own flesh-and-blood hand.

It was mostly made from meteoric steel, but Sam had gilded the metal, and unasked had added an extra layer of Charter spells atop the ones that made the hand work and even feel like flesh, so it also glowed faintly with a golden light.

Already, many people were calling her Lirael Goldenhand. Lirael didn't like the name very much, or the soft glow from her golden fingers. She had worked out how to unravel the part of the spell which provided the light, and planned to do so as soon as she could without hurting Sam's feelings. Having an artificial magic hand attracted enough attention as it was, without the soft golden light as well.

Though she had to admit to herself it was probably too late to avoid attention. It seemed everyone in Belisaere knew who she was. She'd gone out incognito numerous times, wearing a broad-brimmed hat and gloves and simple, unadorned clothes rather than her distinctive surcoat that bore the silver keys of the Abhorsen on a blue field, quartered with the golden stars of the Clayr on green. But this disguise, if it could be called that, never worked for long. People always discovered her true identity.

Just the day before she'd tried to wander through the market near Lake Loesere but she'd had to give up, because so many people were following her around, and the store traders kept giving her whatever she enquired about for nothing, in gratitude for saving the kingdom from Orannis the Destroyer. Within fifteen minutes she was so overloaded with a sack of blood plums, three bottles of wine, several different cheeses, a wheel-like loaf of fine white bread and a giant bunch of asparagus that she had to retreat to the palace, trailing a crowd behind her.

She hoped the message from Ancelstierre was going to offer her the possibility of escape from all the attention. In Sabriel's absence, it was her duty to deal with any Dead or Free Magic creatures, though admittedly the Abhorsen and the King had only consented to go on holiday – to the island of Ilgard – because everything had been largely quiet for the last six months.

Lirael was very eager to take up her duty. Any duty. She still keenly felt the loss of the Disreputable Dog, and being busy was an excellent way to not dwell on that. Or on the difficulties of adapting to a whole new life as the Abhorsen-in-Waiting, with a much older half-sister who was also now her mentor. Though she greatly respected Sabriel, Lirael was also very much in awe of her, and could not easily talk to her about anything other than the work they shared.

Then there was her nephew Sameth and niece Ellimere, though she could never think of them that way, since she was only a little older in years and felt considerably younger in terms of experience with the world. Just being suddenly a part of the ruling family of the Old Kingdom was an almost overwhelming challenge, particularly for someone like Lirael, who was used to spending a great deal of time alone, or in companionable silence with her dear dog.

Now it was nearly impossible for her to be alone, even for a few minutes. The previous six months had been occupied with recovering from her wounding; beginning to learn how to wield the seven bells of the Abhorsen and all the associated magics that went with that art (something she now realised would go on for her entire life; it was not the sort of thing you could ever entirely know); having her replacement hand fitted and fine-tuned, which took absolutely hours; going along with the bare minimum of social activity organised for her by Ellimere, who did not at all behave like a dutiful niece but much more like a bossy, matchmaking sister; and just trying to fit in with a busy family who knew one another very well.

The messenger girl who was leading the way turned at the top of the stairs and held her finger to her lips.

'Um, please remember to speak quietly and walk slowly,' she said nervously. 'So as not to disturb the hawks.'

'I know,' whispered Lirael. She had some experience with the hawks in the Clayr's mews, high in the rocky peak of Sunfall above the Glacier, and she had also visited Mistress Finney's domain before.

The falconer raised a hand in greeting to Lirael as she climbed the last few steps and emerged into the long room, half open to the sky, the shutters all pulled back to allow easy access for the hawks. The rain had eased and the clouds parted, and the warmish, weak sunshine of early spring was pouring in, a welcome light after the winter's darkness.

'Greetings, Lirael. You came quickly,' said Mistress Finney. She held out a sheet of thick, linen-rich paper. One of the first things Touchstone and Sabriel had done when restoring the Kingdom to rights had been to help the guild of paper-makers rebuild several small mills. Touchstone had wanted paper to assist with communications and trade, Sabriel for other reasons. 'I have the message ready, and a hawk waiting should you wish to send a reply.'

Lirael took the proffered paper and read the message quickly, and then once again more slowly, to be sure she had fully taken in everything it conveyed. Which wasn't all that much, when it came to it, save that Sam's friend Nicholas – Nick – had sent it, requesting the aid of the Abhorsen to deal with a Free Magic creature that was a very unlikely distance south of the Wall.

But then Nick himself was very unlikely, in that he had survived carrying a fragment of Orannis within himself, tainting him with Free Magic, deep into his blood and bone. Or to be more accurate, he hadn't survived it. He'd died, but had been brought back from Death by the Disreputable Dog, who had also given him the baptismal Charter mark, somehow containing the Free Magic contamination within his body. No one had been quite sure what the result of this would be, and Nick had quickly been taken away to the south of Ancelstierre, where everyone had presumably hoped it wouldn't matter.

'I had better go and talk to Ellimere and Sam,' said Lirael thoughtfully, though she had already decided she would go, and go straight away. Part of her last six months' training with Sabriel had been spent learning to fly a Paperwing. She was already thinking of how she could fly west to the Ratterlin and follow its silver path south, swooping down at Barhedrin Hill to get a horse from the garrison there, and someone to help her with it, because though she'd had lessons from Ellimere, riding horses was still a new thing and she didn't want to fall off and break her leg before she even left the Old Kingdom. But she would have to ride, because the Paperwing would not cross the Wall, and walking would be too slow. Once across the Wall, she could ride in one of the

Ancelstierrans' noisy, stinking vehicles, like the truck that had taken them west to Forwin Mill to confront Orannis . . .

'And a reply?' asked Mistress Finney, breaking in on Lirael's thoughts. 'To Magistrix Coelle?'

'Oh . . . please send word that I shall come as soon as I may,' said Lirael. She thought for a few moments. 'I should be there within a day, I think. I'll go to Wyverley first, to consult the Magistrix for directions and so forth.'

'I will send a hawk at once,' replied the falconer, but she spoke to empty air. Lirael was already clattering down the stairs in her eagerness to be on her way, to once again be so busy she had no time to dwell upon the past.

She almost ran into Ellimere halfway down, coming up rather more slowly than Lirael was descending, the princess almost dropping the sheaf of messages she was bringing for the message-hawks to send.

'You're in a hurry,' said the princess cheerfully. 'What's happening?'

'Urgent message from Sam's friend Nick in Ancelstierre,' gabbled Lirael. 'A Free Magic creature; they need help. I thought I'd take a Paperwing and fly down –'

'Wait! Wait!' cried Ellimere. She was still smiling, but there was the beginning of a frown on her forehead as well. 'Have you got the message?'

Lirael handed her the paper. Ellimere read it, her frown intensifying.

'But no formal message from the Crossing Point Scouts at the Perimeter, or the government via our embassy in Corvere?'

'Mistress Finney only had that one,' said Lirael.

'Strange there should be nothing official,' said Ellimere. 'And several hundred miles south, there's no chance it could actually be a Free Magic creature. You can't even feel the Charter that far into Ancelstierre. There must be something else going on. I wonder if it's some sort of trap, to lure Mother into another assassination attempt . . .'

'I hadn't thought of that,' said Lirael, suddenly acutely aware that she had let her eagerness to get busy overrule any deeper thinking. She should have particularly thought of a trap aimed at Sabriel. The Abhorsen and King Touchstone had almost been killed in Ancelstierre seven months before by assassins from the Our Country party, who had been secretly funded and directed by Hedge, the necromancer servant of Orannis. Though the leadership of that party and the few surviving assassins were all in prison now, there might still be some outlying groups who intended harm to Sabriel, not knowing there was no longer any purpose in doing so.

'You'd think the Clayr would have Seen anything serious coming up, too,' continued Ellimere. 'I mean, the aged parents only agreed to go on holiday because it's been so quiet and the Clayr said they hadn't seen anything nasty on the horizon.'

'The visions aren't always clear,' said Lirael, who, though she lacked the Sight to see the future, had grown up among the clan of female seers in their fortress under the Glacier. 'I mean, they See many possible futures, and have to look for patterns or recurring visions. And sometimes their Sight is clouded by other magic.'

'They normally See the big stuff, though,' said Ellimere. She paused and then added, 'Eventually . . .'

'Almost too late sometimes,' said Lirael, with feeling. The Clayr had been very late in Seeing exactly what Orannis was, and what it planned. 'Besides, they can't See what happens in Ancelstierre, at least not much beyond the Wall. What if there really is a Free Magic creature loose over there? They have few — or maybe no — mages apart from the Crossing Point Scouts on the Perimeter.'

'But there can't be a Free Magic creature that far south,' said Ellimere. 'It just isn't possible.'

It was Lirael's turn to be silent for a moment. She was thinking.

'It may be significant that the telegram came from Nick,' she said slowly.

'Why?' asked Ellimere.

'He bore the fragment of Orannis inside his heart for a long time,' said Lirael. 'I could feel the Free Magic within him. Even after . . . after . . .'

She paused to blink away an incipient tear. 'Even after the Dog brought him back and gave him the Charter mark, the Free Magic was still there, inside him. Only contained by the Charter. In a way, he was like the Dog herself. Or Mogget when he had his collar on. Something of Free Magic, but also of the Charter.'

'I didn't know he still had Free Magic inside him!'

exclaimed Ellimere. 'Did Mother know? We should never have let him out of our sight. What if the Free Magic overcomes him? He'll be incredibly dangerous!'

'No . . .' said Lirael, though she was far from certain herself that this was true, basing her answer very much on the belief that the Disreputable Dog would not have brought Nicholas Sayre back if he was going to be a threat. 'I don't think that will happen. And Sabriel did know about Nick, she wanted him to come back with us, but Nick didn't . . . he didn't want to come along, and what with his uncle being the Chief Minister and all, Sabriel said we couldn't just take him with us. She thought he would be far enough south both the Free Magic and the Charter Magic would sleep within him –'

'Maybe *he* is the Free Magic creature,' interrupted Ellimere, her frown deepening further. 'Telegram could have been mixed up.'

'Whatever is happening, I think I should go and investigate,' said Lirael.

'Yes,' said Ellimere. 'Perhaps Sam should go with you '

Lirael shook her head. She'd just been in Sam's workshop for the final adjustments to her hand, and he had been in a hurry himself. He was leaving to go and meet the leaders of the Southerling refugees, and take them to see the lands they were to be given by the crown. Sam had promised the Southerlings a place to settle, guaranteeing it with his word as a prince shortly before the final battle with Orannis, in order to make them get clear of the incipient destruction.

Sorting out where they were to go, and attempting to overcome their cultural disbelief in magic, had become a big responsibility for Sam.

'Sam's got the Southerling leaders here, trying to get them used to Charter Magic and everything before he takes them off to their new lands north of Roble's Town. I'm sure I'll be fine by myself.'

Lirael wasn't entirely sure she would be fine. But she did know she needed to get away for a while, to be kept busy, to escape the long nights in her chambers in the palace, grieving for the Dog. A grief made worse by the fact that she knew the Dog would be cross with her for this and would probably have bitten her to stop her feeling sorry for herself.

'You'd better stop at Barhedrin and pick up a troop of the Guard,' said Ellimere. She turned about and started back down the stairs. 'I'll write a letter to the captain there; they can accompany you to the Wall and make sure you get an escort from the Perimeter Garrison to go with you further south. I'd better let the consulate in Bain know as well; they can send some people north to meet you. Bodyguards, with guns and so forth. Oh, and the embassy in Corvere will need to be informed.'

'I thought I'd go to Wyverley College first and talk to Magistrix Coelle, to see if she knows more,' said Lirael. She felt rather like a horse who has convinced another to bolt from a corral but can't keep up. Ellimere was now even more enthusiastic about the mission than Lirael was herself.

'Good idea, but don't go past the Wall without an escort,'

said Ellimere. 'Just in case this is all a trap for Mother, since it could as easily be a trap for you. Those Our Country idiots would be as happy to kill an Abhorsen-in-Waiting as the Abhorsen herself. Do you have everything you need to take?'

'As much as I can fit in a Paperwing,' said Lirael. One of the first things Sabriel had taught her was to be ready to be called upon at all times. The Dead and Free Magic creatures did not wait on the convenience of packing a travelling kit.

'You settle on a new sword?'

'One that will serve, for now,' said Lirael. She had also lost her sword Nehima in the binding of Orannis. With the royal armouries open to her, she had tried several swords, good weapons of fine steel imbued with Charter marks, but none felt entirely at home in her hand. Sam had said he would make her one, but the hand came first, and in any case it would take him a year or more. But as she had told him, the latest blade she'd tried from the armoury was good enough.

So she had a Charter-spelled sword, her armoured coat of gethre plates, and the seven bells of an Abhorsen. Few would dare stand against her, so equipped.

'What are you waiting for?'

'I'm not waiting . . . I'm going!' said Lirael. 'I mean, I'm talking to you, then I'm going.'

Ellimere laughed and gave Lirael a quick hug, before taking several quick steps up the stairs towards the mews, pausing there for a few final words.

'You're too easy to tease. I'll come see you off in the Paperwing courtyard in half an hour. With a letter for the Barhedrin captain, and I'll have Mistress Finney send a hawk to Wyverley now. I've got a bunch of messages to answer anyway.'

'Anything important?' asked Lirael.

'Don't think so!' called out Ellimere, once again racing up the stairs. 'The Bridge Company reporting some incident with the nomads, a few other things. Routine!'

But she was wrong. It wasn't *routine* trouble with the nomads.

chapter three

an offering to the river

Greenwash river, northern bank, the Old Kingdom

Ferin finished tying off the bandage and inspected her handiwork. The quarrel hadn't gone through her leg as she'd initially feared, instead scoring a deep furrow on the side of her calf just above her ankle. If it had been in the middle and higher up she would probably be already dead, the bone fractured and blood pumping out too fast to stop.

She'd been lucky, so far at least. But the wound could still turn bad, despite the healing paste she'd liberally smeared on it, hoping to stave off infection. Now her leg stank of bear fat and gwassen berries, the principal ingredients of the paste. The smell made her a little homesick. It was a long way from the mountains and the squat gwassen bushes with their bitter, restorative fruit.

With the bandage secure, Ferin gingerly hopped up on her good foot. She was concealed in a thick clump of black alders by the riverbank, but she still took care to move slowly and stay hidden. She hadn't got close enough to be sure which clan the horse nomads who'd caught up with her came from, but it didn't matter. The shaman's immediate unleashing of the wood-weird confirmed her early suspicions: the word had spread to all twenty tribes now, to find the Athask woman far from her mountain. Find her and kill her.

All the clans that gave tribute to the Witch With No Face would obey that instruction. Which, as far as Ferin knew, was nineteen of the twenty tribes. Only the raft people who drifted across the bitter sea in the far west had managed to avoid the tribute and the retribution of the Witch With No Face, by the simple expedient of taking their rafts to the far side of their salty waters. The horse-folk of the steppe, and even her own mountain-dwellers, they all gave the Witch With No Face the required offerings.

'Offerings,' whispered Ferin, and smiled. That was how she had got her use-name. The name she had been given at birth was lost, all record and memory of it destroyed when she'd been chosen to be a tribute to the Witch. But later, her very smallest not-sister had tried to call her 'offering' like the adults did, but only 'ferin' had come out. While the adults carefully always called her Offering, as was traditional, nearly all the children called her Ferin.

At least they did when she was allowed to see them, which was not very often. Each clan's chosen offerings had to live away from the rest of their people, a league or more from the main camp, to be overseen by the tribe's best teachers, who ensured the offerings would grow up to be physically and mentally strong. Fast and lithe, supple in mind and body, trained with bow, sword and knife. Taught to speak the common language of the clans and the Old Kingdom, even to read and write as well, something most nomads never bothered with unless they were to become a witch or shaman.

The Witch With No Face wanted only the best when it came time to move into her new body.

Ferin grimaced, both from the thought of that and from the pain in her leg. No muscle or tendon was severed, and it would support her weight if absolutely necessary. But it hurt, a pain that not only inhabited the wound but sent stabbing outriders up her leg and into every toe.

The tribute had been going on for centuries, the Witch With No Face demanding girls be kept ready, choosing one every dozen years or so, depending on how hard she had treated her current body. When that grew too old – and her bodies aged far faster than they would have simply from the normal passage of time – or was injured, the Witch With No Face would leave her old body and move into the new one.

If an offering achieved the age of seventeen without being chosen by the Witch, she was killed and her body burned, the ashes sent to the Witch as proof of the deed. After all, there were always plenty more. If one clan ran out, another would have a suitable candidate, a new body for the Witch With No Face.

But not any more, thought Ferin with grim satisfaction.

Something had happened to the Witch some eight moons past, a great defeat that had completely destroyed the body she inhabited. This had briefly been a cause of rejoicing, on the first news, until it became clear that the death of her body did not mean the Witch With No Face was actually dead herself.

She had returned from Death as a terrible spirit, something like the entities which inhabited wood-weirds and spirit-walkers, or even the tiny, malignant things trapped in spirit-glass arrowheads. But much more powerful, because the shamans and witches could not control her, and even the most powerful spirit-glass arrows simply enraged her, instead of ensuring her final end.

The usefulness – or not – of spirit-glass arrows against her had been tested several times, to the archers' cost. There were many among the clans who hated the Witch, and had lost children as offerings. Now the survivors had even more reason to hate her, but were powerless to do anything about it.

There had been a brief hope that on becoming a bodiless spirit, the Witch With No Face wouldn't need any more offerings, and would even let the current crop walk out of their solitary dwellings and return to their tribes. But this was not to be. Word had come that they must all be killed, their bodies burned on pyres, stacked high with fuel and kept extra hot.

For some reason, the Witch either feared the offerings, or perhaps wanted them killed to remove a reminder of the bodies she could no longer inhabit, the physical life she could no longer have.

All through the north, the offerings had been slain, and urns containing their ashes dispatched as evidence that the order of the Witch With No Face had been carried out.

Except in one place. The people of the Athask, the

red-stitched goatskin-clad people of the mountains, had sent an urn containing human ashes, sure enough, but they were *not* those of their offering.

They did this because another witch had told them to. A witch who had died some nine years before and had stayed properly and sensibly dead. This witch had told the elders what was to come, seeing it in the frozen waterfall that hung jewel-like in the winter, above the summer camp, the highest point in the mountains where the clans regularly pitched their tents.

Ferin had only vague memories of the Cave Witch, as her people came to call the visitor, but she recalled a woman with blue eyes and skin a different shade of brown than the mountain-folk, her hair the colour of dry grass. Ferin had been told how the witch had appeared one summer, taking up residence in a cave off the mountain trail between the winter and summer camps. She had slain five of the clan folk soon after her arrival, including a lesser shaman. They had tried to kill her and take the rich and strange things she had brought with her, along with the two mules that had carried her goods. Mules were rare beasts on the mountain, and tasted even better than horse.

But the Cave Witch had killed her attackers with unusual magic. Old Kingdom magic, from the far south across the great river. Recognising her power, the elders treated with the foreign sorcerer. Normally they would have also sent word to the Witch With No Face, but this was one of the first things the Cave Witch told them not to do, as it would bring them ill luck. As she also correctly told them about an imminent raid from the Ranash people – the Moon Horse clan – who lived in the highest part of the steppe, close to the mountains, they listened to her. When she told them other useful glimpses of what was to come over the years, they continued to listen.

In the months before she died of the wasting sickness, the Cave Witch told them of her most important vision. She foresaw that the Witch With No Face would be killed but not killed, and would no longer need her offerings of young women. Instead, she would require something more, something that would end in the complete ruin of the clan, the death of the Athask people.

The blue-eyed woman told them the only way to stop this happening was to send a messenger to her own people, and it was then that she told the elders about the tribe of seers who lived around and under and beside a glacier in the Old Kingdom.

People she called the Clayr.

She'd written a message to be sent to them, in particular for her own daughter. She'd repeated that, over and over. Saying her daughter's name as if it meant everything.

Lirael.

Lirael of the Clayr.

The elders had taken the message, but had not sent it. The foreign sorcerer had not *always* been accurate in her foretellings, and they thought there was a chance she was wrong.

But then the Witch With No Face *was* killed, and she came back from Death, and two moons past, the messengers had come with the new demands that were exactly what the foreign sorcerer had said would lead to the end of the Athask people.

So the elders had belatedly decided they must send the message to the Clayr. And who better to take it than the Offering, the best of her people, whose life was in any case forfeit?

Ferin had that message now, secure in her head and safely memorised, for anything written could be stolen or lost. She had to get across the river and go to the Glacier, to deliver the message and save her people.

Without being killed by those who served the Witch With No Face, who almost from the moment she had left the mountains to cross the steppe had pursued her as if they knew what she was, and where, if not where she intended going.

But Ferin didn't spare any thought for how her enemies were always close behind, or on anything else, like the fact that she had no idea where the Clayr's Glacier was on the other side of the Greenwash. She lived in the moment, and was entirely focused on her immediate goal.

To get across the river.

She looked out over the water. The snow was still falling, but lightly, and the last sliver of the sun was disappearing in the west, so she couldn't see very far, certainly not to the other side of the river. The Greenwash was at least three thousand paces wide here, and was roaring with snow-melt, its furious current made visible by the chunks of ice that whirled past, remnants of winter that had lingered in the more sheltered parts of the banks until the spring floods scoured them out.

There was no way Ferin could swim across, even if she were uninjured. The current was far too swift, and the water too cold. She would be drowned or frozen before she got even part of the way.

The bridge was now out of the question. The only way onto it was through the North Castle, and the shaman and his keeper would have been only the vanguard of other nomads who would be watching there, waiting for her to approach. If there were enough of them, they might even start searching along the riverbank and to the north, in case she'd doubled back. But it was more likely now they'd wait till morning, and light.

Which meant Ferin had to somehow get across this great, swollen, ferociously cold river in the darkness.

She tore off a strip of the alder bark – it was good for wounds – and chewed on it thoughtfully, looking along the riverbank in the fading light. There was a large clump of some kind of rushes nearby. Not the same as the ones that grew in the high alpine lakes of her home, but similar.

Ferin lifted her head and listened to the noises about her. The rushing waters of the river were so loud she had to focus deeply to hear anything else. But her hearing was acute, and well trained. She stood silently, behind the alder trunk, putting all the small sounds together. None of them suggested other people, particularly people sneaking up on her.

Ferin left the alders and crawled carefully along the bank,

making her trail look like some small animal's so she left no obviously human marks in the snow and mud. When she reached the reeds, she stopped and listened again, while watching for any signs of movement in the knee-high grass beyond the riverbank.

Again, there was nothing untoward. Ferin drew one of the tall reeds down and examined it as best she could in the fading light, and by touch. Its long stem was hollow, like the lake reeds she knew, but it had a large, flowcry head instead of a closed, spear-like point.

Ferin cut it off close to the base with her knife and laid it down in front of her. Again, she waited and listened, then slowly cut another and put it down, before listening once more.

In this patient, laborious way, she spent the next several hours watchfully cutting reeds. It grew colder as the sun departed, but it was nothing like the piercing winter cold of the high mountains, at least not under the *athask* cloak, reversed so the white fur warmed her, and the goatskin lining, deeply oiled, shed the snow and did not give her away.

The snow eased off around this time, and the clouds began to move away, revealing a crescent moon and a bright swath of stars. Ferin scowled at the brightening sky, for she did not need the light, but those who hunted her might be encouraged to set out at night now, rather than wait for the dawn.

Ferin had spread the reeds into nine separate bunches. She quickly bound each of these bundles together individually, and then made a raft, using four bundles for the base and one on each side to make low gunwales. The ninth she only bound halfway and splayed the other end, for a makeshift paddle. All of this took every bit of her available cordage: the twine normally employed as the first stage of lofting a rope by arrow or grappling hook; six ells of the beautiful braided silk rope all the Athask people coveted; and three of her four spare bowstrings.

It did not look like much of a craft to tackle the Greenwash in full flood, but any doubts Ferin had about using it were dispelled when she heard sounds in the distance that were not part of the natural small noises of the night. Horses moving, the creak of saddles, the faint chink of armour, the whisper of commands given in low voices. Whoever it was they weren't even being careful, probably because there were lots of them and they felt secure in their numbers. They were not wrong. Ferin might shoot two or three before they got her, but she knew she probably wouldn't even kill one, not if there were many more archers sending an arrow storm back towards her.

Quickly, Ferin made sure everything on her person was securely fastened. She put her pack and bow case on the raft and tied them to the loose ends of the reed bindings, drew her cloak tightly around herself, and pushed the raft into the shallows, diving on top of her pack as the river immediately snatched up this new gift and dragged it spinning into the heart of its turbulent waters.

chapter four

a man and a creature lie as if dead

Ancelstierre, near the Wall

'You had better stay here,' said Lirael, 'until I see what kind of creature lurks beyond.'

'We should come with you, milady,' countered Captain Anlow. The thirty guards she led were gathered behind her, in a single line stretching back along the tunnel through the Wall and out the northern side, into the Old Kingdom. They had come with Lirael from Barhedrin, where she had landed her Paperwing. 'There might be other dangers. The wind is from the south, their weapons are working. Those sharp barks we heard earlier are called gunshots, and some guns are very deadly at a far distance. They are always fearful here, and shoot too readily; they often have accidents —'

'I have been in Ancelstierre before, and I know about their guns,' said Lirael firmly. 'This is Abhorsen business. You stay here until I have dealt with the creature.'

They stood by the gate that Anlow had just opened. Behind

43

them, on the northern side of the Wall, a meadow full of wildflowers proclaimed the beginning of spring and the sun was just beginning to set, a red light falling across the land.

On the southern side, the crisp chill of winter still prevailed, and it was the middle of the night. A waning moon and cloud-obscured stars did little to illuminate the broad no-man's-land of bare earth ahead, criss-crossed with a veritable bramble forest of rusted, red-brown barbed wire, overlaying the craters and shell holes, evidence of a continuing belief in the use of high explosive, despite the fact it did not stop many of the things that came across the Wall.

Among the hundreds of rusted, bent star pickets that supported the wire, there were wind-flutes. Lirael could hear them, and feel their power, even though she couldn't see them in the darkness. Created by the Abhorsen, the wind-flutes whispered a song redolent with the same power of her bells, helping to close the border between Life and Death. There had been many, many deaths here. Without the wind-flutes, the Crossing Point would not just be the place where travellers went from north to south or vice versa, but would also be a yawning, open door for the Dead to slither, crawl or stride out into the world of the living.

Lirael could feel the closeness of Death, the chill of that inexorable river, the weight of so many dead in this blood-soaked ground. That was to be expected here. But she could also smell the corrosive, hot metal tang of Free Magic, and sense its presence, not least by the beginnings of an unpleasant shivering ache that was spreading through her bones and teeth.

Powerful Free Magic, something that should *not* be here. She had felt it as soon as they opened the southern gate in the Wall, making her stop in her tracks and order the guards to halt, and then to remain where they were.

'I really must insist that I, at least, come with –' Anlow started to say.

'Stay here,' interrupted Lirael. For a moment, she wondered at herself, ordering a captain of the Royal Guard around. Many things had happened in the last half a year. She was no longer a shy Second Assistant Librarian. She was the Abhorsen-in-Waiting. Sometimes that was hard for her to believe, but not when it mattered. Like now, when something awaited that was her responsibility.

Lirael drew her sword and the bell Saraneth. Commonly called the Binder, the sixth bell was a comforting, powerful presence in her hand. She paused for a second then, taking a moment to feel the Free Magic presence that lay somewhere in the night ahead, to feel Death so close, but not yet with any open breach to Life. Then she slowly walked out from the gateway, narrowing her eyes against the darkness ahead as she left the brilliant, constantly moving Charter marks in the stones of the Wall behind.

It got very dark very quickly as Lirael moved away. It was quiet now, too, a sharp contrast to when they'd first arrived at the Wall, hurrying because of the cracking sounds of gunshots and the deeper thud of artillery coming from the south, accompanied by the blossoming of star-shells, tiny suns in the sky. All things Lirael had experienced before in the desperate rush to Forwin Mill the previous summer.

Lirael trod carefully, sword and bell in hand, every sense attuned to the hunt. Many Free Magic creatures were expert ambushers. Some could lurk under the earth, or take the shape of a tree or boulder, or perhaps here in this wasteland a coil of rusted wire.

But this creature did not seem to be even trying to hide. The taint of Free Magic was like a visible trail to Lirael. She could feel where it came from, and though she did not speed up or spare her caution, she followed it to its expected source.

A Free Magic creature.

Lirael's every muscle tensed. Saraneth moved slightly in her hand, wanting to speak, to bind the monster, and she had to grip it more tightly and will the bell to wait. The Charter marks on sword and bell shone with sudden light, and moved restlessly, reacting to what lay before them.

But Lirael didn't ring Saraneth or swing her sword, because the creature was lying motionless on the ground. It wasn't crouched to spring. It wasn't lurking in ambush. It just lay there on the bare earth, with its long, long arms stretched out beside it and its barbed, club-like hands perfectly still.

Lirael studied it for several long seconds, taking in its wasp-like waist; the violet, cross-hatched crocodilian hide; the long neck on which balanced a vaguely human head, though it had hearing slits in place of ears; the pear-shaped eyes, now shut; and a mouth as wide as Lirael's two extended hands, crammed with teeth as black as polished jet.

There was blood around that wide mouth, on the black teeth, trailing down its pointed chin.

'A Hrule,' whispered Lirael, remembering a book she had read long ago in the Great Library of the Clayr. *Creatures by Nagy*, a bestiary which described several hundred Free Magic entities. It was one of the better books of its type, though it was by no means comprehensive. There were a multitude of Free Magic creatures, ranging from mere nuisances to the very dangerous indeed.

The thing in front of her was in the very dangerous category.

She stepped closer very cautiously, wondering why it lay there so still, while trying to recall everything she had read in the bestiary. Hrule were very rare. Drinkers of blood, she remembered that, or was reminded of it by the stain about its mouth.

There was an oddity about this one, beyond its dormant state. It had a chain of daisies around its neck, signifying that someone else had already tried some magic against it. Certain flowers, herbs, spices, metals and scents used in particular shapes or patterns could briefly compel Free Magic creatures into action or inaction. A chain of day's eye flowers would make some creatures pause, if nothing more, and the more powerful and intelligent, like the Hrule, could sometimes be negotiated with in that state.

But a chain of daisies could not have rendered the creature unconscious, as this one seemed to be. Lirael frowned, thinking about possible ways the Hrule could have been stilled. There was something on the very edge of her memory, half-remembered from *Creatures by Nagy*, concerning how to imprison such a thing, also involving some flower or herb lore . . .

Lirael took another step, and over the sharp, almost painful ache of Free Magic, she felt the presence of life.

A life ebbing away.

Somewhere close, a man was dying.

She walked around the creature, quickening her steps, following that sensation of Life, even as it trickled away into Death.

There was the body of a young man a dozen paces from the creature. A young man in a khaki tunic, once-white shirt and black trousers, sprawled upon the ground. A torn bandage on his hand was sodden with blood, and more had pooled under his wrist, spreading out across the broken ground.

Lirael knelt by his side and looked at his face under the light from the glowing marks on her sword and bell.

It was Nicholas Sayre.

She gasped, the sound loud in the silence. Lirael hadn't expected to see Nick so soon, and not here. A wave of emotion struck her, feelings she found difficult to understand or even acknowledge. She had been eager to see him, because she had felt some sort of kinship or something, she wasn't sure what, when she had met him before. Even when he was under the sway of Orannis. Though she had felt sorry for him then, and kind of maternal. Or sisterly. Or something. And after the breaking and binding of the Destroyer, they had lain side by side on stretchers, both deathly hurt, talking of her friend the Dog . . .

Now all those feelings came back, but were overlaid with a much stronger emotion.

Fear. Fear that he was about to die, before she even had a chance to . . . a chance to what?

Lirael took a deep breath and forced herself to attend to the situation rather than her emotions. Nick was wounded and close to death. She had to see exactly how, and take action. And also make sure the Hrule didn't suddenly leap up and drink her blood, as well as . . .

Lirael looked from the creature to Nick's wrist, suddenly realising what must have happened. The Hrule had been drinking Nick's blood. Blood tainted, or perhaps empowered in this context, with the power of Orannis. The Ninth Bright Shiner, one of the most powerful Free Magic creatures to have ever existed. It must have been too much for the Hrule. Though perhaps it was only a matter of digestion, and time. Like when a cave python got into the rabbit hutches back in the Clayr's Glacier and ate so well it lay down in a torpor.

The only serious wound she could find on Nick was the deep cut on his wrist, though his feet were also bloody and scabbed. She was about to rip off the sleeves of his tunic to make bandages when she thought to look in the pockets, and found a tin marked with a red cross that held several very tightly wound dressings of some very thin cloth, and two glass vials she didn't know were surettes of morphine.

With Nick's wrist and feet swiftly bandaged, Lirael felt for his pulse. Nick had lost a lot of blood already, and his heartbeat felt weak and irregular when she pushed her fingers against the big artery under his chin, against the neck. She used her right, magical hand without thinking, and was surprised that she could somehow feel his cool skin and the beat of his heart through her metal fingers, even though they were Charter-spelled. Sam had made her hand even better than she had thought, though she did check again with her left hand, repeating the process. Just in case.

The pulse confirmed what Lirael already sensed. Nick's hold on life was anything but secure. It would be very easy for his spirit to slip away into Death. He had been brought back once by the Disreputable Dog, but that could not be done again, not to keep him as a living person. Indeed, Lirael didn't know how the Dog had managed to do it the first time without making Nick some sort of Dead creature, rather than be simply alive again.

Bandaging his wounds was not enough. She needed to use a healing spell, and quickly. Even as she thought this, she reached into the Charter, finding comfort as she let her mind move through the great flood of magical marks, focusing on the ones she needed, bringing them together by force of will, her fingers sketching the air to help her visualise each mark and how it would fit in the spell she was building.

But the first spell she tried didn't work. It was a fairly simple one, often used. All it took was six marks, none of them very difficult. She had drawn them from the Charter with the ease of long practice, linked them together to form the spell, and tipped the glowing network of marks into Nick's chest.

But the marks ran off into the earth on either side, like spilled water, and immediately dispersed.

Lirael frowned, and thought for a moment. Then she cautiously touched the baptismal Charter mark on Nick's forehead, half-expecting to find it had become corrupted in some way. But she felt a true connection to the Charter. He was still very much a part of the constant, ever-changing flow, deeply joined to the Charter that defined and described everything upon, under and above the earth.

It must be the Free Magic in him, Lirael guessed, resisting interference. The legacy of Orannis. The baptismal mark had built a shell of Charter Magic around the Free Magic that lurked within every part of Nick's physical being, but it was this deeper magic that resisted, indeed repelled, any further intrusion by the Charter.

So she would need to use a stronger spell.

Which would take more time and effort, and thus give the Hrule longer to digest the powerful blood it had drunk. Lirael vacillated for a moment. She had just remembered how to deal with the Hrule, but it would require some minutes searching along the Wall, though she thought she had seen what was required near the gateway. But in those few minutes, Nicholas might die.

'Best heal Nick first,' muttered Lirael. She kept one eye on the Free Magic creature as she once again reached for the

Charter, this time delving deeper into the eternal flow. Seeking out rarer, more powerful marks, which required both certain knowledge of them and a great effort of will to draw them out. When she had them all arranged and held in her mind, she spoke the word that would call a master mark from the Charter. It came out, slowly turning like a brilliant wheel, with the other marks following in a long spiral. Lirael moved the master mark with her golden hand and the direction of her mind, setting it against Nick's chest. The spiral tightened to become something like a golden, shining tornado and very slowly began to spin its way into the young man's body, the golden light of its passage spreading down through his torso and out along his limbs.

Lirael wiped her forehead and rather shakily got to her feet, still watching the miniature spiral of gold and silver Charter marks patiently wind its way into Nick's chest. She was weary now, the effort of casting such a spell taxing her strength. But there was still the Hrule to deal with, and for that she needed both a spear-shaft and a thistle. The spear-shaft she could get from the guards back at the gateway, and she had seen a patch of thistles by the Wall nearby.

It would take her only a few minutes to get both. Lirael hurried back towards the gate, not noticing that behind her the Hrule's black, violet-pupilled eyes had flickered open, and the muscles around its hideously wide mouth were beginning to twitch.

chapter five

the various uses of spirit-glass arrows

On the Greenwash river, the Old Kingdom

The current took Ferin's raft quickly out from the shore, which was just as well, as a nomad appeared there only minutes later and fired several arrows after her. With the benefit of good moonlight to aim by, these came perilously close but did not hit. Ferin was pleased to see that the woman then tried to wade out to get a closer shot, but was tumbled over by the river and only just made it back ashore, without her bow.

In less happy news, the exertion of launching the raft made the wound on her leg bleed again, soaking through the bandage. As she carefully rewound it, trying not to tip the raft, Ferin noticed her makeshift transportation was already sinking lower in the water as the reeds grew sodden. It wasn't going to sink, but it certainly wasn't going to be buoyant enough to keep her entirely dry.

The water was very cold. Ferin shivered, grimaced and

locked her jaw tight to stop her teeth chattering. Slowly drawing herself up, she tried to move to a sitting position atop her pack. But the river was too rough, and the raft too unstable. She had to lie down over her pack, and try to use her makeshift paddle as a steering oar rather than as a means of propulsion. The current was too strong for her to make any headway paddling.

After twenty or thirty minutes of striving with the paddle, Ferin knew that she couldn't steer the raft either. Even a proper wooden oar, rather than her splayed reed paddle, would be useless. The river was flowing too swiftly, and it would take her where it willed.

There was only a slim chance this would be to the southern shore.

Still, she kept up her efforts with the paddle. Not because it did anything to change the direction of the raft, but simply as a physical activity to try to keep from freezing to death.

The night grew colder as the sky continued to clear, the stars and moon growing brighter, while giving no warmth. Ferin paused in her paddling to draw her fur cloak around her more tightly, and to eat some dried goat meat and lumps of crystallised honey. The food would help somewhat, she knew, but she also knew she was too wet and too cold. She would be dead before dawn unless something happened.

And as nothing would happen unless she made it happen, Ferin considered her last, not very attractive chance of survival.

The one spirit-glass arrow remaining in her arrow case.

The chief shaman of her tribe had given her three, all the Athask people possessed, and told her how to use them. Generally they were simple weapons, to be fired at certain points of a Free Magic creature's anatomy, like the head, if it had one, or, if being shot at a shaman or witch, aimed at their navel where their power was centred.

But spirit-glass arrows had other uses. Dangerous uses.

One of these was to start a fire, when all other fire-starting methods had failed. Once started, such a fire would burn of its accord, without fuel, for a day or more. But unlike a normal fire, one started in this way could potentially draw other Free Magic creatures to it, and the smoke was poisonous.

Given definitely freezing to death against only *possibly* drawing more enemies or inhaling the smoke, Ferin thought there was not much choice. Though as an added complication, such a fire would be quite capable of burning her reed raft to ashes, regardless of how wet it was. The fire from a deliberately broken spirit-glass arrow would continue to burn underwater. Or earth. It could not be extinguished, save by other magic, or the passage of time.

Ferin thought about that for a while, until she realised she was slowly slipping into a dazed sleep, a cold sleep from which there would be no awakening. There had to be some way to have the benefit of the fire, without burning the raft . . .

Sometime later, Ferin snapped back into consciousness again. She had gone to sleep, she didn't know for how long. She couldn't remember where the moon had been in the sky. All she knew was that she was very, very cold, and her legs, which were sodden and not covered by her cloak from the knees down, could only be moved with great effort, and she could no longer feel her feet. Even the pain from the wound above her ankle was only a dull ache, but this was not a good sign.

Ferin forced herself to move her recalcitrant limbs, flexing her feet backwards and forwards, wriggling her toes and fingers and arms and every part of her body that could move. The raft rocked a little, but though it was even lower in the water, it was steadier as well. After a few minutes of wriggling brought some life back into her hands and feet, Ferin managed to sit up without oversetting the raft.

She had to use the spirit-glass arrow to make a fire, she knew, and she had to do it very soon. Desperately she tried to get her cold and frozen mind to think of some way of containing the magical flames.

Slowly an idea did rise to the surface, rather like the lumps of ice that were popping up here and there in the river. Suddenly there, and then gone again. Ferin made sure this idea didn't go, concentrating all her willpower to both remember it and put it in action.

Fumbling with frozen fingers at her pack, she managed to get one strap undone. Reaching inside, she groped about until she felt – or thought she felt, because her fingers were so numb – the ceramic pot of wound grease she'd used before. Dragging it out, she wedged it between two bundles of reeds on the floor of the raft, as far forward as she could reach.

The pot had a wooden plug which it took great effort to pull out with uncooperative fingers, but she did it.

Then she took the spirit-glass arrow from the quiver. Removing the leather hood was also quite a trial, but she managed it. Holding the arrow high, she eyed the pot, focusing her mind. The trick would be to bring the arrow down with enough force to shatter the head but make sure all of it fell in the pot . . .

She was just about to try this when she realised the pot might shatter instead, and in any case, bits of arrowhead would go all over the place. There was an easier way; she was just so cold and tired the dramatic method had come to her first.

Settling the arrowhead over the pot, keeping her eyes somewhat averted so she didn't have to look at the fierce glow of the writhing figure trapped inside the dark volcanic glass, she took out her knife. Reversing it, she took a deep breath and struck the arrowhead hard with the pommel.

Spirit-glass shattered, the fragments falling into the pot at the same time a blazing white flame shot up to a height of several feet. Ferin flinched back, making the raft rock dangerously, and turned her head aside to avoid the piercing, metallic smoke that spun in circles around the white flame.

Don't let the pot break, thought Ferin. Don't let the pot break!

Even through tightly lidded eyes, she could see the white flame. There were sparks flying up from it too, and she had the sensation that it wasn't so much a flame as an incredibly thin, capering creature of intense light that was trying to bend itself over to her.

She inched back as far as she could, the raft rocking again. The pot tilted a little as well, the sight of that almost stopping Ferin's heart. But it did not go over, and slowly the tall white flame diminished, shrinking back down and becoming somewhat redder, more like a normal fire. The smoke changed colour too, turning black and lessening until it was no more than a narrow, steady stream.

Ferin watched it as she might watch a coiled snake, until she could bear the cold no more and approached the pot. She could feel the heat from it on her face as she slid over her pack towards it. The raft bobbed again, the pot tilting back just a fraction. Ferin stopped moving, sensation returning to her nose. She hadn't realised it had started to freeze as well. Her ears were protected by the hood of her cloak, but her face was open to the chill.

The pot began to glow red, and the water slopping around it to hiss and boil. Ferin watched with alarm. If it got hotter still, the pot might crack and fall apart, or burn through the reeds and sink, and she would freeze to death after all.

But it didn't. The pot glowed entirely red, but it didn't crack, and the constantly slopping water through the bottom of the raft cooled it enough that it didn't burn through the reeds. Every time the raft shifted and another small wave sloshed around the bottom, Ferin thought she might hear the hissing suddenly become a terrible cracking sound and she braced herself for disaster, but each time the pot just sat there steadily giving off heat.

Eventually, she realised it probably wasn't going to crack and sink her. Ferin drew herself up on the pack and slowly rotated herself around to put her feet near the fire. She could feel the warmth of it even through her moccasin-like low boots, which were of triple-thickness goat hide lined with the fur of the pine martens the *athask* cats liked to hunt and eat.

As her feet warmed, they were shot with sudden pains, and by the time those pains had subsided, her hands and face were cold again. Slowly rotating herself around the pack, she got in position to warm the top part of her body.

Judging by the moon, there were only three or four hours to dawn. The sky was almost entirely clear now, with no hint of cloud. She had the pot, which, barring an accident, would keep her warm until the sun came up. With the warmth, her mind was starting to work again as well, beginning to grapple with the next problem.

She was in the middle of a very big river in full spring flood. It was taking her east at great speed, faster than a horse could trot, and unlike a horse, it was going to keep doing it without rest, until the raft sank, or it ran into something . . . or they reached the sea.

Ferin had been shown a map back at the Athask clan's spring camp. It wasn't very detailed, nor very accurate (though she didn't know that) but it did indicate that the Greenwash Bridge was a long way upstream from the open ocean, perhaps thirty or forty leagues. But a swiftly flowing river could go such a long way in a relatively short time, taking whatever it carried with it.

Ferin looked at her makeshift paddle. She could swim well, and had direct experience with rivers and lakes, though none anywhere so broad and swiftly flowing as the Greenwash. But she knew almost nothing about the sea, or what would happen when this river met it.

It would be best if she could get ashore before the raft reached the ocean, she told herself. Perhaps in daylight it would be easier to work out some way to escape the clutch of the current. If she was lucky, some swirl or eddy might even get her close enough to swim, and she could drag the raft behind her.

There was still quite some time before sun-up. Ferin moved again, until she was lying across the raft, slightly curled up, so her entire front was warmed by the pot. Admittedly every now and then the raft rolled so far her head got a slight dunking, or her feet, but it was worth it.

All she had to do now was stay awake until dawn, she told herself. Then she would begin paddling again, and try to reach the southern side of the river.

But staying awake was not easy now she was relatively secure, warm and totally exhausted. Even the dull ache of her wound was not enough to keep sleep at bay. Slowly she drew herself into a tighter ball on top of her pack as the river grew a little less wild and the raft steadier.

The current was slowing because the river was broadening

out. Ferin couldn't see this in the dark, and in any case did not know this was a sign it was beginning to approach its confluence with the sea. There were still a dozen leagues to go, but as the river spread wider and the current lessened, Ferin lost her battle against weariness.

She slept, and the raft spun and bobbed onwards towards the mouth of the river and the open sea, the little pot glowing red all the way, a thin drizzle of black smoke rising from it to mark her passage.

The smoke was as good as invisible now, in the night. But come the morning, that plume would be like a sharply drawn line of charcoal against the blue sky, declaring to all with eyes to see that there was something unusual adrift on the Greenwash.

chapter six

the general looks dead

The Wall

As Lirael made her way back to Nick, fixing a thistle to the head of a spear-shaft with a simple mark of attachment, the Ancelstierrans fired star-shells again, four in a line abreast, several thousand feet above. With a southerly wind, they actually worked for once, and the white flares slowly descended on their parachutes, illuminating a huge stretch of no-man's-land in stark black and white, all colour lost in the harsh glare of brilliantly burning magnesium.

In the light from the star-shells, Lirael could see a party of around twenty soldiers climbing out of the forward trenches. Some carried stretchers and were presumably healers of a sort, but there were more with rifles, their bayonets gleaming in the monochrome light of the drifting flares.

Behind her, she heard Captain Anlow call out to the guards, ordering them to come forward. Clearly the Guard officer feared the Ancelstierrans might do something foolish, perhaps even attack Lirael. Or there might be an accident.

The Ancelstierrans might want to take the Hrule back,

Lirael suddenly thought. It had come from the south, and it was still on their side of the Wall. That could not be allowed; it had to be dispatched before they arrived.

She hurried, and was greatly relieved to see the Free Magic creature was still lying in the dirt, not moving. Lirael kept an eye on it as she rushed over to Nicholas, who had regained consciousness and was trying to lift his head. She knelt by his side, brushing back her hair from her face so she could see him properly. And he could see her.

'Can you hear me?' she asked. He was conscious, but his eyes were only partly open and his wits might well be wandering. She could feel that the healing spell was still working on him, but was surprised to see the Charter marks moving about just under the skin at his throat and on his face, faint golden symbols rising momentarily only to vanish again, carried around in his bloodstream. That didn't normally happen, but she had to presume it was a good thing.

'Yes,' whispered Nick. He smiled and said, 'Lirael.'

Lirael brushed her hair back again nervously, not noticing that her golden hand was glowing rather more brightly than it had been. She didn't smile. She was too anxious about the healing spell, and the Hrule, and the approaching Ancelstierrans. At least she told herself that was why she felt unsettled. It couldn't have anything to do with Nick smiling at her.

Focus, she told herself sternly. Be the Abhorsen-in-Waiting.

'The spells are working strangely on you, but they are working. I'd best deal with the Hrule.'

'The monster?'

Lirael nodded. She kept flicking her gaze away to keep an eye on the creature, not acknowledging to herself that this was also because she was nervous looking at Nick up so close.

'Didn't I kill it?' asked Nick. 'I thought my blood might poison it . . .'

'It has sated it,' said Lirael, once again looking at the beast. At least that's what she thought had happened. 'And made it more powerful, when it can digest it.'

'You'd better kill it first, then,' gasped Nick. He tried to lift his head again, but was too weak.

'It can't be killed,' said Lirael. She had remembered pretty much the whole entry in *Creatures by Nagy* now. Though it would be more accurate to say that no one *knew* how a Hrule might be killed, this was hardly the time to start such a discussion. 'Nothing of stone or metal can pierce its flesh. But a thistle will return it to the earth, for a time.'

It was a postponement more than a solution. For a year and a day, the Hrule would be bound under the earth. Lirael frowned, thinking about the slim, red leather diary Ellimere had given her, insisting that she keep it for forthcoming social events. Dealing with a Hrule a year hence would be an unusual entry.

She took up the thistle-headed spear and walked over to the creature. Its violet-pupilled eyes followed her, but the thing still didn't move. Presumably it couldn't, or it would have already attacked her. That was another thing Lirael remembered. Hrule were very fast.

Lirael lifted the spear high, and drove it down at the creature's chest. She wasn't sure what she'd expected, but it wasn't for the thistle-point to enter the Hrule's body almost without resistance. The crocodilian hide that could turn swords and Ancelstierran bullets simply parted, and the thistle went deep into the creature's flesh.

The spear-shaft quivered for a moment, then it gently puffed away, turning into dust so that her fingers clutched at empty air. The dust fell in a tight cloud upon the Hrule, and where it fell, the tough hide and the flesh beneath became like water, which sank into the ground. Soon there was nothing left, not even a stain upon the earth.

'How did you know to bring a thistle?' asked Nick, his voice wavering as he tried to get up or just roll onto his side. Lirael went to him and put her hand on his chest, gently pressing him back down.

'I didn't. I arrived an hour ago, in answer to a rather confused message from the Magistrix at Wyverley. I expected merely to cross here, not to find one of the rarest of all Free Magic creatures. And . . . and you. I bound your wounds and put some healing charms upon you, and then I went to find a thistle.'

'I'm glad it was you,' said Nick. He was already feverish, Lirael thought. She looked down, letting her hair fall across her face again, and felt the pulse in his neck, trying to act as unconcerned as possible. Intent on the healing, making sure all was correct.

'It's lucky I read a lot of bestiaries when I was younger,' said Lirael conversationally. She paused, wondering what she could talk about. She looked over at the approaching Ancelstierrans and then across to her own guards, who were lining themselves up about twenty yards away. Captain Anlow was closest, trying to attract Lirael's attention. She waved at them to go back. They did retreat a little, but stopped as soon as Lirael turned away.

The last star-shell fizzled out as Lirael looked back at Nick. She found it easier to talk to him in the dark. The Ancelstierrans would arrive shortly, and she presumed they would take him away again.

'I'm not sure even Sabriel would know about the peculiar nature of the Hrule.'

That sounded too much like boasting, Lirael suddenly thought. She stood up, a little flustered, and continued.

'Well, I'd best be on my way. There are stretcher bearers waiting to come over to take you in. I think you'll be all right now. There's no lasting damage. Nothing from the Hrule, I mean. No new lasting effects, that is . . . I really do have to get going. Apparently there's some Dead thing or other further south – the message wasn't clear . . .'

Lirael stopped talking and didn't exactly bite her lip, but rather gripped it with her teeth in an agony of embarrassment. She'd just spouted a lot of nonsense; Nick would think she was a fool, since obviously he'd sent the message and the creature mentioned in the telegram was the Hrule, and it was dealt with and she wished she had never come, except that if she hadn't Nick would probably have died and the Hrule would have done who knew what –

'That was the creature,' said Nick, but it wasn't in the tone of voice of someone pointing out the blindingly obvious. 'I sent a message to the Magistrix. I followed the creature all the way here from Dorrance Hall.'

'Then I can go back to the guards who escorted me here,' Lirael said. She gestured behind her, oblivious to the fact that Anlow and the whole company of Guards were sneaking forward again like guilty children. 'They won't have started back for Barhedrin yet. That's where I left my Paperwing. I can fly by myself now. I mean, I'm still –'

'I don't want to go back to Ancelstierre,' Nick burst out. He tried to sit up and this time succeeded. Lirael reached out to help him, and touched his arm for a moment before immediately letting go. She felt foolish again, because of course he was just a wounded man who needed help; there was nothing about the touching that was anything else.

'I want to come to the Old Kingdom,' said Nick. He looked up at Lirael, but she looked away, towards the approaching Ancelstierrans. They were following a zigzag lane through the wire and somebody was shouting very officiously, though she couldn't make out the words.

'I want to come to the Old Kingdom,' repeated Nick.

'But you didn't come before,' said Lirael. She still didn't look at him. 'When we left and Sabriel said you should because of what . . . because of what had happened to you. I wondered . . . that is, Sam thought later, perhaps you didn't want to . . . that is, you needed to stay in Ancelstierre for some person, I mean reason –'

'No,' said Nick. 'There is nothing for me in Ancelstierre. I was afraid, that's all.'

'Afraid?' asked Lirael. She did look at him, but hesitantly, half-hiding behind the hair that fell across her face, as she had used to do back in the Glacier. 'Afraid of what?'

'I don't know,' said Nick. He smiled again, a hesitant smile, seeking her approval. 'Can you give me a hand to get up? Oh, your hand! Sam really did make a new one for you!'

Lirael flexed the fingers on her golden, Charter-spelled hand, and once again regretted Sam's desire to show off his work. Her hand was glowing like a candle, soft behind gold-coloured glass. It was warm, and charming, but just too visible for her liking. There and then she decided the spell would go, whether it hurt Sam's feelings or not.

Nick held up his hands, one still bloody. He seemed confident she would take them.

'I've had it for only a week,' said Lirael, slowly turning her golden hand, opening and closing her fist. 'And I don't think it will work very far south of here. Sam really is a most useful nephew . . .'

Lirael looked directly at Nick this time. He was still holding up his hands. She knew if she reached out to them, she would be beginning something, making herself vulnerable, open to more hurt. If she took his hands, and he came to the Old Kingdom, what would happen? Or not happen, which might be even worse . . .

She wished the Disreputable Dog was there, to help her understand her own feelings, and to offer comfort if once again she found herself alone among all the other people who seemed to instinctively just *know* how to make friends and find lovers –

Focus, Lirael told herself. One step at a time.

'Do you think you can walk?'

'If you help me,' said Nick.

Lirael leaned forward, and their hands joined, just as the Ancelstierrans arrived and Lirael's guards closed in, Captain Anlow gesturing so they spread out in a wide crescent about the Abhorsen-in-Waiting they were there to protect.

With a distant boom another star-shell blossomed high above, casting its harsh light across the barren landscape as it slowly drifted down on its silken parachute.

The sudden illumination was accompanied by more shouting. It came from a tall, remarkably slender and very pallid Ancelstierran general. He was so pale that for a moment Lirael almost reached for a bell, thinking he must actually be a Dead creature, even though she had not felt the presence of such a thing.

But he was alive. Alive and protesting.

The general wasn't wearing a helmet or hat, his completely bald head white under the flare. Nor was he wearing khaki and mail like the others; he had on a swallow-tailed coat of scarlet with many miniature medals on his breast, though a keen observer would note none of them were for valour or wartime service. His black trousers had a broad red stripe down the sides, and his dress shoes were very much the worse for crossing the mud and debris of no-man's-land. He looked extremely out of place compared with the other Perimeter troops.

'That's him!' cried the pale general, pointing at Nick. 'Arrest him at once! And get these other people out of here!'

chapter seven

fish are more important

At sea, near the mouth of the Greenwash, the Old Kingdom

The raft of reeds slowed as the river lost its frantic pace, the spinning and rocking giving way to a gentler movement as the makeshift vessel moved out into the mouth of the Greenwash and began to simply ride up and down with the long ocean swell. It was relatively calm, the sky clear with the promise of a fine spring day ahead, once the sun deigned to lift itself above the horizon. Though still very cold, it had stopped snowing hours before as the clouds departed.

The unnatural fire in the small pot continued to burn, and the black smoke continued to climb and drift. It would be visible from some distance now, a dark wavering line drawn vertically against the pale predawn sky.

Ferin slept on. Worn out from her journey, pursued and hunted most of the way, she would have been hard to wake even before she was wounded as well. With the shock from that on top of her general exhaustion, her body had retreated into a very deep sleep indeed, almost a coma. The transition from swirling river currents to the slow rise and fall of the sea had not impinged in the slightest upon her, though in the mountains she prided herself on being alert at all times, and it was true she would usually wake at the slightest noise or a change of light or sensation.

But now she didn't even wake when a fishing boat came up carefully alongside, and two pairs of strong arms hauled her up and over the gunwale, while others pushed the raft away with oars, in order to part company as quickly as possible with the unnatural burning pot, its all-too-visible trail of black smoke and the faint but persistent reek of Free Magic.

There were four fisher-folk on the boat, all from one family. Two sons and a daughter, under the command of their mother and captain, a woman named Karrilke. They were all of middle height, but broad-shouldered and with mighty forearms from drawing heavy nets, their skin cured by sun, wind and sea to a shade that matched the timber of their boat, which, as was the fisher-folk's custom, had no name.

Karrilke bore the Charter mark on her brow and knew a few spells. Most were simple charms, to find the way at night or in fog, to locate the bigger shoals of fish, to gain warning of storms. But the captain also knew a healing spell, one employed many a time to quell the bleeding from a knife cut or to soothe a bad rope burn.

She cast that spell upon Ferin's wounded ankle, or tried to. Though she was sure she had found the right marks in the great swim of the Charter, and joined them just so, the bright symbols skittered from the nomad's skin and broke apart into nothingness.

The spell did, however, wake Ferin up with a fierce and very sudden pain which stabbed her in the navel, sharper even than the pain when the crossbow bolt had creased her leg. It was as if a sharp blade had punctured her right in the stomach, pushed all the way through and out her back.

Ferin came up with a jerk, hands fumbling for her knife, a fumble that turned into a wild flailing action as she realised she was wrapped not in her cloak, but in several dry blankets of scratchy wool. The flailing lasted only a few moments before she was held fast by two fisher-folk gripping her limbs, the one who held her injured leg careful of the wound, collecting a kick for her pains.

'Steady there, steady,' called Karrilke. 'We mean you no harm. We are fisher-folk, pure and simple. We sell our catch both sides of the Greenwash, to your people as well as our own.'

Ferin flexed against her captors one more time, but finding their grip impossible to loosen, and with the pain in her navel going away and so clearly not the result of *actually* being stabbed with a spear or knife, she let herself relax. Hopefully they would too, and give her a chance to escape a little later, when they were off guard. Though with four of them, all strong and wiry, she figured she would probably have a better chance of talking her way out of trouble. They all had knives, she saw. Not fighting knives, but a fish-gutting knife could end a life as easily as any other blade.

'Not my people,' she said. There was a trace of bitterness in that. The other tribes should have respected her as a messenger, but they did not.

'Not yours?' asked Karrilke. 'You have the look of the Twenty Tribes, though your clothes are unfamiliar.'

'I'm of the Athask; we are of the mountains, not the steppe,' said Ferin slowly. She was coming fully conscious, eyes slowly moving to take in her situation, to gauge the strength of her enemies. If they were enemies. 'Though it is true we usually count ourselves kin to the horse-lovers. Cousins, not sisters.'

'So, cousin of the horse people, my name is Karrilke. What do we call you?'

Ferin was silent for a moment. She wondered if she should simply adopt a name to make it easier to go among strangers. But what name? It was easier again to simply give them what her little not-sister Lilioth called her.

'Ferin,' she said.

'Ferin from the far mountains,' said Karrilke. 'What brings you to the mouth of the Greenwash, in a raft of reeds, with a burning pot that reeked of Free Magic?'

'I am a messenger,' said Ferin. 'I am taking a message to the other side of the great river, to the witches who live in the ice mountain.'

'There is a bridge upstream,' said Karrilke. 'Easier to walk across that than take to a raft of reeds.'

'I tried the bridge,' said Ferin slowly. She was looking at Karrilke's eyes, trying to gauge who this fisherwoman was, how she would react. 'Enemies were watching; I was wounded in the fight. They will be watching still, it being the only bridge. I had to take to the water. And it has worked out, has it not? If you take me to the southern shore, I will give you gold.'

'You don't think we will just steal whatever valuables you have?' asked Karrilke.

'No,' said Ferin. 'I do not think so. Your eyes do not slink about when you talk. Besides, you have the magic mark on your forehead, like the witch in the cave whose message I bear. That is an omen that you will help me.'

'Is it?' asked Karrilke, but she smiled. 'A witch in a cave? In your mountains? Who bore the Charter mark?'

'Yes,' said Ferin. 'She came from the witches in the ice.'

'You mean the Clayr?' asked Karrilke.

'Yes,' said Ferin. 'But I do not say so, because names may call the named, or others who listen for the name, on the wind. Already I know there are many who do not want my message to arrive.'

'The strange fire in the pot, that is the work of what we would call a Free Magic sorcerer,' said Karrilke slowly, as she tried to puzzle out this strange catch from the sea. 'But you do not seem to be one yourself. They do not readily take to the water and, among your people, are chained at the neck, are they not?'

'I am no witch,' said Ferin. 'The fire . . . it came from a spirit-glass arrow. I would have died of the chill else.'

'I have heard of those arrows,' said Karrilke. 'Treasures, are they not?'

'My message is very important, both for my people and your own,' said Ferin. 'I carried three spirit-glass arrows when I set out. Now, tell me. Will you take me to the southern side of the Greenwash?'

Karrilke did not answer immediately. She looked away from Ferin, huddled in the blankets on the swaying deck, and out over the sea. The shore could be seen in the distance as a dark smudge on the horizon; they were now north of the Greenwash, so that land was at least notionally claimed by one of the clans. Drifting near this shore, but still too close for Karrilke's liking, a thin line of very dark smoke rose from the raft.

'We should have sunk it,' she said, half to herself.

'What?' asked Ferin, as the captain grabbed a stay and stood up on the gunwale, to look in all directions.

'We should have sunk your raft and that fire with it,' said Karrilke. 'That smoke may invite interest from those it is better to avoid. Now tell me, will you swear upon . . . what do you mountain-folk swear upon?'

'We do not swear upon anything,' said Ferin. 'We simply keep our word.'

'Then if you will agree to keep the peace, and follow my orders, we will release you.'

'Will you take me to the southern shore?' asked Ferin. 'I will pay.'

'Our home port is Yellowsands, twenty leagues south of the Greenwash mouth. We will take you there. But not until our hold is full of salted batith.'

Ferin looked puzzled.

'Batith are fish,' whispered one of the crew who held her.

'But . . . but I have said I will pay!' exclaimed Ferin. She began to struggle again, and found the grip of the fisher-folk had not relaxed. 'I have gold. Enough to pay for any cargo of fish.'

'I have never sailed home to Yellowsands without a full hold,' said Karrilke. 'The fishing has been good; it should take only three, perhaps four more days before we can strike for home.'

'My message is very important!' cried Ferin. 'I cannot waste *any* time! Let me show you the gold!'

'Time is never wasted fishing,' said Karrilke. 'Money is only money.'

'Can you sell me one of your . . . your little boats?' asked Ferin desperately, seeing two dinghies lashed down on the other side of the deck.

'Do you know how to sail one?' asked Karrilke.

'No,' said Ferin. 'I would work it out.'

'In any case, we use them for fishing,' said Karrilke. 'Now, will you agree to be peaceable and follow orders, and work with us, and in three or four days you will most likely be landed alive and undrowned at Yellowsands.'

'Most likely?'

'Nothing can ever be entirely certain at sea,' said Karrilke. 'Perhaps I should say we will all do our best to see you safe ashore, south of the Greenwash, once we have caught our fill of fish.'

'I see no choice,' said Ferin slowly. 'But I tell you, even the delay of three days may mean the deaths of many of my people, and perhaps of yours too. My message is truly important.'

'You are young, and a long way from home,' said Karrilke. 'I expect they told you your message is more important than it really is. Otherwise they would have sent an older messenger –'

'I am the best messenger!' interrupted Ferin. 'I have been trained since I could walk to be the best at everything. Let me stand and I will show you!'

Karrilke smiled.

'In any case, if it is anything of great significance, the Clayr will have Seen it. Now we are wasting time. Will you swear, and in three days be landed safe to take your message onwards?'

'I must,' said Ferin despondently. 'I swear to be peaceable, and obey, in return for being taken ashore to the south, when you are ready.'

'Good,' said Karrilke. She signalled to her son and daughter, who readily let go and backed away. 'Your first task is to lie there, to sleep if you can. The wound in your leg would not take a healing spell, but it should improve with rest. Lie still, I mean it!'

She added that last because Ferin was struggling to sit up, to see more than the bottom of the boat and the sky above.

'I would like to see,' said Ferin respectfully, her eyes cast down, as she would address an elder of the tribe.

'Tolther, Huire, lift her carefully and put her back against the mast,' said Karrilke. 'But you, Ferin, keep your legs straight out, and do not fidget. Hurry, there is fishing to be done!'

'I'm Tolther,' said the young man as he helped lift Ferin. 'Mother is strict, but she's fair. We'll sail at all speed for home once the hold is full.'

'And I'm Huire,' said the young woman. 'What did your white fur come from? It's so soft and warm.'

'A big hunting cat,' said Ferin. Now that she had given her word and so could not dive over the side and swim for the distant land or make some other stupidly desperate effort to continue her mission, she felt very weary again and her leg was extremely painful. The fisher-folk set her down very gently, but even so, she had difficulty not showing how much the wound hurt. Though she was sure they could not tell. She did not want to be the first of the Athask people to show pain in front of strangers, being certain none ever had.

'I thank you for your kindness,' she managed to get out, and then through hooded eyes caught a brief glimpse of the sea about them, a huge blue-grey wave lifting the boat for a few seconds before they slid down its side into the trough, with the white spray flying up, all of it strange to Ferin, who had never left the mountains before.

Then she passed out again, and slept, as Karrilke shouted commands and the mainsail was hoisted and trimmed to a useful, arching billow. The slap of the waves on the hull became louder as the vessel drew closer to the wind and moved faster, heading to the northeast and further away from land. Aiming for the banks, the uprising of the seabed fifty or sixty leagues distant, where the great shoals of batith swarmed, waiting to be caught.

unruly bells which wish to ring

No-man's-land, near the Wall

There was no response to the pallid general's demand for an immediate arrest. He grew even louder at that and turned to the closest soldier in a rage, almost gobbling as he shouted.

'Arrest this man! And clear these other people off to where they came from!'

The soldier he was shouting at was a scarred veteran with a warrant officer's crown on his sleeve, a Charter mark on his forehead and the painted badge of the Crossing Point Scouts on the side of his steel helmet. He didn't answer, but looked away idly as if he hadn't heard the officer even speak.

'I'm giving you a direct order!' bellowed the general. He pointed his skinny, almost skeletal forefinger at Nick. 'Arrest . . . that . . . man!'

The warrant officer continued to stare vacantly at the Wall. A sergeant stepped up closer to him. Also from the

Crossing Point Scouts by his badge, he took out his pipe and began to pack it with tobacco.

'I will brook no dumb insolence! I am General Feversham, from Army Headquarters in Corvere, do you hear? Arrest that man or I'll have all of you in the stockade for the rest of your lives!'

Lirael looked over the Ancelstierran soldiers and saw they were *all* from the Crossing Point Scouts, all bearers of the Charter mark, and every single one of them appeared to be in deep communion with the night, the sky, the Wall, the ground, or in fact everything else *except* the bellowing general in front of them.

'I'll do it myself!' roared the general. He fumbled at his belt, looking for a revolver, realised he was in mess dress and so unarmed, and reached out to take the rifle from the nearest soldier. Who, while pretending nothing was happening, also did not let go.

'No,' said Lirael calmly as the general continued to tug at the weapon. She reached for the Charter, gathered five marks swiftly from the shining torrent flowing through her mind, and flung them from her hand as a net of golden light that settled over the general's bald head.

He let go of the rifle, lifted one hand towards his ear, emitted something between a burp and a hiccup, and collapsed to the ground, caught at the last minute by the sergeant next to him, who dropped his pipe and cursed.

'Sorry about that, ma'am,' said the warrant officer, turning to Lirael and saluting her smartly. 'Sergeant Major Nield, of the Scouts. Ah, you do have matters in hand here? With that creature that came up from the south?'

'Yes,' said Lirael. 'The creature has been dealt with, though either I or the Abhorsen herself will need to return in a year and a day, for it is only temporarily banished, and will rise out of the earth at that time.'

'What was it?' asked the sergeant major curiously. 'Begging your pardon, ma'am, but none of us ever saw anything like that before, and we've seen a lot come across the Wall.'

'A Hrule, a self-willed Free Magic creature,' said Lirael. She felt Nicholas drooping at her side and quickly glanced at him. He was barely conscious, struggling to stay on his feet. 'I'm sorry, but we must go.'

'With Mr Sayre?' asked the sergeant major. 'It is Mr Nicholas Sayre, isn't it? Captain Tindall said so, when he hopped up to us and sent us ahead.'

'Yes,' said Lirael. She hesitated, then said, 'He needs to come with me. You may know he was affected by the . . . the events at Forwin Mill. He should have returned with us then.'

'We have orders from the very top not to let him go,' said the sergeant major doubtfully. 'I mean, not just from some visiting old busybody like Feversham; *he* was just all wrangled up because his dinner got disturbed. He thought it was an intruder on a motorcycle. The general, I mean. He caught sight of Mr Sayre in pursuit; he never saw the creature at all. But there's orders from General Tindall and Colonel Greene, who commands the Scouts. Mr Sayre not to be allowed to cross.'

'He needs to come with us,' repeated Lirael calmly. She heard her guards shifting about behind her, preparing to support her with force, she supposed. There were only twenty or so Scouts, though one did have one of those rapid-firing weapons, a Lewin machine gun. 'You know I am the Abhorsen-in-Waiting?'

'Yes, ma'am,' said the sergeant major, his face troubled.

'Nicholas Sayre is . . . um . . . infused with Free Magic,' said Lirael, choosing her words carefully. 'We need to take him back to the Old Kingdom to make sure he doesn't . . .'

She felt Nick grow heavier, his knees buckling. He was falling into unconsciousness again, all his weight now on her arm. She could barely hold him up.

'We need to help him remain human,' whispered Lirael, hoping Nick couldn't hear. 'Let us go, and I will send message-hawks to become telegrams to all who need explanation. It will not be your responsibility.'

'We should take the general back anyway, Roger,' said the pipe-smoking sergeant. 'I don't reckon we ever caught up with whatever was going on here anyway. Do you?'

The sergeant major looked down at the cadaverous general. He really looked dead now he was on the ground, though the miniature medals on his chest were rising and falling with his slow breath.

'He won't remember,' said Lirael quickly. 'I didn't just put him to sleep. He won't wake till dawn, and he'll have forgotten everything that happened past sunset.'

Sergeant major and sergeant both lifted their eyebrows in

surprise. This was powerful and subtle Charter Magic, beyond anything they could do.

'I guess you're right about nothing going on,' said the sergeant major, low-voiced to the other NCO. He didn't look at Lirael. 'Nothing to see here. Let's pick up the general and head back.'

The sergeant major gestured to two of the stretcher-bearers who were waiting behind. They came up quickly, and rolled the general onto their canvas litter, not at all gently, and one made a rude comment under his breath, at which the other laughed, stifling it as the sergeant major turned to look at him.

Two of Captain Anlow's guards hurried to Lirael's side and picked up Nick. Lirael was both relieved to not have to hold him up any more but also reluctant to let him go. When she did, she looked closely at his unconscious, relaxed face, so pale in the moonlight. She was comforted to see faint Charter marks moving across his skin, indicating the healing spell was still at work.

'Let's go back,' said Lirael.

Captain Anlow bellowed orders. More of the guards moved around Nick, one of them unrolling a kind of hammock that served the same purpose as a stretcher, with two guards carrying each end. Lirael walked ahead of them, to the tunnel through the Wall, thinking deeply about what to do with Nick. He should recover from the loss of blood relatively quickly, with rest, but there was the greater problem of the Free Magic inside him. What if the Charter mark and whatever else the Disreputable Dog had done was merely like a cork pressed into a bottle of sparkling wine? Or like a layer of lacquer upon something that, if flexed, would break and crack? Then all that Free Magic would come out, and Nick, at least as a normal person, would be consumed . . .

Charter marks flared in the stones of the Wall as Lirael passed the gate. She reached out to touch them, comforted by the warm, familiar sensation of connection, joining with the endless flow of the Charter. It made her feel less pessimistic about Nick. There was such quiet, pervasive power here in the stones. After all, in the end even Orannis had been defeated and bound by the Charter, acting through Lirael and others. Whatever power inhabited Nick would be nothing in comparison.

She walked on, still thinking, until surprised by a shout of alarm from behind her. Lirael spun about, hands reaching for bell and sword. Half a dozen paces behind her, the guards carrying Nick quickly put him down and backed away. But there was no sudden, acrid stench of Free Magic, no flashes of white lightning. Whatever power lurked within Nick had not risen forth.

Rather, it was Charter marks flowing *into* him that had alarmed the guards. Marks were floating off the stones of the Wall as if some strange, invisible tide lifted them. Spinning in the air, they spiralled down to fall upon Nicholas Sayre, everywhere from his toes to his pale forehead. The marks lay there for a moment like freshly fallen snowflakes, and then sank in, passing through cloth and flesh.

More and more marks, multiplying by the second, emerging from every stone. Falling so densely they formed small rivers, waterfalls of golden light. So many marks they could not be seen individually, and when Lirael rushed to Nick's side and caught some in her open hand, they were not marks she knew.

'What do we do?' asked Captain Anlow anxiously. 'I've never seen *this* before.'

'They're not defensive,' said Lirael slowly. 'The Wall isn't trying to stop him crossing.'

She let the marks she'd caught fall. They did not go straight down, but drifted sideways to Nick. She'd felt something of their nature, something akin to the depths of a Charter Stone, though she could not place them more accurately than this. And she had no idea why they were flowing so strongly into Nick, or what spell all those marks might be weaving together.

'Pick him up and let's get through.'

Though all the guards were Charter Mages, of many differing abilities and familiarity with the Charter, there was a notable reluctance from all of them to pick Nick up again. Unknown Charter marks and unknown Charter spells were incredibly dangerous, but even so Lirael was surprised how slowly the guards were moving.

Until she realised it wasn't Nick they didn't want to approach. It was her, and they were afraid because the bells in the bandolier across her chest had begun to shiver in place, and despite their tongues being locked by leather, the faint echo of their voices could be heard, like distant music.

All the bells, sounding together.

Dampened and muffled, but somehow ringing even within the bandolier! Lirael could feel their vibration, and far worse, feel their power. All seven of the bells, from Ranna, who brought sleep, to the greatly feared Astarael, the bell who cast all who heard her into Death. None were strong enough yet for their unique powers to take effect, but they were growing louder. And who could say what the combination of all seven bells would do, when rung together in such circumstances, without a human hand? The only time Lirael knew all seven bells to sound as one before was in the binding of Orannis, and the seven had been very much under the control of their wielders, for a very specific spell.

Whatever was going on with Nick and the inherent magic of the Wall, it was also waking the bells, or upsetting them or something, and it was beyond Lirael's knowledge or experience. In a second she went from a confident Abhorsen-in-Waiting to a very frightened young woman who could think of only one thing to do.

Get out. Get the bells away from the Charter Magic in the Wall, before she and all the guards and Nicholas were made to sleep, or stripped of their memories, or forced to walk where they would not . . . or worst of all, be sent unwillingly into Death, never to return.

'Bring him! Fast as you can!' she shouted, and sprinted north, her hands clasped across the bandolier, willing the bells to be silent.

chapter nine

the sky horse clan never go to sea in spring

At sea, off the mouth of the Greenwash, the Old Kingdom

Ferin was still asleep at dusk of the day she came aboard the fishing boat, but it was not a normal sleep and she did not wake from it when the boat heeled, clipped a wave, and spray fell across her face. Nor was it an easy or restful sleep, judging by how she writhed under the blanket and tried to push it off, her cheeks bright red with fever. Her injured ankle stuck out, the bandage heavily stained with dark blood and her leg swollen above the ankle.

'She'll likely lose that foot,' said Tolther. He did not need to say 'you were wrong' or add 'unless we take her back to Yellowsands and the healer there'. They all knew that. However, none of her crew afloat would ever dare say Karrilke was wrong. Not at sea. When they were simply family again, ashore, they might venture such an opinion. Very carefully, no doubt, and in a roundabout way.

'How full are we?' asked Karrilke.

'Just over the fourth line,' said Huire. That meant the single, central hold was half full of salted fish. Karrilke had never returned from a fishing expedition without a full hold, not in twenty years. Sometimes that meant staying out a week longer than normal, with everyone on half rations of fresh water and nothing to eat but fish. She was famous for it. 'Full Catch Karrilke,' she was called, though not to her face.

'Ma . . .' began Tolther, but Karrilke gave him the look, one she hadn't had to use for a long time. 'I mean, Captain . . .'

'Yes,' said Karrilke. She didn't look at him. She had one foot up on the gunwale and was staring out to sea. Doubtless looking for the silver flecks of the batith schooling near the surface.

'She will lose the foot,' said Tolther carefully. 'Maybe die.'

'I reckon you're right about that,' said Karrilke.

'So me and Huire . . .' Tolther took a deep breath. 'Me and Huire think we should take her back. You can take the loss out of our pay.'

'That'd mean no pay for the pair of you,' said Karrilke. 'This voyage and the next.'

Tolther nodded.

'Make ready to go about,' said Karrilke.

Tolther looked across at Huire. Her mouth was open in amazement, catching the breeze.

'Well, what are you waiting for?' asked Karrilke. She pointed off to port. 'Be quick about it. I don't like the look of that craft.'

Tolther looked surprised as well now. Both he and Huire

spun to look over the port side. There, only just visible on the horizon, was a black blot that years of experience helped them instantly identify as a nomad raider, a long, sleek craft rowed by upwards of sixty warriors. It was typical of the kind used by the Yrus clan, the only one of the Twenty Tribes that was almost as at home on the sea as they were on horseback. Though it was very unusual for them to be voyaging in spring, which was a busy time with their herds upon the steppe.

Tolther and Huire leaped to the foresail and mainsail sheets as their brother, Lown, prepared to lean on the tiller. He was the oldest, and laughing now.

'You just gave up your pay for something Ma was going to do anyway!' he roared. 'Going about!'

The fishing boat came about and began to run before the wind. In the distance, they could hear the faint shouts of the rowers aboard the raider, calling cadence.

'Never catch us with this breeze,' said Lown to his mother. 'Why they out, anyway? Truce till after midsummer, ain't it?'

Karrilke glanced down at Ferin, still tossing and turning on the deck.

'Truce is custom, not any kind of law,' she said. 'Might be to do with her . . . or they've come to see what that smoke was about. As for the wind, let's hope they don't . . .'

Her pale eyes narrowed, the wrinkles come from gazing against salty wind and sun now heavily pronounced.

'Don't what, Ma?'

'Don't have a shaman or a witch on board,' said Karrilke. 'A wind-raiser, or worse, a wind-eater.'

'Why would they have one of *them* on board?' asked Lown. 'Sorcerers fear the sea, don't they?'

'They do, but if that's where their keepers want them, that's where they go,' said Karrilke. She was still watching the raider, and listening to the faint, wind-born chanting of the rowers. 'They're rowing faster.'

Lown looked over his shoulder and then back at the sails, which were full and taut, expertly trimmed by his brother and sister.

'We're drawing away,' he said. 'Keep on this course?'

'For now,' said Karrilke. 'Unless the wind shifts, which it shouldn't.'

'We do anything for the girl?' shouted Tolther towards his mother, the wind blowing his words back into his face.

'Healing spell wouldn't take,' Karrilke said. 'Best leave the wound for now. If the wind doesn't turn too much at dusk, we'll be home by dawn. Let's hope Astilaran can do something, save that foot.'

Ferin heard nothing of this, and did not feel the nor'easter that blew the fishing boat south. She was lost inside her own fevered mind, caught in a bubble of time from years ago. A very small part of her knew it was a dream, a memory, but that corner of her mind could gain no leverage to break her free and bring her to a conscious present.

She was in her own tent, made, like her clothes, of red-stitched goatskin. The dye for the red thread came from a scale insect in the oaks that grew on the lower slopes; the yarn was made from goat hair. Ferin neither spun nor dyed herself, nor did she look after goats, as would be normal for the children of the Athask people. All her time was spent in training and learning, readying her mind and body for its eventual occupation by the Witch With No Face.

In this fever dream, Ferin was having the Talk with the elder who had most to do with her, a woman named Jithelal, Jith for short. She thought of it as 'the Talk' because it was a common subject, often returned to, particularly before the few festivals when Ferin was required to join the clan. At such a time she could almost feel she was another daughter, another sister, one of the Athask without difference.

'You are the Offering,' said Jith. 'That means you are the best of us, or you will be. Strongest, fastest, most cunning.'

Ferin bent her head. She did not speak during the Talk.

'You live apart from us, not because you are not one of the Athask. You live apart because what you do is for all the people, not for one family. We are all your fathers and mothers; we are all your brothers and sisters; we are all the children you will not bear.'

Ferin bent her head again.

'You must be the best, for if we were to give less to the Witch With No Face, she would be displeased. In her anger, she would kill and despoil, perhaps slaying many of the Athask people. You, Offering, stand against her in the same way the strongest of a war party must turn against over-whelming pursuit, selling their life dearly so the others may escape. You are our hope, our shield.'

Ferin nodded again.

The dream blurred and changed, and all of a sudden Ferin was in the Offering's Chair, which was really only a cushion set into the hollow in the middle of the great round stone that sat above the Athask people's lower camp, where they wintered.

A huge bonfire burned on the flat before the stone, sparks flying up to the clear, cold sky and the full moon above, a ring of ice around its luminous disc. The dancing had finished, and now all the clan were engaged in the traditional act of gratitude to the Offering. The line had begun with the oldest, each person passing the Offering and taking her hands, just for a moment, to whisper their thanks for what she must do. Then the adults in their prime, the hunters, the warriors, the goat-herders, the spinners and dyers, the gatherers and others. Last came the children, those nearly full grown aloof and self-conscious; the middling ones tired and grumpy, and then the toddlers, last to come, for the babies were too small.

The very little ones, though they could walk, could not reach Ferin's hands, and she was not allowed to bend down to them, for the Offering must bow to no one on this night. So they touched her feet and mumbled the words and toddled away to waiting embraces and straight to bed.

All save the last, who did not touch Ferin's feet. Ferin looked down wonderingly, for this child did not look like the others. She felt a flash of fear as he . . . no, it . . . looked up, for instead of a face it had a mask of dull bronze, a half mask that did not cover its mouth, a mouth full of sharp teeth that it lowered upon her ankle and began to gnaw at Ferin's flesh with horrible grunting noises, like a boar ripping with its tusks. Pain shot through Ferin and she choked trying not to scream, and then she kicked, trying to throw off this horrible thing that she knew was no child, but somehow the Witch With No Face herself, chewing on her leg –

Ferin woke up, still choking. For a moment she thought she was in another dream, for the night sky above was strangely slanted, and she smelled a scent she did not immediately know, until it came to her that it was salt, the salt of the sea, mixed with the reek of fish. She was on a boat, a fishing boat, and her ankle was not being chewed upon, but had been hit by a crossbow bolt.

'Drink again, if you can,' said someone, and a face came into view, a blurry face that sharpened as Ferin blinked, once, twice, three times.

'Tolther,' said the young man. 'Remember? Feeling better? Your fever's broke. That's a good . . . good-ish sign.'

Ferin raised her head and tried to raise her injured leg at the same time. A stab of pain struck her in the head and she flopped back, gasping.

'No, best not move it,' said Tolther. He tucked the blanket back around her, careful not to touch her close. 'You stay rested. We'll be home safe at Yellowsands soon enough, get the healer to look at you . . .'

Something in his voice, some uncertainty or doubt she could hear, made Ferin turn her head towards him.

'There is trouble?' she asked.

'A raider follows us,' said Tolther. 'Has been since before sunset. And they have a witch or shaman aboard, a wind-eater who keeps taking the breeze away from us, so they're catching up.'

'A raider? Another boat?' asked Ferin. She struggled to sit up, Tolther helping her after a momentary hesitation. Her bow and arrow case were by her side, she noted, but it wasn't light enough to see much else, save the dim outline of sails and rigging above.

'From one of the clans,' said Tolther. 'Sky Horse. But that's not what they call themselves. They come from the parts of the steppe nearest the shore north of here.'

'Ah,' said Ferin. 'I know the clan. Sky Horse people . . . what they call themselves is Yrus, as we are Athask, though others call us Mountain Cat. I didn't know the Yrus go to sea . . .'

'They don't in spring, at least not normally,' said Tolther. 'Only late in summer, into the autumn, and never in winter. At least I guess so; we lay up in winter as well, so maybe they're out . . . but the storms are so bad I doubt it.'

'I feel the breeze now,' said Ferin. She could feel it on her face, cool and strong. 'This wind-eater is not so powerful, perhaps?'

Almost as she said the words, the breeze died away. Tolther grimaced.

'When the wind shifts, even by only a few points, we get it for a while, then whoever it is eats it up again.'

'Will they catch us?' asked Ferin.

'Not if I can help it,' said Karrilke, suddenly appearing next to her son. 'Tolther, stand ready on the foresail sheet; trim it for any gust we can catch.'

'How close are they?' asked Ferin. She struggled to sit up higher, but found she couldn't move her leg without suffering intense pain, which lessened if she kept still. Looking down, she saw it was greatly swollen around and above her ankle. Slowly, she looked away again, as if there were nothing of importance there, and instead picked up her bow. 'Are they within bowshot?'

Karrilke looked down at her odd nomad passenger.

'Maybe for you,' she said. 'From the stern. But I came to ask if you know how they can still be rowing at full pace. It's been nine hours, more or less. The wind-eating, I've seen that before. Not often, but it's known. But this rowing . . . any normal folk would have collapsed a long time since.'

'I know nothing of the sea,' said Ferin. 'If you help me to the . . . the stern? I will look, and perhaps even kill the witch or shaman who steals our breeze.'

'You shouldn't be moved,' said Karrilke. She hesitated, then said, 'As it is, the healer might have to take off your foot.'

Ferin shrugged.

'My foot, as my entire body, is nothing,' she said. 'I must get the message I carry where it needs to go, and that means this boat must get to shore. Help me up.'

'It is easy to be brave when you are young,' said Karrilke.

'And have little knowledge of pain. But you are right. Better to lose a foot than a life.'

The broad-shouldered woman bent down and lifted Ferin up under the arms. As her ankle dragged across the deck and her leg jerked and hung down when she was upright, Ferin blacked out from the sudden, intense pain. Only for a few seconds, but when she came back, the pain was still there, and she gasped several times as she tried to steady her breath. Her hand had also opened, and her bow had fallen.

'Bring . . . bow . . . and . . . arrow case,' Ferin managed to get out.

'I'll go back for 'em,' muttered Karrilke. She manoeuvred Ferin over her shoulder and carefully made her way astern, keeping one hand ready to grab at a stay or rail as the deck rolled and pitched under her feet, far less than she would have wanted, for it meant they were slowing again. There was almost no breath of wind, and the sails hung limp and useless.

The rowers' chorus could be clearly heard now, even without the benefit of a breeze to blow their chant to the fishing boat. They were close, and closing.

Karrilke laid Ferin down by the post of the tiller, as gently as she could. Ferin hung over the rail, fighting back the pain, trying to focus her eyes on what lay behind, the dark mass that looked like a monster eating up the silver wake of their own passage.

There were small fires aboard the pursuing raider, spots of red light, that perhaps to some would suggest lit torches, a strange thing to have on a wooden ship. Ferin knew better. As she continued to look, and her eyes adapted to the starlight, she noted that most of the ship's oars, though over the side, were held or lashed high. Only six oars a side stroked the water, but those six moved deep and with inexorable force.

'Only six a side are actually rowing,' she said. 'But those twelve are wood-weirds, or something similar. Untiring, and easily four or five times as strong as the strongest warrior. There must also be at least twelves witches or shamans aboard, with their keepers. No, thirteen, for the wind-eater could not also command a wood-weird.'

'No ordinary raider,' said Karrilke, who had returned with Ferin's bow and arrow case, and her fur cloak, which the captain laid over the girl's legs.

'Sky Horse is a small clan; they could not have so many sorcerers. A dozen such: that is the full strength of two clans, at least,' said Ferin. She felt a leaden weight forming in her stomach, which she refused to accept as the beginnings of despair. 'The tribes never normally ride together. And all sent to sea, which they hate and fear, as they do all deep water? This must be the doing of the Witch With No Face.'

'The Witch With No Face?' asked Karrilke.

'If we live, I will tell you of her,' said Ferin. She nocked an arrow, but did not draw, peering into the night while trying to ignore the pain that began in her ankle and coursed its way along her leg, stabbing at her in time with her heartbeat.

No targets presented themselves on the raider. It was

directly in line behind them, some eighty paces back, but drawing a little closer with every dip and sweep of its oars, pushing ahead as the fishing boat wallowed with flapping sails.

The wind altered. A few points. Sails filled, Karrilke's children hauled on sheets, and Karrilke herself took the tiller and heaved it, hoping to catch as much of the wind as possible.

A silhouette, something a shade darker than the night sky, appeared atop the long curved prow of the raider, someone standing for a better look.

The wind-eater.

Ferin caught the acrid stench of Free Magic, carried in on that blessed wind, the wind that was already fading, pulled back from their sails by sorcery.

She was sitting, on a swaying platform, a drumbeat of pain echoing from ankle to leg to head, her eyes blurred. It was night.

Ferin drew and shot, and her arrow sped across the starlit waters.

chapter ten

the threat of free magic

Northern side of the Wall, the Old Kingdom

The bells fell silent as Lirael ran from the Wall. They quietened almost as soon as she left the northern gate, back into a warm spring evening and the last soft light of day, with the stars just beginning to be visible in the darkening sky. Despite the bells' stillness, she ran on another fifty paces before she stopped and took her hands away from the bandolier. Her golden hand was glowing more brightly than usual, she noted, a corona of unknown Charter marks floating around her fingers, none that were anything to do with the spells Sam had cast there. But these marks faded as she glanced at them, and were gone even as she tried to memorise them for later research.

The guards came running out, six of them carrying Nick, or rather what she presumed must be Nick, because right now what they bore was a cocoon of golden fire, almost too bright to look upon. Marks from the northern face of the Wall were still rushing across to join this brilliant shroud of Charter Magic, but as the guards continued on, the rivers of light fell back. Then, a dozen or more paces away, the marks that enclosed Nick either faded or sank into him, and Lirael could see him again. Still unconscious and unaware of what had occurred in crossing the Wall.

Lirael cautiously walked towards the guards, as they moved towards her. She kept her hands across the bells, in case they should begin to stir again, but they did not. This confirmed her suspicion that it was an interaction that required the power inherent in the Wall, not just the Free Magic that lurked within Nicholas Sayre.

Captain Anlow came hurrying out of the gate, followed by the remainder of her detachment. She came straight to Lirael, looking more anxious than she wished to show, Lirael was sure. Up until a few minutes ago, the captain had been the very model of a tough officer of the Guard, willing to take on anything and, in the process, show the young Abhorsen-in-Waiting that she knew best.

'Is that going to happen again?' asked Anlow. 'And . . . what was it?'

'I don't know,' said Lirael. She gestured to the guards to lay Nick down, and knelt down next to him as they did so. She hesitated for a moment, then touched two fingers to his baptismal Charter mark.

She felt the warm welcome of the Charter and fell into the endless flow of marks. There was no corruption here, nothing that was anything different from when she touched any true mark. But she could feel a massive force of Free Magic behind the Charter . . . or under . . . or somehow kept back from somewhere else that was undefined . . . something she could not conceptually grasp, because the Charter was endless, but then there was something *beyond* or *behind* it . . .

A slight headache began to form between her eyes.

Lirael leaned back and stood up.

'I don't know, Captain,' she said. 'His Charter mark is unsullied, he is as much part of it as we are . . . but he is also deeply . . . deeply *full* of Free Magic. And he has lost a lot of blood. My healing spell still works upon him, but he is very weak . . .'

Lirael's voice trailed off as she tried to think what she should do.

'Selemi's back at Barhedrin,' said Anlow, her voice dubious. 'Our chief healer. He has much experience with common wounds and illnesses, as healer and mage.'

'Thank you,' said Lirael. She was already forming a plan in her mind. It was one she was reluctant to adopt, though already she knew it was the only choice. 'But this is a most uncommon . . . um . . . condition.'

'You'll take him to Belisaere, then?' asked Anlow. Lirael could hear the relief in the captain's voice.

Lirael had thought of that. But this wasn't the kind of thing that even the most experienced of the healers in the city hospital could deal with. Even if Sabriel and Touchstone were there, she doubted they would know what was going on with Nick. They were both very powerful Charter Mages, of course, and fine healers themselves. But this wasn't a medical problem but a mystery, one rooted in the nature of Free Magic and the Charter.

The best place for solving any kind of mystery like that, or even beginning to work out the nature of such a mystery, was in the Great Library of the Clayr. And in conjunction with that, the very best healers of all the Kingdom were to be found in the Infirmary of the Clayr.

Which meant it was finally time for Lirael to go back to her childhood home, something she had been putting off for months, despite a number of invitations and even some quite pointed suggestions from Sabriel. To return to the Clayr's Glacier, where she had been both extraordinarily unhappy, and never happier. But all those happy memories of the place were deeply entwined with memories of the Disreputable Dog, once her only and still her truest friend. Even though the Dog was no longer in the living world, and Lirael knew she would never see her again.

'No,' said Lirael slowly. 'Not Belisaere.'

She took a deep breath, shutting away memories she hadn't wanted to face, blocking off the feelings that rose in her when she thought of the Glacier, her life there, the Dog, all her cousins and aunts and relatives. The Clayr, the great family she had never really belonged to, and never would. Who had, in the end, effectively cast her out. Even if they didn't think of it that way.

'No,' repeated Lirael, after a long pause. 'Not Belisaere. I'll take him to the Clayr's Glacier. That's the best place.'

'We'll rig a proper stretcher between two horses, then,' said

Anlow, visibly more cheerful with the prospect of this particular problem departing from her area of command. 'You'll fly him back in your Paperwing?'

'Yes,' said Lirael. That was another thing. She'd grown somewhat used to flying Paperwings, but it was only six weeks since she'd first flown alone, and she'd never flown with a passenger, let alone one who was some kind of Free Magic reservoir. Hopefully the Paperwing would agree to carry him . . .

The Paperwings weren't simply magical aircraft, but had a level of self-awareness that was difficult to gauge. They were more like a free-willed Charter Magic sending than anything, a created entity that could, to some degree at least, think for itself.

Nick would have to sit behind her, an unsettling thought even though she was fairly sure he wasn't going to be consumed by Free Magic and become some sort of sorcerer or sorcerous monster. But even without such considerations, he'd need to be propped up or maybe lashed in place somehow, if he hadn't regained consciousness by the time they got to Barhedrin.

Lirael looked down at Nick again. He was very pale, almost as pale as she was herself, but in her case, though she had been pale to begin with, she had become much more so from travelling in Death, the cold river which leeched all colour from even the darkest skin. In Nick, the pallor was from dangerous loss of blood. She felt a sudden urge to just rest her hand on his forehead, and almost reached out before she stopped herself and turned away.

'Yes, by Paperwing,' she repeated herself gruffly. 'And I'll need to send a message-hawk to Belisaere, to Princess Ellimere. And one to Mistress Coelle, for a telegram to General Tindall, explaining why we took Nick with us . . .'

'We have a score or more of hawks in the mews,' said Anlow. 'Always need them, where we are.'

'I'm sure,' said Lirael absently. She was wondering what exactly she should say to Ellimere in the limited space provided by a message-hawk's little brain. Sabriel and Touchstone also needed to be informed, of course, though perhaps not until they returned . . . Ellimere had been very insistent they were not to be bothered save in a real emergency. But Sam should also be told. In fact, Sam might well be able to help work out exactly what was going on with Nick. He had already explored different paths of Charter Magic from most mages, and though it was mostly to do with making things, he might have a particular insight. Besides, Nick was one of Sam's closest friends . . .

Lirael blinked and brought her attention back to whatever Anlow was saying.

'What was that?'

'I was thinking it would be best to keep him away from the Charter Stone,' said Anlow. 'The one atop Barhedrin Hill.'

'Yes,' said Lirael. Anlow was thinking more clearly than she was, she recognised. The Wall and the Charter Stones were both taproots into the greater power of the Charter. Though whatever had happened to Nick crossing the Wall did not appear to be dangerous, they had no way of knowing what potential spell might have been placed within him, and though the Charter was generally benevolent, that benevolence might be a weighted thing, where some greater good would be gained at the cost of trouble to those locally involved. Even death, blindness or permanent stilling of a tongue, as happened when people tried to command Charter Magic beyond their ability or experience, thus preventing larger trouble by stopping an individual doing something irrevocably stupid.

'Your Paperwing is quite close to the stone,' continued Anlow.

Lirael stared at the Guard captain.

'I'll move it,' she said.

'But why take him . . . Nicholas Sayre . . . to Barhedrin anyway?' suggested Anlow. 'If you go ahead, you can fly back, easily land on the flat here, and take him away.'

'Oh, right,' said Lirael. She blushed, something made worse by the pallor of her skin. 'I'm sorry, Captain. I've not been thinking.'

'You dealt with the Free Magic creature,' said Anlow. 'The Hrule.'

'That might have been the easy part,' said Lirael. She glanced at Nick again, and brushed the hair back from her eyes in the nervous gesture she did not realise was familiar to anyone who had known her for more than a few days. 'I'd best go, then . . .'

She hesitated, thinking it through. It was only a few hours' ride to the Guard post at Barhedrin; she would be there well before midnight. But flying back would not be so easy . . . and Nick would be left with only the guards for the night. If something happened . . .

'Paperwings don't like to fly at night. I might not be able to make it back before morning.'

'We'll make camp over by that copse,' said Anlow, pointing to a stand of trees another few hundred paces further away, on the flat, grassy plain that accompanied the Wall's northern side from sea to sea. Nothing more significant than ankle-high grass ever grew there, some further magic from the Wallmakers, making it easier to watch for people or things who sought to cross.

'Keep a careful watch, Captain,' said Lirael. 'Free Magic, even contained as it is in . . . in Nicholas . . . may draw the Dead or other things.'

Still, she hesitated. Anlow saw that.

'You are feared for us? Or for him?'

'A little of both,' said Lirael, honestly. She frowned. 'Still, I agree it is best he doesn't come near the Charter Stone. If . . . if something does show up in the night, it might make sense to take him back to the gate, go into the Wall.'

'Even not knowing what happened back there?'

Lirael nodded slowly. 'The marks were not attacking him, or us. It was only their waking the bells. In any case, I hope nothing does eventuate . . . and my healing spell should hold for at least another day.'

'I can cast that spell myself,' said Anlow. 'The spiral cure-all. I saw that was what you did.'

'It was much more difficult than it should have been,' said Lirael. She looked at Nick again. Whatever had happened crossing the Wall, there was no evidence of it now. She couldn't sense any Free Magic 'leaking' out of him, and though he had lost a lot of blood, he was stable and in a healing sleep.

Lirael shook her head, but it wasn't in negation; it was to tell herself to stop dithering and get on with things.

'I'll be back as quick as I can, come the morning.'

chapter eleven

the sky horse clan never pursue past the greenwash

At sea, approaching Yellowsands, the Old Kingdom

A high-pitched, long, drawn-out scream echoed across the sea. The figure on the bow of the raider fell backwards, and the scream became a series of shouts and oaths, likely from the same person. The rhythm of the rowers and the chanting did not change in the slightest.

'Only wounded,' said Ferin with disappointment and some embarrassment, despite the difficulty of the shot. She drew her arm in clumsily, feeling her weakness, almost dropping her precious bow over the side. It had been made for her only a dozen moons past, by the finest bowyer of the clan, using the best of her stock of horn, sinew and mulberry wood, the latter particularly precious because it did not grow in the Athask people's high preserves and had to be traded for, or stolen in raids.

'Good shooting, nevertheless,' said Karrilke. The captain had her head up, nose sniffing the wind. 'If that was their wind-eater . . .'

Ferin nodded. She hoped it was the wind-eater and they were wounded enough to be put out of action, for she had no strength for another shot. She tried to settle down to an easier position, keeping her leg still. She had never felt so weak, and never felt such pain.

'Nothing,' said Karrilke, with regret. The air remained completely still, the raider drawing closer, close enough to hear the groan of the oars, the slap of the blades on the sea, and that chanting, now very clear. It didn't come from human rowers at all, the cadence, Ferin suddenly realised. It was the sorcerers keeping time for their Free Magic constructs.

'Push me over the side,' croaked Ferin. All was lost now. Her message, the Athask people . . . but there was no reason for these kind fisher-folk to die as well. 'It's me they want. They'll not pursue.'

Karrilke didn't reply for a moment. When she spoke, her words came at the same time as a fresh, spray-laden gust of wind. The nor'easter was back, and the captain was not answering Ferin.

'Haul! Haul fast!' roared Karrilke to her crew, leaning on the tiller to send the boat slanting on her best possible course. Ferin choked back a scream as the bow plunged through the crest of a wave and the hull shuddered, sending yet another stab of still greater pain through her leg.

But even with the wind in their sails, the fishing boat was

not yet sure of escape. The Free Magic sorcerers aboard the raider sped up the rhythm of their chant, urging their inhuman constructs to row faster.

A moment later an arrow narrowly missed Karrilke at the tiller. She ducked down, but it was hard to stay low and manage the heavy oar. Ferin twisted around to look. A dim bent-over shape at the bow of the raider was about to straighten up, probably after nocking a new arrow. Almost certainly it was the keeper of the sorcerer Ferin had wounded. Keepers were rarely good archers, but that first arrow had passed very close to Karrilke.

Or so Ferin thought, until the next shot flew a hand's breadth over her head, and she realised the archer was not only very good, he or she wasn't aiming at the captain. *Ferin* was the target, and only the vagaries of breeze and darkness had caused the last shot to miss.

She let herself fall back, only a moment before another arrow hit the hull with a loud *thock*. A few inches higher and it would have hit her in the head.

The next arrow went wide, as Karrilke steered the boat a little off the wind and then on again, their wake showing a sudden kink. The arrow after that went into the sea, a dozen paces short. Even rowing at ramming speed, the raider was now falling back, unable to keep up with the nor'easter lifting the fishing boat south.

'Lown! Take hold here!'

Lown came back to the tiller. Karrilke bent down over Ferin.

'You're a brave lass, and your shot saved us, I reckon,' said the captain. 'Nothing's ever sure at sea, but there's a good chance now we'll have you ashore soon after dawn, and to the healer.'

'How far is it from your Yellowsands to the place where the . . . the Clayr are?' asked Ferin. 'In the ice.'

'The Clayr's Glacier?'

Karrilke scratched her head. Ferin noticed that all the while they were talking, the captain kept a sharp eye over the stern. The chanting and the splash of oars from the raider could still be heard, though more faintly.

'I don't rightly know,' continued Karrilke. 'I suppose you'd take the south road to Navis, and keep going southwest to Sindle and from there north again, following the Ratterlin. On the royal roads, that is. There'd be lesser ways, I suppose, going west from Navis. Maybe five or six days, mounted. Someone'll have a map in Yellowsands.'

'Good,' said Ferin. She tried to say more, to fend off what she thought of as shamefully passing out, but was unable to resist the tide of weakness and pain that was rising in her body.

Karrilke caught Ferin's head as the young woman's eyes rolled back and she slumped sideways. Laying her carefully on the deck, the captain looked over the stern again. The raider was still lit by the red fires that were not fires; the oars were pulling at the same swift pace, as called by the sorcerers. But it was falling behind with every minute.

Despite this, the raider was *still* following them.

For the first time, Karrilke wondered what would happen

if it followed them all the way into Yellowsands. The Sky Horse raiders had never done so before, not in her memory, but then Karrilke had also never been pursued before by a raider full of Free Magic things that rowed all night and did not rest . . .

Yellowsands was a fishing village, not a walled and garrisoned town. The fisher-folk would fight to defend it, of course, but even if most of the boats were in, there would only be sixty or seventy people of fighting age, with perhaps half a dozen Charter Mages. And these latter were not expert in fighting spells; they knew only simple magic, mostly to do with the sea and fishing, like Karrilke herself.

Presuming the wind kept up, as it promised to do, Karrilke reckoned they would get to Yellowsands soon after dawn, perhaps an hour or even two ahead of the raider. But that was very little time to prepare a defence against a dozen wood-weirds and as many shamans and witches, in addition to their keepers.

The closest Guard post was in Navis, sixty leagues south. There was a rural constable in Yellowsands, but only one. Megril, a young annoyance if ever there was one, always poking her nose into honest fisher-folks' business. Karrilke tried to remember if Megril had the keeping of a message-hawk for emergencies. Long ago, Yellowsands had maintained its own militia and message-hawks, but there had been peace for years, ever since King Touchstone and the Abhorsen Sabriel had set everything back to rights.

Karrilke cleared her throat, and tried to speak conversationally. She was never really afraid at sea, or had long ago trained herself not to show it, but the thought of Free Magic constructs rampaging through her village scared her. She had three more children at home, and her husband, a wood-cutter . . . he would be first into the fighting with that long double-bladed axe of his . . .

'Lown,' she said. 'Do you recall if that Megril has a message-hawk? Or anyone in the village?'

Lown made a face, the usual reaction to the mention of the rural constable.

'Don't know about Megril,' he said. 'Doesn't Aulther have a pair, for the markets?'

'Aye, I'd forgot,' said Karrilke, brightening. Aulther was the fisher-folks' factor and banker, who sold most of their catches to the Fishmongers' Guild in Belisaere and arranged the cargo vessels that took the salted batith south. His birds probably only flew to and from the fish market in the city, but it would be a way to send a warning and to ask for help.

Not that any help could possibly arrive before the raider.

'As soon as we berth, you run to Aulther,' said Karrilke. 'Ask him to send a bird to the closest Guard post if he can, or to the Fishmongers' if he can't, asking for help as the village is about to attacked by a dozen Free Magic constructs, their sorcerers and keepers, from the Sky Horses and maybe other tribes with them.'

'We are? I mean, we will be?' asked Lown. He was young and had never seriously fought against anyone, so he was more excited than afraid. For the moment.

'I reckon,' said Karrilke. 'Soon as you done that, you run

home and have Da gather up everything for travelling he can get together real quick and meet us by the Charter Stone. Tell him about the raiders, and to pack food and water for all of us, three days, for travelling.'

'Food and water? Travelling?'

'We can't fight off a dozen wood-weirds,' said Karrilke. 'Have to get everyone in the village out, take the road and try to stay ahead of 'em, get to the old tower on the south road. Tolther and Huire will bring the girl to the stone, I'll go to Megril and get her to sound the alarm, and I'll fetch up Astilaran. Oh, get my harpoon from the house, and the old leather cuirass. It's hanging up with the garden tools.'

'What . . . what about the catch?' asked Lown.

'We leave it.'

'We . . . leave it?' asked Lown, his voice squeaking high in surprise.

'Better to stay alive,' said Karrilke. She slapped the deck affectionately with her bare foot. 'No point dying over salted fish. Besides, it'll keep, provided she stays afloat.'

'What do we do if they sink her?' asked Lown. He was the least imaginative of Karrilke's children, which was helpful sometimes, sometimes not.

'Raise her,' said Karrilke. 'Build another. Worry about that if and when it happens. How long till Yellowsands, you think?'

Lown looked up at the sky, roughly fixing their position in relation to the six stars that made up the Beggar; cross-checked that with the Buckle of the North Giant's Belt, sometimes called Mariner's Cheat; and finally imagined an invisible line drawn through Uallus, the fixed red star a little east of north. After that he sniffed the air a few times, and gazed out upon the sea, taking note of the swell and other indications. A land-dweller would have sworn all the sea looked the same: dark and mysterious, barely illuminated by stars and moon. But to Lown it was familiar, and he knew where they were.

'Reckon we should hear the Mouth Buoy soon,' he said. 'Even over that racket those raiders are making.'

The 'racket' was the continuing chanting of the sorcerers, now only a far-off conjoined sound, that could have been some great seabird calling in the night.

'Aye,' said Karrilke. 'Listen for it and make the turn. I'm going for'rard to talk to Tolther and Huire.'

'Will do, Ma,' said Lown. He bent his attention ahead, listening for the harsh ring of the cracked bell that swung atop the ancient barrel buoy, once a tun of western wine, triple-caulked with tar to keep it afloat. The buoy marked the mouth of the Yellowsands channel, the only sure entrance to the winding way through the treacherous drifts and bars of sand that gave the village its name.

Karrilke had considered silencing the bell on the buoy, so the channel entrance would be harder to find, but she dismissed the notion as it would take precious time. The raider was a shallow draught vessel and so could pass many of the sandbars anyway, and she suspected the Sky Horse raiders were following them by some sorcerous means in any case.

The captain forgot the buoy and went forward, one eye on the sails, ready to call for them to be trimmed if she saw them shiver or heard them flapping.

Ferin lay on the deck near Lown's feet. She was quiet, no longer writhing with fever. Simply a lump under her fur cloak, the only sign she was still alive the occasional quiver of her lower lip as she breathed in and out.

chapter twelve

a quiet conversation, everything important left unsaid

Flying to the Clayr's Glacier, the Old Kingdom

Nicholas Sayre woke slowly, his teeth aching and his eyes blurred from a cold wind that was blowing hard across his face. For several seconds he couldn't work out where he was, because there was only blue sky above and when he tried to move he found himself restrained, tied around the waist and secured behind his back. He was sitting, too, which was strange particularly as he was also slumped at an angle, his head hanging down over the edge of something . . .

He tried to sit up straight, and found that as he did so, he moved out of the freezing-cold wind into an area of still, warm air. His dulled mind processed that he was sitting behind someone; he was tied to some sort of hammock-like suspended chair, which was in . . . in the open cockpit of an aircraft.

Nicholas had flown before, several times; he had an interest in aviation and the physics of flight, and in consequence had gone for joyrides with the barnstormers from the flying circus who visited the ten-acre field near his family home on regular occasions. But this was no Heddon-Hare or Beskwith. It was completely silent, to begin with. There was also warm air in the cockpit, which was impossible, since there wasn't even a windshield.

Looking around, the flimsy contraption seemed to be little more than a kind of canoe body, with long, hawk-like wings that were far too frail to sustain flight. And as he examined the side closest to him, he saw the hull was made of something very insubstantial, some kind of thin laminated plywood or something even lighter.

Still dazed, feeling like his arm was much heavier than usual, he tapped the person in front of him on the shoulder. Whoever it was started and turned her head to look back. Even in his confused state, Nick recognised her.

'Lirael!'

As he spoke her name, memory came flowing back, like a river returning to its course after some temporary dam had burst. First came small trickles of thought, images and sounds, and then the whole lot swept into his mind. Dorrance Hall, the creature in the case, the pursuit north, making the monster drink his blood, and then . . . Lirael. She had finished off the creature . . . no, banished it for a while . . . with her thistle-tipped spear. But everything after that was lost. He had a dim recollection of golden light, light all around, like waking to sunshine through a bedroom window, so bright you can't immediately open your eyes, not until you look away.

Now he had opened his eyes.

To find himself in a silent, far too fragile-looking aircraft that presumably worked by the magic he had for many years refused to recognise as being possible. Piloted by a young woman who he had dreamed about ever since meeting her, or even before meeting her, since he didn't know that his encounter with Lirael near the Red Lake had actually happened.

'Are you all right?' asked Lirael. He could hear her easily; somehow the wind created by their speedy flight was diverted around the cockpit.

'I . . . I think so,' said Nick. 'But I can't remember what happened . . . after you got rid of that creature.'

'The Hrule,' said Lirael. 'You've been in a healing sleep since then. We brought you through the Wall and then this morning loaded you aboard this Paperwing.'

Nick put his hand against the thin material at his side. Small symbols of golden light emerged where his fingers touched, flashed brightly, and then receded again.

'This craft is made of *paper*?' he asked.

'Laminated paper,' said Lirael. 'And a great deal of Charter Magic. Hold on a moment, I need to catch a higher wind.'

She looked to the front again, and whistled: pure, clear notes that seemed to echo inside Nick's head, and out of the corner of his eye he saw more of the strange, shimmering gold symbols appear in her exhaled breath, apparently in answer to the whistling, only to whisk away out of sight as he peered forward to try to get a better look at them.

The Paperwing tilted back and to the side as it began to spiral upwards, passing through a wispy cloud that Nick observed parted in front of the Paperwing's long nose. He saw thousands of tiny droplets of moisture spatter the wings, but none came in the cockpit.

'How, how do we stay warm and keep the wind and moisture out?' Nick asked when Lirael stopped whistling, and the Paperwing settled into level flight once more.

'Where we sit – Sabriel calls it the cockpit – is spelled for warmth and to divide the wind,' answered Lirael. 'But it works only up to a point. If we go much faster you'll feel the wind, and heavy rain comes through, after a fashion. I'm fairly new to this, so we're flying lower and slower than Sabriel or Touchstone would.'

Nick looked over the side. He could see green fields below, sprinkled with small groups of trees, and a few buildings, probably farmhouses. Some distance to his left there was a broad river, the water bright under the sun. It was hard to tell how high they were, but it looked to be at least a few thousand feet.

'You haven't been flying very long?' he asked.

'Not long,' said Lirael. Though he hadn't sounded worried, she added, 'But I do know what I'm doing, and to be honest, this Paperwing could fly itself.'

'Oh,' said Nick. 'It can fly by itself?'

'Yes,' said Lirael.

There was silence for a minute or so. Nick tried to gather his fragmented thoughts. He'd wanted to come to the Old Kingdom for many reasons, not least a desire to see Lirael again, though he had not fully recognised that himself. But he had not thought through what he would do once he got here, in part because it had seemed he would have time to write to Sam before he would be allowed to cross the Wall, and that everything would take a long time and allow careful thought and consideration.

Now here he was, feeling weak and stupid, tied to a kind of hammock chair in a silent flying vehicle that worked by magic. With Lirael, but not in circumstances where he felt he could easily talk to her, or impress her. In fact, he feared quite the reverse. He'd helped a Free Magic creature escape from its prison, inadvertently begun the process of making it even more powerful, and had only been saved by Lirael's arrival, when she had immediately and competently taken care of matters.

Nick shut his eyes and groaned inwardly. She probably already thought of him as a dangerous fool for his prior involvement with Orannis, a reputation he'd now enhanced, or possibly dehanced or whatever the word might be, by his freeing and empowering the Hrule. Once again meddling in things he didn't understand and endangering others.

'Um, I'm taking you to the Clayr's Glacier,' said Lirael, after several more minutes of rather uncomfortable silence. 'Do you . . . do you know about the Clayr?'

'Sam's been writing to me,' said Nick. 'About lots of things. I was . . . well, I was just ordinarily stupid before, when we were at school. I mean, I didn't want to believe any of Sam's stories; it didn't fit with what I knew about science and everything. And then . . . then when I first came here . . . it's all rather vague, my memory, but I seemed to get even worse, refusing to acknowledge what was in front of my face –'

'But that wasn't your fault!' protested Lirael. 'You had the shard of Orannis in your heart, controlling you.'

'It was in my heart!' exclaimed Nick. He couldn't help but look down, almost feeling some phantom pain in his chest. 'Sam didn't tell me that! But surely it would have killed me when it came out?'

'No . . .' said Lirael. 'It travelled through your bloodstream, reversing the course it must have taken to go in, and then burst from your finger, to rejoin the hemispheres.'

Nick lifted his hand and looked at his forefinger. There was a star-shaped scar there above the top joint, and it was always somewhat numb, though he could feel a pinprick or other sharp pain. He had wondered what caused that numbness, and the scar.

'Sam should have told me,' he said quietly. 'I suppose he thought it would be too upsetting . . . Um, the Clayr . . . the women who can see the future, in the ice. They live in an underground city, built around a glacier. Is that right?'

'Yes, for what it's worth,' said Lirael. 'It's more complicated than that, of course.'

'But why are you taking me there?' asked Nick. 'I mean,

I'm grateful, very grateful, don't get me wrong. Thank you for dealing with that thing, the Hrule. I wouldn't want any more people to suffer from my stupidity, which seemed likely . . . there . . .'

His voice trailed off and he shook his head, wondering why he found it so difficult to talk intelligently to Lirael. He never had any problems talking nonsense to the debs at the balls in Corvere, or pretending academic conversations with the bluestockings at Sunbere, or even taking part in intelligent discourse with the students who saw through his act. Everyone said he was charming. It couldn't all be to do with his powerful and influential family, which meant nothing here. Could it?

'*I'm* curious how you ended up by the Wall with the Hrule,' said Lirael. She didn't sound at ease, either, Nick thought miserably. He was probably just a task she had to take care of, part of her duty as the Abhorsen-in-Waiting. Though he was very glad it was she who'd come along, not Sabriel. He was intimidated by Sabriel, though she had always been perfectly nice to him on the rare occasions she'd visited Sam at school.

'It all started with me visiting Dorrance Hall,' Nick began, continuing in a rather disjointed way to tell Lirael the story of how the Hrule had been brought there in the first place as a kind of museum exhibit and the mad Alastor Dorrance had tried to bring it back to life with Nick's blood, all too successfully*.

---

* As told in 'The Creature in the Case' in *Across the Wall*.

124

'So now you know about my latest idiocy . . . why are you taking me to the Clayr's Glacier?'

'I'm taking you there because . . .' Lirael continued, then stopped. She cleared her throat, seemingly uncertain about what she wanted to say. 'I'm taking you to the Clayr because, as you probably know, there is still a remnant of Free Magic power within you, left over from the shard of Orannis. Which would normally be incredibly dangerous. You would be a Free Magic sorcerer for sure, unable to resist using that power. But in your case, the . . . my friend the Disreputable Dog . . . she baptised you with the Charter mark, and somehow it took, so you are a part of the Charter *and* you have Free Magic within you. Which is . . . unusual . . . and the best place to have such things, I mean situations . . . or . . . circumstances . . . looked into is at the Glacier, where there are many very learned Charter Mages of all kinds, and also the Great Library, where there might be books or other . . . sources . . . of knowledge that can help you. I mean us. All of us, that is. Not just the two of us . . . So that's why we're going to the Glacier. We should be there before nightfall.'

Nick could only see the back of Lirael's neck, but he noticed a blush spread across her pale skin, above the high collar of her armoured coat. He grimaced, thinking it was even worse than he thought. Not only had he caused trouble, he *was* trouble, and Lirael was embarrassed to have to tell him so.

Change the subject, he thought. Change the subject!

'Um, this kind of flying is much better than back home,'

he said, grimacing again at how vacuous this sounded. But he pressed on. 'I mean, in our aeroplanes, it's very noisy. Last time I went up I was covered in oil from the engine, sprayed all over me. And it was freezing, even with a fur coat. This . . . ah . . . Paperwing is a far superior way to fly.'

Lirael didn't answer, but the Paperwing responded to the compliment by suddenly dropping forty or fifty feet and wiggling its wings, both of which scared Nick quite a lot but did not upset Lirael in the least.

'I do like flying in Paperwings,' she said affectionately, reaching out to pat the side of the fuselage. 'It's much more comfortable and far easier than flying in owl shape.'

'Owl shape?' repeated Nick quietly to himself, with an intense feeling of déjà vu. Lirael's voice and the memory of an owl, the two together, resonated in his mind, though he couldn't quite place the connection. An owl with golden eyes. And a dog with wings . . . Was that something that had actually happened?

He was thinking about the owl and the dog with wings when he finally noticed Lirael's golden hand again, still resting on the lip of the cockpit. It looked almost like normal flesh and blood, save for the faint golden tinge, until he stared at it, mesmerised by how it did look almost normal, and not quite, all at the same time. This was because every few seconds there would be a faint shimmer and Charter marks would move, revealing a glimpse of the metal structure underneath the illusion of flesh.

'Your new hand,' said Nick. 'It's . . . quite incredible. And to think Sam made it. He wasn't that great at woodwork classes in school.'

'Yes,' replied Lirael, quickly drawing her hand into her lap so he couldn't see it any more. 'Yes. It's a marvel, really. I often forget it isn't my . . . isn't really part of me.'

Nick resisted a strong impulse to slap himself in the head. Sam had told him all about the events at Forwin Mill, and how Lirael had lost her hand in the final binding of Orannis. Of course the loss of her hand, and in fact all the events of that time, were incredibly traumatic, and no matter how good the replacement hand was, she wouldn't want to be reminded of it.

It would be better to just keep his mouth shut before he stuck his foot in it yet again, Nick thought. Particularly since Lirael had lost her friend the Disreputable Dog at the same time as her hand. The Dog he had seen himself; she had brought him back from Death. Nick thought about that, his forehead crinkling with the effort. The dog with wings. He'd seen her with the owl who had Lirael's voice. It was the same dog . . . maybe it *was* a memory, not some fragment of delusion . . .

They flew in silence for some time, until Nick became aware of the alarming reality that he had to go to the toilet. The sun was high above them, so it must be well after noon. They had flown closer to the river too, Lirael obviously following it north. Nick looked down at it, but was not helped by the view of all that water, rushing along . . .

Finally, he couldn't stand it any more. It would be extraordinarily embarrassing if he wet himself, rather than just mildly embarrassing to ask for a toilet stop.

'Excuse me,' he said, blushing himself now. He felt like he was six years old again, back at prep school, and almost raised his hand. 'I'm afraid I need to . . . um . . . stop somewhere. Nature calls, don't you know.'

'Nature calls?' replied Lirael, looking over her shoulder with a very puzzled expression on her face. Nick looked away, not wanting to meet her eyes. She evidently had never heard that particular turn of phrase.

'Uh, I mean I need to . . . ah . . . pass water.'

'Oh!' replied Lirael. She quickly peered over the side, and a moment later, Nick heard her whistle and once again saw Charter marks in the air around her head, forming and moving and spinning around to enter the Paperwing. The craft immediately began to descend in a long, shallow dive towards one of the many sandy islands that dotted the river.

The Paperwing landing was almost as much a surprise to Nick as its flight, for as they drew close, it simply turned into the wind and touched the ground as gently as a petal falling from a flower, quietly and easily sliding to a stop across the sand in less than ten yards. It was very different to the bucking, bouncing and generally alarming landings Nick was used to in an Ancelstierran flying machine.

Lirael got out first, stretching before she turned to take out a sword from within the cockpit to buckle on her belt. Nick tried to look at her without being too obvious he was looking, which just made him appear very shifty. But in those few moments he saw both the Lirael who stood in front of him, but also, superimposed on the present, he saw her up to her waist in marsh water, wreathed by reeds. Both Liraels wore the same strange armoured coat of small overlapping plates; the same surcoat of silver keys on blue quartered with golden stars on green; the leather bandolier holding the seven bells of different sizes, their mahogany handles hanging down.

But the swords were different. The Lirael in the reedy swamp bore a different, somehow more impressive blade, though it was no longer or heavier, and in fact it had only one small green stone in its pommel and quite a dull silver-wired hilt, compared with the newer sword Lirael now carried, which had a gold-chased hilt and a pommel cast in bronze to resemble a snarling lion.

Nick blinked, and the two Liraels became one. She bent behind him, and undid the buckle of the strap that kept him secured to the hammock-like seat.

'We had to strap you in,' she said. 'I wasn't sure when you would wake, and I didn't want you falling out, of course.'

'Thank you,' said Nick gravely. He rested his hands on either side of the cockpit and slowly stood up, fighting off the dizziness that came over him. Lirael was quick to hold his elbow. He didn't really need it, but he didn't shrug her off. Instead he turned to look at her, really look at her, his eyes meeting hers.

'Did you . . . when I first met you, were you an owl?' asked

Nick slowly. 'I know it sounds as if I might be insane, but perhaps here —'

'Yes,' said Lirael. 'I was wearing the Charter skin of an owl. A barking owl, to be exact.'

Nick nodded. He could almost grasp the memory. It was like a shimmering oasis close by, where all else around was a bleak, featureless desert. Nearly all his time with Hedge, once he'd crossed the Wall to go to the great pit near Edge, was like that. A desolate emptiness in his mind.

'And the dog, the dog with wings,' Nick continued. 'That was the same dog who . . . who brought me back from Death?'

Lirael's eyes brimmed with quick tears. She blinked them away and said, 'Yes. The Disreputable Dog. My greatest friend.'

'Thank you,' said Nick. 'I thank you both.'

He looked down, gently moved his arm away from Lirael's grasp, and stepped out of the Paperwing. The island was mostly sand, but there was a higher part to the north, where low bushes grew. Nick mumbled something and began to walk over to it.

He hadn't got very far when he realised his trousers were coming apart along the seams, and his shirt and the khaki officer's coat he'd 'borrowed' were tearing with every swing of his arms. He stopped and looked down. His shoes were fine, but every other part of his clothing was in danger of falling off, leaving him standing naked on the pebble-dotted sand.

'My clothes!' he exclaimed, turning back to Lirael. 'They're falling apart!'

chapter thirteen

charter stones and free magic talismans

Yellowsands, the Old Kingdom

Ferin regained consciousness as she was being lifted out of the fishing boat to the jetty, one of a dozen rickety constructions that lined the waterfront of Yellowsands. The harbour was sheltered from the sea by a high breakwater, an ancient and much more imposing edifice than the jetty, made of huge blocks of black stone expertly placed together so there were no gaps for the sea to exploit.

'Welcome to Yellowsands!' said Tolther. 'Huire's going to put you on my back, so I can carry you more easily. Is that all right?'

'Yes,' said Ferin. 'Where do you carry me?'

She was pleased to have come closer to delivering her message and to see another day, a day that felt more promising. It was warmer already, the sun was coming up over the ocean, the sky was a soft blue, and her foot didn't hurt as much as it had. Though she wasn't sure whether this was a good thing or not, and when she looked her leg was very swollen above the ankle.

'To the Charter Stone,' said Tolther. 'We'll meet Astilaran there, the healer, get your foot looked at while everyone's getting ready to go.'

'Go?' asked Ferin. She screwed her eyes shut for a moment as Huire hoisted her onto Tolther's broad back, the pain in her foot returning like a surprise charge on an unsuspecting enemy. She told herself shutting her eyes was not a sign of weakness if no one could see.

'That raider's still following, or it was,' said Tolther. 'Put your arms around, a bit lower, not on my neck. We haven't the strength to fight them here, the village can't be defended, so everyone's heading out to the old tower a ways off.'

'Ah,' said Ferin, trying to keep the pain out of her voice. 'I have brought this on you, and I am sorry.'

'Oh well,' said Tolther, carefully picking his way along the jetty, with Huire walking behind, carrying Ferin's bow and arrow case, and her pack. 'With the Sky Horses coming so far south and everything, your message *must* be as important as you said to Ma. So best we help you.'

'Yes.' It took considerable effort to talk without showing that she was in pain, but she managed it. She was glad Tolther hadn't said anything requiring a longer answer.

Ferin looked about as Tolther carried her from the jetty onto the paved waterfront, with its big open-sided timber building for sorting and packing fish, where right now a cluster of fisher-folk were talking excitedly with Karrilke rather than working. They hurried past this fish-packing shed and Ferin saw a line of well-made houses stretching up both sides of a road that speared directly up a low hill. The houses were all whitewashed stone with red tiled roofs, very different from the goatskin tent camps of the Athask. From the dockside they followed the cobbled road, Tolther puffing as they began to climb, though the slope was gentle.

Fisher-folk came out of the houses as they passed, and asked what was happening. Huire told them, quickly. The result reminded Ferin of shooting ducks on the high lakes: one bird would drop to the first arrow and most of the others would take flight, quacking in alarm. But there were always some ducks who didn't fly with the rest. They were the ones that would fall to the next shot. Most of the people here started to run back into their houses, shouting as soon as they understood what Tolther had told them, but a few stood where they were, their mouths agape. They were like the sitting ducks on the lakes.

Tolther and Ferin were near the top of the hill, where the houses stopped, when a loud, low-voiced horn sounded from somewhere about the harbour below, immediately followed by another two sharp, loud blasts.

'Alarm,' puffed Tolther. 'Guess Ma got Megril to act fast for once.'

'But it's the same as the one for fire,' said Huire doubtfully.

'It'll get everyone out, and word travels fast,' said Tolther.

Ferin turned her head to look below. Even more people were running about, and there was also more shouting. It didn't look very organised, but she thought it might just be the different way these southerners did things. Among the Athask, there were many different horn blasts for various situations; if one was sounded, the response would be ordered and disciplined, and above all, quiet. There would be none of this excessive shouting, and particularly there would not be any of the screams Ferin could hear.

Huire had paused to look too. She pointed out to sea and said, 'The raider *is* coming! See, two fingers left of the sun?'

Tolther turned around. Ferin grimaced as her leg was swung about and her neck jolted. She looked over Tolther's shoulder, squinting against the rising sun.

Sure enough, there was the raiding ship, making its way along a broad channel, a black smudge amid the blue-green sea and golden sands. From the hill Ferin could see many other channels: forking, joining, splitting, rejoining, a complicated tracery of darker arteries and capillaries cutting through the great drifts of yellow sand that formed the banks and bars.

Some of the channels looked wide to begin with, but soon narrowed or led nowhere, and at sea level Ferin thought it would be very easy to take the wrong one. But the raiders hadn't done so, or at least hadn't taken one that would greatly slow them down. They were not in the widest and most direct channel, but one parallel to it that would rejoin soon enough. From the wake of the ship, the wood-weirds were continuing to row at an unnatural pace.

'Pity the tide's in,' said Tolther. 'They might've gone aground otherwise.'

'Might have been and could have done, neither worth thinking on,' said Huire, repeating one of their mother's favourite sayings.

'They'll be inside the breakwater, lay alongside a jetty inside of an hour, I reckon,' said Tolther. 'Not much of a start for us . . .'

He increased his pace, puffing harder. He was very strong, Ferin thought, but did not have the endurance of her people. At least not for walking and running, no doubt due to spending most of his life on a boat.

'Stone's up ahead,' said Tolther. 'I'll lay you down there to wait for Astilaran and run back to help Da get our gear together. Huire, you stay with Ferin.'

'Why don't *you* stay!' protested Huire. 'I've got things I'd like to get too!'

'It isn't about that,' said Tolther. 'I'm older, so do as I say.'

'I will stay but not because you're older,' said Huire. 'Someone sensible has to be with Ferin.'

'I am grateful for all your help,' said Ferin. She felt very old all of a sudden, an adult among small children. They clearly had no idea of what wood-weirds could do, or the powers of the shamans and witches on board the approaching raider, or they would not spare energy for childish squabbles. Or be helping a wounded stranger, because if they knew what was coming after them they would run away right now. 'From both of you.'

The top of the hill was a pleasant, flat area that when spring became fully established would doubtless be under grass. The first shoots were coming through now, patches of green dotting the bare earth, legacy of the past winter. In the middle of this flat soon-to-be pasture, there was a tall grey stone, reminiscent of a fir cone in shape, round at the bottom and tapering to a point at the top. It was about twice as tall as Ferin, and as they drew closer she saw many strange symbols were carved everywhere, all over the stone, from foot to crown.

As she watched, the symbols moved, and suddenly shone bright as if they were made of beaten gold that had caught the sun. Ferin blinked several times, wondering if she was becoming feverish again. But she didn't feel feverish, and the symbols were very definitely moving, crawling about and shifting position. Some were also changing, flowing out of one shape into another, and they shone brighter and brighter, as bright as molten gold poured from a crucible, so bright Ferin had to hood her eyes and look away.

'What . . . what is that?' croaked Ferin.

'The Charter Stone,' said Tolther. 'Good magic. The marks aren't always so bright, though. Something must have stirred them up. Help me put Ferin down, Huire.'

The brother and sister laid Ferin down on the grass about ten paces from the stone, arranged her bad leg straight out and put her pack behind her so she could sit up against it. She stared at the stone in fascination, continuing to watch the symbols move and change. Some even drifted off into the air, moving like leaves caught by the wind, slowly fading until they were mere wisps of light and then no more.

After a minute or two, most of the radiant marks dimmed, and the moving ones became slower, and soon the rock simply looked like a much-carved-upon standing stone again.

'The little carvings, what do they mean?' asked Ferin. 'Are they letters? There are so many . . .'

'Need to be a Charter Mage to know,' said Huire. 'Ma is one, a little bit. We've all got the mark, Ma insisted, but I never had time to study. I know how to make a light, that's about it. You don't want to mess with marks you don't understand.'

Huire pushed her fringe back and showed Ferin the charter mark on her forehead.

'I thought that was just a brand, marking your clan,' said Ferin. 'I have one such, here.'

She tapped her stomach, just above her navel.

'It does look just like a painted sign or a brand,' said Huire. 'Until someone else with a Charter mark touches it, or if you touch a Charter Stone. Then it will shine and move, like the ones over there, and if you have one, you feel . . . joined to the Charter. It's kind of difficult to describe –'

'I'm going back down to help,' interrupted Tolther. 'You stay with Ferin, Huire.'

'I am staying, aren't I?' snapped his sister. 'Get my blue cloak and the woollen hat with the long bit at the back if you're going home, and make sure Da remembers to bring all the good knives.'

'All right,' said Tolther, and he was away, running back down the road.

'Boys,' said Huire. 'Thinks he'll miss out on some fighting. Should be hoping it doesn't come to that.'

Ferin nodded, saving her strength. Huire had laid the bow and arrow case close by, which was good. Ferin wished she had some spirit-glass arrows left, or rather that she had many more than she had started out with. But even without them, if she could shoot the keepers, then there was a chance the shamans or witches would run off, or turn on their masters. If even two or three of the sorcerers and their wood-weirds attacked the others, that would be a great help.

A hawk swooped down above them. For a moment Ferin thought it was going to attack and reached for her bow, but it flew over Huire's head and landed atop the Charter Stone. It was brown but had streaks of pale yellow in its wings, and fierce amber eyes. As it perched on the stone, Charter marks shimmered up and wrapped themselves around the bird's feet and talons, wreathing it in light. The hawk launched itself into the sky again, the marks falling back into the stone, becoming dull carvings once more.

'Message-hawk,' said Huire. 'Astilaran, that's the healer who's coming to sort you out, he says that in the old days, I mean the real old days, Charter Mages could make messenger birds just with magic, they didn't need an egg to start with, or to train up a real bird. Imagine that!'

Ferin nodded again, watching the quick beat of the hawk's wings as it rose up into the sky. Magic birds that flew messages would be extremely useful, particularly in raids on other clans. She had never been allowed to go on a raid herself, being too valuable to the clan, but she had joined many practices. Things often went wrong because the five or six parties in a typical big raid had no way to quickly send messages to one another.

A stab of pain from her leg brought Ferin back to the present. She leaned forward and saw that the swelling above the ankle was so great that her breeches leg was tight against the skin, adding to the discomfort. She took her knife and carefully unpicked the red thread along a seam, opening the goatskin from the knee down.

She was thinking about cutting off the dirty, blood-encrusted bandage as well but was prevented from doing so by the sudden arrival of a short, very thin man of indeterminate age with bulbous eyes and something of a permanent frown. He wore a strange sort of pale blue robe which was liberally equipped with at least a dozen buttoned pockets, many of them bulging, and carried a leather satchel over his shoulder.

'Now, now!' he called. 'Let me see if there is cutting to be done, for if there is, I'll do it. I am Astilaran, doctor and Charter Mage, neither of these things in any extraordinary manner, but perhaps sufficient unto your needs. What a very impressive fur cloak.'

He crouched down low by Ferin's side and sniffed around the bandage like a small dog unsure of whether it might find a snack or something that would bite its nose.

'A crossbow bolt, I believe?'

'Yes,' said Ferin.

'And Karrilke tried a healing spell which didn't work?'

'Yes,' said Huire. 'The one she always uses.'

'Hmm,' said Astilaran. 'Have you any talismans, charms or suchlike about you? Ferin, that is your name?'

'Yes, I am Ferin. I have no charms. Our shaman gave me three spirit-glass arrows, but those I have used.'

'I will essay another healing spell in a moment,' said Astilaran. 'But first I want to take a look at the wound. It does not smell bad, not yet, though there is some reason to fear corruption will occur.'

He unbuttoned several pockets, taking a clean bandage from one, and small silver bottle from another, and a tube of canvas from his satchel, which he swiftly unrolled to reveal a number of very sharp-looking short knives. Taking one of these, he swiftly and expertly cut off Ferin's makeshift bandage, using the point to pry away pieces that were stuck on with dried blood. The mountain girl forced herself to watch as if this were nothing, though she did almost cry out when Astilaran poured whatever was in the silver bottle over and into the wound. It wasn't water.

The wound began to bleed again. The blood was welling rather than rushing out, but there was enough to alarm Ferin, who instinctively moved to press her hand against the flow.

'No, no, stay as you are, I'll not let you bleed too much,' said Astilaran. 'I want to allow the ill humours that have suppurated near the surface to flow away, and I will cast a spell to both cleanse and mend in a moment. Does it hurt a great deal here?'

Ferin nodded very slightly as the healer pressed his finger just below her knee.

'Hmm,' said Astilaran. He looked at her intently. 'You wouldn't say if it did, would you? Your people believe in not showing pain?'

'Pain is a challenge to be met and overcome,' said Ferin through clenched teeth, as Astilaran pressed in several other points.

'Fortunately for my purposes, observation of your pupils, skin and that clenched jaw provides me with sufficient response to my questions,' said Astilaran. 'Now, I am going to cast a Charter spell of healing. You have seen this done before?'

'No,' said Ferin. She'd been unconscious when Karrilke had tried to cast the healing spell on the boat.

'You have seen the marks move on the Charter Stone,' said Astilaran. 'I will call marks like that and join them to make a spell, which will enter your leg. Do not move, or be alarmed. The spell will take away most of the pain, knit the flesh together, and cleanse the wound.'

'We do not have any such spells,' said Ferin. 'Our shamans and witches only have spells to cause harm, destroy things, bend others to their will. That is why they must be kept in check with neck-rings and keepers. Our healers have no magic; they use herbs and make potions and pastes.'

'I do that too,' said Astilaran. 'Charter Magic is not without cost, or danger, and if healing can be done in other ways, I do it. Now, as I said, do not move.'

The healer shut his eyes and reached up with his hands, stretching his long and surprisingly elegant fingers wide. Glowing Charter marks began to form around his hands, marks slowly drifting around one another, linking and changing. After a few seconds, he held a chain of glowing marks, which stopped shifting about as they settled into position.

Astilaran lowered his fingers and the glowing chain fell upon Ferin's ankle. As it did so, a savage, overwhelming pain struck her in the stomach. She made a choking sound, her eyes rolled back, and her head lolled to one side. The chain of marks broke and the individual marks rolled away, sank into the ground, and disappeared.

The spell had failed.

'Hmm,' said Astilaran. He raised his left hand, clenching his fingers into a claw, which he pointed at the Charter Stone, closing his eyes in concentration again. This time, Charter marks came boiling up out of the stone and danced across the air to his clawed hand, surrounded his fingers, and continued along his arm into his body. More and more marks came, making a flowing vine of golden light from stone to man.

Ferin recovered consciousness a few seconds later, the pain in her belly dissipating, and saw this line of light and Astilaran kneeling by her side. She tried to say something, but her mouth was extraordinarily dry, so she could merely growl and cough.

Astilaran spoke a word and a particularly bright Charter mark appeared in the air above her leg and began to slowly turn, as it did so sending out a shower of small, cool sparks of brilliant light. Other marks joined this one, coming out of Astilaran's mouth, and then he suddenly brought his right hand down on Ferin's ankle and the super-bright Charter mark and all the others with it that had come from the stone flowed from his hand into her leg with a flash like sudden, close lightning out of a clear sky.

The pain in Ferin's stomach struck again, more intense than ever, and she fainted from the shock.

When she came to, perhaps a minute later, Astilaran was examining the clan sign above Ferin's navel, his hands hovering above her skin as if he were warming them at a particularly hot fire he dared not approach too closely.

Like all the Athask people's, Ferin's clan sign had been made when she was very young, using the point of a red-hot knife to carve a very simple, stylised design of the mountain cat from which they took their name. The resulting scars were no wider than a knife's edge, and slightly red, though in most of the older people the red faded until all that was left was lines of white.

'This is the trouble,' said Astilaran. He seemed all of a sudden to be very tired; his eyes were hooded and his hand shook. 'There is something under the skin here. A Free Magic charm of some kind, a very strong one. Perhaps even something necromantic . . . there is the hint of Death . . .'

Ferin stared at him blearily. The overwhelming pain in

her stomach had certainly been centred in her clan sign. But it was gone now . . . and so was the pain in her ankle. She sat up straighter and looked at her leg. The swelling had receded, the wound no longer bled, and in fact it looked as if it had been healing well for at least half a moon. Small glowing symbols – Charter marks – were still crawling about, but they did not enter her skin.

Ferin flexed her foot experimentally. There was a dull ache there, but it was nothing compared to what it had been. She put her hands down and began to get up.

'Slowly, slowly,' said Astilaran. 'I was forced to draw upon the stone and use a master mark to make the spell powerful enough to break through against the Free Magic talisman you have under your skin. The spell will make you feel stronger than you are for some time, but you still need rest.'

'You say there is a magic charm under my skin?' asked Ferin, her voice rasping. She took out her knife and set its point against the clan sign on her stomach. 'I will cut it out!'

'No! No, you can't do that!' protested Astilaran, grabbing her wrist. 'It can only be removed using magic, Charter Magic. Or by whoever put it there in the first place, I suppose.'

'The Witch With No Face,' muttered Ferin. 'It has to be. That is how my pursuers know where I am.'

'Very likely,' said Astilaran. 'But you are going to the Clayr, Karrilke tells me. There are many mages among them who have the skill and the power to remove such a horrid thing.'

Ferin slowly resheathed her knife, her face set in a scowl. With Astilaran helping her, she stood, pausing halfway to pick up her bow and arrow case. She glanced at her pack, but Astilaran shook his head.

'As I said, you feel stronger than you are. Let someone else carry it, for now. The pain and weakness will return all the sooner if you extend yourself too far. I also do not know how my spell will fare with that charm in your belly; it is possible it will wane all the sooner or take some unusual course. You must be careful.'

Ferin took a step, slowly putting her weight on her injured leg. The ache grew stronger, but her ankle would support her. She could walk, perhaps even run. Most important, she could stand well enough to shoot.

Many people were coming up the road now, scores of them, all carrying packs and bags, some even pushing little carts. They were quieter; there was none of the shouting and screaming that had gone on when the news first came.

Out beyond the breakwater, the raider was nosing into the last part of the channel. Very soon, the ship would tie up at a jetty, the wood-weirds would be freed from the rowing benches, and they would come ashore, with sorcerers and keepers close behind.

Then the hunt would begin.

chapter fourteen

nicholas learns about real librarians

En route to the Clayr's Glacier,
following the Ratterlin, the Old Kingdom

'Oh!' exclaimed Lirael. She held her hand to her face, hiding a sudden bubbling up of laughter at Nick's stricken face. He seemed more concerned about the prospect of sudden nakedness than he had been by the prospect of bleeding to death. 'I should have thought of this . . . things made with machines in Ancelstierre, they fall apart once past the Wall. I have a spare cloak; I'll get that for you.'

'Thank you,' said Nick, clutching his rags about himself. That prompted another memory. The owl and the dog, in his tent near the Red Lake pit . . .

'Um, I seem to recall I've been . . . ah . . . without clothes before . . . I mean, you've seen . . .'

'Yes,' said Lirael, coming over with a cloak in her hands. 'You were not yourself, of course, under the sway of Orannis. You were very, very thin.'

'Oh,' said Nick, taking the cloak and quickly wrapping it around himself. What did that mean? Very thin? Did it mean 'super-ugly very thin,' or was it just 'extremely unhealthy very thin,' or did it not mean anything, just an observation, like 'that flower is yellow,' of no importance to Lirael, who had more pressing things to think about?

'I'll just go over there,' he said, scuttling off like a large blue beetle, shedding various pieces of torn and disintegrating Ancelstierran cloth from under the cloak.

Lirael watched him for too long, realised when he got to the low bushes that they didn't conceal him as much as he evidently thought they did, and looked away again quickly. The river rushing past reminded her that she also needed to go to the toilet, but she didn't know whether to go around the far side of this small island now or wait for Nick to come back and then go, only deeper into the bushes, and then she wondered why she was thinking about this as being difficult. When she had been travelling with Sam both of them had simply diverted off a ways as required and done their business without even thinking about it, just like the Disreputable Dog; she didn't make a fuss about necessary ablutions. It wasn't because Sam was her nephew, because she hadn't even known that straight away. He'd just been a young man to her, like Nick. Only not like Nick for some reason . . .

When Nick came back, Lirael offered him a small leather bag.

'Bread and cheese, and a water bottle. It's empty; fill it from the river, the water is good to drink. I'm just . . . I'm just going over there. Like you. Also. I mean, um, your cloak is coming open –'

She fled, with Nick hastily winding the cloak around himself another half turn, making it so tight that he almost fell over as he sat down to eat some bread and cheese.

At the other end of the island, Lirael went to the toilet, then washed her hands and face in the river. The water was very clear and cold, even this far from its source under the Clayr's Glacier. Lirael had seen the spring where the river was born, far beneath the inhabited parts of the Clayr's sprawling underground fastness.

There is a spring. A very old spring. In the heart of the mountain, in the deepest dark.

The Dog had said that, when they were exploring together, shortly before Lirael had found the Dark Mirror and the pan pipes, the instruments of a Remembrancer, which in her case had been but the first step towards becoming an Abhorsen.

Lirael dipped her hand in the cool, clear water again, and sighed. When she was with Sabriel, dealing with the Dead or walking in Death, learning to be an Abhorsen, she didn't have time to think about what she had become, or was becoming, and even less to think about her former life with the Clayr. Not only that, her office as Abhorsen-in-Waiting had proved quite a shield in social situations against the people who Ellimere was always trying to get her to meet and do things with; she need only say that she had Abhorsen business and they left her alone.

But the other side of that coin, Lirael knew, was that she

still had almost no experience with how men and women could get together and become friends, let alone lovers, and not much more with how women and women could get together, as some of the Clayr did. Or mixing and matching, as even more of the Clayr considered perfectly straightforward and usual.

It always seemed easy when everyone else did it. Lirael frowned as she thought of various cousins pairing up with each other or venturing down to the Lower Refectory to laugh and drink with the traders and supplicants, later to bring them up to their beds.

Lirael really didn't know how they went about these activities. She had been a loner all her life, one who had the great fortune to make one wonderful friend in the Disreputable Dog. Literally, in this case, since she had somehow summoned the Dog or helped her into existence. But the Dog was gone.

Now Lirael did have a kind of family, even sort-of parents in Sabriel and Touchstone, since she could never think of them as half-sister and brother by marriage. Sam and Ellimere were more like brother and sister to her; certainly they never treated her as an aunt.

But they were all a very work-obsessed family. Or maybe that should be responsibility-obsessed, Lirael thought. She was too, she supposed – but when there weren't Dead creatures to battle or Free Magic entities to be bound, or some immediate problem to face, only the ordinary social interactions of normal people . . . she didn't know what to do. Even Ellimere, who seemed to be able to make any social situation work exactly as she wanted it to, hadn't been able to fit Lirael into any group of friends or introduce her to potential lovers.

Lirael almost sighed again, but swallowed it. The Disreputable Dog would not have approved of all this sighing. Lirael smiled, a wry, sad smile, and reached into the little pouch she'd affixed to her bell bandolier, beneath Ranna, the smallest bell. Inside that pouch was the soapstone statuette of a black-and-tan dog with sticking-up ears, a wide grin and a lolling tongue. The statuette she had snatched up from the strange room of the Stilken, many years before, which in some way had been the seed of her conjuring of the Disreputable Dog.

Lirael scratched this little figure between those ears with the edge of one fingernail, then fastened the pouch closed again. She could almost hear the Dog telling her to simply get on with it.

Back near the Paperwing, Lirael saw Nick tying the belt from his shredded trousers around the cloak he now wore, to keep it together and not suddenly part in ways unbecoming to his modesty. Which he seemed to care about more than Lirael did, but she had to remember he was from a very different country and upbringing.

'Handmade belt,' he said, and pointed with his left foot. 'Like my shoes. Though the laces seem to be going . . . I will need to have words with Mr Jollie when . . . if I get back to Corvere.'

'Mr Jollie?' asked Lirael.

'My cobbler,' said Nick. Lirael was pleased to see that he

had a little colour in his face, and generally looked better than he had the previous night or even that morning. 'Machine-made laces! Can you imagine!'

'We will get you new clothes and boots at the Glacier,' said Lirael.

'Oh, good,' said Nick. He hesitated, then added, 'I seem to recall Sam said it was all women. I mean the Clayr were all women.'

'We . . . they are,' said Lirael. 'Um, does that matter?'

'Clothes,' said Nick.

Lirael still looked puzzled.

'Men's clothes,' said Nick. 'Will I be able to get men's clothes?'

'There are frequent male visitors,' said Lirael. 'But . . . we don't really wear different clothes, I mean a few underthings . . .'

She gestured around her chest. Nick nodded and looked away.

'I mean, breeches, a tunic, boots, they're all the same, let out or taken in as required . . .'

'Oh, I see,' said Nick. 'Stupid of me. Now, you wear armour and have a sword and those . . . those bells. I suppose you need them. All of it, I mean. Will I get a sword and armour, too? I can fence, reasonably well, fenced épée for the school all the way to the national championship, though I can't say I've ever worn armour, real armour I mean. Will I need it? Armour and a sword?'

'I think at first you will need to rest and fully recover,'

said Lirael carefully. She wasn't entirely sure what the Clayr would make of Nick, but she knew it was important to discover what was going to happen with all the Free Magic contained inside him. 'You will be quite safe within the Glacier. I mean as long as you stay out of the Library and places like that.'

'Oh, fierce librarians, then?' asked Nick, with a rather forced laugh. 'Tell you to shush and that sort of thing?'

'Some of them *are* fierce,' agreed Lirael. She smiled. 'Going into battle, at least. Though I'm not sure what "shush" means.'

'To be . . . to be quiet,' said Nick. 'That's what librarians do, back home. I mean at school they did; the ones . . . the ones at the university are different.'

He did not mention that his knowledge of the university librarians was very limited, as, though he had been up at Sunbere for two terms, he had been following his own studies, had rarely attended a lecture and only looked into his own college library once, and had never even visited either of the university's two major libraries. He had already been fully under the sway of Orannis then, the Destroyer directing his thoughts and plans.

'They tell you to be quiet?' asked Lirael. 'Because you might attract the attention of something dangerous, that has escaped the collection?'

'No, not exactly,' said Nick. 'Er, your librarians go into battle?'

'When they must,' said Lirael. 'The Library is very old, and deep, and contains many things that have been put away for good reason. Creatures, dangerous knowledge, artefacts made not wisely . . . books that should not be opened without proper preparation, some books that should never be opened at all.'

'Creatures?' asked Nick quietly. The few memories he'd managed to retain about his previous time in the Old Kingdom were often brief moments of seeing . . . hearing . . . smelling strange creatures, things come back from Death, and other monstrosities that his mind wished he had never seen. And the Hrule, of course, the creature in the case . . .

'Yes,' said Lirael. She was thinking of the Stilken, the creature she had found and inadvertently freed in the room of flowers in one of the Old Levels of the Library. She had been very lucky to survive that first encounter – and indeed, the second one – when she had dealt with that creature. Though not without considerable assistance from the Disreputable Dog, even though the hound would have claimed she didn't do anything and wasn't involved.

'I like libraries,' said Nick. He had loved the library at his prep school, but this love had turned sour at Somersby because of Mrs Knipwich the librarian, who had been soured herself from dealing with several generations of irritating overprivileged schoolboys, and treated all of them as pests on a par with the cockroaches who ate the bookbinding glue. 'Though not necessarily librarians –'

'I was a librarian,' interrupted Lirael stiffly. 'A Second Assistant Librarian. Red waistcoat. I suppose I still am one. As well as being Abhorsen-in-Waiting.'

'I'm sorry,' said Nick. 'I didn't mean to offend. I liked the librarians at my first school. Just later, I mean Mrs Knipwich was probably our librarian for too long; she got old and very cranky, a right horror . . .'

His voice trailed off as he realised he was talking nonsense, and worse, nonsense offensive to the librarian in front of him.

'I apologise,' he said.

'It is no matter what you think of librarians, or of me,' said Lirael. She hoped she'd managed to say it as if she didn't care in the least, though in truth she was quite deeply wounded. Becoming a librarian had saved her life, in many ways, giving her an identity she had lacked when she was a Sightless Clayr. It hurt to hear Nick talk disdainfully about librarians, almost as if he were talking about her.

'Please, if you're ready, get back in the Paperwing. We still have a long way to fly and we must arrive before nightfall.'

'You don't want any bread and cheese?' asked Nick, offering the pouch. 'Or water? I filled up the bottle.'

'No, thank you,' said Lirael, though she was quite hungry. 'I can eat as we fly; the Paperwing knows the way.'

'Right . . .' said Nick dubiously. He glanced over at the eyes painted on the canoe-like bow of the craft. The Paperwing winked at him and he dropped the food bag, the bread and cheese tumbling out into the sand, instantly attracting a layer of grit to become inedible.

'Or not eat,' said Lirael shortly. 'Please do get in. Do you need to be tied to your seat again? You don't feel faint?'

'No, I'll be fine,' said Nick. He felt quite cross now, both at himself and at Lirael. She seemed far more miffed about an innocent remark than was reasonable. How was he to know about her being a librarian and everything? And this constant harping on about him being weak and probably fainting, it was too much. He climbed into the Paperwing and settled into the hammock-like seat, noting that he too had a kind of long pocket on the left side to hold a sheathed sword, and a broad pocket on the right side for other odds and ends.

As Lirael put away her sword and climbed in front, Nick eyed the sandy ground ahead. There was only about twenty yards of island in front of them, and no aircraft he knew could possibly take off with a runway so short.

'How do we take off?' he asked, quite anxiously. 'We'll end up in the river, won't we?'

'I *do* know how to fly,' said Lirael. 'So does the Paperwing, as I've said. All I have to do is whistle down the wind to lift us up.'

chapter fifteen

retreat from yellowsands

Yellowsands, the Old Kingdom

There were eighty-nine villagers, all told, including twenty-three children too young to fight, even by Athask standards: they would give a five-year-old a knife if necessary. Ferin had counted the fisher-folk as they began to straggle away from the village, along the road that continued past the Charter Stone down the other side of the low hill and then carried on in a very straight line through a broad, empty valley that lay between a modest grassy hill to the southeast and a much higher line of grey shale hills to the northwest.

The valley road was perfect country for horse nomads, or in the current case wood-weirds that could run as fast as horses, Ferin noted unhappily, looking at the paved road and the bare ground either side. Now her foot was so much better, she could manage a good pace herself, far faster than the villagers were actually going. The fisher-folk were *so* slow, even after those with barrows and push wagons and even chickens and ducks had been forced by the constable to set them aside or release them. Megril the constable was bringing up the rear now, a very identifiable figure – the only person in a mail hauberk with a shiny steel helmet and a sword at her side.

She was urging the laggards on, running back and forth and chivvying them along, but it made little difference to the overall speed of the strung-out column of trudging fisher-folk, who were nearly all much more at home on a boat's deck than land.

Ferin closed up to where Karrilke was striding along between her son Tolther and an older yellow-bearded man who wore a sleeveless leather jerkin with studded wrist bracers, displaying sinewy, muscled arms. He had a double-bladed axe slung across the heavy pack on his back, and a long knife thrust through his belt.

'Captain,' said Ferin, 'this won't work. The wood-weirds can run as fast as a cantering horse, and we have too short a start. They'll catch us in the open.'

'I know,' said Karrilke heavily. 'I'd planned to get to where the road turns south; there's an old watchtower, built over the estuary there for defence against the Dead. It is large enough to shelter us all, and is high and strong. We could make a good stand there, against any odds. But as you say, we go too slowly . . .'

Ferin looked ahead. She could see where the road began to turn behind the hill, but neither tower nor estuary. They had to be least a league away, and the wood-weirds would catch them long before that. Even the shamans and witches would, for that matter. They might be horse nomads, but even the horse nomads could run when they needed to, much faster and for longer than these fisher-folk.

'I am the one they pursue,' said Ferin. 'If I turn aside, they will follow me.'

Karrilke shook her head.

'No. You said your message is important, and it must truly be so for such a pursuit. Besides, you are our guest. It would be as if we gave you to them.'

It was Ferin's turn to shake her head.

'I do not plan to be easily caught.'

She pointed across and up towards the northwestern hill of grey shale that rose to a razorback ridge, the ridge continuing in a twisting line as far as Ferin could see.

'There is a path along the ridge, up there, I think?'

'Yes,' said the axe-bearer next to Karrilke. 'A very dangerous path. In some places the ridge is like a knife edge, and you can only pass at a crawl, gripping either side with hands and feet.'

'My husband, Swinther,' said Karrilke. She looked at him with a wry smile. 'Who I trust has not gone that way since he was a boy, and was dared to take it, as they will.'

'If I go that way, I am sure they will follow,' said Ferin. 'Wood-weirds do not go well along narrow ways, or on uncertain ground. There is much loose shale I can see from here, and even a wood-weird cannot survive a great fall.'

Karrilke hesitated.

'That *would* give us time to reach the tower . . .'

'You'll need a guide,' said Swinther. He seemed to accept the idea immediately. 'It looks straight enough from down here, but there are several false ridges, and if the cloud comes down you'll be lost.'

'I don't know . . .' murmured Karrilke.

'The lass is right,' said Swinther to his wife. He gestured at the long, straggling line. 'They'll speed up when the first few at the rear are slain, but it won't make a difference. Not if these things are as fast as you say, Ferin. I'll show you the way.'

'No, Pa,' interrupted Tolther. 'Let me go!'

'Nay, lad,' said Swinther, tousling his hair. 'You've not been past the first crest, have you?'

'I've been halfway along,' said Tolther. 'Let me do it!'

'No,' said Swinther and Karrilke together. There was a moment of silence, then Karrilke added, 'I'll need your help, at the tower.'

Tolther looked away, face set in a scowl. Ferin restrained herself from shaking her head. The boy still didn't realise this was a serious, life-or-death matter.

'We'll need shields,' said Ferin. 'The sorcerers won't have bows, but their keepers will. And at least one of them has a good eye.'

'Best we have someone to shoot back as well,' said Swinther. He caught Ferin's look of bridling indignation and added, 'Besides yourself, I mean. Where's Young Laska?'

'Up ahead,' said Karrilke. She filled her lungs and bawled out in her seagoing voice, honed to be heard over the fiercest gale, 'Ahoy! Young Laska! You're wanted!'

Up ahead, a middle-aged woman walking alongside a much older man looked behind, raised her hand, and came loping back. Her skin, hair and clothes were so much all the same deep shade of brown she had the look overall of a deeply weathered old chestnut tree. Of greater interest to Ferin was the longbow on her back and a quiver of goose-feather-fletched arrows considerably longer than the ones the tribespeople used.

'Young Laska was with the Borderers for years, till she came home to make Old Laska's dying comfortable – that's her pa,' said Karrilke. 'Only he's taking a long time about it. She hunts still, and I believe is as good an archer as anyone could wish.'

'As for shields, we don't have any as such,' said Swinther. He looked back along the line of stragglers, his eyes narrowing against the glare of the morning sun. 'But there might be . . . I'll be back. Keep walking on; I'll catch you up again before we need to strike towards the ridge.'

He ran back the way they had come, moving easily, unlike most of his neighbours a man accustomed to a vigorous day outdoors, over hill and dale, cutting down trees and dragging heavy timber.

Young Laska arrived from the front at much the same time as Astilaran came hurrying up from further back. The healer scowled at Ferin, who was carrying her pack again, made heavier by the fur she had packed away, as the day was now too warm for such a coat.

'I told you to rest as much as possible,' he said, talking as he matched his pace to hers. 'Your foot is not better; my spell is merely holding back the pain and assisting your body to heal itself. Which it cannot do if you test yourself beyond enduring.'

'I cannot rest,' said Ferin. 'The pursuit will soon begin in earnest, and I must lead the wood-weirds away from your people. After all, I was the one who brought them here.'

'What? What's this?' asked Astilaran.

'I will take the ridge path, along the shale,' said Ferin, pointing. 'They will follow me. You others will go on to take refuge in the tower.'

'You will break the spell!' protested Astilaran. 'Climbing the shale . . . it is bound to stress the wound.'

'Ferin says the wood-weirds can run as fast as horses,' said Karrilke. She lifted her eyes to the rear of the slow column of villagers.

'Hmm,' said Astilaran. He looked back too, scratched his head and grimaced, his ever-present frown deepening even more. 'We had best sort out some kind of rearguard. Megril alone would be overborne in moments. I recall a few spells that may be of use; I could probably deal with one or two of these creatures −'

'There are twelve wood-weirds,' said Ferin. 'At least. Perhaps more. With the sorcerers who command them, and the keepers who watch the sorcerers. Your only chance is if they follow me, rather than you. On the shale, the wood-weirds may fall, the sorcerers too for that matter −'

'They may fall!' snorted Astilaran. 'You certainly will

when my spell fails and your foot gives way again. I do not like this.'

'It is a reasonable plan,' said Young Laska. She spoke with calm certainty. 'The only one possible, given the circumstances. You called me back, Karrilke . . . is it to suggest I go with our visitor?'

'If you would,' said Karrilke. 'Ferin, this is Young Laska.'

Ferin inclined her head, and received a similar movement in return.

'How far can you shoot that great bow?' asked Ferin.

'Up there, in the wind?' asked Young Laska. 'Perhaps three hundred paces with any certainty of hitting what I aim at.'

'Better than I could manage with my bow, and the Yrus with theirs,' said Ferin. She was not sure Young Laska could be believed, for three hundred paces was more than half as much again as far as she could shoot accurately with her own bow. But she had heard the southern longbows could send a shaft a great distance. Though she still thought it was too big and cumbersome for general use. You could never shoot such a bow from a horse, or up a tree, or from hiding.

'The wood-weirds cannot be harmed with normal arrows, of course, and the sorcerers may be warded with spells or charms. But if you can shoot even some of them, or their keepers . . . it will help.'

'I have five Charter-spelled arrows ready, imbued with marks to cut, unravel and flense,' said Young Laska. As she spoke she lifted her head, her broad-brimmed hat tilting back to show that she too bore the Charter mark on her forehead. 'And I have some small store of knowledge when it comes to the more combative marks, as do all Borderers. Some should work against these wood-weirds, and I am happy to put all to the test.'

'Better and better,' said Ferin. She looked up at the sun, noting how much time had passed since Tolther had said the raiders would make landfall. She thought they must be close to that point now, and the wood-weirds would soon be loping over the Charter Stone hill and coming down towards them. 'But we must get up to that ridge, and soon.'

'Swinther's on his way back,' said Karrilke. 'Path to the ridge starts over there – you see the gap between those first two great shards where they break through the earth?'

Ferin nodded. She could see the beginnings of a path, a line of bare earth bordered initially by grass and then by the loose shale, fallen from the great folds of rock that thrust up out of the ground, the first buttresses of stone for the larger hill behind.

Without noticing it, they had begun to walk more slowly as they talked, so the stragglers at the rear of the fisher-folk column had gained ground, and were now only two or three hundred paces behind. Swinther came running back, carrying two round metal shields, which, as he got closer, Ferin saw were actually the heavy lids from two large cast-iron pots.

'Thought Gebbler would try to bring his pots,' he said, handing one lid over to Ferin and the other to Young Laska. It was heavy iron, with a large handle, and would serve quite well as a shield for the time being, though she would not want to be carrying it about all the time. 'This way. I'll lead. You want to take the rear, Young Laska?'

'Aye,' answered the former Borderer, before Ferin could protest. The older woman looked at her and something not quite a smile twitched across her mouth. 'You'll have plenty of targets yourself, young mistress, I'm sure. I'll not be hogging them all.'

'Good fortune,' said Karrilke. She briefly touched hands with Ferin and Young Laska and then gave her husband a business-like kiss on his cheek.

'You also,' said Ferin awkwardly.

Before she could say anything else, a screeching cry echoed behind them from the Charter Stone hill, like a hawk's that had mistimed its swoop on a juicy pigeon and was complaining of it, but far louder.

'Already at the stone!' exclaimed Karrilke. Her hand fell upon her knife. 'We are too late!'

'No, no,' said Astilaran hurriedly. 'That is a warning spell I set, to be triggered at the first touch of Free Magic upon the jetty, the warning to be repeated by the Charter Stone. They have landed. But we must hurry, to be sure! I hope we may meet again!'

With those parting words, he ran back to the rear of the column, shouting to the laggards.

'The enemy has landed! You must go faster, or else be slain upon the road!'

chapter sixteen

an unlooked-for return

Clayr's Glacier, the Old Kingdom

The clouds came rolling down as the Paperwing flew the last few leagues up the Ratterlin towards the Clayr's Glacier, a shining blue-white monolith of ice nestled between the dark grey rocky peaks of Starmount and Sunfall, the Glacier's attendant mountains. It grew colder, even within the magically warmed cockpit, and then somewhat miserable as it began to rain. Even though the heavy raindrops were *mostly* repelled by an almost invisible shield of Charter Magic, they broke into a mist which soon saturated both Lirael and Nick.

'I'm sorry I didn't get you better clothes,' said Lirael rather worriedly over her shoulder. She had forgotten her irritation from his comments about librarians, and now was only concerned for his well-being. 'You must be uncomfortable.'

'It's nothing,' said Nick, though he was shivering. In normal circumstances he thought he'd be fine and just shrug this off, but in his current weakened state he did feel very cold and ill, and highly uncomfortable. He was basically naked under the borrowed cloak, which would keep billowing open every time he shifted to try to find a better position.

'It's not far now,' said Lirael. She peered ahead, though she could see little through the rain. 'Fortunately the Paperwing is very familiar with the way, or I wouldn't dare go into this cloud and rain so close to the mountains.'

'We're going straight into that?' asked Nick, peering over her shoulder towards the vast cloud-wreathed glacier and the mountains either side. 'Where do we land?'

'There's a terraced landing field carved out of the side of Starmount, about two-thirds of the way up,' said Lirael. 'I'm sure the Clayr will have Seen us arriving, so we should be able to land and slide straight into the hangar, and get warm immediately.'

'We're landing on a terrace two-thirds of the way up one of those mountains?' asked Nick. 'They must be at least ten thousand feet high!'

'Feet?' asked Lirael. 'Oh, your Ancelstierran measure, much the same as our pace. They're not that tall. Starmount is the higher of the two, about eight thousand paces compared to Sunfall's seven and a half. There are higher mountains in the Kingdom.'

'Those two are high enough,' said Nick, with feeling. He was suddenly glad to be in a magical aircraft, for a Beskwith or a Humbert Twelve would crash here for certain, if anyone was fool enough to try to land on the side of a *mountain* over a glacier, under thick cloud. While it was raining no less or as it was now, beginning to snow. It would be crazy at any time, at least back in Ancelstierre.

Nick tried to think about something else.

'What happens when we get there?'

'Ah, I'm not entirely sure,' said Lirael, who had been thinking about this herself. 'But first of all a hot bath, clean clothes, dinner . . .'

'I meant beyond the immediate necessities,' said Nick. 'Though all of those will be very welcome.'

'The Infirmarian will need to look at your wounds and see how you are, in general,' said Lirael. 'And . . . I think probably the Librarian and some others should investigate the Free Magic that is a result of you . . . of you having had the shard of Orannis in your body.'

Nick was silent for a moment. 'Sam wrote to me about that, a little, and tried to explain your Charter Magic as opposed to Free Magic. I'm not sure I entirely understood. He said I somehow have both within me . . . and I *need* to understand. I need to know what I have become!'

'The Clayr will help you do that,' said Lirael.

'Yes,' said Nick. He had forgotten his momentary irritation as well. 'I . . . um . . . want to thank you again. For coming to get me.'

'I wanted to,' said Lirael, almost without thinking, and blushed at this honesty.

'Good,' said Nick. 'I'm . . . I'm happy you did. That it was you.'

Both were suddenly very aware of their closeness in the

cockpit. For a few seconds, they were suspended together somewhere else, a kind of shared space and time, suddenly gone as the Paperwing tilted and began to climb, bursting through the fall of wet snow and into whiter, less heavy cloud that was still sufficiently dense they could see no further than the nose of the craft.

'Oh!' exclaimed Lirael. 'We're climbing up to the landing ledge. I had better whistle the wind around to the south, make it easier for our friend.'

She reached out of the cockpit and patted the side of the fuselage fondly, much as she used to do to the Dog. The Paperwing wiggled the ends of its wings and continued to steeply climb as Lirael began to whistle, golden Charter marks blowing out of her pursed lips, joining a cloud of frosted breath.

The wind shifted in answer to Lirael's whistled spell, Nick marvelling that it did so. He could see the cloud moving, shredding apart as the wind changed, the slushy snow going with it, so that all of a sudden there was a gap between wisps and he caught a glimpse of a flat white area to their left and now somewhat below them, with one side the patchy grey rock and ice of Starmount continuing ever upwards and the other side a frightening absence, a drop down to the blinding blue-white glacier far, far below.

Nick shut his eyes and would have crossed his fingers, but he somehow thought the Paperwing might be able to tell if he did that, and become offended. So he had to be content with fixing his eyes *very* closed, leaning back in his hammock chair, and hoping that Lirael's extreme confidence in their magical craft was entirely justified.

A few minutes later, when he had felt no sudden bump, or for that matter, a half-expected smashing impact with the mountainside, Nick opened his eyes again. He blinked several times, for he couldn't believe they had actually landed. It had happened so gently he hadn't even felt it as any different from the tiny bumps and adjustments of their travel in the air.

The Paperwing was in the middle of that flat ledge, in front of a vast gate in the mountainside. By Nick's estimate it was at least seventy feet across and twenty-five feet high. The gate was made of some dark wood, perhaps ebony, and was studded all over with greeny-bronze bolts arranged in the shape of stars, dozens of star patterns in different sizes.

'The Starmount Gate,' said Lirael, a note of puzzlement in her voice. 'I'd have thought it would be open, and someone here to meet us; they always See visitors at least a few hours ahead of time, if not days before. Stay here, it will remain warm . . . or at least warmer . . . in the cockpit.'

She climbed out, her boot heels crunching through the thin layer of icy snow on the landing terrace. Nick noticed there was a lot less snow there than there should be, as there were high drifts to either side. It was as if the terrace had been freshly swept and raked, though there was no sign of anyone doing such work. He also noted that Lirael took up her sword and buckled it on, and she hadn't taken off the bell bandolier at any stage. So even here, where he would have supposed it must be safe, she took no chances. He wished he had a sword himself, or at least a knife.

Nick watched as Lirael went over to the corner of the gate and opened a small sally port there, leaning close to use a key or perhaps a spell; he couldn't see clearly as her back was to him. She vanished inside, and the sally port closed behind her.

He felt very alone all of a sudden, and damp and uncomfortable, and tired and weak, and wondered if he had done the right thing. But at the same time he was thinking about Lirael's words.

'I wanted to,' Nick repeated to himself. She had wanted to come and get him. For her own sake? As a favour to Sam? Was she one of those people who just said nice things without meaning them? He didn't think so; she seemed quite serious. He liked that, but it was hard to be sure of her true feelings on such a short acquaintance.

He must look a complete joke to her at the moment, he thought. A scrawny, pallid wreck in a borrowed cloak, shivering away with a red nose that was beginning to drip. A far cry from how he had imagined returning to the Old Kingdom.

Or how he had imagined it would be to meet Lirael again.

Nick wiped his nose with the edge of the cloak and looked back at the sally port. It remained stubbornly closed. The cloud was closing around the landing ledge once more, reknitting itself into a solid expanse of white flecked with black streaks, and it was beginning to snow again. Wet, slushy snow.

After ten minutes, though it felt much longer to Nick, he grew tired of waiting. Clutching his cloak together at the front, he laboriously climbed out of the cockpit, gasping at the savage impact of the cold as he left the protective magic. His breath puffed out immediately like smoke, and the wetness on the end of his nose felt like it had been suddenly snap frozen. His shoes, now bereft of laces, were loose on his feet and let in snow at the sides, which melted at once on what had been up until that moment his relatively warm feet.

Nick crept to the sally port, thinking to knock on it. But he had barely gone more than a few paces from the Paperwing when there was a flash of light under the thin layer of snow ahead, as if hundreds of the magnesium flares photographers used had suddenly fired off, without the usual puffs of white smoke. Nick stopped and peered at the ground ahead. There were golden lights moving about under the snow there, tracing a picture, as if some huge unseen hand were painting in lines of sunshine.

He was still staring when the lines all came together at once, there was another even more blinding flash, and when his vision cleared save for several dancing black spots, there was a giant worm between him and the gate.

A worm easily seventy feet long and twelve feet in diameter, with a mouth of that same disturbingly wide diameter occupying all of the end closest to him, a mouth completely ringed with six serried layers of different-sized teeth, from enormous grinding molars at the back to tiny, delicate flesh-rending pointy ones at the front. Thousands of teeth, each the size and shape of a murderous small knife.

Nick gulped and stumbled back several steps to stand next to the Paperwing, which he hoped might lend him some protection, as his mind furiously tried to come to terms with the sudden appearance of this vast monster.

The worm reared up at the front, its middle segments scrunching together, but it did not pursue him, nor make any move elsewhere. Its whole posture, if a giant worm could be said to have a posture, was that of a watchful sentry.

It was guarding the gate, Nick realised. He really hoped that also meant it would not attack him unless he tried to go closer.

He was feeling very slightly relieved about this when he heard the faintest sound behind him. Half-turning, he found the very sharp point of a sword near his throat, and his cloak gaped open again from the speed of his spinning about. He started to pull it closed, but stopped as the sword touched his skin.

'Stay still!' commanded the woman who held the sword, which was glowing with Charter marks, warm and bright upon the cold steel blade. She was dressed entirely in white to match the snow, a thickly bundled figure with a hooded cloak showing a few errant strands of very pale blonde hair, deep brown skin, and bright blue eyes under the green glass goggles which she had slid up on her forehead. Another brown-skinned, blue-eyed blonde woman, also dressed in white furs over armour, stood nearby with an arrow nocked on a short bow. The point of the arrow was aimed at Nick's head, though she had not actually drawn back the bowstring.

'I am a guest,' said Nick, trying very much to be the First Minister of Ancelstierre's nephew, even standing bare naked under a rather gaping cloak. He remained very still. The sword point was just pricking the skin of his windpipe, and it was as sharp as any razor he had ever used. 'Or so I have been assured.'

'Is that so —' the swordswoman started to say, but she was interrupted by the sudden return of Lirael, who was trying to come out of the sally port. Finding it would only open halfway because of the worm, she put her head out, looked at the huge creature that had taken up residence in front of the greater part of the gate, and stamped her foot much as Nick might do when one of the dogs at home tried to come in where it wasn't allowed.

'Shoo!' said Lirael, waving her golden hand.

The worm flexed itself back far enough to allow her to open the lesser door and she came striding out towards the Paperwing. 'What is going on? Lower your sword at once!'

'Who are you?' asked the swordswoman. She did not lower her sword, and the archer with her transferred her aim to Lirael.

'The Abhorsen-in-Waiting! As you can see very well from my surcoat, bells and the royal Paperwing right in front of your eyes, Calleset!'

The sword did go down this time, rather waveringly, and the archer lowered her bow.

'Lirael?' asked Calleset. She stepped away from Nick, who took the opportunity to wrap his cloak back around himself and look nervously at the giant worm. It remained by the gate, which was only slightly comforting, as its rows of teeth were rotating, each layer moving in a contrary direction to the next.

'There is only one Abhorsen-in-Waiting, isn't there?' commented Lirael testily. 'Why isn't the gate open? And I would have expected *someone* from the Watch up here to meet me!'

Calleset looked at her, open-mouthed, then mumbled something about 'having grown taller'.

'Well, where is everybody?' repeated Lirael. She gestured at the archer. 'Lower your bow before you have an accident. Jelesray, isn't it? I didn't know you were in the Rangers.'

'I . . . I just joined three months ago,' said Jelesray haltingly. She was much younger than Calleset, perhaps seventeen to the latter's early twenties.

'I'm sorry, Lirael,' said Calleset stiffly. 'I was just surprised. I've never heard you talk so much. You never did before. We used to call you Chatterbox, remember?'

'No,' said Lirael. She was surprised to have had any nick-name at all, particularly from someone older like Calleset. It all seemed so long ago, her life as a Clayr. Or as she had always thought, not really a Clayr, since she didn't have the Sight. 'Did you?'

'Um, well, some people did,' said Calleset, suddenly recalling that Lirael was no longer a very shy and retiring

Second Assistant Librarian but the Abhorsen-in-Waiting, and not only that, but a great hero of the Kingdom.

'Why isn't the gate open?' asked Lirael. 'Has something happened? All the Watch busy, and only two rangers available to meet me and my guest?'

She indicated Nick, who was nervously watching the worm, still with a certain amount of disbelief and a great deal of caution. He was trying to work out where to run if it suddenly lunged forward with that vast mouth and all those teeth. Lirael was very trusting to turn her back to such a thing . . .

'Who I should say is Nicholas Sayre, a . . . a prince from Ancelstierre,' continued Lirael. 'Or as good as, his uncle being their ruler –'

'That's not quite right,' interrupted Nick. He still didn't take his eyes off the worm. 'Technically the Hereditary Arbiter is the head of state; he's my cousin. Uncle Edward is the Chief Minister –'

'So I would have thought someone from the Watch could be here to greet him at least, even if everyone just thinks I am still the same old Lirael!'

'I don't think anyone thinks *that*,' blurted out Calleset. 'It's . . . it is just that we . . . they . . . the Nine-Day Watch didn't See you.'

'Oh,' replied Lirael.

The Clayr *always* Saw visitors, even if they missed other things. But set against that certainty there was also the case that she herself had never been Seen by the Watch when

175

she was growing up, even when the normal Nine-Day Watch of forty-nine Clayr was reinforced to the rare Fifteen Hundred and Sixty-Eight Clayr, all concentrating their power in an attempt to distil the myriad possible futures into a mere several that could be Seen clearly in the ice of the observatory.

The Watch had in fact only Seen Lirael once, at the very last moment, when the action against Orannis was critical. Lirael had thought that from then on the Clayr would see her as much as they Saw everyone else. But perhaps not . . .

'There is also the . . . the Starmount Guardian,' added Calleset, indicating the giant worm arrayed in front of the gate. 'We came from the next post up the mountainside when the alarm sounded, indicating the guardian was active. It only comes out when danger threatens, or enemies are without the gate.'

'It c-c-ame out of the g-g-ground when I walked t-t-towards the little d-d-door,' said Nick. His teeth were chattering from the cold now, much as he tried to keep them still. 'Is it . . . um . . . r-r-real?'

'It's a guard Sending,' said Lirael. 'Made of Charter Magic. Real enough, if you had to fight it, though I have to say whoever made it – a long time ago – got the teeth wrong. Real drill-grubs don't have pointy teeth in the front ring, or pointy teeth at all, for that matter. But we need to get you in out of the cold. Come on!'

Lirael took Nick by the arm and began to lead him towards the gate. But as they approached, the great worm reared up before them, its teeth rotated faster, and gobbets of purple slime began to drip from its mouth.

'Drill-grubs don't drool. That is pure invention,' said Lirael crossly, but she stopped as Nick flinched back. 'However, it does seem to be triggered by your presence, Nick.'

'We can't let anyone in whom the Starmount Guardian refuses,' said Calleset uneasily. She pulled a small leather-bound book from the pouch on her belt and flicked it open. 'That's rule thirty-six: "Should the Starmount Worm, the Sunfall Lion, or –" well, there are others I shouldn't mention – it says "appear of their own volition, then look to your swords and bar entry to those the guardians scorn."'

'Scorn?' asked Nick.

'It's old-fashioned,' said Lirael hurriedly. 'It just means keep out.'

Calleset put the book away and stood at attention with her chin up, which unfortunately did nothing to counter her general air of uncertainty.

'So . . . um . . . we can't let your guest in. Even if he is a prince from over the Wall. I'm sorry.'

'Because of rule thirty-six,' said Lirael. 'And you have to follow the rules.'

'Yes,' said Calleset.

Lirael looked at the Guard Sending and thought for a moment. She could probably send it away with a spell, or disable it, but this would only create more problems. Two young rangers would never go against their rules and regulations. They might even feel they had to fight her . . . Lirael felt suddenly ill at the thought of fighting her kin, and hastily dismissed any notion of forcing her way in.

'I presume more rangers will be on their way, from the other posts on the mountain and from inside? Someone of higher rank?'

'Yes,' said Calleset. 'The alarm will have sounded everywhere.'

'So we can expect Mirelle or some other officer who can send the guardian back to rest fairly soon?'

Mirelle was the commander of the Rangers, those Clayr who patrolled the Glacier, the mountains and the river valley, and who also guarded the outer gates.

'Maybe just a lieutenant,' said Calleset. The expression on her face suggested that she hoped it was not the commander herself who would show up. 'Qilla's the closest on duty, up here.'

'Qilla got made a lieutenant of the Rangers?'

Qilla was only five or six years older than Lirael, very young to be promoted so high. A lieutenancy in the Rangers was the equivalent of a First Assistant Librarian. Not that ranks in the various employments of the Clayr were considered all that important by the inhabitants of the Glacier; everything was subsidiary to their main task of Seeing the future, or trying to make sense of the many possible futures they Saw.

'Acting lieutenant,' said Calleset, then shut her mouth as if she had said too much.

'We'd better wait for her, then,' said Lirael. 'But could

Jelesray please go inside and fetch some of the Paperwing flyer's furs for Nicholas? If that isn't against the rules?'

Calleset inclined her head at the younger ranger, who quickly ran to the sally port. Nick noticed that she went as far around the worm as she could, obviously not really believing it knew the difference between those who should be allowed in and those who should not. He was relieved to see he was not the only person there who found the drill-grub Sending frightening. He wished he could be as uncaring about it as Lirael, who had barely spared the giant worm a glance after she had first shooed it away from the gate.

'Perhaps I should explain that Nicholas was involved in the binding of Orannis,' said Lirael. 'And from that, carries the taint of Free Magic in his blood and bone. I suspect that is what the worm reacts to; that kind of Sending is generally not very discerning.'

'Or it simply doesn't l-l-like my face,' said Nick, attempting a joke, which fell flat, as Lirael and Calleset both looked puzzled.

'Drill-grubs are blind,' said Lirael, after a moment. 'They sense vibrations. Though this Sending may have been given other senses in its creation, you can see it has no eyes.'

'Yes,' mumbled Nick, teeth chattering. He felt even more miserable now. 'How s-s-illy of me.'

chapter seventeen

loose shale and charter-spelled arrows

Near Yellowsands, the Old Kingdom

The first wood-weird came scuttling over the Charter Stone hill a little less than thirty minutes after Ferin had parted company with the main body of villagers. It skirted around the stone, keeping well clear. This particular Free Magic construct was long and low, rather like a cockroach or spider in shape, one made from a rough-hewn hickory trunk and branches, trailing strips of partially sloughed-off bark. The creature had eight legs made from tree roots, joined in multiple segments. Free Magic fire burned at the joints, and also in the eyes and mouth that had been gouged in the end of its central trunk with auger and adze.

It was very quick, faster than any wood-weird Ferin had seen before, as swift as a galloping horse, though it moved in a series of long lunges, with short pauses in between. Well ahead of its fellows, it got down into the valley within a few minutes. There it continued its horrible speedy, scuttling movement: rushing forward, stopping for a moment as if to test the air, then rushing forward again.

Ferin and her companions were a little more than halfway up the shale hill, the ridgeline looming above them. They stopped to look down, and there was a collective pause in everyone's breath as the wood-weird did *not* turn aside to follow their path, but continued down the road, following the fleeing villagers. The last dozen or so of the fisher-folk were still in sight, well short of where the road turned behind the southern hill towards the estuary and the tower.

The wood-weird would catch the stragglers in ten minutes at the most, though these last villagers had seen it too, and were now running rather than walking. But there was no way they could escape such a swiftly-moving creature.

More wood-weirds appeared on the crest of the village hill, again giving the Charter Stone a wide berth. These were like the one that had attacked Ferin at the Bridge Castle: tall monsters of fir and spruce and ironwood, timbers greatly valued on the steppe, where all trees were rare.

Once again, Ferin wondered at the profligate use of the wood-weirds so far from the steppe. The cost in sorcerers, keepers and rare timber was extreme. She had said the raider must carry the sorcerous strength of two clans at least, but perhaps it was nearer three or even four clans working in concert, at the behest of the Witch With No Face. Her own Athask people had only two shamans and three witches, and of them, only the most senior could create a wood-weird. It took years to make the body, carving the timber and infusing it with spells, preparing it for habitation by a powerful enough Free Magic spirit, which had to be taken from wherever the sorcerers found such things.

'Charter, please make it turn aside and follow us,' whispered Swinther, his words echoed by Young Laska. The woodcutter was not looking at the slower creatures marching down the Charter Stone hill, only at the spider-like, eight-legged wood-weird on the road below, which drew closer and closer to the rearguard of the fisher-folk. If you could call it a rearguard, since in terms of effective fighters it consisted only of Constable Megril and Astilaran, the former kicking a well-known dockside lounger along in an effort to make him run faster.

'Can we draw the creature's attention?' asked Ferin. 'With some of your magic?'

'Yes,' replied Young Laska. She smiled a wry smile. 'I am more used to trying to conceal myself from such things. But there is a signal we use . . .'

She bent her head and held her hands cupped near her mouth, a look of intense concentration in her eyes. The Borderer blew out a tiny breath, and Ferin watched in fascination as glowing marks tumbled from Young Laska's lips and gathered in her hands, winding together like a tiny serpent, the head gripping the tail. She took another breath, deeper this time, laid her hands flat, and blew the spinning circle of marks out into the air. Rather than tumbling down the hillside, the glowing ring shot up into the sky and a second later exploded into dozens and dozens of brilliant small stars that fell a dozen feet before disappearing with attendant thunder-claps, not loud and close, but as if from a far-off storm.

It was enough to attract the attention of all the wood-weirds in the valley below, and indeed the sorcerers who were loping along with their keepers behind them holding their silver chains close, like huntsmen keeping dogs of uncertain temper on short leashes.

'The spider-thing turns,' said Ferin. She waved her arms and called out, 'Here! Here!' and then made several rude gestures common to all the tribes, though these would mean nothing to the Free Magic creatures, and the sorcerers and their keepers were probably too far away to see her clearly.

Young Laska chuckled at her side. Ferin looked at her.

'You know what that meant?'

The Borderer nodded.

'I was assigned for several years to the Northwest Desert, one of the most distant parts of the Kingdom that borders the lower western steppe. There are several oases there where the Moon Horse clan and the Blood Horses come to trade, and sometimes to raid. So I know a little of the tribes, and even of sand-swimmers, wood-weirds and spirit-walkers, though I confess to having seen a wood-weird only once before. They were very uncommon in the desert.'

'But you survived,' said Ferin. 'That is good.'

'I hid from it, and ran when I could, and I was lucky,' said Young Laska. She pointed downwards, where the fast wood-weird had already turned and was running towards their hillside. 'I think it is time we also quickened our pace, if not to run.'

'No running,' said Swinther. 'The path narrows even before the ridge, and it will be broken shale underfoot soon; you will need to set each footfall very carefully, and crouch low. Watch where I go, do what I do. Follow!'

The path grew steeper and more difficult almost immediately. Either frequent passage, or active work, had cleared away the deeper piles of loose shale so that there was bedrock or earth beneath to actually step upon, and here and there in the trickier parts iron staples had been driven deeply into the rock to use as foot- or handholds, though some were so rusted Swinther tested them very carefully before use.

Ferin was pleased the path was difficult, for it would slow the wood-weirds a great deal. But then again, she did not want them to turn back too soon, and go on to catch the fisher-folk before they reached the haven of the old tower.

But after a very steep section, liberally seeded with deeply seated iron spikes, they reached the ridge and the going became much easier, at least at first. The path was six or seven paces wide, and almost level, rising or falling only a few feet for quite some distance. The shale underfoot on the path was loose, but in very crushed, small pieces, so it was reasonably easy to keep one's footing, unlike the much more treacherous many-layered sheets of stone to either side. The shale there would undoubtedly break at once and slide away if trodden on, taking the unfortunate walker with it.

They had only gone on another hundred paces when

Young Laska stopped and held her hand up to test the breeze. There had been little enough below, and not much more on the ridge, but now the wind was freshening and swinging around. It was colder, and brought with it the tang of rain.

'Wind's changed,' said Young Laska. She looked to the west. 'A westerly now, from the mountains. Not natural.'

'They had a wind-eater aboard,' said Ferin. 'I shot her. Or him. But they were not killed.'

'Bringing clouds,' said Young Laska. 'I wonder –'

She was interrupted by the sound of falling shale. They looked back and saw the speedy wood-weird get its two leading tree-root legs over the top of the steep climb, scrabble for a moment, then haul itself up onto the ridge. It paused there for a few moments, burning eyes looking straight at Ferin and her companions, then immediately started along the path, its movement now reminiscent of a hunting spider.

Young Laska had her bow off her back and an arrow nocked in seconds, with Ferin only a moment behind. Two arrows flew, Ferin's striking the body of the creature only to shatter without effect. But Young Laska's Charter-spelled arrow stuck fast in the hollow of the thing's eye, a great gout of white sparks spraying out where it lodged.

'Save your shafts!' snapped Young Laska to Ferin, sending another arrow speeding into the creature's other eyehole. Again, there was a shower of sparks. The wood-weird stopped, and for a moment Ferin thought it was mortally wounded. But it was only blinded, and it started forward again, carefully feeling the path ahead with its forelegs.

Young Laska shot again, at one of these forelegs, her arrow sticking in a joint, which became wreathed in golden fire, Charter Magic competing with the sickly red burn of Free Magic within. But her next arrow missed the other leg, striking shale, and the creature rushed forward, opening its rough-cut mouth wide, the fire within roiling, white smoke jetting forth, accompanied by the nauseating, hot-metal reek of Free Magic.

Young Laska dropped her bow to wield a Charter-spelled arrow in her hand, but Swinther nimbly slid past her, his double-bladed axe lifted high.

'For Yellowsands!'

the avoidance of responsibility

Clayr's Glacier, the Old Kingdom

Qilla, newly made acting lieutenant of the Rangers, did not feel she was of a sufficiently elevated standing to ignore rule thirty-six and send the guardian drill-grub Sending back into its quiescent state under the stones of the landing ground and admit the visitor, despite Lirael's entreaties.

'Oh, for Charter's sake!' exclaimed Lirael. 'Can someone send for Mirelle? Or the Voice of the Nine-Day Watch?'

'The Voice?' asked Qilla. She pursed her lips and shook her head. 'I don't think this calls –'

'Qilla,' said Lirael. 'I know it's hard for you all to come to terms with the fact, but I am not just some junior cousin any more, I *am* the Abhorsen-in-Waiting. If it were Sabriel here asking you to let her guest in, would we all be standing around in the cold?'

'Uh, no,' said Qilla. 'But . . .'

'Get Mirelle,' said Lirael. 'Or the Voice.'

Qilla looked as if she was about to say something, but shut her mouth as Lirael looked at her, her golden hand resting on the handle of Saraneth, the sixth bell, the one used to bind the Dead to the wielder's will. There was no trace of the meek, withdrawn girl Qilla had known vaguely by sight, as all the Clayr knew one another, if not better because of closer kinship or the propinquity of either work or shared participation in the Nine-Day Watch.

'I'll send word for Mirelle,' said Qilla, and walked away to confer with one of the other rangers. There were four of them on the landing ground now, standing about and gazing outwards, down and up, as if they were guarding Lirael and Nick from a surprise attack from without, rather than surreptitiously keeping an eye on these unexpected and complicated arrivals.

Lirael looked down at Nick, who she had made sit back in the relative warmth of the Paperwing's cockpit. He was dressed in a leather-and-fur flying coat and woollen breeches now, and he felt much warmer and more secure, now sufficiently well-clothed not to be embarrassed by a sudden movement or a gust of wind. But, although he did not know it, he still looked awful, very pale and weak, and he shivered from time to time, no longer from cold but simply from lack of blood and weariness.

He smiled at Lirael and said, 'I go a thousand miles, to another kingdom, somewhere that feels like another world entirely, and it is just like being back home! Trying to get into the Moot when it is in session, to see my father or uncle, with some flun– that is . . . with a guard or an official wanting a particular pass or someone else to take responsibility for letting me through the door.'

'Thank you for not being . . . for not being angry,' said Lirael. *She* was angry, quite furious that they had not been admitted at once. It made her look stupid and ineffectual in front of Nick, and though she did not want to admit it, even to herself, she had hoped that when she did eventually return to the Glacier that she would finally be treated as someone of note, a handsome frog rather than an ugly tadpole, as in the children's story.

Mirelle arrived some thirty minutes later, slightly out of breath from running up the Starmount Stair, something that would have left most Clayr half her age, or anyone else for that matter, puking and half-dead. It was a very long way and the steps had much higher risers than was normal, as if they were built for a race of eight-foot-tall people. Yet for the leather-skinned, grey-haired commander of the Rangers it was apparently no more than a mild stretch on a spring afternoon.

'Greetings, Abhorsen-in-Waiting,' said Mirelle, bowing. She raised her hand, two fingers extended, and said, 'May I test your mark?'

Lirael nodded. This was correct etiquette, but she doubted Mirelle meant it that way; it was probably her being wary of a potential enemy, some sort of substitution or deceit. Particularly as she noted the older Clayr kept one hand on the hilt of the small but doubtless extremely sharp knife she wore on her left side, next to her sword. Lirael had always found Mirelle rather frightening on the few occasions they'd crossed paths, but this time she was not intimidated. She thought about that for a moment, remembering her earlier self. But that younger Lirael had not fought Free Magic constructs, many Dead creatures, Chlorr of the Mask and ultimately Orannis itself.

The commander reached out and touched the Charter mark on Lirael's forehead, even as Lirael did the same to her. Both immediately felt the deep connection, the sudden immersion in the endless sea of marks, some very familiar, some known, so many unknown, flashing past in an instant.

Mirelle withdrew her hand and smiled.

'I apologise for my caution, Lirael,' she said. 'We are so rarely blind to the future on our own doorstep, and you were not Seen at all. May I test your companion's mark?'

'Sure,' said Nick, even though she hadn't asked him. He smiled wearily. 'Whatever it takes to get closer to a hot bath and a meal.'

'Before you do,' said Lirael, speaking quietly so only Mirelle and Nick could hear, 'you should know this is Nicholas Sayre, who bore the fragment of Orannis within him, and unwittingly aided the necromancer Hedge. The . . . the Disreputable Dog, that is to say Kibeth, used her power to restore him to Life and baptised him with the mark. But there is a great deal of Free Magic within him as well. That is why I have brought him here, to see . . . to see what we may discover of the nature of this combination. And . . . and to deal with his wounds, both old and new.'

'I see,' said Mirelle. She bent over and touched the mark on Nick's forehead and kept her fingers against his forehead for several seconds. Then she slowly withdrew her hand, but didn't straighten up.

'Now you touch my mark,' she said. 'That is the normal courtesy. We do it to assure ourselves the mark is not faked, or corrupted in some way, by Free Magic or artifice.'

Nick glanced at Lirael. She nodded encouragingly, so he reached out as Mirelle had done, and touched the mark on her forehead. It was just under the lip of her steel helmet, which was wrapped in white cloth and somewhat resembled a turban.

Nick gasped as he felt himself suddenly surrounded by glowing Charter marks, the normal world somehow dull and removed. He knew he still sat in the Paperwing, he could feel the cool air, but at the same time he had the sensation of sinking – no, diving – deep into some other place, an endless sea of glowing Charter marks that had no beginning or end, and he became afraid that he would be lost in it as he began to feel separate from his own body, a detached intelligence caught up in this rushing current of magic, and he had to exert all his willpower to pull his fingers back, breaking the connection and restoring himself to himself.

'So that is what Sam talks about,' he croaked. He felt very small and insignificant all of a sudden, a mere speck, suddenly aware of so much more around and about him and how it was connected. 'The Charter.'

'I am afraid you present a problem,' said Mirelle. 'Your mark is true, but you also contain a great amount of Free Magic, as much or more than any of the creatures who are our mortal enemies. That is what the Starmount Guardian senses, no matter how it is overlaid with Charter Magic. We are expressly forbidden to allow you entry to the Glacier . . . as a guest or visitor.'

Lirael noted the phrasing of Mirelle's reply. She seemed to be suggesting something, some way around the prohibition, without actually saying so. But Lirael wasn't sure what the ranger meant.

'Can the Voice overrule this prohibition?' asked Lirael. 'Who is the Voice at the moment, anyway?'

'She could,' said Mirelle, in a tone that suggested this was not going to happen. 'But it is your aunt Kirrith. At least for the next five days.'

'What!' exclaimed Lirael. 'Not Sanar and Ryelle?'

Kirrith was the Guardian of the Young; she had held that office for the entirety of Lirael's life, and it was one that usually excluded the bearer from participating in the Nine-Day Watch and thus the potential to become the Voice. Being the Voice was an honour and responsibility which usually went to the Clayr with the strongest vision, which meant it was the province of people like Sanar and Ryelle, whose Sight was very powerful. One or the other of these twins, or both of them concurrently, usually occupied the post for many consecutive terms of the Watch. But Lirael knew that some-times, when everything was quiet and there wasn't much being Seen anyway, the post was assigned to those worthy in other ways, as a mark of distinction and gratitude for their everyday work in the Glacier.

'They have the influenza,' said Mirelle, with the faintest of shrugs. 'It is not very serious, but a great many people have needed to take to their beds these last few weeks. It was Seen coming, and with little else happening, it looked an appropriate time to honour some who perhaps would not otherwise ever be the Voice.'

Lirael suppressed a groan. She did not hold a high opinion of her aunt Kirrith's intelligence. Worse, Kirrith was deeply suspicious of anyone or anything from outside the Clayr's closed world. She would never overrule any tradition, regu-lation or even old habits of the Clayr.

'I take it your aunt is not likely to look fondly upon my visit?' asked Nick. 'I have some aunts of my own who aren't too keen on me, either.'

'Nick needs to be somewhere warm soon, where he can rest,' said Lirael to Mirelle. 'I never thought to be turned away here! We should have gone to Belisaere.'

'The King, of course, could order us to take him in,' said Mirelle. 'But I understand the King is taking a holiday?'

'Yes,' said Lirael. 'Not to be disturbed by message-hawks, save for dire news of the first importance. Which I suppose this isn't . . .'

She looked up at the sky. It was growing dark quickly, and

the wind was increasing, a very cold wind. Soon it would be too cold even in the cockpit of the Paperwing, which would not be comfortable overnight in any case. Nick was visibly shivering all the time now, and she thought his lips were looking bluish. It was ridiculous to be so close to warmth and shelter and not be allowed to take him in. Lirael was sure the Free Magic was contained; it would not simply break out. It wasn't as if she was trying to smuggle a Stilken inside.

Her mind wandered to how the Stilken had got into the Library in the first place, though of course it had probably been there for centuries, if not longer. The Clayr could not possibly guard all entrances, every nook and cranny in two mountains and a glacier. It was possible it had even been brought in on purpose, inside that glass coffin, to be studied . . .

A smile slowly spread across Lirael's face.

'Nick,' she said, looking down at him, her eyes suddenly bright. 'There is a way we can get you inside.'

'Good,' said Nick faintly. He smiled back at her. 'I *really* wouldn't mind that hot bath you mentioned . . .'

Lirael turned to Mirelle. She was surprised to see a very faint look of amusement on the ranger's generally stern and forbidding face.

'I believe the Library has a general dispensation for importing items of interest, including living things and even Free Magic?'

'Indeed,' said Mirelle.

'Then please send word ahead to the Librarian or her

deputy that the Abhorsen-in-Waiting and once and perhaps still Second Assistant Librarian Lirael presents her compliments and is bringing a temporary addition to the collection, a person to be studied. And can you put that Sending back under the ground and open the gate so we can get the Paperwing inside as well?'

'As you wish,' said Mirelle. The faint look of amusement became a definite flicker of a smile, which crossed her face for a moment and was gone. She bowed, waved the other rangers in, and walked across to the great worm. There she spoke several words heavily imbued with Charter marks. The worm immediately blurred, like a sketch being erased, and became once again an outline drawn in light. This hung in the air for a few moments before it sank into the ground, leaving behind thousands of tiny glowing marks like strange wildflowers on the snow, which slowly faded, leaving no trace of the worm's former presence . . .

Lirael helped Nick out of the Paperwing, and whistled, three short sweet notes, Charter marks leaping with her breath to the Paperwing's nose. It shuddered and lightly flicked its wings. Lirael held Nick as they walked to the slowly opening gate, the Paperwing drifting along behind them a few inches above the ground.

chapter nineteen

battle on the ridge of shale

Near Yellowsands, the Old Kingdom

Swinther's axe bounced from the ensorcelled wood-weird's leg, but the sheer force of the blow pushed the creature off balance. At the same time Young Laska took a great risk, lunging past the woodcutter with one foot on the loose shale off the path. Somehow she kept her balance, driving an arrow by hand into the top joint of the wood-weird's left foreleg before turning on the spot to jump back.

White sparks geysered from the wound with a sound like a massive snake hissing. The wood-weird snapped down at Young Laska as she spun away, but Swinther swung his axe again, knocking the certainly fatal bite aside.

'Back! Swinther! Back!' shouted Young Laska, grabbing her bow and crawling away along the path as fast as she could. Ferin also retreated, sending another useless shaft into the wood-weird, the arrow again simply bouncing off and falling down the hillside.

Swinther backed up, swinging his axe in fast diagonals, but the blade did not cut; no wood chips flew. He could knock the forelimbs aside, but that was all. The wood-weird continued after him, though it did not move as swiftly as before. White sparks continued to fountain from its eyes and joints, but otherwise it did not seem to be much damaged.

'Go!' shouted Swinther. 'I will slow it! Go!'

In answer, Ferin reached off the path and grabbed the corner of a slab of shale half her own size, though only three or four inches thick.

'Help me!'

Young Laska saw at once what Ferin intended. Dropping her bow again, she picked up the other side of the stone.

'Duck!' they shouted together, and as Swinther dropped low, they heaved the stone against the wood-weird's already damaged foreleg. Once again, it did not affect the ensorcelled timber. But the stone broke into pieces and fell under the creature's questing forelimbs, making it pause for a dozen seconds as its long root-like legs tentatively felt for solid ground amid the rubble.

Useful seconds, which allowed Swinther to back away and Ferin and Young Laska to retreat several more paces around a corner where ridge and the path upon it turned sharply north.

'Small stones!' shouted Ferin. 'Break them in front of it!'

She started picking up smaller pieces of shale, hurling them to shatter in front of the wood-weird. Young Laska copied her, both of them picking up and throwing slabs as quickly as they could, covering the path with pieces of broken stone.

The wood-weird, blinded by the still-sparking Charter-spelled arrows in its eye sockets, came on cautiously, feeling about in the broken shale with its forelegs. It moved more erratically now, the Charter-spelled arrows working away in the joints to sever the Free Magic that articulated and drove the cleverly fashioned timber.

Swinther retreated around the turn in the path, dropped his axe behind him, crouched down, and started to throw slabs of shale as well. Ferin and Young Laska were now using both hands to scoop and throw, so that the path ahead of the creature was piled high with broken shale.

The wood-weird, blind and probing with its crippled fore-limbs, and now confused by the shale everywhere and no clear path to find, missed the turn. It continued straight ahead, several steps too far. Its forelimbs slipped and it fell forward, rear legs scrabbling as the shale in front collapsed. For a moment it looked as if it might draw back, but then a whole great layer of shale slid down the hill, precipitating a sudden avalanche of stone.

The wood-weird surfed down the side of the ridge amid a clattering wave of broken shale, until it came to a halt several hundred feet below with a sickening crack. A second later it was buried by the several tons of shale that came down after it, and a great cloud of grey stone-dust rose up to the sky.

As the dust rose, there was a scream of rage from further

back along the ridge. A shaman climbed up to the path, ignoring the keeper who was heaving on the silver chain about his neck to keep him still. The shaman tried to run towards Ferin and the others, but only managed two or three steps before the neck-ring closed and he fell, choking.

The keeper climbed up behind the fallen shaman, knelt on his back, and jerked the chain savagely several times, as a warning or to ensure compliance. Then she let go, dropped the chain, and stood up to take the bow from her back.

Even before this keeper could take an arrow from the case at her side, she was struck by one of Young Laska's ordinary, unspelled arrows. The yard-long shaft should have killed her, piercing her through and through, but just before it hit, some unseen force sent it spinning away.

'Charmed!' spat Young Laska, and sent three shafts in quick succession at almost exactly the same target: high on the left of the keeper's chest.

Two arrows spun away like the first, diverted by the Free Magic charm. But the power of the defence failed with the last arrow, or at least did not entirely work. The arrow veered, but only by a few inches and the keeper fell, transfixed through the neck by a bloodied shaft.

Ferin had drawn too, but not shot, thinking she was likely to miss at that range, and with the wind blowing.

The shaman, freed from the restraint of his keeper's silver chain, slowly got to his feet. He paused for a moment, then came staggering along the path, face set in a mask of anger. He was just beginning to raise one hand in a spell-casting gesture when Young Laska sent three quick arrows at him as well. Either he had no defensive charm, or it was not ready, for all three struck. The shaman was spun about and fell from the ridge with one last screech of pain and anger, his descent accompanied by a cascade of shale. A few seconds later the stone-dust rose again, just as it had for the wood-weird he had made.

'Eleven to go,' said Ferin.

'I have no more Charter-spelled arrows,' said Young Laska in a matter-of-fact tone. 'And only eight ordinary shafts.'

'We'd best not let them catch us, then,' said Swinther. He was examining the front of his leather jerkin, which had been ripped open by the sharp foreleg of the wood-weird, and was bloody underneath.

'You're wounded?' asked Ferin. Her ankle was hurting much more, as Astilaran had predicted, but it was still nothing like as painful as it had been. She could move without restraint.

'No . . .' replied Swinther, wiping his bloodied hand on his breeches. 'It swiped me, sure, but those limbs were strangely hot. It cauterised as it cut. A bite would have been a different matter, those snaggled splintered teeth . . . stay still, I will come around you. The path grows very narrow soon and forks with a false dead-end ridge in the offing. Then there is the sharpest part of the ridgeline to pass, where we will need our hands and bare feet to grip. I do not think even that eight-legged creature could cross there.'

Young Laska looked up at the clouds that were drawing

closer, and then down below. She was puzzled by what she saw, for only one silver-chained figure and his or her keeper were beginning to ascend, and they had no wood-weird with them. The other keepers were gathered close, their sorcerers kept in a huddle between them. From the look of all the gesticulating and the faint sound of shouts, there was an argument under way, one that had so far fallen short of blows.

'There's only one sorcerer and keeper coming up,' said Ferin.

'Can you see which tribes the keepers are from, in the main body?' asked Young Laska.

'No. They are too distant to see the colours on their sashes,' said Ferin. She gestured back along the path. 'That one you killed, he was Yrus. Sky Horse. Are you thinking they will fight each other? They will not, not when they are under orders from the Witch With No Face.'

'I think they don't want to send their wood-weirds up the shale,' said Young Laska. She pointed where the ring of keepers was suddenly expanding, sorcerers being dragged back by chains, wood-weirds rising up on their tree-root legs. 'Look, they are heading back towards the village.'

'To loot and burn, most like,' said Swinther heavily. 'Still, better we lose our houses and boats than our lives.'

'They will not go away unless they are sure I will be taken or killed,' said Ferin, a note of puzzlement in her voice. 'But to send only one shaman, one keeper, not even with a wood-weird . . .'

Young Laska looked up at the clouds again – darkening

clouds, moving quite rapidly towards the sun – and then she gazed back down at that lone shaman.

'I would hazard a guess their wind-eater is also a wind-caller,' she said slowly. 'And not only that, a necromancer to boot. I can think of no other reason they would want to block the sun.'

As she spoke, the shadow of the clouds rolled over them, blotting out the sun, and the ridge was suddenly cool. Ferin stared down at the shaman below, who was still in sunshine for a few more seconds, and saw that he did indeed wear the seven bells of a necromancer in a bandolier across his chest, and his head was helmetless and freshly bandaged around the ear, testament to the closeness of the arrow she had shot from the fishing boat. In addition to his bells, the shaman had a strange tarred box upon his back, doubtless containing some adjunct to his dark art.

He did not wear traditional garb, and it took Ferin a moment to work out that the off-white coat he wore was a kind of armour, made from hundreds of small bones, linked with dark iron rings. It was almost certainly imbued with charms against ordinary arrows, and other mundane weapons too.

The keeper behind him was a woman. Ferin knew her sash colours, and observed that she kept a very a tight hold of the silver chain, and in her gloved right hand she carried an unwrapped spirit-glass arrow, a thin coil of white smoke rising from its tip.

'He *is* a necromancer,' said Ferin. 'The keeper is of the Ghost

Horse clan; they are one of the three tribes that keep necromancers. He must be very powerful; she is so fearful of him she must carry a spirit-glass arrow at the ready, in addition to the neck-ring and chain. They will both have stronger charms against arrows.'

'Something to test, if the opportunity presents,' said Young Laska. 'But for now, I suggest we open the range, rather than closing it.'

'Yes,' said Ferin. She looked at the necromancer again, then at Swinther. 'Are there dead buried up here at all?'

Swinther thought for a moment, knowing all too well why Ferin was asking. A necromancer needed something to work with: bodies, a cemetery, a battlefield, a place of many deaths . . .

'Not on the ridge itself,' he said. 'But below this hill, to the north, there were once a dozen farms in the valley, maybe more. One was bigger than the others, a place called Nangan Rest. There was a feast there; everyone for leagues around attended. No one knows what happened, but they fell to fighting each other, and nearly all were killed. Nangan Rest was burned to the ground, farmhouse, outbuildings, tower and all. Later, the bodies were put into the ground and a mound raised. This is fifty . . . fifty-four years gone, you understand. In the bad times, when there was no King.'

'How many farmers died?' asked Ferin. 'And how close, exactly?'

'Hundreds, to hear the tale,' said Swinther. 'Just below us, as I said. You can see the mound still, that small green hill, perhaps half a league beyond the last of the shale.'

He paused, then added, 'And . . . there are also those who have died along the ridge. One every few years or so. The farm boys will do it as a sort of initiation, they always have, and sometimes ours will join in, as I did myself, long ago. The fallen will be under the shale; the bodies can never be recovered.'

'He will have plenty to call on, then,' said Young Laska. 'And the closest swift water?'

'Where the others are, the tower built over the estuary to the south,' answered Swinther. He had not seemed overly frightened by the wood-weird, but he was pale now, and there was sweat on his forehead despite the sudden drop in temperature that had come with the disappearance of the sun.

The prospect of encountering the Dead had that effect upon the living.

'Can we get there?' asked Ferin. She had to work hard to keep her voice even. She had never seen a Dead creature, but she had heard tales. The Athask people did not approve of necromancers, and would not allow their kept sorcerers to dabble in necromancy. But every now and then someone would encounter a free-willed Dead thing in their mountains. Caves and narrow mountain ravines were good places for creatures that feared the sun.

'Can't go back, of course,' said Swinther. 'We *might* be able to get down from High Kemmy – that's the third peak along – there's a better path down from there at least, and then we could cut across the valley. If . . .'

His words trailed off. There was no need to speak the 'ifs' aloud, for there were too many. Night was coming early, and soon the necromancer behind them would be summoning the Dead . . .

chapter twenty

old furniture and the prospect of baths

Clayr's Glacier, the Old Kingdom

There was an easier but much slower way down from the Paperwing hangar than the Starmount Stair. Called the Long Stretches, it was a series of switchbacked, gently inclined corridors that gained their name from the two and a half leagues they took to drop two thousand paces. It was a long way to walk after a day's flying, much too far for Nick in his current state. He was once again put into a hammock-like stretcher, and carried by four rangers at a time, taking turns. There were eight rangers walking with them now, Mirelle having summoned more of an escort. The commander accompanied them, but stayed well ahead like a racehorse that can't help but be in front.

Lirael trudged by Nick's stretcher, sunk in weariness and deep in her own thoughts. No one talked, and they did not meet anyone, hardly a surprise this high up in the Clayr's abode. Any sensible person with business in the Paperwing hangar would take the stairs.

At least it was pleasantly warm in the Long Stretches. As in most of the Clayr's vast subterranean habitat, the corridors were heated by steam pipes from the hot springs far below. Ancient clever engineering was aided by judicial use of Charter Magic, and the constant labours of the usually rather grimy engineers from the Steamworks. Charter marks in the ceiling and walls, refreshed and recast every decade or so, also provided the soft, constant light.

Though she had rarely used the Long Stretches, walking in that particular Charter light and feeling the unique, humid warmth provided by the steam pipes stirred up Lirael's confused feelings of both being home and not being at home. She had always felt something of an outsider here, but growing up had known nowhere else. Back then she had never considered the possibility of living away from the Glacier, or having a life that was not as one of the Clayr. This had lasted right up until the final revelation that she would never have the Sight, and instead had an entirely different destiny as an Abhorsen.

Now she was experiencing what it was to return to the place of her childhood, where she had always desperately hoped she would one day permanently and properly belong. With it came the clear understanding that though this was her heritage, it was only that: something of her past that would not come again. She had become someone and something else, whose life and future lay apart from being one of the Clayr.

Lirael was thinking about this, and how she now felt so different from her younger self, as if she were an entirely new person in a way. She was thinking so deeply about this that she was slow to notice a party of librarians coming up the Long Stretches to meet her and the new addition to the Library's collection.

When she did see them, the sight made Lirael's heart leap in a joyful recognition that had not come with her entrance into the halls of the Clayr. She smiled to see the familiar uniforms and faces, and most particularly at one of the junior librarians at the back who was trying to read and walk at the same time, thinking herself far enough behind to be hidden from view.

It was a formal procession. The party was led by the imposing figure of Vancelle the Chief Librarian herself, in a night-black waistcoat with the sword Binder at her side; followed by two deputies in white waistcoats, ceremonial axes on their shoulders, though these were only ceremonial in the sense of being gilded and adorned – they were still useful weapons; then four First Assistants, their waistcoats blue and ceremonial weapons short-staved halberds with blue tassels; eight Second Assistants with curved scimitars, in red waistcoats like Lirael's own, which was in a chest with camphor balls back in the palace in Belisaere; and a gaggle of Third Assistant Librarians in yellow waistcoats, bearing long spears, the heads bright with new-laid Charter marks placed there only on very special occasions.

All of them, of course, bore dagger, whistle and clockwork

emergency mouse, the standard equipment of the Clayr's librarians. They would not set foot outside the great Reading Room far below without these essential items.

Lirael had herself been a member of such ceremonial parties, as a Third and then Second Assistant Librarian, greeting notables such as the King himself, or Sabriel, or the Lord Mayor of Belisaere. But always far back in the throng, like the Third Assistant who was still reading her book. Lirael had never thought to be at the forefront, or to be greeted in such a way herself.

Both groups stopped a dozen paces short of each other, and Vancelle came forward and bowed to Lirael, who returned the greeting. But that done, the Librarian moved closer and embraced the younger woman, which was a surprise.

'You have done great things,' said Vancelle. 'And all of us in the Library are very, very proud of you.'

'Thank you,' said Lirael. She fought back the tears in her eyes, because though she no longer felt she was one of the Clayr, she still felt she was a *librarian* and always would be, no matter what else she had become as well.

'We have some gifts, long prepared for your return,' said Vancelle, indicating two First Assistants who carried ornate boxes: one long and thin; the other almost a cube. Both were made of dark red cedar with elaborately cast hinges, edges and lock plates of shining gold. One of the First Assistants was Lirael's old friend Imshi, who had carried out Lirael's induction to the Library almost six years before, assigning her dagger, whistle and mouse. Imshi smiled and waggled her little finger in greeting, all she could move without dropping the box.

'But perhaps having waited these last months, they can wait a little longer, until you are settled,' said Vancelle, noting the weariness in Lirael's eyes. She peered past the young Abhorsen-in-Waiting to where Nick was asleep in his hammock, looking very pale and sick. 'That is Nicholas Sayre? The young man from Ancelstierre who was an unwitting servant of Orannis? And you bring him to us for examination?'

'Yes,' said Lirael. It was a relief to tell Vancelle about Nick; it seemed to lessen the responsibility she felt herself. 'He bears an unsullied Charter mark, but he is also deeply contaminated with Free Magic, almost as much as if he were a creature himself. But he isn't! And I am sure will not become one, though I have no real . . . I have no real facts to support that. It is a mystery I would like to unravel, and so I thought to bring him here. To the Infirmary first; he was wounded again, only last night –'

'The Infirmary is full of those struck down with this current influenza,' said Vancelle. 'But we will take him onwards now, so Mirelle's people can return outside. Perhaps he would be best put in your rooms?'

'My room!' exclaimed Lirael. 'My old room? There's no space, I mean, there's only one bed –'

'No, no, you have the Abhorsen's Rooms,' said Vancelle, smiling. 'On the Southscape. A dozen bedrooms at least, several sitting rooms, a very extensive bathhouse . . . all from the days when the Abhorsens were more populous, and a score or more might visit at the same time.'

'Oh,' said Lirael. She hadn't thought beyond getting Nick settled in the Infirmary, and it had never occurred to her she would have such important guest rooms. The adjustment of being the Abhorsen-in-Waiting she had begun to make elsewhere was slower to take place here. 'Yes. That would be good. But perhaps if someone from the Infirmary could come and take a look at him? He proved very resistant to my healing spells, but I would like to try another . . . I mean, I would like someone else, more skilful in the healing arts, to try another spell to speed his recovery from loss of blood.'

'I'm sure the Infirmarian herself will come as soon as possible,' said Vancelle. 'But in the meantime if you do not object, I will see what I may do. You may not know it, but I worked in the Infirmary for more than three decades, before I went to the Library.'

'Oh, th-thank you,' stammered Lirael. She was often surprised by the older Clayr, who had all done so much. They generally looked much younger than their true ages so it was easy to forget they might have had several different, long-term careers within (or without) the Glacier. Vancelle had ash-grey hair and some powerful lines upon her face, but even so Lirael did not think she looked any more than sixty-five. However, she had to be in her nineties at least. Even this was not a great age among the Clayr. Most did not take to their dreaming rooms until they were well past their century, and the majority didn't die for a few decades after that. This extended lifespan was generally accepted to be somehow related to the Sight, and exposure to the use of Charter Magic in the observatory.

'I will leave you to these most capable librarians,' said Mirelle. She bowed to Lirael, and then to Vancelle. Though she spoke with no apparent lack of sincerity, Lirael knew there was a long history of rivalry between the librarians and the Rangers, one protecting the Clayr mainly from without, the other mainly from within. Both provided most of the soldiers on the rare occasions the Clayr sent an expeditionary force away.

'Thank you,' said Lirael. 'I am glad you didn't leave us out in the cold, despite rule thirty-four.'

'Rule thirty-six,' corrected Mirelle, straight-faced as ever. 'Rule thirty-four is concerned with the ways and means of traversing the Glacier, and when not to do it. Which is most of the time.'

She bowed to them all again, and seeing that several Third Assistant Librarians had given their spears to others to hold in order to take over Nick's hammock-stretcher from Calleset and her companions, Mirelle indicated for the rangers to follow. She set off back up the Long Stretches at a fast jog, lesser rangers loping behind. Lirael watched them for a moment, feeling a strong sense of relief she had never been silly enough to ask to join the Rangers rather than the librarians.

Lirael talked quietly with Vancelle as they walked, telling her how she had found Nick and what she had done; what he had told her about the Hrule in the south; and the strange behaviour of the bells when Nick was being brought through the Wall. The Librarian asked few questions but kept Lirael talking, and the young Abhorsen-in-Waiting found herself opening up about far more than just the recent events, at least until she realised she was doing so and immediately clammed up.

The Long Stretches eventually joined the Westway for a brief distance, and from there they took the little-used Second Back Curve to the Southscape, that most important corridor where many of the senior Clayr lived, which included the Chief Librarian's official residence. Walking past it, seeing the symbol carved by the door, Lirael was reminded of stealing the sword Binder there one midnight, aided by the Dog. She'd needed it to confront the Stilken, and the Dog had returned it before Vancelle woke up. At least that's what Lirael had always supposed had happened, but as they went by she cast a nervous sideways glance at the imposing straight-backed old lady who was marching along next to her, and wondered how much the Librarian knew about that, and perhaps more besides.

The Abhorsen's Rooms were not much further along. Word had obviously been sent ahead, or someone had finally Seen something, because a gang of young Clayr from the current roster on general duties were there in their probably-clean-that-morning aprons, busy mopping the stone floor in the corridor outside and dusting the front door, which was an imposing slab of black granite without any visible doorknob, handle or lock.

'You'll need to open it,' said Vancelle. 'These rooms haven't been used in a long time. Sabriel prefers the royal chambers. A touch should do it.'

Lirael nodded and wearily laid her hand upon the cool stone slab. It shivered under her palm, and then slowly swung inwards. It was dark inside at first, but Charter marks for light slowly began to blossom, many of them set in patterns in the ceiling to mimic the stars at night, arranged in familiar constellations.

'After you,' said Vancelle to Lirael. The Librarian turned to her deputies and spoke to them quietly as Lirael went through the door. Most of the staff departed, going back to their duties, leaving only Vancelle, Imshi and the other present-carrier, and the four Third Assistants carrying Nick in his stretcher.

Lirael halted as what appeared to be a forgotten piece of sacking near the door rose up in front of her, Charter marks swirling, trailing lines of light as they stitched together a human-shaped servant to inhabit the decayed tunic. When sufficiently materialised, this Sending bowed before Lirael. As it bore no weapons, it was not a guard Sending, but some sort of door warden she guessed. It bowed to the others as they came in, hesitating at Nick, bending forward like a suspicious dog sniffing something it was unsure about. But it did not try to bar his passage, and finally bowed to him as well.

The reception room was not at all like Lirael's old, rather bare room in the Hall of Youth. There was a rich woollen carpet on the floor, in deep blue with silver keys embroidered around the edges and an abstract but recognisable bell motif in the centre. Several comfortable but low armchairs of supple dark brown leather lined one wall, with small tables between them for books and drinks. There was a hatstand of wrought black iron near the door, adjacent to a sword-rest of carved mahogany with ivory inserts with space for a dozen swords; and a strange narrow bookshelf that shimmered with Charter marks. It took Lirael a few moments to work out this was another kind of rest, for bell bandoliers to be laid upon one of the felt-lined shelves.

'The furniture here all came from Hillfair, the Abhorsen's rambling palace they built in the times of peace, and then had to destroy some four hundred years ago,' said Vancelle. 'It was a surprising folly, being completely indefensible against the Dead. But they took the furnishings away first, some to their ancient House on the Ratterlin, some to Belisaere – where it was lost in the later interregnum – and some here. There is a catalogue of the pieces and what is known of their history in the Library, of course, should you wish to read it. The door to the left leads to the bedrooms, and to the right, a complete bathhouse. It has been several years since Sabriel last stayed in these rooms, but there are a quite a number of domestic Sendings who should have kept the place in order.'

'Thank you,' said Lirael. She felt very, very tired and very hungry now. She glanced over at Nick, concerned that he was sleeping so deeply, worried that he might have slipped into a coma. But even as she looked at him, his eyes flickered open and he gave her a somewhat disoriented smile.

'We've arrived,' said Lirael. 'The Abhorsen's Rooms in the Clayr's Glacier. Allow me to introduce you to Vancelle, the Librarian. The chief of all librarians here. Nicholas Sayre.'

'I am very happy to be here,' said Nick. He nodded his head respectfully, not needing to be told that this was a very different kind of librarian from Mrs Knipwich at his old school. 'And to meet you, Chief Librarian.'

'Call me Vancelle; I do not stand on my title. Do you think you can get up, with assistance?'

Nick nodded and, with help, managed to stand. Though he was still very weary, and his wrist ached, he felt considerably better than he had.

'I apologise for appearing before you in such a state,' he said, with a sideways glance at Lirael. He looked down at himself, indicating the badly fitting Paperwing flyer's furs, which were now much too hot. 'If I could clean myself up somewhere . . .'

Vancelle looked him up and down, assessing his general state, before she nodded in approval.

'There are a number of baths to the right,' said Vancelle. She gestured to one of the young Clayr who was on domestic service duty. 'Zarla will assist you –'

'Oh, I don't need assistance,' said Nick, looking around at all the women about him. Several of other young Clayr had stepped forward with Zarla, as if they wanted to help bathe him as well. 'I'd prefer to . . . ah . . . take my bath privately . . .'

'Of course,' said Vancelle quickly, noting his apprehension.

'In any case there are Sendings in the bathhouse. They came from Hillfair too, by the way, Lirael. So they're very old, but still functional. They will attend you.'

'Sam mentioned Sendings; they're like . . . um . . . magic servants . . .'

'After a fashion,' said Lirael. 'They are made with Charter Magic, in various shapes and with various powers, and have limited self-will. They generally want to help, regardless of their nature.'

'All right, then,' said Nick. 'I guess if I need assistance . . . bath through there?'

He began to walk over to the door, but faltered and leaned against the wall. There was a surge of movement from all the Clayr present, but Lirael was first to his side, taking his arm. But he waved her off, smiling crookedly.

'No, no, I can do this,' he croaked. 'I don't want to be a burden all the time.'

'You're not a burden,' said Lirael, not without some exasperation. 'It will take a while to recover from your blood loss, not to mention being stuck out in the cold.'

She was still quite cross about the delay in getting inside, and would be crosser still if Nick ended up getting a cold. Or this influenza that was going around the Clayr, as happened every few years. Many of the Clayr believed the steam pipes spread colds and influenza; certainly once some of them caught something, it was usually only a matter of time before they all did.

'I can do it,' repeated Nick. Leaning on the wall, he walked slowly to the bathhouse door, which was opened by a tall and very old Sending, judging by the pale Charter marks in its body and the threadbare robe it wore. It put one arm around Nick, which Lirael saw with some annoyance he did not resist. As it did so she noted that the old Sending glowed more brightly and the Charter marks that had been moving so slowly across its magical skin sped up and became more active.

'Interesting,' commented Vancelle, who had also noticed this effect. 'I do not think he is in immediate danger, unless he should somehow reopen that wound on his wrist. I will leave you for an hour, so you may also bathe, Lirael. On my return, with or without the Infirmarian, we can take a look at Master Sayre's wound and general state. Imshi, if you would stay with Lirael and help her with whatever she may need? Do try to remember she is the Abhorsen-in-Waiting now and must be treated with great respect, not as someone to go and fetch your spare waistcoat because you've spilled tea on yourself.'

'Yes, Librarian,' said Imshi, her eyes downcast. 'It was only the once. Or maybe twice. And Lirael offered, didn't you . . .?'

Imshi stopped talking because Lirael was chuckling, and Vancelle was already gone.

chapter twenty-one

red glints mean gore crows

Shale Ridge near Yellowsands, the Old Kingdom

It grew brighter briefly as the last red light of evening sneaked in under the clouds, but when the sun finally dipped away it became very dark indeed upon the ridge of shale. Ferin and her companions had used the light well, climbing faster towards the peak called High Kemmy. But they were still several hundred paces short of the top, where they hoped to find the downward path that would take them to the valley floor, and then across to the estuary and swift water to protect them from the Dead.

But the necromancer did not plan to let them even reach the peak.

Ferin saw the attack first, a cloud of fiery sparks descending from above as she and her companions inched along the ridge. They were feeling the way forward, aided only by the very faint light of a single Charter mark that Young Laska had just cast upon the handle of Swinther's axe, which he held reversed to probe the shale ahead and test their path.

The sparks were in fact Free Magic fires burning in skeletal eye sockets. The many eye sockets of creatures flying through the air.

'Gore crows!' shouted Young Laska.

Ferin swung her makeshift cookpot-lid shield in front of her face; Swinther wove a defensive pattern with his axe, and Young Laska whipped her bow about to be a makeshift staff only a few seconds before they were charged by dead birds, an assault of animated lumps of decaying flesh, broken feathers and shattered bones. Half-rotten beaks and skeletal claws gouged at every inch of exposed skin, most particularly at their eyes.

Gore crows, prepared by the necromancer long ago and kept in the closed darkness of the tarred basket he carried on his back. Birds ritually killed and then infused with a Dead spirit, a single slain man or woman animating a flock of dozens, so they moved together with one fell purpose.

Ferin crouched and swung her shield blindly, covering her eyes with her right arm. She heard Swinther cry out, a bellow of pain, and then Young Laska shouted something inaudible. Her words were followed a moment later by a blinding light. Ferin peeked and saw the Borderer's bow outlined with golden light, bright Charter marks falling from it like liquid fire. Where the bow hit, a gore crow fell and did not rise.

With the light, Swinther and Ferin were able to strike more accurately, smashing the remaining gore crows down. But even broken into something resembling porridge, the horrid lumps of feather and bone tried to move. All three companions were kept busy for several minutes, kicking the gore crows off the ridge and down the slope, once again precipitating an avalanche of shale.

'Nineteen of them, by my count,' said Young Laska. She was bleeding from her hands and on both cheeks, but not badly. She held her bow high, the light falling on the others. 'I doubt he could have more crows prepared in that basket . . . at least I hope he hasn't. Swinther! You are wounded?'

The woodcutter held one hand to his right eye, and there were rivulets of blood leaking out between his fingers and running down the back of his hand.

'Cursed things!' he swore. 'Bind it up. We must get to High Kemmy and on the path down before worse comes.'

'Hold my bow away from your body so you stay at least a little in darkness, and keep watch,' said Young Laska, handing the still-brilliant bow to Ferin. 'Sit down, Swinther.'

Swinther sat. Young Laska took a square of cloth and a rolled bandage from her belt pouch, folded the cloth four times to make a pad, and gave it to Swinther, telling him to press it against his eye as she unrolled the bandage around his head.

'You are well prepared,' said Ferin.

'My old kit from the Borderers,' said Young Laska, tying off the bandage so it held the pad in place. 'If we had time and I the strength, I'd try a healing spell, but we do not. In truth, I am weary from bringing light to my bow, though I hate to admit it. My old mates would laugh at me now, to be so out of practice.'

'We should use the light to hurry,' said Swinther. 'That necromancer seems to know where we are anyway, in darkness or in light.'

'Indeed I do!' called a voice from shockingly close back along the ridge. 'As will my servants, when they come. Give me the Athask woman, and you others will go free.'

In answer Young Laska snatched the bow back from Ferin, nocked an arrow, and sent it speeding towards the unseen voice, all blindingly fast. But there was no sound of an impact, just a faint clatter of shale.

Laughter sounded, further back and to the right, and then a moment later arrows lofted high came down from above, nomad arrows at the full extent of their range, the necromancer's keeper aiming at the light from Young Laska's bow. Ferin heard them and was quick to raise her shield, deflecting one shaft. Young Laska dropped to the path, and several spent arrows bounced harmlessly from her armoured back.

Swinther was not so fast. An arrow struck his shoulder. It had no force either, simply falling from on high, all the power of its launching spent. But it upset his balance. He put one foot back. Shale cracked under the woodcutter's heel and slid away. He lunged forward, arms flailing, but even as Ferin and Young Laska reached for him, more and more shale slid away beneath his feet.

'The second path —'

Swinther's words were lost in the rumble of shale. A few

seconds later, they heard the impact and the now-familiar roar of an avalanche of loose rock.

Young Laska touched her bow and it went dark, so they could not see the column of stone-dust rise where Swinther fell. But they could taste its grim finality on their tongues, and feel the grit of it in their eyes.

'And so another joins my happy band,' sang the voice in the darkness, now sounding as if he were far to the left, where there was nothing but empty air. The necromancer was throwing his voice, or utilising some magic. 'You will see him again, but I doubt he will be welcome.'

Ferin felt Young Laska touch her arm.

'We must move,' whispered the Borderer. 'Crawl and feel the way ahead. Hurry!'

Ferin needed little encouragement. She crawled a dozen paces forward, as quickly as she could, pausing to drop the cookpot lid on one side before continuing. The makeshift shield was too heavy and awkward; and she was already tired and her foot was getting worse. Ferin hoped the necromancer's keeper would not get close enough to be able to shoot with greater effect.

She felt Young Laska touch her heels, and could hear the crunch of shale. It was not too difficult to feel the path ahead, but she was already cut by the broken shale on her hands and knees, and now her fingers were also bleeding. The cuts were not serious in themselves, but fresh blood was a lure for the Dead. With the scratches from the gore crows, Ferin and Young Laska were like bait being dragged for hunting dogs.

Her ankle sent out more stabbing pains, a sure sign Astilaran's spell was weakening. Ferin ignored this, as she ignored all the lesser pains from scratches, cuts and bruises, and the pang she felt from Swinther's death. Karrilke's husband, father to six children, who had been so keen to help her.

Ferin was no stranger to death; the Athask people looked upon it with considerable fatalism, considering that death could come at any moment, unlooked for or otherwise. It was to be faced bravely, and if circumstances allowed, the dead were to be mourned and their lives celebrated.

If circumstances allowed. In battle, or on the hunt, any death was locked away in its moment, not to be considered until some later time permitted.

This Ferin tried to do, but she felt a great responsibility, knowing that she had brought this death to Swinther and to his family. For the first time, she wondered if her message really *was* so important. But it was only a fleeting thought, instantly banished as she refocused her mind on the path ahead.

The ridge began to slope up, suggesting they were nearing the peak. Before the light had completely gone, Ferin had managed a look at High Kemmy ahead. It was also shale, of course, but it seemed to her the ridge rose and widened to make a large flat area, and then there were several ridgelines running down again from that. One of these would be the path that led to the valley and from there to the river tower. But without Swinther they did not know which one and in the dark they could not see . . .

The second path . . .

Ferin wondered what Swinther had tried to call out as he fell. Did he mean the second path they would meet upon the peak? Counting from where? Second on the left, second on the right? Or was he calling out something entirely different?

They could not choose the right path from his dying shout. They would have to do something else.

Ferin kept thinking about this as they crawled forward, her questing hands checking the path ahead. Several times she had to force herself to slow down, as she almost missed a slight turn or deviation that would have had her move off the ridge and begin a slide to certain death. Always she was aware of Young Laska at her heels, and somewhere behind her, there was the necromancer and his keeper, and who knew what Dead things the necromancer had dragged back into Life.

Ferin stopped and reached behind her to pull on Young Laska's hand, drawing the Borderer up close enough to hear a whisper.

'We have to try to kill the necromancer's keeper,' said Ferin, very quietly. 'Without the keeper, he will be free to make his own choices and may turn aside, go elsewhere, or even choose to let us go.'

'I doubt it,' said Young Laska. She hesitated. 'But . . . I can think of nothing else. Have you an idea how we might do this?'

'Shoot lots of arrows at her,' said Ferin.

'That has the virtue of simplicity,' said Young Laska. 'But in the dark —'

'I was hoping you could put one of your marks on the shale, so that when the necromancer or the keeper steps upon it, there will be light,' interrupted Ferin quickly. 'We wait on the peak, and we shoot.'

'They will be very close behind, if we fail,' said Young Laska. 'I think we should keep moving. There is always a chance we can stay far enough ahead, get down and to the tower –'

'Do you know which ridge to follow down?'

'No,' said Young Laska. But she too had noticed Swinther's final words. 'The second path, Swinther tried to tell us, didn't he?'

'Perhaps,' said Ferin. 'But can we be sure what he meant? And we'll have to feel for it, in the dark. It will be very hard to find *any* path down.'

Young Laska did not answer for a full minute. Finally she spoke. 'All right. We are fairly close to the peak. I will set the mark here.'

It took the Borderer a few minutes to place the Charter mark, tense minutes with Ferin staring back along the ridge behind her, trying to make out any slight changes in the darkness that might indicate movement, intently listening to every sound. She could hear the occasional crack of shale, the shuffle of displaced stone. From that she knew the necromancer and his keeper were still following, but it was very difficult to tell how far away they were. They were definitely getting closer.

Young Laska cupped her hands to hide the momentary

spark of the mark's appearance, before it sank into a lump of shale in the middle of the path. It would burst into bright light for several minutes when anyone trod on it, or passed nearby.

'Go on,' whispered Young Laska urgently. 'It's done.'

Ferin resumed her crawl. The ridge and the path upon it were climbing more steeply now, making the way more diffi-cult. Ferin probed ahead with her fingers, feeling where the shale was in bigger pieces, piled higher on either side of the slight depression of the path.

She was reaching forward as usual when she noticed the sky was growing lighter. Ferin paused for a moment, and stared up. The dark clouds summoned by the necromancer's wind-raising were beginning to split apart. There were stars shining through. In their faint light, Ferin could now see the ridgeline ahead and the dark silhouette of the peak, High Kemmy.

Looking behind, Ferin could also now just about see Young Laska's face, or rather the reflection of starlight from her eyes, and the faintest suggestion of an outline for her head.

'The clouds are moving,' whispered Ferin. 'The necroman-cer's hold on the wind has weakened.'

'Or he uses his powers otherwise,' said Young Laska. 'Hurry!'

Ferin resumed crawling. It was easier, now she could see a little, and her heart was lifted by the presence of the stars above. But she had hardly gone on a dozen paces when that slight relief was entirely lost, as the necromancer behind them rang one of his sorcerous bells.

It was Mosrael's voice they heard, though neither Ferin nor Young Laska knew this, or even knew it was a necromantic bell. To them it was simply a terrible, harsh sound that entirely filled their bodies with a sickening vibration, a sound that plucked at their bones as if it might draw them out of their flesh, force the teeth from their jaws and explode their joints.

Mosrael was the Waker, the bell which brought Dead spirits back into the living world, back into whatever flesh might be found to house them.

The sound of the bell went on for what seemed a very long time, though it was less than a minute. Ferin lay flat on the path, her teeth clenched, her eyes screwed shut, her hands pressed hard against her ears. None of this in any way lessened the sound or reduced the effect of the bell's awful call.

Finally, the harsh, bone-jangling peal faded. Ferin slowly took her hands away from her head and numbly began to crawl forward again, not knowing what else to do. Some primal instinct made her just want to get further away in case the sound came again.

But the bell did not speak. Ferin's wits slowly returned. She kept mechanically crawling forward, but she also began to notice the world around her again. The sky was becoming brighter still, one point of the crescent moon poking through the parting clouds. Under its light, Ferin reached the peak, a flat area some twenty paces wide where five ridges met, and all the loose shale was gone, providing a welcome platform of solid rock.

Ferin immediately dropped her pack to one side, took up her bow, shifted her arrow case for quick use, and turned back to look down the ridgeline where they'd come. Young Laska stood next to her, longbow in hand. The light was now strong enough to cast the faintest moonshadow, and the ridge was a faint pale line running through the deep darkness of the depths to either side.

But they could not see any movement on the ridge, and the cloud came and went across the moon. Ferin's ankle throbbed with pain; it was getting even worse. She had to put her weight mostly on her left foot. It was not ideal for shooting well.

'See anything?' whispered Young Laska.

'No, I —'

Light flared on the path, the Charter mark blossoming into golden fire. But it was not the necromancer and his keeper who were suddenly illuminated.

It was a Dead Hand. A shambling, broken and twisted corpse given the semblance of life by the spirit that now inhabited its cold flesh, a spirit summoned out of Death by the necromancer, a spirit totally subservient to the necromancer's wishes.

There were three more Dead Hands close behind, though these bodies were almost skeletons, only small strips of flesh remaining on their bones. Unlike the first Dead Hand, for this had once been Swinther. The horribly crushed and flattened body that stalked towards them was only recognisable by the remains of the woodcutter's leather jerkin that hung from the creature's torso. Apart from the damage, the spirit within was already corroding the remaining flesh, and red flames flickered where once were eyes.

Far behind the creatures, safely out of bowshot, the necromancer crouched upon the path, his body covered in a thin layer of ice. His spirit was in Death, sent there by the seesaw effect of Mosrael, to balance the four Dead spirits he had returned to Life as his servants.

There was nothing Ferin or Young Laska could do against the Dead. They had no Charter-spelled arrows, no spirit-glass shafts, not even a fire. As one they snatched up their dropped packs, replaced their bows, and hurried to the second ridgeline path to their left and started down.

Both hoped desperately this path would lead them off the shale hill, and both greatly doubted it was the right one.

The Dead Hands followed, as ordered by their master, but goaded even more by their hunger to feast upon the living.

chapter twenty-two

preliminary discoveries and presents

Clayr's Glacier, the Old Kingdom

Lirael had her bath in a room next to Nick's, one of several in the surprisingly luxurious bathhouse that she thought must also have been outfitted from the Abhorsen's former Hillfair palace. The Clayr's normal baths certainly were not carved out of single giant blocks of black marble veined with silver, and did not have gold-plated taps and pipes, as hers did, even if the gold had mostly worn off. Lirael idly wondered about those long-ago Abhorsens, who were clearly keenly more interested in luxury than the later generations. Or perhaps just had more opportunity to indulge themselves.

It was a great treat to have a very deep, hot bath. Lirael soaked in it, letting her cares wash away, topping up the hot water every five minutes. Like all the hot water in the Clayr's Glacier it came with a waft of sulphur, since it came from hot springs far below. But Lirael was long used to that and very swiftly adapted to it once again, so she soon didn't smell it at all.

She tried not to think as she floated, wanting to simply relax. But it was very difficult to clear her mind. It was full of thoughts about Nicholas and what was going to happen to him, and furthermore, what she wanted to happen. To him, or with him, or between them . . . it was all quite mixed up. Then there were other thoughts, about the Clayr, and her childhood, and Aunt Kirrith, and being the Abhorsen-in-Waiting and what the future held; was she going to always be looking for tasks and danger, always flying off in a Paperwing to confront Free Magic creatures or the Dead, in no small part because when she was in such circumstances she didn't have to think about how to live her ordinary life?

Eventually, the hot water and the scented oil she poured in helped to banish these thoughts some little distance, at least for a time. Lirael floated and turned the tap with her big toe, and almost fell asleep. She would have stayed in for hours, only she knew Vancelle was coming back, and there was dinner to think of, and as soon as food came to mind she realised she was very hungry indeed so she jumped out of the bath.

A Sending brought her a very large and fluffy towel that was also not at all like the ones Lirael had grown up with, and fresh clothes. The underwear was the Clayr's normal linen garments from the common stock, but she was surprised to be brought a dress rather than her usual more utilitarian clothing. The dress had long sleeves, swallowtailed at the wrists, a shaped bodice, and went almost to her ankles, where it flared out. Made of a dark blue material akin to silk, but not something Lirael recognised, it was dotted with tiny keys wrought in silver thread. It was clearly old, but not often worn, though it had been freshly laundered. It also fitted very well, suggesting one of the Sendings had altered it. They were like that, always keen to serve their creators or their heirs. Sometimes the Sendings were so eager to help they became annoying.

Lirael felt odd wearing something she knew had been worn by other Abhorsens long before, and was slightly uncomfortable because it was not a uniform. She was used to hiding herself behind either a librarian's waistcoat or an Abhorsen's hauberk of gethre plates.

The Sending also brought a red belt of very soft leather, one in the old style without a buckle, to be tied at the waist to show the points which were adorned with matching cats' heads in silver with ruby chips for eyes.

The belt points reminded Lirael of Mogget. Not for the first time, she wondered where that cat who was not a cat had taken himself since the binding of Orannis. Sam had seen him several times, Lirael knew; the two of them seemed to have some kind of friendship or at least an understanding of some sort. But Lirael had been too busy to ask Sam what the newly freed Eighth Bright Shiner was up to. Part of her hoped she wouldn't ever meet him again, for though Mogget had proved an essential ally at the very last moment in the battle against the Destroyer, she was not sure he would ever be such an ally again.

When Lirael came out, there was no one in the reception room save the doorkeeper Sending, who pointed at the hallway. So Lirael went along it, and looked in the next two rooms, which proved to be quite sumptuous bedchambers. Each had an imposing four-poster bed, the posts gilded and carved, with dragons' feet at the base and heavy curtains of dark blue velvet and gold brocade. It was not to Lirael's taste, and it was not at all like the simpler furnishings of the Abhorsen's House on the river, or the palace in Belisaere for that matter.

The next room made Lirael pause, for there was a long window here, which she knew must look straight out and down into the Ratterlin river valley below the Glacier. It was night outside, and with the cloud and light snow falling, it was impossible to see anything but soft darkness beyond the spill of light from the Charter marks in the room. But she knew in daylight, on a clear day, there would be a wonderful view here. She had once looked through a similar window, sneaking into the Chief Librarian's own rooms, which were nearby.

This reminded her of the Disreputable Dog again, and Lirael instinctively reached for the little soapstone sculpture, before remembering her bell bandolier with its extra pouch for the little dog was back on the shelf by the front door, just as her sword was on the sword-rest there.

Lirael returned to the hallway and tried another door. It

opened onto a large dining room, dominated by a long table of very pale timber, its legs and edges carved in ornate patterns. There were seventeen rather spindly chairs with gilded legs around the table, and an eighteenth chair at the far end which was basically a throne, covered in gold and gems and looking decidedly uncomfortable.

Imshi was sitting next to this throne on an ordinary chair, with the two boxes that were Lirael's welcome home presents on the table in front of her. She was watching what was going on at the closer end of the table with great interest, while also maintaining a familiar pose that Lirael recognised stemmed from having been told to stay out of the way by someone in authority.

What drew Imshi's attention, and Lirael's, was Nick. Now dressed in a plain linen shirt, woollen breeches and stockings, he was lying stretched out on the table, with a padded seat taken from one of the chairs under his head as a pillow.

Both Vancelle and the Infirmarian – a short but supremely confident and decisive woman in her sixties called Lealla, who had assumed the post some five years before when Lirael's great-great-grandmother Filris had died – were leaning close around Nick, in the middle of casting a complicated healing spell which Lirael didn't recognise. They were both working on it, Vancelle drawing Charter marks with her fingers in the air, which flashed into existence and fell like large and extremely brilliant raindrops, the Infirmarian snatching them to swiftly join together a thick ribbon of golden light which she was looping around Nick's wrist. One end of this ribbon was moving into his skin, the marks growing brighter as it did so.

'Concentrate,' Vancelle was saying to Nick. 'Will the marks to be stronger, and invite them into you, to help you heal. It may be easier for you to focus on one at a time.'

'I'm trying to,' said Nick slowly. 'They move about so much, and they're so *bright* —'

'It is working,' said Vancelle. 'The marks *are* responding to you. Aren't they, Lealla?'

'Yes. I am only preparing the spell, not sending it in,' said Lealla, who had just the tip of her right forefinger resting on Nick's forehead Charter mark. It took great skill to be able to touch a baptismal mark and not be drawn into the Charter yourself, but it was part of a healer's technique. 'This is very interesting. He seems to be able to strengthen the marks, to make the overall spell much more powerful. But it does not seem to lessen the Free Magic I feel within him, behind or perhaps *underneath* the Charter Magic that contains it.'

'It's lessening me all right, though,' said Nick anxiously. 'I feel like I've run a mile . . . I can't keep looking at the marks, they're too . . . it's too difficult —'

'Then you should rest now,' said Lealla. 'We will finish directing the spell. Close your eyes, relax. Fall asleep if you like.'

Nick's eyes closed with relief. He had not seen Lirael, she thought, where she watched from the door. Both Vancelle and Lealla had glanced her way, but neither indicated she should come in, until they finished with the spell a few minutes later.

'Well met, Lirael,' said Lealla. She stepped back from the table and bowed. As she did so, Nick sat up and looked across. He seemed surprised to see Lirael, and stared at her with his mouth open. She did not realise he had never seen her out of an armoured coat.

'Thank you,' said Lirael. She avoided looking at Nick, who was *still* staring at her. 'How is the patient?'

'He does very well,' said Lealla breezily. 'There is still debilitation from some time ago, but it is not serious. The wrist injury is not significant in itself, though the blood loss could have been. You did well with your healing, Lirael, as I would expect. Also . . .'

She paused, and looked at Vancelle, who nodded for her to continue.

'Furthermore, though it is still very early and much more work needs to be done, with the Librarian's invaluable assistance I think we have begun to establish that he has become or is becoming something very interesting indeed; in fact, in some fashion he is a −'

'I'm right here,' interrupted Nick plaintively. 'You don't have to talk about me as if I'm not here.'

'I beg your pardon, young man,' said Lealla, though she continued to ignore him and address Lirael. 'Now, when you came in we were in the process of having Nicholas attempt to prove our early postulation.'

'Which is what?' asked Lirael, who was having some difficulty arriving wherever Lealla was heading.

'We *think* Nicholas has become something akin to a Charter

Stone,' said Vancelle gravely. 'That is to say, a source of Charter Magic, somehow fuelled by the Free Magic within him. And in our rather limited experiment just now he has shown that he can direct this power, to strengthen Charter marks and spells, and presumably to lessen them as well, should he so desire.'

'Oh,' said Lirael. She looked at Nick, who smiled at her. She smiled back, but quickly smoothed her mouth flat as she noticed Vancelle and Lealla were watching her rather than him. She couldn't tell from their expressions what they were thinking.

'It is potentially a very dangerous power,' said Lealla, 'if Nick cannot control it. Certain spells, augmented beyond control, or made to fail could be fatal both for himself and those nearby . . . and it may be only one expression of his particular condition. We will need to investigate more thoroughly.'

The Infirmarian now looked directly at Nick and tapped him on the head.

'You must learn how to master your gift, as I believe it to be,' she continued. 'Though others might consider it something of a curse. Now, I have many very reluctant, sneezing and watery-eyed patients back in my Infirmary, who will try to sneak out if I'm not present, so I must be away. Abhorsen, Librarian, Mister Nicholas Sayre, Imshi. Good evening.'

With that, she whisked past Lirael at her customary speedy pace, swinging the leather bag that was both the mark of her calling and a repository of all the non-magical adjuncts needed for healing.

'I must return to the Library myself,' said Vancelle. 'I will call upon you in the morning, Lirael. With your permission we will continue to investigate Master Sayre's interesting powers.'

'What about my permission?' asked Nick.

'That too, of course,' said Vancelle. She hesitated, then added, 'But it is perhaps best you know that as someone brought here for investigation in the Library, you are not precisely our guest but, shall we say, a ward of the Abhorsen-in-Waiting. I do not think the powers that lie within you will present a problem, yet it is ever best to take care. There will be two Second Assistant Librarians on guard on the Southscape outside your front door, Lirael, and Nicholas must not leave the Abhorsen's Rooms unless it is with me, the Infirmarian or yourself.'

'So I am a prisoner,' said Nick quietly.

'No,' answered Vancelle. 'Should you wish to leave, we would arrange your return to Ancelstierre. You are more a puzzle, one that is potentially dangerous. Dangerous to yourself as well. We would like to help you work out how you can master your unexpected power, but there *is* an argument that you might be best going back to where neither the Charter nor Free Magic exist. After all, I doubt there is another creature like the Hrule in the south, and you could go even further away from the Wall, from us. Is that your desire?'

'No,' said Nick quickly, flashing a look at Lirael. 'No. I want to stay here. And learn. Learn what I am, and what I can and can't do.'

'Good,' said Vancelle. 'And goodbye, for now.'

She bowed, turned on her heel, and left.

'Finally!' exclaimed Imshi. She bounded down the table and took Lirael by the hand. 'You have to see your presents, Lirael!'

'Presents!' exclaimed Nick, swinging himself up and then off the table. He seemed very much recovered, though Lirael noticed he did not use his right hand. 'Um, I missed what they're for . . . is it your birthday?'

'No,' said Lirael.

'They're welcome home gifts,' burbled Imshi. 'Gifts from the librarians and from the Great Library of the Clayr. For a librarian who has become one of the great, a hero of the Kingdom and beyond!'

'Not *very* far beyond,' said Lirael, embarrassed by Imshi's exuberance, but determined she would not show it in front of Nick. She felt a strong urge to dip her head and hide behind her hair, but she fought it off.

'A joke!' asked Imshi, laughing. 'I've hardly ever heard you make a joke.'

'I was very shy growing up,' said Lirael to Nick, though she did not directly look at him. She hoped he would understand that she was still very shy. 'Now, which box do I open first?'

'This one,' said Imshi, patting the larger box and visibly restraining her enthusiasm in a vain attempt to appear more dignified. 'This one is from all the librarians together, something we had made.'

Lirael turned the key in the golden lock plate and lifted

the lid. First she saw several layers of very fine, very thin pale yellow paper, which she lifted up and put aside. Underneath there was a librarian's waistcoat. A unique waistcoat. Lirael stared at it for several seconds before she picked it up, as always noting the surprising heaviness. The waistcoats were only covered in silk; they were stiff canvas underneath, to provide better protection.

This waistcoat was blue like a Deputy Librarian's, but the deeper shade of the Abhorsens' surcoats, and it was embroidered with hundreds of tiny silver keys and golden stars. As Lirael held it up, she noticed there was quite a wide variation in the quality of the sewing.

'We all did a star or a key,' said Imshi proudly. She pointed at a star near the front pocket, *not* one of the expertly embroidered examples. 'There's mine.'

The waistcoat had a new clockwork emergency mouse in the pocket, and a bright new silver whistle already looped in place near the collar. Lirael had a distinct feeling of déjà vu as she touched it, remembering when Imshi had told her the whistle was positioned up there so a librarian could always blow it, even if someone or something was holding her arms.

'It's beautiful,' she said, unbuttoning the front of the waistcoat and slipping it on over her dress.

'There's more,' said Imshi, reaching into the box herself in excitement, to take out a librarian's dagger and a bracelet. The dagger had the usual silver-washed steel imbued with Charter marks, but the hilt was of finer work than Lirael's old one. The bracelet was of beaten silver three fingers wide, and it was set with seven emeralds. The stones held spells to open doors in the Library, and as Lirael slipped it on, all seven began to glow, indicating they were active. This was a far cry from the single key spell she had started with as a Third Assistant Librarian, though she had surreptitiously activated several more. But with this bracelet, Lirael could open any door, hatch, grill and lock within the whole Library, a level of access only comparable with the Chief Librarian herself.

'Thank you,' said Lirael. She hugged Imshi, who enthusiastically hugged her back, and then Imshi turned away and hugged Nick as well.

'Hold on!' laughed Nick. He didn't put his arms around Imshi, Lirael was pleased to note. 'Why are you hugging me? I'm not the returning hero.'

'I just get carried away,' said Imshi. She jumped back from him and flung her hands in the air. 'This is so exciting! Oh! The other box has the official present! Open it!'

The second box was long and narrow, so Lirael already suspected it held a sword; she was not surprised to find one inside. But she was shocked to see one so similar to her lost Nehima. The hilt had a sapphire set in the pommel rather than an emerald, but the silvered blade was the same length and width, and Charter marks flowed like oil on water with a rainbow effect, rippling around the inscription etched into the blade.

'Raminah,' Lirael quietly read aloud the single word. As she spoke, both Charter marks and the ordinary letters shimmered and changed, a new inscription appearing, surrounded by different marks.

'Wallmakers made me to wield with Wisdom, and to wield well.'

'Some tongue-twister,' muttered Nick, and he almost laughed, but gulped it down when he saw Lirael was very serious, her focus entirely on the sword. She took it up and held it high. Charter marks flowed down the silver blade, over the sapphire pommel and joined those moving on her golden hand, and Nick saw something of what it might be like to face Lirael as an enemy, and quail before her.

'I wonder how many sister-swords of Nehima are still in this world,' said Lirael quietly. 'For Raminah must be one, like Binder, the Librarian's blade.'

'There's a scabbard too, in the box,' said Imshi. She had grown serious again. 'Deputy Wenross found the sword a week after Forwin Mill, while cataloguing one of the Sorting Rooms that hasn't been touched in centuries. It was tagged as "Wisdom", which perhaps is its use-name. A few days later, you were Seen holding it, here in the Glacier. Even if we didn't See you arriving, we knew you would come for it.'

'Sooner or later,' said Lirael. She took out the scabbard, which was lacquered black leather with silvered steel reinforcements, and sheathed the blade.

chapter twenty-three

well-met by moonlight

Near Yellowsands, the Old Kingdom

The Dead were slow and clumsy at first, the spirits within unused to inhabiting bodies again, and they had also to make damaged and broken limbs work by sheer force of Free Magic. But soon they became faster as they relished having physical form and began to stretch and change the bodies to suit their needs. Joints moved through many more degrees than normal, muscles restitched themselves in curious ways, toes and fingers grew longer, bones protruded and spread to armour the remnants of flesh beneath, nails and teeth lengthened and became sharper and tougher. . .

Ferin and Young Laska were going downhill as fast as they could safely manage along the descending ridgeline. Whatever the necromancer was now doing, he had not tried to call back the clouds, which continued to disperse as the wind reversed back to its previous nor'easter. Soon the whole crescent moon hung in the sky amid a swathe of stars, so there was plenty of light for experienced night travellers like an Athask clanswoman and a former Borderer.

'They're getting faster,' said Young Laska.

'Yes,' said Ferin. She could hear the crunch of shale and the clicking of dry joints getting louder and closer. 'At least the light is better. I think we have to do what Swinther told us we must not do.'

'What?'

'Run,' said Ferin. 'Better to fall than to be caught by those things, I think.'

She immediately put her words into action, lengthening her stride, focusing all her attention on getting her feet on the path. The flat top of the ridge was fairly wide at this point, without too much small, loose shale on top. Even so, in the first ten steps Ferin almost slipped, a slip that would have taken her over the side of the ridge. She recovered without a word, and kept up the pace. Young Laska was close behind, holding her bow horizontally across her chest like a balancing pole.

The Dead Hands behind them also sped up their pace, the leading one – being a little smarter than the others – going down on all fours to scurry like an ape. As this idea percolated through the slow minds of the other three, they followed suit, but the rear-most one somehow managed to put its hands down off the path. Long fingers slid on shale, hands flipped backwards, the wrists completely mobile, and the Dead Hand did a somersault over the edge.

Ferin heard the crash and tumble of shale, and smiled a grim smile. One less Dead Hand meant a slightly greater chance of survival. She was fairly sure now they had interpreted Swinther's final words correctly; the ridge they were on was descending quickly on a diagonal course towards the valley. If they could keep ahead of the Dead, and there were no wood-weirds on the flat, there was a chance they could make it to the tower on the estuary.

Just as she thought this, her wounded ankle gave way. Ferin toppled forward, only a desperate twist keeping her on the path. She slid on loose shale for a moment, taking skin off her hands, but did not go over. A moment later she felt a glancing blow as Young Laska, unable to stop, jumped over her. There was a sudden rattle of shale, but not with an accompanying scream or the greater roar of an avalanche.

'You hurt?'

'No, no,' gasped Ferin, getting up as quickly as she could with the weight of her pack and her weakened ankle. She hopped for a moment, testing it. The pain was intense, but her ankle would take her weight.

'Go on!' she exclaimed. The Dead Hands were closer still; a glance over her shoulder showed them clear in the moonlight, dark shapes against the grey shale. 'Go on!'

Now with Young Laska leading, they ran on, a little slower but still too fast for any kind of safety. Both of them slipped every dozen steps or so, but managed to catch themselves before falling. Each time, Ferin's ankle sent a jolt of pain through her, and she feared that if it kept happening, she would be blasted unconscious and fall.

And still the Dead Hands closed the gap.

Ferin made a momentous decision. She had been told she

must only tell her message to the Clayr, and most particularly to the one called Lirael. No one else.

But that was foolish, she thought. The elders had been too mistrustful of others; they did not know there were true people like Karrilke and Swinther and Young Laska, people who could be trusted as much as any of the Athask. Ferin knew she would fall soon, or be taken by the Dead, but there was a chance the Borderer ahead would get away. She wasn't wounded, and could certainly run much faster once they got off the hill of shale.

Young Laska could take the message. The Athask people would be saved by another, but what did that matter? The message was far more important than the messenger.

'Young Laska!' gasped Ferin, not slowing her pace. 'I need to tell you my message for the Clayr. It is for one of them called Lirael. Lirael! Now listen!'

She spoke the message as she had memorised it, line by line, words spilling out between the sharp cracking of shale, the terrible sound of stone slipping under feet, the racking gasps of her breath, and always the sound of the Dead Hands getting closer and closer, the repulsive ratchet of bone on bone, the wet plop of pieces of rotten flesh falling, jarred loose by the creatures' passage.

Ferin finished the message just as they reached the bottom of the hill, their feet suddenly pounding on dirt, not shale. Young Laska fell back a step and took Ferin's arm, hustling her forward, taking some weight from her bad ankle.

'Do you . . . have the message in mind?' gasped Ferin.

'I do,' said Young Laska, pulling harder on Ferin's arm as the young mountain woman started to slow. 'But better two deliver such a message than one.'

'I . . . I only slow you down.'

'Save your breath,' said Young Laska. 'Run!'

Behind them, the Dead Hands also left the hill, the three forming a line abreast, already breaking into a loping stride that was as fast or perhaps a little faster than their quarry.

Two or three hundred paces later, Young Laska and Ferin reached the road. But they could hear the Dead Hands so close behind now that Ferin pushed Young Laska away, slowed to a stop, and turned to make a final, and doubtless very short, last stand.

'Athask!' roared Ferin, holding her knife high, the blade bright. 'Athask!'

Young Laska stopped too, and reached deep into the Charter. She had the strength for only one spell, she knew, but it was a trusted one, drilled into all the Borderers. They learned to cast it even when wounded, or utterly exhausted, or both. A spell of last resort.

She found the marks almost instantly, gathered them into hand and mouth, the use-names of the marks that would make them active rising up in her mind like fish to a lure.

The closest Dead Hand sprang at Ferin as Young Laska unleashed her spell.

'Anet! Calew! Ferhan!'

Silver blades flew from the Borderer's outstretched fingers, striking the Hand at neck, groin and knees. Golden fire exploded around the gaping wounds they caused, but still the Dead Hand came on, clawed hands reaching for Ferin, who dodged aside, hacking with her knife. The Hand continued past her, staggering away, the spirit within unable to control the body but unable to leave it either, until the Charter-spelled blades dissipated and the golden flames died.

The other two Dead Hands stepped out onto the road, cautious now, both moving towards Ferin, one from the left, one from the right.

'Run!' croaked Ferin. 'Deliver my message!'

Young Laska did not run. She reached for the Charter again. She had never been able to cast the spell of the silver blades twice, but she had never needed to so badly. Yet even if she could manage it, there were two Dead Hands . . .

The creatures crept forward warily, suspicious of the magic that had ended their companion. Red fires grew brighter in their eyes as they felt the life they would soon devour. Their newly curved and lengthy toenails made horrible screeching sounds upon the stones of the road and their bony jaws hung low in their almost fleshless skulls, showing teeth that had grown long and serrated.

One had a tongue, a kind of whip of leathery flesh, that lolled and flicked as far as the holes in its skull where once were ears. Both Dead Hands hungered for the life they were about to consume; if they were able to, they would have drooled.

Young Laska tried for the third mark of her spell, but it

was too much. She fainted, the first two Charter marks falling from her mouth to dissipate upon the wind.

Ferin snarled and ran at the closest Dead Hand, her knife raised for slashing. But her ankle gave way and she rolled under it, trying to hack upwards from where she lay, knowing it would be as much use as stabbing dirt.

The Dead Hand, not expecting her sudden fall, leaped over her. It turned to come back and rend her apart, taloned hands raised – and then suddenly there was a brilliant flash of light and Ferin caught the gone-in-an-instant sight of a golden rope of Charter marks looping over the Hand's head to jerk it sharply away from her. The rope tightened and pulled the Hand's head completely off its neck. The rest of the creature whirled off into the darkness, arms flailing, as the Dead spirit within frantically tried to find some other flesh it could anchor itself in to remain in Life. But it could not, and with a despairing, silent scream it returned to Death.

There was another explosion of golden fire off to Ferin's right. She shut her eyes against the terrible brightness. When she opened them again, Astilaran the healer was looking down at her and offering his hand, and Megril the constable was bending over Young Laska and peeling back her eyelids.

'How many Dead?' asked Astilaran urgently as Ferin wriggled out of her pack and hauled herself up with his help. She did not even try to pick up her bow or arrow case.

'Three followed close,' said Ferin. 'But the necromancer is somewhere behind . . . You came back for us?'

'No,' said Astilaran. He was looking behind Ferin, his eyes

narrowed. 'We came to scout in general. Just as well we did. A necromancer, you say?'

'Yes,' said Ferin.

'Swinther?'

Ferin pointed to a figure limned in golden fire, capering and bounding in circles some distance away. Young Laska's first spell was still burning, tormenting the Dead spirit inside. The leaping corpse did not look at all human.

'He fell,' she said, her voice sombre and regretful.

'His body was used by the necromancer?'

'What was left of it,' whispered Ferin. She hopped forward, testing her ankle again.

'And you have overdone it and broken my healing spell, just as I said. Lean on me. Megril!'

'Aye?'

'A necromancer, close behind, probably more Dead. We must hurry!'

'Oh, aye!' called Megril. She deftly stripped the pack from Young Laska and threw it aside, then bent and hoisted the Borderer onto her shoulders. 'Quick as I can!'

chapter twenty-four

dinner for two plus one

Clayr's Glacier, the Old Kingdom

Lirael had just returned Raminah to the scabbard when there was a knock on the door, and one of the young Clayr on domestic service duty shyly poked her head around.

'Dinner's coming up,' she said. 'Do you want it in here?'

'Yes!' said Lirael eagerly. She was starving and also curious: she'd never had a meal brought to her in the Glacier; she'd always eaten in one or another of the refectories or taken snacks to eat in her study in the Library or in her room. There were three refectories in the Glacier: the Lower, which served mainly visitors; the Middle, which was by far the biggest and most used; and the Upper, which catered to those whose places of work lay highest in the mountains.

Several young Clayr came in bearing trays which held numerous dishes covered in silver domes to keep the heat in; behind them came three Sendings carrying baskets of crockery and silverware; and behind them some sort of superior major-domo Sending who held a folded blue and silver-edged tablecloth of very heavy linen. This Sending bowed to Lirael, flung the cloth over the table and straightened it, then gestured to the other Sendings to lay out plates, numerous glasses and bright silver cutlery. The Clayr domestics were sent to a long sideboard, where they set down the dishes and then retreated, all of them trying to get a good look at Lirael and Nick while pretending they were not doing so.

'From the Upper Refectory,' said Imshi, gesturing to the covered dishes. 'Nothing but the best for our important guests. Did you know there's even a wine cellar here? Lots of famous old wine; I'm surprised no one's tried to requisition it, though I suppose it is the Abhorsen's, not like normal property.'

The Clayr typically had very few personal possessions, but could requisition anything they needed from the common stock. Such requisitions were governed by a relatively informal code policed by one's peers, unless the requisitioning got out of hand and higher authorities needed to become involved. This was rare, but it did happen from time to time. When Lirael was a child she remembered the shamefaced Jasefel having to carry back more than a thousand pieces of soap, one bar at a time, held above her head so all would know.

Lirael was thinking about Soapy Jasefel and wondering if she ever fell back into her over-requisitioning ways when she noticed the table was only set for two.

'Only two places for dinner?' she asked.

'Oh, I ate ages ago!' declared Imshi breezily. She turned her head to Lirael and winked, so Nick couldn't see. 'I'm sure you two must be famished, and have lots to talk about. Besides, I have an appointment with a visitor myself, in the Perfumed Garden.'

'A garden?' asked Nick. 'Here? On the mountain?'

'Inside the mountain,' said Lirael quickly. She didn't want Imshi to start talking about the main reason people went to the Perfumed Garden in the evening, as it was for assignations with lovers. 'A very large open space, full of scented plants and flowers, with Charter marks set high to mimic the sun and the night sky, in turn. But what have we been brought for dinner?'

She went over to the sideboard and began to lift the covers. Nick came to look as well, and neither noticed when Imshi slid out of the door, leaving only the Sendings behind.

'Rabbit,' said Lirael. 'Roasted with garlic.'

'Some kind of fish,' said Nick. He bent low. 'It smells good.'

'That is eel,' said Lirael. 'From the eel ponds, we . . . the Clayr eat a lot of eel. But here is fish, freshly caught from the Ratterlin. Pike fillets.'

'Pike?' asked Nick. 'Always thought that was too bony to eat, but this looks very good. Expertly filleted.'

Lirael felt a slight touch at her elbow and found the major-domo Sending holding a plate for her, while a second Sending offered one to Nick.

'Potatoes came to us from Ancelstierre, three hundred

years ago,' said Lirael, pointing to another dish. 'I read a beautiful book about potatoes once, in the Library, by the gardener who first grew them here. She was a wonderful artist too, though perhaps sixty or seventy hand-tinted colour plates of potatoes would be too much for many readers.'

'Colour plates?' asked Nick. 'You have printing, then? Oh, I didn't mean to be . . . It's confusing, you have swords and armour and things seem sort of medieval, but then there are the magical lights, and the hot water, and the heating . . .'

'My limited experience of Ancelstierre was confusing to me, too,' said Lirael, helping herself to some roasted rabbit. 'Have some of this, we call it a twisty green. It is a leaf vegetable, peppery and very refreshing. But yes, there are a number of printeries within the Glacier, and dozens in Belisaere and the towns. Most do simple broadsheets and the like, but you could have a proper book of almost any size printed and bound here, or at any one of three or four printers in Belisaere. There is also a considerable body of Charter magic to do with books and printing. Some of our most distinguished printers and typographers are also very powerful Charter mages.'

Lirael kept piling food on her plate as she talked, not really thinking about it until a potato almost rolled off and she had to quickly tilt the plate to stop it, and then tilt it back again before the piece of rabbit slid off. She looked at Nick, feeling clumsy, but he smiled with her, not at her.

'Caught it?' he asked. 'I once catapulted a serving spoon full of mash across the table and hit a very important visitor in the face. An ambassador. He was very cross. Everybody else was too.'

'Mash?' asked Lirael.

'Mashed potato,' said Nick. 'You don't have mashed potato? Do you have sausages?'

'Oh yes, we have sausages,' said Lirael.

'Thank goodness for that,' replied Nick. He turned and set his plate down on the table. 'I don't know what I'd do if you didn't have sausages. And the possibility of mash . . . here, give me a potato and I can make some. Is that butter? I take my fork and presto!'

The fork came down, but instead of pressing the small potato and the dab of butter into something resembling mash, it shot out from under the tines and zoomed across the table, striking a crystal wine glass which fortunately rang with a clear, vibrant note rather than shattering.

'Oops,' said Nick.

Lirael put her plate down and started to laugh. She laughed so hard she almost choked, and after a moment where Nick seemed unsure whether to join in, he laughed as well.

After that, the dinner was a very relaxed and enjoyable affair. The major-domo Sending brought several different wines in beautiful decanters of silver-collared crystal, which they tasted before settling on one straight out of a dusty green bottle, an effervescent wine the colour of pale straw, which was infused with hundreds or maybe thousands of tiny bubbles.

All through dinner, they talked. More than Lirael had ever

talked with anyone save the Disreputable Dog. They talked about their childhoods, finding common ground in early loneliness, for though Nick had two living parents, they had never paid him much attention. He had been sent to boarding school at the age of six, and in his first holidays (and many thereafter) had not gone home, for his parents were away travelling, but had been sent to stay with his uncle Edward, which really meant staying with his uncle's servants, for even then Edward Sayre was Chief Minister and had very little time for his small nephew.

Lirael's mother, always fey and somewhat lost in the future – even for a Clayr – had left the Glacier when her daughter was five, following her visions. Word had come years later that Arielle was dead, somewhere in the North. Though child-rearing was very much a communal activity among the Clayr, particularly as the children got older, it was still more difficult for someone without her mother or close aunts or great-aunts who took an interest. Or as in Lirael's case, it could be made *more* difficult by a relative who did take an interest.

Given the nature of the Clayr's community, fathers were only ever seen as of passing interest. Though many were regular visitors and had good relationships with their daughters, they could not fully participate in the lives of those within the Glacier and were indeed only allowed into certain parts of it, around the Lower Refectory, the Guest Quarters and recreational places like the Perfumed Garden and the Sun Steps.

Lirael's only close relation was her aunt Kirrith, though of course almost everyone in the Glacier was some sort of cousin. Kirrith, for her part, was not known for empathy or understanding, and had always completely failed to understand Lirael's feelings of loneliness and despair when she did not gain the Sight and so felt herself not truly one of the Clayr.

From families and childhood, their conversation turned to friends. They talked briefly about Lirael's great and in some respects only friend, the Disreputable Dog. But Nick saw she found this difficult and painful, so he quickly changed the subject to Prince Sameth, who was one of his closest friends and also Lirael's friend and, strangely, half-nephew, so they could laugh together about his idiosyncrasies and be justly proud together of his ability to make things, which also gave Nick an excuse to take Lirael's golden hand across the table and bring it up to look at the Charter marks that flowed and swirled over the gilded metal.

As he lifted her hand, the marks grew brighter on her fingers, and some blossomed on Nick's skin as well, seeming to emerge from deep within his flesh. Both of them felt the sudden presence of the Charter everywhere about them, as if instead of them falling into the Charter, as happened when touching a baptismal mark, it was about to fall on them like some great, irresistible wave.

Nick's grip loosened and his eyes flickered anxiously, but Lirael closed her hand so he could not let go.

'No,' she said quietly. 'Hold on. This is your power manifesting. Relax; *let* the Charter wash over us. I do not think it will be harmful.'

Nick gulped but tried to follow her instructions. He found himself looking into her eyes, and for once Lirael didn't lower her head and let her hair fall across her face. He grew calmer, though he could still feel the pressure of the Charter, all those millions and millions of marks all around and through him. In the corner of his vision he could see them too, or almost see them, so many it was as if the room were misted with some golden gas.

A great weight of magic was building around them both, drawn to the other energies he could feel deep inside himself, the Free Magic. Nick wondered with sudden fear if this manifestation of the Charter was indeed like a flood, building up to rush in and snuff out the strange fire within his blood and bone, to quench forever that legacy of Orannis, which surely would also kill him –

'I wanted to see you again,' said Nick hurriedly, suddenly feeling that if he didn't speak now, he might never have the opportunity. 'I wanted to ever since Forwin Mill. Perhaps from before then, though that time is like a dream.'

'I wanted to see you too,' said Lirael. 'I . . . I'm not very . . . I don't find it easy to talk, let alone . . . but I hoped. I hoped you liked me.'

'I do,' said Nick. 'When you came in tonight . . . you are very beautiful, Lirael.'

'I am?'

'Yes. But . . . you like *me*? Despite everything?'

'Everything?'

Nick shrugged unhappily. 'Orannis. And . . . and Hedge. I helped them –'

'That wasn't your fault! It was the shard of the Destroyer within you. It is amazing you survived at all.'

'But then there was the creature in the case,' continued Nick. 'The Hrule. I actually made it stronger. If you hadn't come when you did, it would have killed dozens, maybe hundreds of people . . .'

'You tried to do something,' said Lirael. 'That is better than doing nothing. And the Hrule is imprisoned under-earth, and you are here . . .'

'We are here,' said Nick. He smiled, his whole face lighting up. 'We are here. Together.'

'Yes,' said Lirael. She was smiling too, a tide of happiness rising inside her like the bubbles in her wine glass, streaming to the surface. 'But you should . . . you should know . . . I don't really know what . . . I don't know what to do, I mean, next . . .'

Nick smiled and leaned across the table, and they kissed, and at that moment the Charter marks that had saturated the room, building to some imminent conclusion, simply vanished. There were just two young people kissing across a table, one with his elbow on a piece of leftover eel and the other with her left hand in a pile of salt from the knocked-over salt cellar.

The kissing would probably have gone on for much longer, with even greater damage to the leftovers and table settings, if it were not for a sudden knock at the dining-room door. Lirael and Nick just had time to wrench themselves apart and sit back when the door opened, and one of the Third Assistant Librarians who had been on guard in the Southscape outside the front door came in, rolled her eyes to the ceiling, and in a very formal voice made an announcement.

'The Voice of the Nine-Day Watch!'

Lirael's aunt Kirrith followed very closely on the heels of her announcement. Kirrith was a large and muscular woman, both broad and tall, and in her white robes rather resembled an immense block of marble. She was wearing a very ornate crown of silver set with moonstones, which Lirael recognised as an antique not used by the Voice for centuries; it was usually stored in an exhibition case in the Library's Reading Room. Kirrith's large-knuckled hand clutched the metal-tipped ivory wand that was the mark of her office, at least for another five days.

'Lirael!' she boomed. 'Welcome back! And you must be the curio for the librarians to look at, the Ancelstierran? Welcome, welcome.'

Nick had stood up when she strode in. He bowed, though Lirael noticed his mouth quirked at being addressed as a 'curio'.

'Allow me to present Nicholas Sayre, who is the nephew of the Chief Minister of Ancelstierre,' said Lirael coldly. She also stepped back to put her chair in the way as Kirrith came forward with the obvious intention of giving her a hug. She knew her aunt had no real affection for her, but Kirrith liked to go through the motions as if she did.

'Oh, across the Wall!' said Kirrith easily, flicking her fingers and somehow giving her words the same intonation as if she were talking about a neighbouring and rather noisome dunghill. 'But let me look at you, Lirael! You have grown taller, I swear.'

'I stopped growing years ago, Aunt,' said Lirael.

'The blue suits you, and the silver details,' said Kirrith. She sat down at the head of the table and gestured to one of the Sendings. 'Wine. Not that bubbling rubbish. Something red and full-bodied.'

The Sending did not move. Kirrith frowned.

'Some of our Sendings, they are so old and stupid –'

'It isn't that,' interrupted Lirael. 'These are the Abhorsen's Rooms, Aunt. It will not answer to any of the Clayr.'

'I am not just any of the Clayr!' boomed Kirrith. 'I am the Voice of the Nine-Day Watch. And not before time, too. You would not believe how badly organised it is in the observatory, so many excuses about people being sick with this influenza, which I'm sure can be fought off if you have the force of will to do so . . . Order it to get me some wine, Lirael. I have only a few moments and then must return; we're finally Seeing something useful again, and I cannot be spared.'

'Please fetch some wine for my aunt,' said Lirael quietly to the major-domo Sending, who bowed in response. She glanced at Nick, who raised one eyebrow just a fraction. She didn't know he could do that, and the corner of her mouth twitched just a little in return, though she wanted to beam all over her face and gather him in and start kissing again and perhaps . . . Lirael blinked hard and brought her mind back to whatever nonsense Kirrith was spouting.

'Free Magic beasts! Attacking one of our villages! Can you believe it?'

Suddenly all of Lirael's attention was on Kirrith.

'What?' she asked. 'Free Magic creatures? Where? And when?'

'Yellowsands,' said Kirrith, waving with her wand in a direction she supposed to be northeast, but was actually due south. 'North of Navis. A dozen of them, with keepers and all that rigmarole the nomads carry on with. And a necromancer. Can you imagine the hide of it?'

'When?' asked Lirael grimly. 'How soon?'

'How soon?' repeated Kirrith. 'Today, or so Oreana calculated, you know, by sun and moon. In fact, right now –'

'Now!'

Lirael stood aghast, all thoughts of kissing entirely banished. She looked at the tall water-driven clock in the corner. It was already almost midnight. Around seven hours till dawn, when she could fly the Paperwing, and she hadn't replenished the food and water in her pack, or cleaned her armour . . . but Kirrith was still talking.

'Don't worry. We sent message-hawks this morning as soon as we Saw what was going on . . . to the Guard post at Navis, and to Belisaere. I'm sure Sabriel will be there soon enough to sort them out, though we haven't actually Seen that yet; when I go back I'm sure I *will* focus the Sight, whatever that Traienna says –'

'The Abhorsen is on holiday,' spat Lirael. 'I have the responsibility of dealing with such things now! Why wasn't I told of this as soon as I arrived?'

'Don't be silly, dear,' said Kirrith. 'It is a matter for the King and the Abhorsen, as always. You're too young. I know you're the Abhorsen-in-Training, but surely –'

'I am the Abhorsen-in-*Waiting*, and I have fought and won against all manner of Dead and Free Magic creatures, including one of the most powerful, the Ninth Bright Shiner itself,' said Lirael forcefully. 'Now, I need to know exactly what has been Seen.'

'You're just like your mother,' complained Kirrith. 'Always so sure of yourself, and look what happened to her!'

'Tell me what has been Seen or I will send for someone who *can* tell me!' retorted Lirael. 'We're wasting time!'

'Oh very well,' said Kirrith mulishly. She snatched at the wine the major-domo Sending had just poured for her, took a large swallow, and then told Lirael and Nick what the Clayr had Seen that morning, a rambling exposition that included how difficult it had been to focus on the particular vision in question, since Free Magic distorted the Sight, and the great doubt that many had that it was a true Seeing and lots of other unnecessary detail.

At the end of this rambling discourse, Lirael possessed the information that perhaps a dozen wood-weirds with attendant shamans, witches and keepers from several clans were raiding Yellowsands, a fishing village to the northeast some eighty leagues away. The inhabitants had retreated to an old tower on a tidal creek, but a necromancer was pursuing some of them along a ridge nearby, and there were already Dead summoned. And all this was taking place right now, or had taken place earlier in the night.

Nick watched Lirael as she listened to Kirrith. She was furious, he could tell, but also deeply intent on the details. It soon became clear to him she planned to go to Yellowsands as soon as she could, and he became very worried. He did not know what wood-weirds were, but a dozen of them sounded like a great many, and a necromancer and the Dead as well . . . His memory was fragmented, but he still had the nightmarish recollection of Hedge and what he had called his Night Crew, who were in fact Dead Hands, as Sam had told him.

'Very well,' said Lirael, when Kirrith could tell her no more. 'You may go.'

'I am the Voice!' protested Kirrith. 'No one tells me if I may go or stay.'

Nevertheless, she pushed her chair back and stood up, raising her wand. During the course of her recitation, and Lirael's occasional but important questions, it seemed to have penetrated her self-obsession that she had made a major mistake, and though she might be the Voice for another five days, she most likely never would be again.

'I choose to leave!' she said. 'You should be grateful I *didn't* send you word, Lirael. I was just looking after you, keeping you out of danger!'

Lirael didn't answer, the anger clear in her set expression and fierce eyes. Kirrith stalked away, and Nick came around the table and held out his arms. But Lirael did not go to him, or reach out.

'I have to prepare a Charter skin,' she said, almost as if thinking aloud rather than talking to Nick. 'A barking owl. If I start now I can probably leave by three or four, well before dawn, when the Paperwing would fly.'

'But you're already very tired,' said Nick anxiously, letting his arms fall. 'Must you go?'

'This is what . . . this is what it is to be an Abhorsen,' said Lirael. Her gaze was distant; she was already thinking through the first marks she would need to make the Charter skin. 'You should go to bed; the Sendings will show you where. The Librarian . . . someone will come and see you in the morning.'

She hesitated, lunged close, and quickly kissed Nick hard upon the mouth, their noses almost clashing. Before he could fully respond, she broke away and ran from the room.

chapter twenty-five

an unwelcome sleep

Near Yellowsands, the Old Kingdom

It was strange to run on grass after so long upon the treacherous shale. Ferin kept expecting to hear that awful cracking sound and feel the ground shift beneath her. Then her exhausted mind caught up once again that they were in the valley now, and the arm helping her stay upright belonged to Astilaran, the old healer, who was scrawny, but surprisingly strong.

Young Laska had come back to her senses and now she ran alongside, with Megril bringing up the rear. The constable often paused to look back, sword and spell-casting hand ready. But there had been no further pursuit, at least not yet. The necromancer and keeper presumably still followed, but even though the night was now bright from the moon and stars, it would be easy for them to stay hidden provided they kept off the road.

Five minutes later, Astilaran called a halt. Ferin sank to her knees, panting, but still kept one hand on her knife. She regretted having to leave her bow and pack, but it had been the right thing to do. She could not have come this far still burdened.

'Three minutes' rest,' said Astilaran. He bent over and put his hands on his knees, sucking in great breaths.

'Did you . . . did you see what the other sorcerers with the wood-weirds were doing?' gasped Ferin.

'Sacked the village, gone back to their ship,' panted Astilaran. 'Suppose . . . confident the necromancer . . . would get you. You see or hear anything, Megril?'

'No,' grunted the constable. She had gone off the path and was half-hidden by a low bush, ready to spring out if someone came up on them.

'He won't have given up,' panted Ferin. 'Did everyone . . . everyone make it to the tower?'

'We'll talk later,' said Astilaran, with a sideways glance at Young Laska, who still looked rather stunned. She couldn't speak, the failed spell having damaged her throat. 'Save your breath.'

'If . . . he does catch up,' said Ferin. 'Kill the keeper. Necromancer . . . freed, might go elsewhere. Could work.'

'Aye,' said Megril, tilting her sword so the moonlight didn't reflect upon the blade.

Astilaran snorted, a very demonstrative sound of disbelief. 'Rest over; let's go.'

They ran more slowly now. Ferin's ankle was so weak she had to lean heavily on Astilaran. Young Laska was unable to keep to a straight line along the road, whether from simple exhaustion or because she was still somewhat stunned. Only Megril, always at the rear, moved easily.

But the dark bulk of the southern hill could be seen against the sky, and the road was curving to the east. They were within half a league of the tower, perhaps even closer, and there was still no sign of pursuit.

Until a bell sounded behind them.

Not close, but close enough. It was a sweet, gentle sound that entered Ferin's muscles. She felt suddenly warm and cosy, and also pleasantly weak. Before she knew it, she was slowly subsiding to the ground, Astilaran with her. He yawned mightily, and Ferin followed suit, her mouth wide, eyes closing. They laid themselves down on the grass by the roadside. Young Laska already lay sprawled on the stones of the road, her head cradled in her hands.

Only Megril staggered on. Charter marks shone bright on her hauberk, rolling off her armour onto her skin, and other marks dripped from her sword to her hand. Protective spells coming to life, laid there by the best mages of the Guard and Rural Constabulary as protection against just such a force that acted against her now. She had two fingers pressed against the Charter mark on her forehead and her face was contorted with the effort of resisting sleep.

'Bell!' she croaked. 'The Sleeper . . . wake up! Wake up!'

Megril staggered to Astilaran and knelt to touch his Charter mark. The old healer stirred and mumbled something in his sleep, but he did not wake.

Megril groaned and straightened up, shaking her head like

a horse, sideways and up and down. She faced back along the road, sword held at guard, the sweet, beguiling sound of Ranna echoing all around. But underneath that lullaby, there was also the sound of footsteps on the road. Soft, scuffling footsteps, the sound of nomad moccasins, not southern boots.

The constable took a deep breath, and then another, more quickly. She bit her bottom lip hard and then tilted her head back and roared up at the sky, a wordless battle cry that still could not cut through the comforting chime of Ranna.

Megril charged up the road, hoping for the faint chance of surprise. She saw the necromancer, the small bell in his hand. The keeper behind him dropped the silver chain to take her bow from her back, not bothering to grab an arrow because she already had a spirit-glass shaft in her left hand.

Megril was only a dozen paces away when the spirit-glass arrow hit her in the chest. Free Magic exploded through the protection of even Charter-spelled steel, and the bloodied arrow came clear out of her back. Somehow Megril continued on another two or three steps, even lifting her sword as if to strike. Then she stumbled, the blade twisted out of her suddenly open hand, and she fell dead upon the road.

'Garner her spirit,' instructed the keeper, bending to pick up the chain again. She yawned as she did so, and cast a sudden look at the necromancer. 'Spare me the bell's attention!'

The necromancer smiled and rang Ranna again, away from his body, whereas before he had held it close to his chest, the bell's open end pointing ahead.

The keeper snarled and half-straightened, reaching for

another spirit-glass arrow that was tucked through her belt, though this one was safely hooded. But the bell was now almost in her face and she did not complete the movement, suddenly slumping against the necromancer's legs. He kicked her aside, stilled the bell, and replaced it in his bandolier, stifling a yawn himself. Even the most practised necromancer had to be careful with the bells, for they were greedy to bring all within the grasp of their power.

The necromancer reached down to draw out the keeper's own knife. Slitting her throat, he revelled at the sensation of her death, smiling as if he had just taken the first bite of a most delicious and long-awaited meal.

'Now to bring *you* back, my keeper,' he whispered to himself. He looked across at the dead constable. He would harvest her spirit too, before she went too far into Death. If he was swift, he could catch both spirits before the First Gate, use Mosrael to return them to Life, and though he would be seesawed it would not be beyond the Second Gate. He could come back from there quickly enough. It would take no more than thirty minutes, out in the living world, and he now had plenty of time.

For a moment he considered walking ahead to slay the trio he had put to sleep with Ranna, but he decided against it. They would not wake for hours; he could kill them at his leisure. The river of Death was swift, and while he did not care about the constable, he most earnestly wanted to capture his former keeper's spirit before it went too far, or worse, someone else bound her to their service.

Even the Dead could be tortured, if you knew how. The necromancer knew, and he had much to repay.

Even so, he waited a few moments, letting his sense of life and death expand to make sure he was alone. He could feel the sleeping three, and some small animals, hares perhaps, out in the meadow. Nothing else, no one close. This was the only time he regretted the absence of a keeper, or rather, some faithful servant. They would keep his body safe here while he was absent in Death.

But he had no such servant. Entering Death was a calculated risk, as always. But in any case, he could return very quickly to his body if need be, as he had no intention of going deeper into Death than the Second Precinct.

The necromancer drew the bell Saraneth, red flames flickering around its ebony handle. Those flames were echoed in his eyes, but they were not a reflection, rather a hint of the creature that lay bound beneath his skin, the source of his power.

He would use Belgaer later; he chose Saraneth now because it was safer to go into Death ready to bind and command, in case anything powerful lurked close, or had been prowling about in search of some easy doorway into Life. Sudden, violent death made such passage easier, as did freshly spilled blood. There was plenty of that around now, a great puddle of it under the necromancer's boots.

He exerted his will and stepped into Death, his physical body suddenly rimed with ice, the blood of the Keeper growing colder under his feet.

Several minutes later, the first six Royal Guardsmen from the post at Navis advanced carefully along the road. Alerted sixteen hours earlier by message-hawk from the Clayr, this vanguard had ridden out with two spare horses each. They had reached the tower on the estuary an hour before, found out what there was to know there from Karrilke, and had come ahead warily on foot, looking for Astilaran and Megril, wood-weirds and Free Magic Sorcerors.

Finding Astilaran, Ferin and Young Laska asleep upon and by the road, they did not speak, but quietly moved into a line abreast and edged forward with great care.

They halted when they saw the blood pooled upon the road, the two corpses and the necromancer crouched with bell in hand, encased in ice, stark white under the moon like some strange culinary sculpture displaced from an unpleasant celebration.

They paused for only a few seconds, but in that time the necromancer sensed their presence, even though he was about to pass through the waterfall of the First Gate. He spun about at once, fighting the current, and strode as fast as he could back towards Life, cursing himself for being so stupid as to seek revenge over safety.

He was almost at the border, reaching out to his body, when half a dozen Charter-spelled swords struck as one, piercing his throat, his stomach, and his arms and legs. Golden fire burned and silver sparks fountained out, but even so he managed to get back into his flesh, only to find himself pinned by the swords. He tried to speak a spell, but the sword in his throat choked him, and he could not move his arms to gesture, to summon up the Free Magic spirit that was bound to him, lived within him, and was the source of his power.

He died, gargling and cursing. His spirit was drawn back weak and powerless into Death and the Free Magic spirit he had once bound separated from him to go its own way, perhaps one day to return into the living world.

'Jarek, Linramm, Kasad, scout ahead, two hundred paces, then come back,' said the lieutenant quietly. 'Watch for burning eyes. Wood-weirds. Stop and listen too; those keeper's chains rattle.'

Three of the guards nodded and moved ahead, keeping off the road, being careful so that their moonshadows did not fall upon the bare paving.

'Temerry, go back and see if you can wake those three up,' whispered the lieutenant again. 'Should be possible now the necromancer's gone.'

Temerry had a healer's pouch as well as a sword on her belt. When she had gone, the lieutenant turned to the sergeant.

'What do we do about the bells? I've never dealt with a necromancer before.'

'I dunno,' said the sergeant. He let out a deep, slightly shuddering breath. 'I never dealt with one neither.'

'We were lucky,' said the lieutenant. 'A few more minutes, he'd have been ready, with these two as Dead Hands, maybe more we haven't spotted. And whatever else he could do. Hmm . . . we'd better send these two to rest.'

The sergeant shook his head.

'Enemy'll see the fire,' he said, referring to the white blaze of total cremation that came from using Charter Magic to ensure no body remained for further use, and which also assisted the spirit connected to it to go beyond the Ninth Gate. 'Wait till dawn, come back when we can see what's going on.'

'Just leave those bells here?'

'You want to pick them up?'

The lieutenant shook her head. She could smell the Free Magic, a sickening, acrid stench of hot metal, and there was the suggestion of red fire on the black handles of the bells. She couldn't see it when she looked directly, but every time she turned her head it was there in the corner of her eye.

'The keeper's got one of them spirit-glass arrows too,' said the sergeant. 'Ought to smash that. From a distance.'

'Abhorsen's business, this,' said the lieutenant, coming to a decision. 'Sabriel or Lirael should be here tomorrow; word was sent. We'll leave everything as it is for now, withdraw to the tower. I don't want to be out here in the dark any longer if there are still wood-weirds around, and we've got the nomad girl Captain Karrilke says this is all about.'

'Karrilke said her husband was with them,' said the sergeant slowly. 'Woodcutter with a big axe. But he isn't one of the three.'

'Yes,' said the lieutenant. 'Well. Let's take back who we can.'

There was a faint barking crackle in the darkness, the soft cry of a corncrake, repeated twice.

'Nothing sighted,' said the sergeant automatically. 'They're on their way back.'

The lieutenant looked behind to the sleepers. Temerry had the old healer up on his feet, but the other two were still on the road, obviously unable to be roused even with a Charter spell.

'I'll take the tail with Jarek,' said the lieutenant. 'You take Linramm and Kasad. They'll have to carry the nomad and the Borderer.'

'Least she's a *small* nomad,' said the sergeant. 'Wonder what she did with her horse?'

chapter twenty-six

barking owls and night-time visitors

Clayr's Glacier, the Old Kingdom

The two bedrooms Lirael had already seen turned out to be guest bedrooms. The Sendings led her to the actual Abhorsen's bedroom, which was not only twice the size, but also had a ridiculously large and ornate bed that had *eight* posts, each corner featuring a double column of ornately carved and gilded timber. The ludicrously fat mattress must have needed the feathers of several hundred geese, and the bedspread was fringed with silver tassels and had an enormous Abhorsen key some six feet by three paces embroidered in silvery seed pearls.

Lirael's pack was on the dressing table, her new sword, Raminah, on the sword-rest next to it, her freshly cleaned armour on a stand, and her bells upon another strangely shallow bookcase like the one by the front door.

Lirael checked her pack, to discover the Sendings had refilled her water bottle and there were new emergency rations of hard biscuit and even harder cheese wrapped in paper and oilskin. Her cloak was rolled tighter than she ever managed, the clockwork fire starter had a new flint, her knife was sharpened and her spoon polished.

'Thank you,' said Lirael to the Sending by the door. It rose and gestured at another pile of gear, laid ready next to her own. 'What's this?'

There were several folded items of clothing on top of a leather satchel. Lirael lifted the top piece and shook it out, puzzled to see a long, hooded robe. A few, fading Charter marks hung in the close weave of the unfamiliar cloth; she thought it once would have been completely saturated with marks. There were also two elbow-length gloves of the same material in the pile, and under them . . .

A bronze mask.

Lirael felt her heart suddenly race as she lifted the gloves and saw it, and she sprang back, suddenly wary, for it was Chlorr's mask!

But after a moment of rising panic which she fought down, Lirael realised it was not Chlorr's mask, though it could have been made by the same hand. This one had fading Charter marks drifting through the metal; once it too would have been deeply imbued with Charter magic.

Lirael set the mask aside, and examined the satchel. It held three metal bottles, with stoppers of solid silver and armatures of gold wire ready to twist around to seal the bottles shut. Bottles to imprison Free Magic creatures, as she had read about in *Creatures by Nagy* and other tomes.

The robe, the gloves, the mask, the bottles . . . they were all part of some long-ago Abhorsen's equipment for dealing with Free Magic creatures. But dealing with them in a much closer and more involved way than Sabriel ever did, or had spoken of to Lirael. They had not talked much about Free Magic creatures, but Lirael knew Sabriel advocated destroying the lesser ones, if they could be destroyed. The more powerful were very rare, and often had to be forced beyond the boundaries of the Kingdom, or bound in a dry well or some such prison.

These old bottles and the protective clothing suggested past Abhorsens might have kept their Free Magic prisoners closer, to use them in some way, perhaps even in a similar fashion to the sorcerers who were their eternal foes . . .

Lirael put the satchel aside and wondered about all this, and about Chlorr who wore a mask devoid of Charter marks but otherwise of a pattern with this one, surely property of a long-ago Abhorsen. She would ask Vancelle if there was anything in the Library about Chlorr, she decided.

But there were more important things she had to do first.

Lirael sat in the big throne-like armchair, another sign of some past Abhorsen's grandiloquent taste, and at once began to make a Charter skin. It took all her concentration and willpower, which was good, because she needed to let go of a great many feelings. Anger and frustration at Kirrith, and the far more complex feelings that had erupted inside her to do with Nick, of longing and excitement and joy, but also fear. Fear of losing what she had only just begun to know.

Slowly, as she sank deeper into the Charter, finding each mark and knitting it into the complex network of her barking owl shape, she left all these emotions and most of her conscious thought behind. There was only the Charter, the marks, the feel of being an owl, of feathers rather than skin, sensing the shift and lift of different parts of the air, a whole new experience of the night . . .

Three hours later, she had the Charter skin made. It wasn't folded for storage or transport – that would take longer – but Lirael needed at least a little rest before she could do that. She stood up and swayed in place, needing to put her hands down on the arms of the chair to balance herself.

She was very tired. But she knew she had to fly to Yellowsands and do whatever she could. If Kirrith had told her accurately there were probably guards from Navis there already, but they would need help.

Lirael took a step away from the chair and nearly fell over her Charter skin, which, since it wasn't folded, would have destroyed it. She steadied herself and blinked, trying to clear her somewhat blurry vision.

It was no good. She had to sleep for at least a little while. Falling asleep as an owl and crashing into the ground would not help anyone.

'Sending,' she said quietly, to the silent servant who was almost invisible in the corner of the room. 'Wake me in one hour.'

With that, she staggered to the bed and fell face down on the heavily embroidered coverlet. She was too tired to notice the tiny seed pearls sticking her in the cheek, and when she woke would have an abstract part of the larger pattern of the big key imprinted on her face.

But it was not the Sending that woke her, and it wasn't in an hour. First there came urgent knocking, which came through to her as a dream of carpentry and people hammering on inexplicable constructions of wood. Then someone was shaking her, and it wasn't the Charter-magic hand of a Sending doing the shaking, but one of real flesh.

'Wake up! Lirael!'

Groaning, Lirael opened her eyes. A familiar face loomed above her; though the brown skin was flushed with red on the cheeks, the blue eyes were not so bright as normal, and the usual cloud of blonde hair lay flat and dull.

'Sanar!'

The normally extremely beautiful and completely self-possessed Clayr was not her usual self and indeed looked quite ill. It took Lirael a few more moments to process that though she didn't look well, she was wearing the silver circlet of the Voice – the standard one, not Kirrith's antique crown – and had the ivory-and-steel wand stuck through the twisted rope belt of her white robe.

'You're the Voice again? What happened to Kirrith?'

'Reported sick with influenza,' said Sanar. 'I'm sorry to wake you, Lirael. I have been ill too; in fact, Lealla only just agreed I am well enough to be released from the Infirmary. I've been trying to sort out what is going on. Kirrith . . . well, it was hard to make sense of some of what she told me, so I had to go back through all of the last week's messages and talk to Traienna about what has been done in the observatory, and then I had to assemble some sort of Watch from at least half-well people to try for some meaningful visions. Which we have just done.'

'Good,' said Lirael. She shook her head, felt the strange impression on her cheek, and grimaced. 'Did you See what's happening at Yellowsands? I've made a Charter skin, an owl. I'll fly there as soon as I can fold it and go up on the −'

'That's why I woke you up,' said Sanar. 'You don't need to go anywhere. Most of the sorcerers went back in their ship with their wood-weirds; they're gone. The necromancer has been dealt with by the guards from Navis. And Sabriel and the King are flying to Yellowsands at dawn. We didn't See that, by the way. A message-hawk came in just before sundown last night stating their intention, but Kirrith didn't file the message, she just put it up her sleeve.'

'But . . . but their holiday!' protested Lirael. She felt a sudden hollow feeling inside, that she had let down her half-sister, had failed in her duty.

Sanar laughed.

'Can you imagine those two staying on holiday for any length of time?' she asked. 'I expect they were very pleased to be called back, even if Kirrith was wrong to do so. Which she was, by the way. It is my fault too, and I apologise. Well, mine and Ryelle's. We fell into the very traditional error of the Clayr, the one our mother always warned us about.'

'What's that?'

'Thinking we will always See everything important,' said Sanar. 'We all know better, but we forget. We Saw nothing significant ahead, save this bout of influenza, and thought a few sops to those who don't normally get the chance to be the Voice wouldn't go astray. Very worthy folk like Pegrun in the Steamworks, and old Allabet, who makes those lovely confections in the Upper Refectory. And some not-so-worthy folk, like Kirrith. We just got tired of her complaining that no one recognised her value.'

'So I can go back to sleep,' said Lirael.

'For now,' replied Sanar. 'We know from the message-hawk that Sabriel and Touchstone are going to Yellowsands. But not for long, because we have Seen them coming here.'

'Coming here?' asked Lirael. 'What for?'

'They're bringing a messenger,' said Sanar. 'A young woman from the far mountains beyond the steppe, who has had a very hard road indeed.'

Lirael nodded and yawned. Sleep called to her very strongly, and she started to subside back onto the bed, noting for the first time how very comfortable the feather mattress was. It was so much firmer and well-packed than her old bed, and wider too; there was ample room for two people on it. Her and Nick, for example . . .

Sanar was still talking. Words drifted past Lirael's ear, only some of them connecting with her very weary mind, which was wandering off on some pleasant imaginings. But two words did penetrate, and with them came a sudden jolt of wakefulness that brought her right back to the present.

'Your mother.'

Lirael sat up as if a large pin had suddenly been discovered the hard way amid the feathers of the mattress.

'My mother?' she asked sharply. 'What did you say?'

'The messenger from the far mountains,' said Sanar gently. 'She is bringing a message from your mother. And word of some wider trouble ahead. The King has called a council. They will arrive around noon, I should think. Both Sabriel and Touchstone are flying Paperwings, and they will bring this messenger.'

'But my mother is dead,' said Lirael in a very small voice. 'Isn't she?'

'She is,' said Sanar, sitting down next to her on the bed to give her a hug. 'But she was a Clayr, and a very strong one. We think she Saw something years ago, something that is now coming to pass, and she arranged for a messenger to warn you. To warn us.'

'I see,' said Lirael. She gave a small, slightly bitter laugh. 'Or rather I don't See. As always.'

'You have other gifts,' said Sanar. 'Very important ones, as we all know. You are the Abhorsen-in-Waiting, and a Remembrancer. I think Arielle was immensely, immensely proud of you.'

'Of a five year old she left behind?'

'No,' said Sanar quietly. 'Of the woman you have become. I think she Saw you. She knew. Perhaps this messenger will tell us more. You should sleep now.'

She got up and went to the door.

'Your friend is handsome, by the way,' said Sanar.

'Oh,' said Lirael. 'Nick? You . . . you have Seen him? Seen us?'

'Not in time to come. Not in the ice,' said Sanar, much to Lirael's relief. 'But the door to his bedroom is open, and like you were, he is asleep fully clothed on the bed.'

'He's getting more handsome as he recovers,' said Lirael. 'But that's not what . . . that's only part of . . . there's something else about him, that's not obvious . . .'

'It is always important to look beyond a pleasant visage,' said Sanar. 'Sleep well.'

She went out, the Sending shutting the door quietly behind her. But Lirael did not immediately lie back. She was still very, very tired, but she got up and took off her dress, laying it carefully over the chair. The Sending came forward immediately, took a nightgown from the ugly but impressive wardrobe that had gargoyles on its top corners, and offered it to her. Lirael dutifully put it on but didn't go straight back to bed. Instead she undid the strap on the smallest pocket of her bell bandolier and took out the small soapstone statuette of the little dog. Holding it tight in her left hand, she went to the bed; this time she crawled between the sheets, made the pleasant discovery they were fine silk, and dropped immediately off to sleep.

chapter twenty-seven

arrivals and departures

Ferin dreamed terrible dreams. She was back in the Offering's Chair again, and there was not one but many small children chewing on her ankle with their impossibly sharp teeth, shredding flesh and bone, grunting like hogs. Then they were gone and there was another even worse pain in her stomach, and the Witch With No Face, who Ferin had never actually seen but had heard described, was stabbing her in the navel, striking again and again, and her bronze mask was sweating, great beads of molten bronze sweat falling onto Ferin and burning her . . .

Then she woke up, to find herself on some sort of low bed, under a blanket and her own Athask fur coat. Ferin touched the fur gingerly to see if it was real or if she was still dreaming, for she knew it had been in her pack, dropped on the road as they fled . . . She let go and lifted her head, anxiously looking around. Had she been captured by the necromancer? Surely he would simply slay her?

She was in a stone-walled room, the wall curved behind her. She could see the sky of early morning through the narrow window opposite, but not the dusky orange of dawn. It was mid-morning, perhaps two or three hours after daybreak. There was an open door to her left, which was promising. Not a prison. She could see stone steps going down, and up.

A tower. Probably the old tower where the villagers had fled. Ferin grimaced, thinking of what she had to tell Karrilke. But first she had to get up. She put her elbows back and tried, but there really was a pain in her navel. Pushing back coat and blanket, she found she was dressed only in a kind of long white shirt. There was a bandage around her middle. Ferin pressed against it, discovering a wound. She ran her fingers along the small, neat incision, reminiscent of a stab wound. But she didn't remember being struck there, certainly not with a weapon. It wasn't like the many small cuts on her face and hands, from the gore crows and the shale, which had been smeared with some kind of healing grease, but not bandaged.

Her ankle hurt too, but not as much as it had. It was hard to sit up, but she managed it, and looked at her right foot.

It wasn't there.

Her leg ended in a carefully bandaged stump.

Ferin could swear she still felt her toes, and could even wriggle them. But they were not there. For a moment the shock was too great; she could only stare along her leg. But slowly the realisation came. She had damaged it too much, the healing spell had failed, and it had been cut off so it could not poison the rest of her.

Ferin let her head fall back and stared at the ceiling, willing herself to stay calm. She was Athask, and the loss of a foot was nothing important. She would get a wooden foot. There were several people in the tribe who had lost limbs in fighting, or from accidents, or frostbite. Ears and noses too. It did not matter.

Though it would make things a little difficult in the immediate future. Ferin also wondered why it wasn't hurting more. Surely it should be like the blinding pain she'd felt on the fishing boat, so great she had not been able to stay conscious? She sat up once more, grunting with the effort, and looked again. After a few seconds, she saw those strange glowing, moving symbols again, both on her foot and on her stomach. Charter marks. There was magic at work.

'Ah, you're awake,' said Astilaran, climbing up the last few steps into the room.

'You cut off my foot,' said Ferin baldly. 'And someone has stabbed me in the stomach.'

'I *helped* cut off your foot, it's true. But only because it was necessary to do so,' said Astilaran testily. 'But you have not been stabbed in the stomach. The Free Magic charm there has been removed; it was necessary to do so before adequate healing spells could be cast upon you. Fortunately one greater versed than I in all manner of Charter Magic undertook both operations. I merely assisted with my small knowledge and the purely surgical aspects, with knife and saw and my sewing kit.'

'Who took out the charm?' asked Ferin.

'I did,' said the woman who had come in behind Astilaran. She was tall, very pale, and had short black hair. Her voice had the tone of a war chief or great witch, and she wore the bells of a necromancer over a surcoat of deep blue with little silver keys dotted upon it, and under that strange armour of little overlapping plates, something Ferin had never seen before. A sword with a well-worn hilt was at her side, and the little magic marks were everywhere about her, glinting in the shaded part of the room, shining brighter where she moved into the sunlight from the window.

'This is the Abhorsen Sabriel, who is also Queen,' said Astilaran, bowing very deeply. 'Milady, this is Ferin of the Athask people, who bears an important message for your sister Lirael, and the Clayr.'

'Your sister?' asked Ferin, startled. Then she remembered she was talking to someone more important even than the elders of her tribe, and she ducked her head in an uneasy bow.

'Lirael and I had the same father, but different mothers,' said Sabriel.

'Ah, you do not have the look of the Witch in the Cave,' said Ferin. 'From what I can remember. I was small. And no one told me Lirael had a sister.'

'I am sorry about your foot,' said Sabriel. 'But as Astilaran says, it had to be amputated. The wound, and then the conflict between the Free Magic charm under your clan sign and Astilaran's healing spell, made it turn very bad indeed.'

'The blood poison?' asked Ferin. She made a dismissive wave with her fingers. 'Better it is off.'

'Not the blood poison, though that might well have come too,' said Sabriel. 'Your foot was turning into something else, your flesh and bone transformed. It would have spread to the rest of you, in time. Free Magic does that, if it is not constrained. The charm in you had broken free, you see.'

Ferin was silent for a moment, thinking about this. Far, far better to lose a foot than become a monster.

'I thank you,' said Ferin. 'As I thank my rescuers, whoever they may have been. I can remember nothing after I fell upon the road. I must have hit my head.'

'No,' said Sabriel. 'You fell under the sway of Ranna, one of the necromancer's bells. The Sleeper, it is often called. But fortunately it was not long before our people arrived, and the necromancer was careless.'

'I am in the tower on the estuary?' asked Ferin.

'Yes,' said Sabriel.

'The fisher-folk?' asked Ferin. 'They are here? I must tell . . . I must tell Karrilke about her man, Swinther. He died bravely, and saved us with his dying words.'

'The villagers have returned to Yellowsands, with most of the guards who came from Navis,' said Sabriel. 'Karrilke knows what happened. Young Laska did not sleep so long, and she has gone back with them.'

'Young Laska lives?' asked Ferin. 'That is good. She is as brave as an Athask. Perhaps even a better archer. At greater distances, at least.'

'Her father died,' said Astilaran. 'Heart gave out. Old Laska was very old indeed, and more than ready to go. He was the only one, apart from Swinther and Megril. Many more — perhaps all of us — would have been slain if you had not drawn off the attackers, Ferin. We are all grateful for that. Everyone in Yellowsands.'

'I brought the enemy in the first place,' said Ferin. She looked around and saw her pack in the corner. 'There is gold in my pack, nuggets from our river. Take it to Karrilke, and to Young Laska, and Megril's family if she had one, as a blood price. It is not enough, but it is all I have.'

'It is not necessary —' Astilaran started to say, but he stopped as Sabriel inclined her chin, indicating that he should take the gold.

'On their behalf, I thank you for the blood price,' said Sabriel gravely. 'But tell me more of this message. I have already heard from Young Laska that it is of great importance, though she would not tell me exactly what it is, knowing it is yours to give, and you would soon wake and could tell me yourself. Or not. For if you wish to deliver it to Lirael and the Clayr, you will be able to do that soon enough. We will fly to the Glacier shortly, if you feel able to move, and Lirael is there.'

'Fly?' asked Ferin. She thought she did not show her surprise, though the others did see a certain widening of her eyes. 'You ride upon a dragon?'

'No,' said Sabriel. 'A craft called a Paperwing, a kind of magical boat for the sky. I have read about dragons, or what people called dragons in ages past. Have you ever seen one?'

'No,' said Ferin regretfully. 'Long ago, a witch of the Athask had one in her service. Or so the tales tell. Some of the sorcerers of other clans also talk of their dragons of legend. But they are only stories. I thought perhaps here, in your strange land, they might not be mere tales. I would like to see one; it would be something to speak of, at the turning of the seasons when we gather.'

'I am grateful we do not have dragons,' said Sabriel, who had some knowledge of what they were, or had been: Free Magic creatures of great power who assumed a reptilian, flying shape. 'Now, here is the question healers always ask: how do you feel?'

'I am pleased to be alive,' said Ferin, her brow quirked in puzzlement. 'And happy our enemies are dead. Also, that I might be close to delivering my message —'

'No, no,' laughed Sabriel. 'Do you feel sick with fever? Is the pain bearable? I have placed a number of healing spells upon you, but there is always variation in how they work.'

'Pain is nothing to the Athask,' said Ferin. She paused, then added more truthfully, 'But there is less than there was. I can hop, I think. When I return to my people, I will carve myself a foot from the blue ash that grows below our summer camp. And the slicing in my stomach . . . that is nothing.'

'My son might be able to make you a better foot than one of simple oak,' said Sabriel. 'He has had some practice with such things, of late.'

Astilaran looked at her with interest.

'Sameth? I have heard of the golden hand he made for Lirael. But would such a thing work in the North, without Charter Magic?'

'There is Charter Magic in the North,' said Sabriel. 'At least until you reach the Great Rift. It is just much more difficult to reach the Charter, with the nearest Charter Stones so far away.'

'You have been in the North?' asked Ferin. 'To my people, in the mountains?'

'Not to the mountains,' said Sabriel. She had a faraway look in her eyes. 'I have travelled the steppe, both low and high. A long time ago. Now, your message. Do you want to tell me, or wait to tell Lirael?'

'You say Young Laska has not already passed on the message?' asked Ferin.

'No, because it is yours to give,' said Sabriel.

'It is really the Witch in the Cave's message,' said Ferin doubtfully. 'I told Young Laska because I thought I would soon die, and the message should not die with me. But now . . . I wish to wait, and tell Lirael, as my elders instructed, and as the Witch in the Cave desired.'

'Very well,' said Sabriel. 'Rest now. One of the Guard sergeants is carving you some crutches, but I think we'll have you carried down –'

'Pah!' exclaimed Ferin, looking at the stairs. 'I can crawl down there easily enough.'

'You will be carried,' said Sabriel sternly. 'You can practise with the crutches on the flat.'

'But don't overdo it,' said Astilaran. 'Rest! That is the best healer.'

'Food is also good,' said Ferin, suddenly realising she was starving, and thirsty with it.

'Breakfast downstairs,' said Sabriel. 'I will send guards to bring you down. Astilaran, a word, if you please.'

She clattered down the steps. Astilaran followed, and they talked, but though Ferin listened eagerly, she could not catch what was said. For a moment she considered showing them she could crawl down, but decided against it.

After all, it was not against an Athask's dignity to be carried by warriors. Quite the reverse. On their shoulders, of course. Not like a sack.

Two hours later, Ferin was in the cockpit of a blue-and-silver Paperwing being flown at great speed towards the Glacier by Sabriel. After a little while, another Paperwing, of red and gold, caught up with them and took station to their right, and Ferin had to work hard to appear unimpressed when she was told the man who flew that one was the King himself, Touchstone the First, who had been on some errand of his own, but had now joined them to also fly to the Clayr.

Sabriel talked to Ferin for a while during the first part of the flight. She asked about her life in the North, and soon discovered the nature of Ferin's name, and that she was an offering. Sabriel was very interested in that, and in the Witch With No Face and the information that all the clans gave the Witch young women, or had done so until recently.

After a while Ferin grew hoarse. Sabriel stopped asking questions and did not talk very much after that. She whistled occasionally, and Ferin saw the Charter marks come out with her breath, or maybe with the whistled notes. The Athask woman spent most of her time peering over the side of the cockpit, looking at the ground far below. Once she saw an eagle and smiled with recognition; it was the same great russet eagle as in her mountains. She was looking down at it, because they flew higher than the bird, and more swiftly.

Ferin was astonished to be able to see so much, and to move so quickly. If her people had such flying craft, they would be able to swoop down on their enemies. Ferin was tempted to try her bow, which she believed she could shoot from the Paperwing, unlike Young Laska's unwieldy great weapon. But she did not dare try since she was not sure if an arrow would be caught by the onrush of their passage to fling back in her face or into the Paperwing. Besides, it might anger Sabriel, and Ferin did not want to do that.

When the sun was right above them, close to noon, the Paperwing climbed very high, and it became cold despite the warm air that was magically kept around them. Ferin was glad for her fur coat, and she stopped sticking her head out to look down, because she was familiar with the beginnings of frostbite. Though the sky was very clear and there was almost no cloud, the ground was too far away now to see much, beyond interesting patterns of colour indicating forests and fields. There was one large and very long river that was not the Greenwash because it went from north to south and was not wide enough, and snow-capped mountains where the river began.

Not too much later, they began to descend in a series of spirals, heading down towards two tall mountains that cradled a glacier between them. The mountains were respectable, almost as high as the Athask ranges, but it was the glacier that attracted Ferin's attention. It had to be her destination, though she wondered how the Clayr actually managed to live inside a glacier. She did not wonder for very long, as she would find out soon. As always, she did not spare thought for unnecessary questions that would be answered in their own due time.

The King landed his Paperwing first, on a terrace halfway up the western mountain, which Ferin thought should have been covered in snow and ice but had only a finger-thick dusting of snow. Sabriel brought her Paperwing close behind, and it slid to a stop just behind the King's.

Sabriel helped Ferin stand up out of the Paperwing, but stood aside as soon as the young woman got her crutches positioned, an indication she already knew how proud and capable Ferin was.

'Be careful of the stump, and sit whenever you can,' said Sabriel. 'I know you can't really feel it, but that is only because of the healing spells, and the spells are easily disrupted.'

'Yes, I did that on the shale hill,' said Ferin. But she did not speak with regret. She had done what she thought was necessary, at the price of a foot. It was worthwhile, because now she was here, and could fulfil the task she had been given and then make plans to return to her people.

'Stay close to me,' said Sabriel. There were a lot of people coming out of the huge gate ahead, all women, some obviously warriors in armour, but many in simple white robes that were inadequate for the cold, though Ferin could see from the shimmer in the air and the wisps of steam about the edges of the gate that the huge room beyond was warm. It was a place to store Paperwings; she could see three more.

Ferin thought the King must be a bit cold too, at least on the legs, because he was wearing a strange skirt-like garment of leather she'd never seen before, though a sensible fur coat above that. Touchstone had two swords, something else she'd never seen, and she wondered how he fought with them. It would be good to see how it was done. From the look of him, the way he moved and the muscles in his hands and legs, he would be a very dangerous warrior.

Quite a number of the people who were coming out to meet them were sneezing and had red noses. Ferin wrinkled her own nose, remembering the fever she had studiously ignored several moons ago, in winter. At least until Kragorr the healer had told her she must lie down and pretend to be dead for three days, for the good of the clan. That had not been easy to do, suppressing the coughing and trying not to move around at all.

The women were bowing to the King, but he was looking back at Sabriel, smiling and holding out his hand. When he noticed the bowing, he said, 'Oh stand up, do! Sanar, Ryelle, it is good to see you. Though I see the winter influenza is still causing mischief. We had it too, in Belisaere. Let's get inside, out of the cold. Someone will take care of the Paperwings? Good. Come on, Sabriel! My knees are freezing. And you must be Ferin, messenger of the Athask?'

Ferin bowed gracefully, which was quite hard on crutches. The King had pronounced Athask properly, which no other southerner had quite managed. She looked from him to Sabriel and back again, very quickly, thinking that these two were well-matched in power and honour, and in cleverness, owed respect by all who knew them. They were old, of course, perhaps even forty. But they had done so much, and were not yet in decline.

She hoped one day she might be like them. It did not occur to Ferin that this was the first time she had ever thought of a real future for herself. One that extended beyond the present day, or perhaps the next.

chapter twenty-eight

mysterious movements in the night

Clayr's Glacier, the Old Kingdom

Lirael awoke slowly, thoughts of Nick uppermost in her mind, and then second thoughts about how she shouldn't be thinking these first thoughts. There was Abhorsen business to tackle, something serious if Sabriel and the King were flying to the Glacier. And then there was this supposed message from her mother. Lirael couldn't really remember her, or be sure the fragments of memory she had were real or just something imagined or picked up from watching other mothers with their daughters.

These half-asleep thoughts were interrupted by a glance at the Charter marks in the ceiling, which suddenly had her flinging back the covers and twisting around to put her feet on the floor. Like everywhere else in the Glacier, among the many general marks for light there were a few that mimicked the sun or moon. Any Clayr could tell from them almost instantly the rough time of day outside, and Lirael had just seen it was nearly noon. The Waking Bell that resounded through the Hall of Youth and most of the other dormitory levels clearly did not reach the more exclusive rooms on the Southscape. She had overslept by hours!

Sendings emerged from the wall and the door as Lirael leaped out of bed. One gestured to a basin and ewer of water on the dressing table, while the other presented new under-clothes. Lirael raced to the basin, splashed water on her face and ran her fingers through her hair, stripped naked, grabbed the new undergarments, and had them on in moments, hopping on one foot to get the drawers on. It was only then she remembered the Charter skin on the floor and groaned, thinking she must have torn it to shreds with her feet.

But the Charter skin wasn't there, and it wasn't the only thing missing. Lirael stood for a few moments, properly waking up, then looked at her hands. The little dog statuette wasn't in her grasp, though she clearly remembered taking it to bed. She went back there and looked under the pillows, and under the covers, throwing them all the way back. But there was no sign of the soapstone carving.

But while doing this, she noticed the Charter skin was on the side table next to the throne-like chair. It was folded, ready to be packed, which was extremely puzzling. Lirael went over and carefully picked it up. It had been folded at least as well as she could manage, but the making and folding of Charter skins was a very obscure branch of the Charter Magic art, and she did not know anyone else who knew how to do it among the Clayr. Or anywhere else, for that matter.

A knock at the door interrupted her thoughts. Lirael put the Charter skin down and was about to indicate to the Sending to open the door when she thought it might be Nick. Did she want him to see her in her underwear? Utilitarian Clayr underwear of dull linen, with waist-high drawers that bagged out at the thighs? No, and on further reflection she didn't want anyone else to see, either, even if it was a Clayr she had grown up with. She was the Abhorsen-in-Waiting now, and receiving people in her underwear would not enhance her prestige.

'What is it?'

'Message,' said a young Clayr voice. 'King and Abhorsen landed above. Council to meet in the Map Room in one hour.'

'Thank you!' called Lirael. One hour. The Map Room was part of the Library, and had in fact been the Reading Room until the new, even larger one was built some eight hundred years ago. It would take her twenty minutes at least to get there: it was about a thousand paces below the Southscape; she would have to take the Second Back Stairs most of the way, and then . . . but first, get dressed.

A council meeting with the King and Sabriel meant official business. Lirael turned back from the door to see the Sendings had already thought this through. One was holding up her armoured coat, the other the surcoat that would go over it.

'Not the surcoat,' said Lirael thoughtfully. 'Not today, thank you. My new librarian's waistcoat over the armour.'

The librarians would like to see her wearing it, she thought.

It was quite snug over the hauberk, but all the waistcoats were made to be worn over other clothes, and be loose enough to allow for the general librarian habit of shoving all sorts of things into pockets. Lirael checked them at this thought, feeling weight on both sides. The clockwork mouse was in the large left-hand pocket, but she was surprised to find a book in the right-hand side and then not surprised, when she took it out and it grew in her hand, a book bound in deep blue leather with silver clasps. The title of the book was embossed in silver on the spine.

The Book of Remembrance and Forgetting.

Like its close cousin, *The Book of the Dead*, the binding of this tome swarmed with Charter marks, marks of binding and closing, burning and destruction, to ensure only certain readers could even open the book, let alone read it. There was Free Magic inside, constrained and locked by boards, leather binding, glue and stitches that were themselves as much creations of Charter Magic as any mundane process.

Lirael had left this book in her rooms in the palace at Belisaere, but it tended to show up wherever and whenever it would be needed. She had read it several times, but again, like *The Book of the Dead*, the contents changed with each reading according to need, or the phase of the moon, or perhaps even the weather. In the Library there was a whole section devoted to attempted indices and concordances for such books, but they were never complete, and Lirael had never found even an attempted one for this particular book.

She slipped it back into the pocket. Though it was twice

as wide it went in easily, shrinking on the way. Lirael felt something else there as she slipped it in place, but she knew what it would be now the book had appeared, though like it she had left this item back in Belisaere. A small metal case that someone from Ancelstierre would presume held cigarettes, or perhaps a powder compact. But it too was a Charter Magic container or binding for the Free Magic artefact that lay inside, a double-sided mirror, one side bright reflective silver, the other . . . a rectangle of nothing, of absolute darkness.

With the Dark Mirror, combined with the knowledge contained in *The Book of Remembrance and Forgetting*, she could go into Death and look into the past.

The appearance of the book and the mirror meant she was probably going to have to do just that, but Lirael put it out of her mind for the moment. It was not something she wanted to do, but neither was it something she totally dreaded or feared. She just didn't want to dwell on it, not least because the further a Remembrancer needed to look back in time, the deeper they had to go in Death. The last time Lirael had used the Dark Mirror she had been very deep in Death indeed, on the edge of the Ninth Gate itself. She hoped she would never need to look so far back again, and doubted she ever would, for then she had needed to see something from the very Beginning, all the way back to the first breaking and binding of the Destroyer.

A Sending handed her the new sword, Raminah, in its black-and-silver sheath, already fastened to a baldric of the same dark leather with silver buckles. She slipped it over her shoulder and settled the sword at her side. It felt very companionable there. For a moment Lirael considered donning the bells as well, but there would be no need for them within the Glacier. She left them on the shelf, and went out.

She heard Nick before she saw him. All the doors along the hallway were open; his voice was coming from the reception room with the long window that looked out beyond the Glacier, to the valley below. Lirael hesitated for a moment several steps short of the door, unsure of how to behave, or what to do. The intimate feeling she had of sharing a secret world with Nick from the past evening was gone now, and she had a terrible fear he would repudiate whatever had happened.

Lirael shut her eyes for a moment, gathering her strength, at the same time wondering why she needed to do so. If it was a Free Magic creature in there, or some terrible Dead revenant, she would not hesitate so, but would be straight in to deal with it.

Nick was talking to someone. Vancelle, answering now. Something about the Charter, but then Lirael heard her own name, so before anything else was said, either complimentary or detrimental, she forced herself to stride into the room with a cheery 'Good morning,' that sounded false even to herself.

'Almost good afternoon,' said Vancelle. 'But I do not criticise. You were very weary. And Sanar told me she visited you in the early hours to dissuade a sudden departure to Yellowsands.'

'Yes,' said Lirael, but she was looking at Nick. Fortunately, he was looking at her, and there was something in his eyes and face, a special light that told her he was not going to repudiate anything that happened the night before, but indeed wished to repeat the experience, and more. Lirael had caught glimpses of such looks before, between other people, and felt both their power and her uneasiness at being an onlooker to such a private, unspoken communication. She had never shared in such a look before.

'Good morning,' said Nick. He smiled and Lirael smiled back. Their secret, shared world had once again been conjured between them, coexisting with the far more mundane reality around them.

'Nicholas is proving to be a very interesting, if temporary, addition to the Library,' said Vancelle, as always calm and somewhat remote. Though she could not have failed to see how Lirael and Nick looked at each other, she did not remark on it in any way, or show she noticed. 'I have found some reading which may prove useful. I think you should also speak to both Sabriel and Sameth, because there are parallels with the Abhorsen's bells, in that they are Free Magic powers constrained or guided by Charter Magic. Deputy Harquell would also be helpful, I think, given her long study of books that have two such natures.'

'I helped Vancelle cast two spells, and stopped . . . I mean quenched . . . another,' said Nick excitedly. He came forward and took Lirael's hands. Neither of them noticed that Lirael's golden hand immediately glowed brighter, and small Charter marks began to fall from her fingers, like a mist of tiny gold and silver rain. 'So even if I can't cast Charter spells myself, I can help others. I could help *you*.'

'To be fair, you must also remember your several failures,' said Vancelle. 'With little, safe spells, so no harm done. There would be considerable danger to yourself and to others if you test yourself against anything more significant before you have had a great deal more practice. For example, right now you had best let go of Lirael's hand.'

'Oh!' exclaimed Nick. He hesitated for a moment, then released only Lirael's golden hand, keeping her left hand tight in his right and moving to stand next to her. It was a very public statement of how he felt. Lirael edged slightly closer to him, accentuating this from her point of view as well.

Vancelle smiled, something Lirael had never seen before. She was not sure she liked it, and was quite relieved when the Librarian's face settled back into its normal serene detachment.

'Now, I believe all of us have to join the King's council very soon,' said Vancelle. 'It may go on for some time, Lirael, so I would suggest breakfast before you come down to the Map Room. Good morning to both of you.'

As soon as she left, Lirael and Nick were kissing again, twined together near the window. Only a flash of light from the high noon sun recalled Lirael to the time. She reluctantly pulled herself away and they just held each other, Lirael careful not to touch Nick with her golden hand.

'I'll have to work out how to get on with those spells,' said Nick, tilting his head towards her right hand.

'I'm sure you will,' said Lirael. 'But we do have the King's council to get to, and I need to eat something before we go. I don't want to pass out in front of Touchstone and Sabriel.'

'Sabriel?' asked Nick anxiously. 'She always scared me when she visited Sam at school. I mean, his father does a bit as well. Only not so much. If you know what I mean. Do you think they'll be okay with me coming to the Old Kingdom . . . and . . . to be with you?'

'What does okay mean?' asked Lirael.

'Um, it means "all right",' said Nick. 'Will they be all right with me being here, and with you? They won't send me back?'

'No,' said Lirael decisively. 'No. I'm sure they wouldn't, but even if they did, I wouldn't let them.'

Nick kissed her again, quickly.

'You are a fierce librarian, aren't you?' he said admiringly. 'I like the waistcoat.'

'And you admit everything you knew and said about librarians before was completely and utterly stupid?' asked Lirael, kissing him back.

'Yes and yes,' said Nick, when they had to break free to breathe a little. 'Um, am I really supposed to come to this council?'

Lirael nodded, and reluctantly pushed him away.

'Yes,' she said. 'They will want to know about the Hrule and everything, your powers . . . hmm . . . come to think about it, there is a Charter Stone in the Map Room. I hope that's going to be . . . what did you call it . . . okay?'

'Why wouldn't it be?' asked Nick.

Quickly, Lirael told him what had happened when they crossed the Wall. Nick listened intently, his forehead creased with both concern and thought. He looked so much better, thought Lirael. The healing spells had brought back his natural colour, but it was more than that. He seemed so incredibly alive now, so full of excitement and joy.

'I can tell when whatever is inside me wants to . . . to join with Charter Magic,' said Nick. 'And I can let it go, or force it back. I'm getting better at it all the time. So even with a Charter Stone, if I'm conscious and trying to control the reaction . . . it should be all right.'

'There will be many very experienced Charter Mages there, in any case,' said Lirael. 'I mean, besides the King and Sabriel, Vancelle, Sanar and Ryelle I expect, perhaps Mirelle and some of the other senior office holders.'

'Am I dressed appropriately?' asked Nick. He was wearing a dark blue tunic the same colour as Lirael's waistcoat, without the silver keys, trousers of a similar colour and doeskin shoes that buttoned up at the sides with blue buttons. 'Do I need a sword?'

'You can have my old one, from Belisaere,' said Lirael. She thought for a second. 'Though it is Charter-spelled.'

'I could practise with it while you have some breakfast,'

said Nick eagerly. 'It's by the front door, isn't it? I'll get it; meet you in the dining room!'

He whirled out of the door, leaving Lirael reaching at air to hold him back for one more kiss. She smiled and shrugged, and was just about to follow him when she noticed something on the floor, its snout pressed up against the window.

Her little dog statuette.

Lirael picked it up, feeling the familiar soapstone, and looked around. How had it got there? Two Sendings stood in the corners of the room, behind the long leather lounge that was arranged for comfortable viewing.

'How did this get here?' asked Lirael. But neither Sending answered in any way. Lirael looked at the little dog again, then out of the window. It was a clear day, and she could see the Ratterlin, a long line of brilliant blue shot with bright reflections. A small boat was sailing up the river, doubtless going to the Clayr's dock, for it was well past anywhere else it might land. It was not an easy task against the current, and the spring flood; the way the boat moved suggested magical assistance.

There was nothing else of note to see.

Lirael frowned again, tucked the statuette into one of the upper pockets of her waistcoat, and went to see about what would need to be a very hasty breakfast.

chapter twenty-nine

the council of touchstone

Clayr's Glacier, the Old Kingdom

The Map Room was a vast domed chamber, the ceiling of the dome decorated with a mosaic that incorporated a great deal of Charter Magic, so that each tile had many different iterations of design and colour. The whole thing was a map of the Old Kingdom, from the far northwest to the southeast waters by the Wall, but it hardly ever displayed all at once. Rather, the ceiling would show the detail of a town, or a mountain range, or a nautical map with soundings of some part of the Sea of Saere. As it had been made perhaps a thousand years ago, sometimes it showed towns or villages that no longer existed, a forest long since cleared, or curious details that could not easily be understood by the Clayr of the current times.

Apart from this vast, changing map on the ceiling, the Map Room did not seem to contain any maps. Right in the centre, under the top of the dome some eighty paces above, there was a round table of great antiquity. Made of a deep red wood become almost black with age and centuries of polish, it was thirty paces in diameter and could seat forty around it in its companion chairs, made of the same timber, though many had been repaired here and there and the upholstery was fresh and new, the eleventh time the dark green cloth had been replaced.

The table had a hole cut in its centre, for here a Charter Stone rose up from the paved floor – not a grey stone, as was usual, but an obelisk of black basalt. Its surface roiled as normal with Charter marks, which rose to the surface to flash gold or more rarely silver and then sank beneath or, even more rarely, left the stone to rise to the mosaic map overhead.

Apart from the central table, there were a dozen desks lined up in rows of three at the northern end, but they had no maps laid upon them either. Unlike the usual green leather surfaces found elsewhere in the Library, these desks were topped with clean white marble.

At the southern end, perhaps a third of the Map Room was taken up with many curious long racks, each as tall as two Clayr. The racks held thousands of suspended ribbons, each ribbon imprinted with two letters and four numerals in some sort of code. From each ribbon there hung an ivory cube, redolent with Charter marks.

Lirael was used to this, and simply strode in through the main doors of beaten bronze, which had been pushed fully open on this occasion; normally the librarians used a much smaller ordinary door to the left. But Nick stopped on the threshold, staring up at the ceiling and then around the vast room. As they were holding hands, Lirael was jerked back; she trod on Nick's foot and he said, 'Ouch!'

Everyone looked at them, from where they were gathered in a crowd around one of the desks. The King, Sabriel, Ferin on her crutches, Vancelle, Sanar and Ryelle, Mirelle, the Infirmarian, and half a dozen other very important Clayr. Beyond this inner circle were more than twenty seers of less exalted rank, there as note-takers, attendants and messengers. Clayr from the Mews, the Rangers, the Library, the observatory, the storerooms . . .

'Hello,' called out Lirael, her voice echoing under the dome. She was a bit out of breath since they had run the last few hundred steps down the Second Back Stairs. Hand in hand. Remembering this, she gently let go, as did Nick, though their hands stayed close together. 'Sorry we're late.'

She didn't mention why they were late. Nick had been rather too optimistic about how he would interact with Lirael's Charter-spelled sword, and the blade had erupted into actual flames before Lirael could quell it, but not before the hilt had grown so hot Nick had to drop it. There was a sword-shaped scorch mark on one of the carpets in the Abhorsen's Rooms now.

However, Nick was wearing a sword, the major-domo Sending having brought him one of ordinary steel, without any magic, just as they were leaving. This reminded Lirael that she had yet to properly explore all the Abhorsen's Rooms, because there had to be an armoury there, as well as the wine cellar Imshi had mentioned. Explaining the carpet burn to

Sabriel would have to come first. Lirael hoped her sister's general lack of interest in furniture and haberdashery would also apply to ancient Abhorsen carpets . . .

They hurried over to the central group by the desk.

'Do I bow or go on one knee or anything?' whispered Nick as they gave the central Charter Stone and the round table a wide berth to approach the King and Sabriel, the lesser Clayr quietly moving aside to create an alley for them.

'No,' said Lirael. 'They don't go for much ceremony, except on special occasions.'

Sabriel came forward and removed Nick's doubts by taking Lirael on each shoulder and kissing her on the cheeks, and then offered her hand in Ancelstierran fashion to Nick.

'Welcome,' she said. 'A long way from Somersby, I think, Mr Sayre?'

'Yes, ma'am,' said Nick, rather flustered. The last time he'd properly met Sabriel he'd been in the Fifth Form and thought himself very grown up.

'Call me Sabriel. You haven't formally met my husband, I think? He didn't visit the school. Touchstone, this is Sameth's friend Nicholas Sayre.'

'An honour to meet you, sir,' said Nick, shaking hands. He couldn't help himself glancing down at Touchstone's bare knees and blushed as Touchstone saw him do so, and laughed.

'Always worn a kilt,' he said. 'It was the fashion in my day, and a fine, comfortable garment it is. I've been trying to reintroduce it ever since, but when even my son won't wear one, I suppose my efforts are wasted! Sameth should be here shortly, by the way; his boat is tying up now.'

'Sam's here?' asked Nick.

'Yes, come to see what is going on with you, I suppose,' said Touchstone. 'While we are all trying to find out about a host of other things. The first step being for you to meet a messenger, Lirael. Allow me to present Ferin of the Athask people.'

Lirael looked to the odd one out in the group around them, the young woman in strange, red-stitched clothes made of some kind of soft leather, her right foot recently amputated from the look of the bandages and evidence of healing spells Lirael knew well, though the way she moved on her crutches suggested the amputation had taken place a week or more ago.

She was a very young woman, perhaps only sixteen or seventeen. She was considerably shorter than Lirael but looked very wiry and tough, despite or perhaps even because of the many scratches on her face and hands and the way she ignored the absence of a foot, immediately swinging forward on her crutches to bow before Lirael.

'I bring a message from the Witch in the Cave,' said Ferin. 'To her daughter, Lirael of the Clayr.'

'Thank you,' said Lirael. 'I can see it has not been an easy task.'

Ferin shrugged, no small achievement on crutches.

'I have come by land and sea and air,' she said, with a slight sniff as if this were nothing. 'But done no more than the elders of the Athask would expect. I will tell you the message now?'

'Please,' said Lirael. She felt her heart begin to speed up, thumping in her chest. What could her long-departed and years-dead mother possibly have to say to her?

Ferin drew in a deep breath, and then, in the voice she clearly believed to be appropriate for a message of great import, recited a surprisingly short missive.

'Lirael. These words come from your mother. I am dead now, from the wasting sickness. But I have Seen you in the frozen waterfall. An Abhorsen like your father, and Remembrancer, wielder of the Dark Mirror. You have done great things, but there is more to do. A terrible threat builds against the Kingdom, one that will bring death and ruin to many, many, in both south and north, including my friends of the Athask. I will say more, knowing you will hear me in the past, as I See you in the future I will not live for. Come listen, on the third moon of winter, in the year of your tenth birthday.'

There was silence for a few seconds before Lirael spoke.

'That's all? My mother who abandoned me thinks I have "more to do" and wants me to go and listen to her in the past, using the Dark Mirror?' asked Lirael, unable to hide the anger and hurt on her face. Arielle hadn't even bothered to say anything personal, or send her love. Just instructions. 'Has anyone else Seen this "great threat"?'

'We have not,' said Sanar calmly, seeing the emotion on Lirael's face. 'But as you know, the Watch is depleted. Many of our best seers either have the influenza or are recovering from it, and in the North, concentrations of Free Magic may cloud our vision.'

She hesitated, then added, 'It is also possible Arielle succumbed to false visions. She says she was already very ill, near to death. In such circumstances, we of the Clayr often See a great many possible futures, and indeed, even many impossible ones.'

'There may be something to it,' said Sabriel. 'A number of things suggest the Clayr's vision has been intentionally clouded. Even this influenza is untimely, and it started with a party of merchants from the steppe.'

'Can Free Magic make a disease?' asked Nick curiously.

'No, but it can be used to influence an existing one, and there is always influenza in the North in winter, that typically travels slowly to us and is in full force by late spring,' said Lealla. 'It is very early this year, as were the merchants. It may be only a coincidence.'

'And Ferin tells us her clan elders were ordered by the "Witch With No Face" to send the entire fighting strength of the clan to a muster,' said Touchstone. 'To gather at the Field Market. If this same message went to the other clans, it can have only one purpose: a massed attack upon the Greenwash Bridge.'

'I mean no offence to our visitor,' said Mirelle, bowing to Ferin. 'But if none of this has been Seen, can we be sure *any* of the clans are sending their warriors to this muster? Or have been asked? And who is this "Witch With No Face"?'

'The Bridge Company reports nothing unusual,' said Touchstone. 'But they do not scout so far as the Field Market until summer. As for the "Witch with No Face" . . .'

He turned to Sabriel.

'It has to be Chlorr of the Mask,' said Sabriel. 'She came from the North. I had wondered how she extended her life, and it seems by a similar method to Kerrigor.'

There was a stir among her listeners as she mentioned that name. Nick noted it to ask Lirael later. He vaguely recalled Sam mentioning it once, but he'd thought it was merely the name of some pet. A cat. Though perhaps it was a cat like Mogget, he thought. Not a cat after all.

'In fact, she may even have taught it to him; he was known to travel in the North. But in short, many centuries ago Chlorr must have put her original body into a state between Life and Death, suspended there by Free Magic, and her spirit moved into a new body. These she would need to replace every few decades, and it seems she has long done so by demanding offerings from the clans. Our new friend Ferin was bound for such a fate, and indeed, takes her name from being such an offering. When I slew Chlorr's most recent body, she became a Dead spirit, but with her original body hidden somewhere she could not die the final death. Not even when compelled by my bells, or Lirael's. Anchored in such a way, she has been able to consume other Dead and Free Magic powers, to become greater still. I had not thought of this, and presumed she would stay in the North, only needing to be dealt with if she was foolish enough to cross the Greenwash. But if what Ferin tells us is true, or if what Arielle hints at is likewise true, then I was utterly wrong and we must ready ourselves against Chlorr and for the first time in our history, the full strength of all the Northern clans.'

'If true,' muttered Mirelle.

'I suppose the first step is to find out what else my mother wants to tell me,' said Lirael. She looked at Sabriel. 'Will you come into Death with me?'

'I will,' said Sabriel. Her eyes flickered, noticing Nick's instinctive move closer to Lirael, as if he might protect her. 'Indeed I wish to go into Death to investigate something else related to the Witch With No Face.'

She took a small bronze box out of her belt pouch and touched it with two fingers, a Charter mark for unlocking quickly conjured at her touch. The box sprang open, revealing a spindle of bone that flickered with small Free Magic fires. Several people retreated a few steps as it was unveiled, and the acrid hot-metal stench wafted across them. But none of the senior Clayr moved, nor Lirael or Ferin. Nick gulped audibly, and Lirael felt him shift his feet, but he did not step back.

'This is a charm or fetish I removed from Ferin,' said Sabriel. 'It has several purposes, but perhaps of most interest is the necromantic magic it holds, which I suspect links Ferin in some way to the Witch With No Face. I need to examine it in Death; it may provide a clue as to why Ferin was pursued with such strength, and so far. A dozen wood-weirds and their keepers is no small force. When we return, we will know much more, I think.'

'We cannot go into Death here,' said Lirael. 'Most of the Library is too well-warded. We can go down, deep into the Old Levels. Or up and out . . . which is probably better . . . to one of the lookouts, perhaps. Mirelle?'

'Northwest Two,' said Mirelle, without hesitation. 'Sun will be on it longer.'

'I will go and fetch my bells, and join you there, then,' said Lirael to Sabriel.

'Wait a few minutes more,' said Touchstone easily. 'I would like your views, Sabriel. We need to know more, but I think . . . I think we must act as if the threat is real. An army of nomads coming to attack the bridge . . . Can we have a map of that part of the Greenwash, please, cartographer? With the Field Market?'

The cartographer, a Deputy Librarian, had already anticipated such a request. She held several ivory cubes by their ribbons in her left hand. Selecting one, she set it on the marble desktop. Charter Magic flared into life, many marks glowing and shifting about on the ivory faces. A second later, a line of intense black ink ran from the cube as if drawn by an unseen cartographer's careful hand. It continued on, moving faster and faster, far more swiftly than anyone could actually draw, and in half a minute had completed a quite detailed map of a large area around the Greenwash, centred on the bridge, showing Yellowsands to the east, Navis to the southeast, the Clayr's Glacier to the south and the Field Market sixty leagues to the north, a square mile of the steppe where a great market was held by truce four times a year.

'Amazing!' breathed Nick. Ferin too was entranced. The map was far better and more detailed than anything she had ever seen before.

'The bridge is well-fortified, with the North Castle, the mid-river bastion, and the South Castle,' said Touchstone. He touched the map as he spoke, and it changed, suddenly displaying the bridge and its fortifications in much closer detail. 'However, it is not as strongly garrisoned as it might be; each of the seasonal Shifts is understrength . . . but it is the only possible place to cross. The river is in spate, and if there has been surreptitious building of rafts our normal patrols would have spotted that, even if the Clayr do not. So it must be the bridge. You agree?'

'Yes,' said Sabriel. 'What do you think, Ferin? Could your cousins the horse nomads cross anywhere else?'

'No,' said Ferin. 'When I tried, my raft was swept to the sea.'

'You crossed the Greenwash in flood?' asked Lirael.

'I tried the bridge first,' said Ferin. 'They will too. The river is too wide, too cold and too swift. Even for an Athask.'

'Only the Yrus have ships,' mused Touchstone. 'And not many of those. Yes, it must be the bridge. Hawkmistress?'

A rather falcon-faced Clayr wearing the leathers of the Mews stepped forward, two Assistant Falconers at her side with their notebooks and pencils at the ready.

'I have two messages to dispatch immediately.' Touchstone spoke quickly, with great decision. 'And doubtless more to follow. First, to Princess Ellimere in Belisaere. Northern invasion suspected at Greenwash Bridge stop. Order two-thirds of all Guard garrisons north of and including Chasel to march for rendezvous Greenwash Bridge immediately stop. All Trained Bands to mobilise stop. Belisaere Trained Bands to march as soon as able for Greenwash Bridge stop . . . Ah . . . is that about maximum length?'

'Yes, Highness,' said the Hawkmistress. 'But I will break down any message for multiple birds, as required.'

'Good. New message, for the Greenwash Bridge Company, Navis. Northern invasion imminent at bridge stop. By royal order ready all defences stop. Dispatch all Shifts immediately to bridge stop. Going there myself stop. Signed Touchstone. End.

'That's it for the moment,' continued Touchstone. 'Get those away. Sabriel and Lirael, if you could find out whatever Arielle has to tell us from the past, that would be useful. Nicholas, you might care to wait for Sam; he'll come straight here. Mirelle, we'll need as many of your rangers as you can spare, and your librarians, Vancelle, on the road north by morning. And your Paperwing flight, Ryelle. Can they fly to the bridge this afternoon, and to the Field Market tomorrow morning? If we can scout out that area we'll know for sure what's happening.'

'The Paperwings do not like to fly so far across the Greenwash,' said Ryelle. 'The Charter is more remote without stones below; they feel weakened, even as if they are dying.'

'Can it be done?'

'It is *possible*,' said Ryelle. She hesitated, then said, 'But I do not wish to risk all our craft, or flyers. I will go myself, alone. You are sure there is a real threat?'

Her voice carried all the doubt of a Clayr used to the future being at least partially mapped out, rather than entirely unknown.

'No,' said Touchstone. 'But I do know we must act as if there is.'

chapter thirty

arielle

Clayr's Glacier, the Old Kingdom

Nick and Lirael could exchange only a heartfelt glance as Sabriel took the latter's arm and marched towards the doors, with one of Mirelle's rangers leading the way. It was Qilla, Lirael noticed, though she no longer wore the leaping snow leopard badge of a lieutenant on the breast of her hauberk.

'So Nicholas Sayre is the reason none of the young gentlemen Ellimere put forward ever came up to scratch?' asked Sabriel with a smile as they followed Qilla into the Apple Peelings, a tight spiral ramp that led to the Third Back Stair. Lirael didn't know where the Rangers' Northwest Two lookout was located, save it must be high on Starmount.

'No,' she replied, and then blushing, added, 'I mean, yes. But I didn't know it. Not until last . . . not until yesterday.'

'He seems a fine young man,' said Sabriel. 'Sameth thinks highly of him; they were very good friends at school. But this matter of him becoming some sort of avenue into the Charter is troubling –'

'He's getting that under control,' said Lirael quickly, blushing again as she thought about the flaming sword. 'Or at least, I'm sure he will get it under control.'

'Good,' said Sabriel. She did not talk for a few more minutes as they strode up and around and around the ramp; then she suddenly asked, 'Has your Disreputable Dog ever reappeared?'

'No,' said Lirael. The pain was still there, but she found it somehow more bearable now. 'Why . . . why do you ask?'

'Because of Nicholas. In a way, he is akin to the Dog. Something of Free Magic deeply entwined with the Charter. I thought she might have been back to check up on what happened to him, after she returned him from Death.'

'But she's dead,' whispered Lirael.

'The physical *shape* she wore those years with you died,' said Sabriel. 'But she is Kibeth, one of the Seven, and always will be.'

'She said my time with her had passed,' said Lirael. There were tears in her eyes now. She wiped them away and blinked hard, determined not to show her grief.

Sabriel put her arm around her shoulders and gave her a hug.

'I am sorry,' she said. 'I did not want to bring you pain. I thought it possible the Dog might . . . look in . . . as it were. As Mogget still does, from time to time, though his motivations are, as ever, far more obscure.'

'Mogget?' asked Lirael. 'Why?'

'Who knows?' asked Sabriel. She touched a silver ring on her left hand, turning it nervously twice around her finger.

'He comes to see Sameth every now and then, usually when there is the prospect of fish about, though Charter knows he could easily catch them himself. Where he goes and what he does elsewhere is a mystery . . . I just hope he doesn't cause trouble. I have no desire to see if it is possible to bind him anew.'

It took an hour to climb to the lookout, with a slight detour to collect Lirael's bells. Sabriel did not mention the burned carpet in the Abhorsen's Rooms, but only said how much nicer the royal apartments were, uncluttered with the heavy old furniture from Hillfair, and Lirael and Nick were welcome to move. Lirael declined the offer. She was already thinking about the night ahead.

They also had to pause again just before going outside, to put on heavy fur cloaks, hats, snow goggles and scarves to wind around their faces, for the lookout was very high on Starmount indeed. A walled ledge that projected from the ice-encased rock only a thousand paces short of the summit, it was high enough that both Lirael and Sabriel felt the thinness of the air, their lungs labouring to get enough breath.

'Do we cast a diamond of protection?' asked Lirael.

Sabriel hesitated, for this was the normal procedure, to protect their bodies left behind when they went into Death. But Qilla was here, and the four rangers who took turns to watch through the great bronze telescope at the Ratterlin and the paths along the river that led to the Glacier.

'How deep must we go into Death, for you to see back?' she asked. 'Nine years, isn't it?'

'Almost ten,' said Lirael. 'My birthday is in six weeks. I'll be twenty.'

'Twenty,' said Sabriel. She smiled, thinking back to her own twentieth birthday. She had been pregnant with Ellimere then, and alternately very happy and very cross at having to remain in the Abhorsen's House while Touchstone was constantly away, in the very beginnings of the Restoration, with a new crisis to face every week, and a battle of some kind to be fought once a fortnight.

'I'll look in the book,' said Lirael. She took out *The Book of Remembrance and Forgetting*, not noticing Qilla back away as a small fume of white smoke gushed out of the opening pages. As Lirael expected, the book fell open exactly where she needed to look, and she had only to follow a line in a table with her finger to double-check what she thought she remembered.

'Easy,' she said, putting the book away again. 'First Precinct. We won't even have to go past the First Gate.'

Sabriel held up her hand, her expression very serious.

'Never think of entering Death as easy,' she said. 'The river can take you as *easily* in the First Precinct as anywhere else. Enemies may lurk there. You must never forget what it is to go into Death and remain alive. You want Nicholas to see you again, I trust?'

'Yes,' said Lirael, chastened. She suddenly remembered being attacked by Hedge the necromancer on the very edge of Life, and how narrowly she had escaped. 'I . . . I was thoughtless. I won't be again.'

'Qilla,' said Sabriel, addressing the ranger. 'The Abhorsen-in-Waiting and I will enter Death. As time is of the essence, we will not cast a diamond of protection, but instead rely on you and your companions to protect our bodies. Should there be any attack or anything untoward, you must clap me – my body – on the shoulder. But do not touch us unless it really is an attack or something as serious. Do you understand?'

'Yes, Abhorsen,' said Qilla. 'Good luck.'

Sabriel nodded. She drew her sword and Saraneth, assuming the guard position, sword in her right hand, bell in her left. Lirael moved next to her, but not too close. She took out Ranna, the Sleeper, and the sword Raminah.

'Ready?'

Lirael nodded, and together they entered Death.

The chill of the river was of an entirely different nature from the cold of the high mountain. It seemed to blossom *inside*, rather than penetrate from the outside, and as always, it was accompanied by the grasping tug of the current. The first few steps in Death were often the most important, the test to see who was stronger, Abhorsen or river.

Sabriel was planted as firmly as a tree, the strange monochrome water rushing around her thighs. Lirael was made to take one step before she could fully exert her will and resist the current. It grabbed at her heels, twisting and pulling, but it could not move her beyond that first step.

Apart from the rush of the river and the distant roar of the waterfall that was the First Gate, there was no sound. It was impossible to see very far, for the strange grey light stretched to an entirely flat horizon that seemed close, but always retreated.

Both Abhorsens stood for a few minutes, letting their sense of Death expand. Sabriel sniffed; though it was not precisely a smell she sought, it seemed to help. Lirael quirked her mouth, for it seemed to help open her ears, though again it was not sound she listened for with that extra sense.

'Nothing,' said Sabriel. 'For now. How far do you want to go on?'

'A dozen paces,' replied Lirael. She began to trudge forward, careful to make sure she had good footing before taking each step. The river could do tricky things, even reversing the current for a moment, or coming sideways at a wader.

Sabriel went with her, keeping a careful lookout, bell and sword ready.

'Here will do,' said Lirael. She took a deep breath, sheathed her sword and replaced the bell, then reached into the pocket of her waistcoat for the Dark Mirror. It was partly underneath the strap of her bandolier, which she hadn't thought about, so it took several seconds to get it out. But Lirael didn't let herself be distracted. She moved with slow certainty, her feet firmly planted, legs apart and balanced.

'It may be very hard for you when you see your mother,' said Sabriel. She paused, then added, 'I never knew mine at all, you know. But I think it can be worse to see someone you loved as a child so much later on, if she is not at all what you remembered.'

Lirael nodded. She knew Sabriel was warning her that the Arielle she was going to see in the past might be entirely mad. It was rare, but sometimes Clayr did become insane from the pressure of their Sight, seeing too many possible visions, too quickly, so they became lost in many futures and could not relate to the present at all.

Lirael opened the Dark Mirror and quickly raised it to her right eye, though she still looked out upon the river with her left eye. It was hard to focus like that, one eye seeing the interminable grey light and the rushing waters, the other staring into pure, unrelieved darkness. But she knew it was possible, she had done it twice before, so she persevered

Slowly, the Mirror began to clear, the darkness receding. There was a spark of light there, which became the sun. It started to go backwards, travelling from west to east. The process had begun.

Lirael imagined her mother in a cave with snow about, basing her face upon a charcoal drawing she had but making her clothes like Ferin's. Red stitches in soft leather. At the same time, she tried to think of her tenth birthday, another one of cruel disappointment since she had not gained the Sight, though not so fiercely sad as her birthdays would later become.

Charter marks began to fill her mind; she felt the great swim of the Charter, linking her, the bells, Sabriel by her side. Lirael selected the marks she needed, learned from the book, and let them fall into her voice.

'My mother I knew, but never enough,' she said. 'As she

Saw me in her future, show me her past, in the third moon of winter, ten years gone by.'

The passage of many swift suns through the mirror quickened as she spoke, flashing by, days gone in seconds. Then it slowed again, and the sun grew larger and closer. Lirael felt herself drawn towards the Mirror, falling into it, and still the sun drew closer and brighter and brighter still, till she had to shut her right eye or be blinded.

When she opened it again, a moment later, Lirael saw a tent of red-stitched leather, pitched before a frozen waterfall that fell in front of a deep cave. There was a firepit outside the tent, burning high, sparks flying up towards the moon, which was ringed with ice.

A woman in the white fur coat of an Athask walked around the fire and looked directly at Lirael. She was younger than Sabriel, which was the first shock, though of course she had to be, having died somewhere around the age of thirty-five. The second shock was how much she looked like Kirrith, though on a smaller scale, for Arielle did not have the same height or massive shoulders. But her face was so similar, albeit more finely drawn. Lirael could see almost nothing of herself in her mother. Arielle was very typically a Clayr, her skin brown as an acorn, eyes bright blue, hair almost white-blonde.

'Lirael,' said Arielle. For a moment Lirael almost answered her, as if she were truly there. Her lips moved, but no words came as she remembered that Arielle spoke to the future, to the Lirael she felt she knew would come to look upon this moment in the past.

'Lirael. I hope I am indeed talking to you, that you see me through the Dark Mirror.'

Arielle raised one hand and reached out, almost as if she might be able to touch her daughter after all, before she let it fall. The movement spoke much about her health, for she did not move easily, and coughed when her arm came back to rest.

'I have always Seen too much in the ice, been driven to make the future just so . . . to steer matters, as if I alone might make a difference. Arrogance, I suppose, and stupidity. To look too much to the future, and not enough to the present.'

She paused to cough, and when her hand came away from her mouth, it was speckled with fine drops of blood.

'I thought you would be happy in the Glacier, as I was, growing up. I did not See you for so long; I thought you would be no different from all the others. I thought you would be crowned with the silver and moonstones as I was, when I was nine; the Sight has always come early in our family. But not with you . . . I am sorry, so sorry . . .'

The scene before Lirael grew misty, but she knew it was not some fault in the mirror. It was a tear in her eye, another one of the many tears cried over the years for a mother lost long ago.

Arielle visibly pulled herself together, drawing in a racking breath, only to cough again. But when that bout was over, she did not talk of Lirael's childhood. Her demeanour changed to that of a Clayr delivering an important message from the observatory, one that must be acted on immediately.

'Listen. The Witch With No Face has summoned the *entire* fighting and sorcerous strength of *all* the clans to gather at the Field Market by the second full moon of spring in the year you turn twenty. From what I have Seen this is only a week or ten days from when you look at me here. This great host will attack the day after the full moon, at the Greenwash Bridge. Yet the bridge is only part of it; there is some other plan that I cannot See. You must warn the King and the Abhorsen. But force of arms cannot hold back the northern assault; at least I do not think so. I have Seen so many futures where the nomads roam the Kingdom, towns burn, the walls breached at Belisaere, the Glacier besieged . . . so many on both sides dead and dying . . .'

Arielle coughed again, and when she looked back up, her eyes were lit with a feverish light, and Lirael saw sweat beaded everywhere upon her face, though her breath blew out in frosty clouds.

'It is the Witch With No Face who holds the chance of victory. She must be killed. I have Seen you and a young man, you go to do it, you go beyond the Great Rift, to the Empty Lands where the Charter does not exist and the spirit-glass shards lie all about. I don't know how . . . but you do it, that's the main thing. Find her and kill her. That's what you do. Except when you don't. Too many times, too many times, my daughter dead . . . it is a terrible thing to See, so terrible . . .'

Arielle began to weep and clutch at her hair. Lirael reflexively tried to go forward, to hold her, but nothing changed.

She could only watch and listen, until her mother coughed again, and somehow the act of dealing with this calmed her, and she could begin again.

'Beyond the Great Rift. The Empty Lands, where the sorcerers go for spirit-glass. That's where she is, lying in her sarcophagus. The offerings know the way, though they don't know they know. All joined together, the Witch With No Face and the offerings, that's why she wants them burned. Wait? If they're burned, if they're all burned, then there's nothing, no thread to follow . . . but there was one. The one who goes to Lirael. Doesn't she? I can't remember . . . her hand, *your* poor hand, though the golden hand, a hand of gold . . .'

Arielle started to weep again, tears mixing with the sweat upon her cheeks. But once again she stopped herself, wiped her eyes with hands bloody from her coughing, and pulled herself upright, wincing and shuddering at the pain in her chest.

'Lirael. You must go beyond the Great Rift, where the Free Magic sorcerers go to collect spirit-glass. The Witch With No Face's first body is there, in a sarcophagus, a stone coffin. Follow the thread. You must kill her. I have Seen what must be done, though I cannot clearly See if . . . if you succeed. I have Seen where you do not . . . no . . . I must not think of that.'

She coughed a little, but managed to still it.

'Go now, with my love. I always loved you. Always. You probably don't believe it. Perhaps you shouldn't. Love should always be shown, not merely said. I was too slow to learn this, too distracted by my visions. Do better! Go now. Go, Lirael. Do not watch me die. Farewell!'

Lirael shut her right eye hard, and kept it closed for a good two seconds. When she opened it again, she saw only the river of Death and Sabriel by her side, carefully watching.

'You saw her?' asked Sabriel quietly.

Lirael nodded, shut the Dark Mirror, and slid it back under the bandolier and into her waistcoat pocket. Then she drew Raminah and Ranna again. It was best to always be prepared in Death.

'She was dying,' said Lirael. 'She told me about her visions. An army of nomads, gathered by the Witch With No Face, to attack on or soon after the night of the second full moon of spring.'

'A week from tomorrow,' said Sabriel.

'At the bridge,' said Lirael. 'But she said there was some other plan as well, which she could not See. And in many, perhaps most futures, we lose the battle anyway.'

'Not very encouraging,' said Sabriel.

'She told me I had to kill the Witch With No Face's first body. She is in a sarcophagus beyond the Great Rift, where the sorcerers go for spirit-glass,' continued Lirael.

'Ah,' said Sabriel bleakly. 'Unfortunately, that does make sense. Chlorr's original body, her anchor in Life. But beyond the Great Rift . . .'

'I know nothing about that place,' said Lirael.

'We will talk of it when we go back,' said Sabriel. She

stopped to listen and look around again, Lirael doing like-wise. 'But before we do, could you keep watch while I examine this charm I took from Ferin?'

Lirael nodded. She found herself shaking slightly from seeing her mother in such straits, so distressed and ill. But the river would exploit such weakness, so she willed herself to be still, to put aside the emotional turmoil that threatened to rise within her.

Next to her, Sabriel opened the metal box with the bone charm. Red fire sprang up around it, far more than had out in living world, in the Map Room. Outlined by the fire, both Abhorsens saw two threads of absolute blackness connected to the bone.

Both threads led back into Life, but one went to the right, and the other to the left.

chapter thirty-one

threads from a charm of bone

In Death

'How very unusual,' said Sabriel, lifting the box to watch the threads lift out of the river. 'Both go back into Life. We must follow them, see where they go.'

Lirael nodded. She knew about such threads from *The Book of the Dead*. They were typically used by powerful necromancers to control distant spirits in their power, or as trip wires to alert a necromancer to something of theirs being disturbed in Death. But she had not read about two such threads connecting a charm that had been cut out of a living person, or ones which lead from Death back out into Life.

The first thread took them some hundred paces along the border before it went out into Life.

'Watch my back,' warned Sabriel. She went right up to the edge of Life. Even a few steps away, Lirael could feel the warmth of it, the lure of the living world. But if she went out here, it would not be back into her own body.

Sabriel placed her hand in seemingly empty air, feeling for the unseen border where Death met Life. Then she laid her head against it and shut her eyes.

Lirael knew how to look out into Life in this way, though she was by no means as practised at it as she would like to be. She watched Sabriel for a few seconds, then quickly looked away, to concentrate on the river, to listen for the First Gate. If the sound of the waterfall paused, it would mean something was coming through from deeper in Death.

Sabriel did not stay in her eavesdropping pose for long. She straightened up and turned away, holding the bone charm in the box up to lift the second thread, which ran along the border in the opposite direction.

'That first one goes out somewhere in the far north,' she said. 'I would say beyond the Great Rift, which fits in with what Arielle had to say. Let us see where this other one goes.'

Lirael nodded, and followed. As always, it was very tiring to be in Death. The river constantly leeched away heat and energy and hopefulness. She could feel it in every small wavelet that washed around her legs, inviting her to give up, to lie down, to be swept away. A constant refrain that she had to shut out and ignore, in addition to resisting the sheer physical force of the current upon her spirit form.

Sabriel crouched longer where the second thread went out into Life. When she straightened up, it was with a cry of alarm.

'Stand ready! Shadow Hands!'

Irregular shapes of blackest shadow sprang from Life into

the river, goaded by their master somewhere in the living world beyond. Impossibly long claws of stretching darkness reached for Sabriel, but she was retreating fast, and Saraneth was already ringing.

The harsh voice of the bell held the Shadow Hands in place, but there were a dozen of them, and more were coming through. Lirael returned Ranna to the bandolier, slapping home the strap that kept it silent, and as swiftly drew her own Saraneth. Swinging the bell in a long overhand loop, she added its voice to Sabriel's. This was something they had practised together often, for it more than doubled the power of the individual bells. Provided neither of them made a mistake, and a bell twisted in their hand . . .

'Hold them there,' ordered Sabriel. 'We will return to Life.'

Slowly they edged along the border, still ringing their bells, seeking the place where their bodies awaited them. Lirael was surprised by this retreat, because Sabriel usually would want to bind any Dead they found, and send them on to die the final death. The Abhorsen had never retreated in the time Lirael had learned from her, and though there were now sixteen Shadow Hands, that was not too many for Sabriel and her apprentice, at least in Lirael's opinion.

But as they neared their crossing point, Lirael saw why Sabriel had retreated. Scores more Dead were coming through. Dead drawn out of the bodies they were inhabiting in Life, so things of lesser power than Shadow Hands, but there were so many of them! A hundred, perhaps more, and behind these lesser creatures came several hulking shapes of shadow, with burning fire in their eye sockets, flames dripping from their hands. Greater Dead, at least five of them.

Coming from the wrong direction, coming from Life into Death. Even without intervention from the Abhorsens, many of these Dead would be taken by the river. Which meant there was something or someone making them come back to the place they had fought so long to leave.

'Out!' said Sabriel, and stepped into Life, Lirael close at her heels.

Ice cracked and fell from skin and armour as they returned. Clayr rangers turned swiftly to look at them, then resumed their watching, though many hands stayed in spell-casting gestures or on bows or swords.

'Stay ready!' warned Sabriel to Lirael. 'Some might be driven to come through, even with the sun.'

Shadow Hands were fast. As close as they had been, it would not be too difficult for them to come back into Life, particularly here where the border had been crossed and made more permeable.

The tentative attack, when it came, was exactly as Sabriel predicted. A Shadow Hand oozed out slowly into Life, a thin tendril of shadow appearing in mid-air, which immediately smoked and bubbled under the sun. It tried to recoil, but Sabriel was already ringing Saraneth, and under the compulsion of the bell, the entire spirit was forced to emerge.

Rays of sunshine bored holes in its shadowy spirit flesh as it fought against the bell and Sabriel's implacable will. Smoke boiled and eddied from it as it writhed and wriggled, desperate to get under some rock if it could not escape to Death. Yet still Saraneth rang, its commanding voice impossible to avoid, ordering obedience or *else*.

A minute later, the Shadow Hand ceased to exist. The afternoon sun on a spring day was more than strong enough to quickly slay all but one of the Greater Dead, and even they would fear it.

'I do not think more will follow,' said Sabriel, returning her bell to the bandolier. 'But I would double the watch here tonight, you rangers, and summon *many* Charter lights. Come, Lirael. We had best get back to the council, and I need you to tell me exactly what Arielle said. I fear she did indeed See truly. That second thread led to a great host, including many Dead and Free Magic creatures, and it was somewhere on the steppe. Quite possibly the Field Market.'

Lirael told Sabriel as much as she could remember as they raced down from the lookout. The Abhorsen listened carefully, firing off questions as they negotiated stairs and doors and sloping corridors and groups of Clayr who scattered like ants fleeing heavy raindrops when Sabriel charged towards them, calling 'Urgent business!' in a voice that brooked no argument.

After Lirael had recounted twice everything she could remember from looking back, Sabriel told her what she had put together, a rapid-fire assessment of what was a much worse situation than anyone had thought only a few hours before.

'Your mother Saw truly indeed, I have no doubt,' said

Sabriel. 'There is a host on the steppe, doubtless growing by the day. We should know by tomorrow evening if it is at the Field Market, provided Ryelle returns safely . . . Actually, I must send a message-hawk to the bridge, to warn her; there will be gore crows without a doubt. Hey, you!'

A young Clayr pressing herself against the side of the hallway to allow Sabriel to pass made a shivering reply.

'Yes, Abhorsen?'

'I need you to go to the Mews right now, tell the Hawkmistress or whoever is in charge there to send a message-hawk to the Greenwash Bridge from the Abhorsen Sabriel, for Ryelle of the Clayr. Message is: "Beware gore crows and Free Magic at Field Market." Repeat that back to me.'

The girl stammered out the instructions and the message.

'Good work,' said Sabriel. 'What's your name?'

'Blindyl,' whispered the girl.

'Go!' ordered Sabriel, and Blindyl fled. Fortunately in the right direction to get to the Third Front Stair, Lirael noted, the quickest way to the Mews.

'So a host on the steppe, and that other thread definitely led to the Empty Lands, I could tell from the silence. What do you make of that?'

'I don't know,' said Lirael. 'I mean, one thread must lead to the necromancer who made the charm. That would be the Witch With No Face. I mean, Chlorr. Is that right?'

Sabriel stopped suddenly and gripped Lirael by the shoulders.

'Both lead to Chlorr!'

'Oh,' said Lirael, slowly putting it together. 'You mean to . . . to Chlorr's original body as well as her current Dead shape?'

'Yes!' cried Sabriel, striding off again, narrowly avoiding a collision with a Steamworks engineer, who had to swing her toolbox behind herself to avoid tangling it up in Sabriel's legs.

'And your mother told us that too,' continued Sabriel. 'Follow the thread to the first Witch With No Face, the thread from the charm taken from an offering. They're all joined together, just as Arielle saw.'

'But what are the Empty Lands?' asked Lirael, taking Sabriel's elbow to direct her to the left-hand door. 'What lies beyond the Great Rift?'

'There are some inhabitable lands beyond the western arm of the Great Rift,' said Sabriel. 'But beyond the northern arm there is a bleak and featureless plain where nothing lives, nothing at all. That is the Empty Lands. There are no plants, no animals, nothing. There is not even air to breathe.'

'What?'

'Free Magic sorcerers go there to collect spirit-glass, shards of volcanic glass that contain trapped spirits,' explained Sabriel. They were back at the Apple Peelings, and she broke into a run down the sloping corridor. 'They use their magic to make bubbles of air around themselves, which last long enough for a dash into the Empty Lands, a quick scrabble for spirit-glass and an even swifter return. Many die, of course.'

'But how can we go there?' asked Lirael. 'We can't do that.'

'You could make a bubble of air with Charter Magic, though, couldn't you?' asked Sabriel.

'Yes,' said Lirael. 'But I thought . . . Mother said the Charter isn't there beyond the Rift.'

'It isn't,' said Sabriel. 'I think it is the remnant of a world destroyed by Orannis.'

'What!' exclaimed Lirael. She stopped mid-stride, suddenly remembering what she had seen in the Dark Mirror before the binding of Orannis. She had seen worlds destroyed, seen the awful power of the Destroyer, the rings of fiery devastation that exploded from it, each larger than the last . . .

'I think it is the remnant of a world destroyed by Orannis,' repeated Sabriel. 'The spirit-glass fragments are the last surviving things left, Free Magic creatures that were either allies or enemies of the Destroyer, sufficiently powerful not to be entirely annihilated along with everything else. Come on!'

Sabriel took off again, with Lirael following more slowly. She called out after her half-sister, returning to her previous question.

'But if the Charter isn't there, how can we make a bubble of air with Charter magic to go there?'

'By taking the Charter with us!' shouted Sabriel, without slowing down. 'Come on!'

chapter thirty-two

who will slay this troublesome chlorr?

Clayr's Glacier, the Old Kingdom

There were even more people in the Map Room when Sabriel and Lirael burst back in. Several desks were in use with maps displayed; messengers were hurrying to and from the King or waiting to be heard; a group of librarians had brought in a trolley-load of books and were sorting them at another desk; Clayr on domestic-service duty were arranging wine bottles and glasses on the round table.

And Nick and Sam were sitting on a desk, talking rapidly to each other, with hand gestures and shrugging and smiles. Both leaped to their feet as Lirael came running in behind Sabriel, but she could do no more than smile and wave as she followed the Abhorsen in a beeline to the King.

'It's all true,' snapped Sabriel from a dozen feet away. 'A huge host on the steppe, lots of Dead and Free Magic creatures of all kinds, several tens of thousands of nomads. Almost certainly going to attack a week from tomorrow, on the full moon, or the day after.'

'I see,' said Touchstone calmly. 'We might just be ready for them, in that case.'

'There's more to it,' said Sabriel. She went to Touchstone's side and briefly embraced him before continuing. 'Some skulduggery, because the bridge is not their main target.'

'Not?' asked Touchstone. 'But they cannot cross any other way.'

'That we know of,' said Sabriel. 'The assault will come at the bridge, but with some other ploy. Sorcery, no doubt. Chlorr will have a great many Free Magic practitioners in her service. A hundred and fifty, or more. I am not sure what they could do together.'

'We will have as many strong Charter Mages,' said Touchstone, watching his wife carefully. 'And many more, not so strong.'

'It is not just numbers, as you know,' said Sabriel. 'It is knowledge. If they have some prepared spell to cast together, it would be almost impossible to counter in time. In any case, we are fortunate there is a way we might lop off the head that directs this host, and without it, the clans will split and go home. Or fight each other, as they usually do.'

'Chlorr, you mean?' asked Touchstone. 'She is vulnerable in some way? I thought you said she cannot be permanently killed.'

'Not unless her original body is slain,' said Sabriel. 'But now we know where it is, thanks to Lirael and her Dark Mirror.'

'Where is it?' asked Ferin, levering herself between two Clayr by judicious use of elbows and crutches. 'I will kill her!'

'It is in the Empty Lands, beyond the Great Rift,' said Sabriel. 'You are brave, Ferin, but you cannot go there. However, it is the charm I cut from you that will lead us to her. So you have done more than your part in bringing that to us, and in delivering your message.'

'It is not as satisfying as driving a knife home,' muttered Ferin, but no one was listening. Touchstone had got to his feet, his forehead furrowed as he clenched and unclenched his fingers.

'Uh-oh,' said Sameth, and hurried to his father's side, with Nick close behind.

'Lead *us* to her?' asked Touchstone, dangerously quiet. 'You cannot mean to go beyond the Great Rift, Sabriel. The Charter does not exist there. Would you use Free Magic? You know the dangers of that, even for an Abhorsen. *Especially* for an Abhorsen.'

'I do mean to go,' said Sabriel, equally quietly, her voice determined. 'But not to use Free Magic. I will take a source of Charter Magic with me. If he agrees to come.'

Touchstone's head swivelled to look at Nick and he groaned.

'How do you always find some way to undertake the most dangerous, crazy, ill-thought-out –'

'I beg your pardon,' interrupted Lirael, 'but this is not for Sabriel to do. My mother, Arielle . . . she Saw it in the ice of the frozen waterfall. I am the one who must go beyond the Great Rift to slay the original Chlorr.'

Sabriel turned to her, eyes flashing in anger, but Lirael met her gaze. After a moment, the Abhorsen sighed and her face relaxed.

'I wondered if you'd remember that,' she said grudgingly. 'And I suppose there will be plenty to do at the bridge anyway.'

Lirael looked at Nick. He knew what she was asking. She didn't need to say anything, or he to answer. He moved to her side and took her hand. Her left hand.

'Like that, is it?' asked Sam. He smiled and nodded at them both. 'I approve, Auntie. But if you're going to go to parts unknown with my rather magically mixed-up friend, I'd better come with you. You will need someone who knows *advanced* Charter Magic, after all.'

'No one is going anywhere until we sit down and I hear everything I need to know,' said Touchstone firmly. 'Why does this family forever run straight at the first enemy that sticks up its head? We need planning! Forethought and planning, which is based on actually sharing all the knowledge you lot have gained in Death or the past or wherever you have found it!'

'I think you should have a glass of wine,' said Sabriel gently. 'The Charter knows I could do with one.'

It took several glasses of wine, and barley water, and cups of tea before the matter was settled, if not entirely to everyone's satisfaction.

'Time,' said Touchstone. 'Never enough time. As it is, we won't even have half the Trained Bands to the bridge by the full moon. The Bridge Company has managed to let almost the whole Winter Shift go on leave, to Belisaere and parts further south, and may not be able to collect them on time, or at all.'

He frowned, and changed tack suddenly.

'Are you sure you can fly as far as the Rift in owl shape, Lirael? Carrying Nicholas?'

'I flew before, carrying Sam,' said Lirael. 'This will take longer; it is much further. Several days, or nights, rather. I'll need to rest in the day.'

'I will show you on the map the places where you might find safe havens,' said Ferin. 'Anywhere it is hard for a horse to go is good. But there are not many on the steppe. Rocks, areas of nice sharp rocks, these are plentiful. A few hills, lonely hills, but they are very rare. Marshes. Full of biting insects, but no horse nomads.'

'You'll need my jumping frog to eat bugs,' said Sam. 'Lucky I brought it with me; always handy on a boat. Though I still think I should be going too.'

'I can't carry you both,' said Lirael. 'And the Paperwings can't or won't fly that far beyond the Greenwash. Besides, I'm sure you'll be needed at the bridge.'

'You can put spells on my arrows,' said Ferin, her scratched-all-over face beaming with enthusiasm. 'Like Young Laska did to hers. Good for wood-weirds and spirit-walkers.'

'Y-e-es,' agreed Sam. He put his head to one side and looked at Ferin, perhaps seeing past the bloodied and bloodthirsty exterior for the first time to the young woman behind. 'In fact, I'll get everyone to spelling arrows, build up as many stocks as we can. Good idea.'

'And you'll make me a foot later? Sabriel said you would. Better than carving my own.'

'Well, if Mother said I would, then of course I'll be happy to oblige,' said Sam, slightly taken aback by the matter-of-fact way Ferin seemed to be dealing with the loss of an important limb. 'It will take several months at least. You'll need to come to Belisaere, to my workshop.'

'If we live, I will go there,' said Ferin. She eyed Sam up and down, either to gauge his use as a maker of a new foot or to size him up for some other purpose. He straightened his back and sucked in his stomach, before looking away to speak hurriedly to Lirael.

'Speaking of magical prosthetics! As we are. I hope Nick can keep your hand working. It'll just be a lump of metal otherwise.'

'I'll do my best,' said Nick very seriously.

'We would not put you to such a test, not so soon, if it were not necessary,' said Sabriel.

'I know,' muttered Nick. He did know, just as he knew that Sabriel and Touchstone and Sameth and Lirael would not spare themselves either, not from anything. If something needed to be done, they would do it, no matter the personal cost.

He cast a nervous look at Lirael, hoping he wasn't showing his anxiety. On one level he was excited to be going to do something important with her, but he was also very apprehensive about something happening to Lirael.

They had only just found each other, and now, to go into unknown dangers where he didn't really know what he could do to help, and might even end up as a hindrance . . .

Lirael was thinking very similar thoughts. She had tried and tried again to think of some way she could go into the Empty Lands without Nick. But there was no one else who could be a source of Charter Magic. Which reminded her that they needed to practise together to make sure it would work, though this was also greatly influenced by her desire to be alone with him again. Alone somewhere safe, not in the wilds where they would always need to be on guard . . .

'Nick and I need to practise with me using him to access the Charter,' she said.

'And I need to help you remake your owl Charter skin,' said Sam. Lirael had told the group she had one prepared, which they could partially unstitch and just make larger. At least she could with Sam's help. 'I wonder who did fold it, by the way.'

'One of the old Abhorsen's Sendings, I suppose,' said Lirael.

'Hmm,' replied Sam. 'I don't know the ones here. I guess it would be possible to make a Sending who could do that. It would be very difficult . . .'

'Go practise,' said Sabriel. 'And make the Charter skin. Ferin, do you wish to fly with me to the bridge?'

'Yes!' said Ferin, clashing her crutches on the floor.

'We will fly at dawn tomorrow,' said Touchstone. 'Sam with me, Ferin with Sabriel. You should go tonight, Lirael. If your Charter skin can be ready.'

'Oh!' exclaimed Lirael. The comfortable, safe night she'd thought lay ahead popped like a soap bubble in the bath floating under the hot water.

'Time,' said Touchstone. 'Two or three days to fly to the Great Rift, at least another three crossing it, another day searching for the sarcophagus –'

'I have Ferin's charm,' said Lirael. 'I will follow the thread in Death once we are there, find the place quickly.'

'Maybe,' said Touchstone. 'But many things could happen. If you can finish off Chlorr once and for all, it would be best done before we come to battle. It might save many lives. On both sides.'

'This is what my elders feared,' said Ferin, suddenly very serious. 'The Athask are the bravest; we will be the first sent in to battle. And if all our grown men and women are slain, what will become of the clan?'

'Yes,' said Lirael. 'We will go tonight. Midnight, probably, from the Paperwing terrace.'

She thought for a moment, then added, 'Sam, can you see what you can get for Nick in the way of armour, and a traveller's pack? Hard rations and a water bottle too, that sort of thing? Ask Mirelle; the Rangers have good equipment. I'll meet you both in the Abhorsen's Rooms later to work on the Charter skin, and practise with you, Nick. Ferin, I'd welcome your advice on where to stop. Come and look at the map with me.'

'We will all see you off,' said Sabriel. 'Oh, I wish I could go myself!'

chapter thirty-three

across the greenwash

The North/Greenwash Bridge, the Old Kingdom

Lirael was very out of practice flying as a barking owl, particularly as a giant owl carrying a man weighed down with a pack and weapons. Launching from the Paperwing terrace was a nightmare, and she seriously frightened both herself and Nick by dropping at least four hundred feet towards the glacier below before managing to get her wings beating hard enough to lift them up and begin to climb over the massive monolith of ice and head north.

Her right wing was golden, which was part of the reason for Lirael's panic. For a few seconds she thought it wouldn't work, so it didn't. But then it did, and apart from the colour, it seemed to be just as good as the other one.

Once out of the mountains, when she could fly lower, with a warm wind carrying them in the right direction, it grew easier. She could glide a great deal of the time, and even talk to Nick, though he found it difficult to understand the words screeched from her beak, a noise that caused several curious night birds to immediately reverse direction and go else-where.

Towards dawn, Lirael sighted the Greenwash and the bridge, both easily visible from on high with the moon and a clear sky. The bridge was far off to the east, so though she had thought about resting there, she decided against it. She could also see a few hills ahead, eight or nine leagues north of the Greenwash, where the ground began to rise up towards the beginnings of the steppe. She could be there well before the sun was high enough to trouble her huge golden eyes.

Landing, as always, was a problem. Lirael had to make three attempts, almost smashing Nick into the ground on the first two. He was lying in a hammock she carried in her claws, and though he got his legs out and held himself ready, she still approached too fast.

But on the third try she managed to slow to a complete stop, beating her vast wings in a flurry that raised a huge column of dust, hopefully not too visible in the predawn light. Dropping Nick down, she let go of the net, flew up again, and came around to land a dozen paces away.

Nick came over and scratched the feathers on top of her head. They'd landed in a hollow between two bare hills, quite shielded from view, but Lirael hadn't noticed there was a small spring bubbling away on the side of the northern hill. While water would be welcome, it might also be a known supply where nomads came with their horses.

'When do you change back?' asked Nick. 'So I can kiss you again?'

'Arrghhhkkkk!' said Lirael. She'd forgotten to tell Nick she had to stay in the Charter skin until they got to the Rift. It could be worn only once, though it should last for several days.

'What does that mean?'

'Got to stay like this!'

'You have to stay like that?'

'Until Rift!'

'Oh,' said Nick blankly.

'Tired,' said Lirael, trying to keep her bird shriek as quiet as possible. 'Drink. Then sleep. You watch till sunset. Wake me. You sleep tonight while we fly. All right?'

'Okay,' said Nick. He touched the sword hilt at his side nervously. 'Yes. I'll keep watch.'

Lirael waddled over to the spring and drank. She wasn't hungry, which was just as well, because in this shape she felt she'd need to eat a horse. And she didn't want to see any horses, because that meant nomads.

'Love you!' she shrieked at Nick when she came back.

'What?' asked Nick.

Lirael shrugged, very expressively, her head disappearing well past her shoulders, or rather the top of her wings. Nick looked mystified.

'Never mind! Sleeping.'

The giant owl scratched out a shallow pit and settled down in it, putting her head under one wing, and instantly fell asleep.

* * *

When Lirael awoke, Nick was scratching her head again, using both hands and all his fingers, digging deep. The sun was setting in the west, and all seemed as it had been that morning, the spring burbling away, the hills shielding them from view.

'Good,' said Lirael. 'Ready to go?'

'Ready to go?' Nick repeated back.

Lirael nodded.

'Yes, I'm ready,' said Nick.

'Get in net.'

Nick hesitated, clearly slow to understand what Lirael said. Then he climbed into the hammock, keeping one leg out either side while holding the netting up above his head. Lirael very carefully grabbed it with one claw, while balancing on the other and getting her wings started. Again, she began to raise a huge cloud of dust.

The take-off was better than her last one, but she still bounced Nick very lightly once on the ground. He didn't yell, which she took for a good sign. Once fully airborne, she bent her head down to look underneath, and hooked her other foot onto the hammock. Nick smiled and waved at her.

Wings beating rhythmically, Lirael flew to the north under the waxing moon.

At the Greenwash Bridge, King Touchstone was making his discontent felt. The Bridgemaster had already been verbally lashed for not sending out more scouts, and further, and had retreated to pass on this unhappiness to his subordinates, while also urging them to better and faster preparations for a siege.

Ryelle had arrived from her reconnaissance at much the same time Touchstone and Sabriel flew in, so there were three Paperwings in the outer bailey of the South Castle, by far the bigger of the two Bridge Company fortifications. Ryelle confirmed the presence of a vast host at the Field Market, even bigger than Sabriel's estimate, with long lines of reinforcements heading in from all directions, save south.

Gore crows had pursued her, but forewarned by Sabriel's message, Ryelle had been ready for them, flying faster and higher while pushing the clouds away with Charter-spelled winds to allow the sun to beat directly down on the gore crows, hastening their second demise.

Very few of the Old Kingdom troops had arrived – only the small troop of Guards who patrolled the Nailway, and the Summer Shift of the Bridge Company, which was a third understrength.

Sam, true to his word, had immediately gone to work on spelling arrows, setting marks on shafts and flights so they flew true, and on arrowheads so they would cleave Free Magic spells and rend Free Magic flesh. He conscripted the best of the available Charter Mages to help him, but most could manage to do only a dozen at most before they were exhausted. Sam did nearly a hundred before he had to stop and rest. When he moved back from the work table in the armoury and slumped against the wall he realised Ferin was watching him, sitting on the next bench, her crutches leaning against a spear-stand.

'You're better at making magic arrows than those others,' she said. 'I want some of yours.'

Sam yawned, covered it with his hand, and tried to straighten up. Failing, he slid down the wall a bit.

'You need the Charter mark yourself, to use them,' he said, touching the baptismal mark on his forehead. 'Won't work otherwise. Sorry.'

'What!' exclaimed Ferin. 'But I told you to make them, back in the Clayr's place.'

'Yes,' said Sam patiently. 'But I didn't think you wanted them for yourself.'

'You think I can't shoot with a foot missing?' protested Ferin. 'I have my bow. I will go up the tower and lean on the wall. It will be easy.'

'No, no, not all,' said Sam hurriedly.

'But I need magic arrows to kill wood-weirds,' said Ferin. 'How do I get the mark? A hot knife? Can you do it?'

'Yes . . . I mean, no,' said Sam. He was very tired. 'No knives involved, and no I can't do it. It's done when you're a child.'

'Always?' asked Ferin. 'Athask adopt others, sometimes grown.'

'Well, I suppose it can be granted to adults,' said Sam. 'But it's a very serious thing, a commitment to the Charter . . .'

'I will go and ask your mother,' said Ferin. 'She is wise. She will give me the mark. I will come back for arrows.'

'Good luck with that,' muttered Sam, and closed his eyes.

An hour later, a dig in his ribs from the end of a crutch woke Sam up. He blinked, eyes adapting to the dim light. It was almost dark outside and there were no lanterns or Charter Magic lights in the armoury, or none lit.

'Look!' exclaimed Ferin. She leaned on one crutch, reached up, and touched her forehead. A Charter mark glowed there, under her finger. 'See! You touch it, and then I touch yours.'

'Ah, yes,' said Sam gingerly. He pushed himself up using his back against the wall. 'That is . . . that is the custom.'

He reached out and touched the mark, half-expecting it to be faked in some way. But he fell instantly, deeply into a golden sea of marks, and had some difficulty retrieving his consciousness. Weariness, he thought, standing up straight as Ferin touched his mark. She held her finger there for several seconds, then slowly withdrew her hand.

'It is like swimming in the high lake,' she said, grinning, her teeth white in the darkness. 'The shock at first, the sudden cold, then it comes all around and you know what it is to be alive and you go under and it is so smooth and clear and it seems to be forever and it is not cold, but warm . . .'

'Yes,' said Sam.

'Now you can give me magic arrows,' said Ferin, swinging away on her crutches. 'When we are in Belisaere, you making my foot, you can teach me how to do spells, make magic arrows. All right?'

'Yes,' said Sam.

'If we live,' added Ferin casually. She looked over the finished shafts on the bench, which Sam, fresh from his immersion in the Charter, could see all glowed with a light he wasn't really seeing with his eyes.

chapter thirty-four

into the shadowed depths

The Great Rift/Greenwash Bridge,
the Old Kingdom

Lirael and Nick reached the edge of the Great Rift several hours before dawn on the fourth day of their flight from the Glacier, with nothing more anxious over that time than the distant sight of a band of nomads heading southeast. The steppe was deserted, a consequence of Chlorr calling all the clanspeople to her service.

The moon was waxing gibbous, more than three-quarters full, so from the air they saw the Great Rift many hours before they arrived. A vast slash in the earth, it was at least two or three leagues wide, and its depths were too deep to be seen. It ran from east to west ahead of them but slowly angled south, and far off towards the horizon this turn could be seen to increase, marking the western extension of the mighty canyon.

Despite the moon, it was very hard to make out the northern side of the Rift. Even with her owl eyes, Lirael couldn't seem to focus beyond the great canyon. Everything was clear enough immediately ahead. It was all red rocks and little streams cutting through to become narrow waterfalls, but halfway across, something happened. It was as if the air were full of dust, or there were a heat haze. But Lirael knew it was a border of sorts, like the Wall to the south.

Up until now, she had not needed to try to access the Charter via Nick. Lirael had been too tired to make the attempt, particularly in owl form. She could still feel the Charter, and find it, and draw marks from it, though it was much more difficult than it was across the Greenwash, back in the Old Kingdom. However, the Charter was still there, a constant, comforting presence, even one grown remote and more difficult to access.

Somewhere below, crossing the Rift, that presence would vanish. Then Lirael would need to draw upon Nick, and neither he nor anyone else knew how long the Free Magic he had inside him would sustain the Charter Magic that somehow drew upon that power.

By this stage of their journey, Lirael had mastered landing. She set Nick down very gently, releasing the net at the same time, then flew up and around to come back and land next to him, without falling over and flailing about with her wings.

The edge of the Great Rift was two or three hundred paces away, and, most important, so was one of the tattered flags that marked the beginning of the path the sorcerers took to descend, and cross, and go up to the Empty Lands to seek their spirit-glass.

Nick packed away the net, and prowled about the bare, rocky patch of ground where they had landed, his hand on his sword hilt. There was no cover, but Lirael did not intend staying there. Slowly, she began the process of shedding the Charter skin.

Faint lines of golden light began to trace out the lines of her feathers, limning every bar and curve. They grew brighter and began to run together, and then the whole giant owl was golden and bright for a moment and then it was dark again, and there was no owl. Just Lirael lying on her side on the ground, with her pack on her back, her bell bandolier in front, and Raminah at her side.

'Ouch,' said Lirael. 'As always, I hurt. And I feel disgusting. And I probably smell.'

Nick came over and helped her up. His nose wrinkled as he gently embraced her, Lirael moving stiffly to return the hug.

'We both smell,' he said. 'Fortunately.'

Lirael raised both eyebrows, because she couldn't raise one by itself.

'Well, it would be bad if just one of us smelled,' said Nick. 'Do we rest here?'

'No,' said Lirael. She sighed and pointed towards the flag. 'We have to start down. Apparently there are caves where the sorcerers usually rest.'

'What do we do if we meet any?' asked Nick.

'Fight,' said Lirael succinctly. 'But Chlorr should have called them all away. Ferin certainly thought so.'

They walked on in silence for a while, occasionally touching hands, but not holding on. Lirael in particular had to be ready to wield both bell and sword.

'Do you feel different here?' asked Lirael quietly as they reached the head of the path and looked down. It was quite a well-made track, easily ten feet wide, carved into the stone of the canyon wall. If you kept to the side, you might not even notice the massive, apparently bottomless drop on the edge, Lirael thought. She started down, Nick withdrawing to follow a few paces behind her.

'A little,' said Nick thoughtfully. 'When I touch the mark on my forehead, it feels . . . slower . . . The Charter is there, but it takes longer to well up. Or something.'

'And the Free Magic inside?' Lirael asked. 'You said you could feel it, like heat, deep within.'

'Yes,' said Nick. 'Still there. Not spreading. Not breaking out. Not turning into a monster.'

'Good,' said Lirael. She turned and smiled at him. 'Keep it that way, please!'

They walked on in silence for some time, but as the first red light of dawn shone overhead, still hours off from shedding any serious light into the Rift, Nick spoke again.

'Lirael,' he said. 'If I do . . . if I do become a monster, a Free Magic creature . . . you will kill me, won't you?'

Lirael didn't answer.

'I mean it,' repeated Nick. 'Don't give me the chance to hurt you. Strike first.'

Lirael stopped and turned to face him.

'Just don't do it,' she said. 'That's all. Come on. I think there's a cave ahead.'

Dawn at the bridge was neither as quiet nor as lonely as at the Great Rift, so many leagues to the north. Here, there were soldiers everywhere hard at work; most had been roused an hour before. On the northern side, the moat around the castle was being cleaned of debris, the sluice gates that allowed it to be filled from the river temporarily shut, the water pumped back to the river the day before.

'That's him!' said Ferin, pointing down at the muddy ditch where a mixed group from the Bridge Company, the Navis Trained Band and the Royal Guard were raking together broken logs and flotsam and tying them into bundles to be lifted clear. 'That's the one who shot me!'

Aron, crossbowman of the Bridge Company, didn't notice. He was exhausted from all the extra work of preparing the castle for siege, and intent on getting the current awful, muddy job done. Haral, who was working next to him, did look up. She saw the mountain girl in the white fur, hopping up and down and waving one crutch in the air. Next to her was a young, important-looking man; he wore a gethre plate hauberk so he had to be. Haral groaned as she heard what the nomad was saying, and recognised the golden tower symbol on the man's red surcoat.

'That's the girl you shot,' hissed Haral. 'And she's with Prince Sameth!'

Aron stopped trying to drag a particularly recalcitrant

piece of dead tree out of the mud and looked up, wiping his brow.

'Ho!' called out Ferin. 'Lucky you didn't kill me. Tell the woman next to you thanks for spoiling the shot!'

'I'm sorry!' bawled out Aron. He was sorry. He'd been thinking about the young mountain woman ever since their unfortunate meeting, reliving the moment when he'd panicked at the smell of Free Magic. Wishing it had never happened. 'I'm glad you're alive!'

'Me too!' shouted Ferin. She waved her leg out over the edge of the moat. 'They cut my foot off! But I am Athask! I still shoot straight. Straighter than you!'

'Crazy,' muttered Haral, but she was grinning.

'What's your name again?' called out Aron. He was grinning too.

'Ferin! We have come to make magic arrows for your castle. Me and Sameth. Maybe you'll get some, help you hit what you aim for!'

She waved, and swung away on her crutches. Sameth followed, vaguely disturbed by the way the young Bridge Company soldier down below had looked at Ferin.

'What do you mean *we've* come to make magic arrows?' he asked as they crossed the drawbridge over the moat.

'I do one Charter mark,' said Ferin proudly. 'On every arrow.'

'For light,' said Sam. 'They don't even need it.'

'It helps you see the fall of shot at night,' said Ferin. 'But you are right. You need to teach me more marks. If we live.'

chapter thirty-five

no air to breathe

Beyond the Great Rift

'I have never slept with a man before,' said Lirael, as she swung on her pack and readied herself for the day's climb. It had taken them a day to descend the southern side, a day to cross the dry, rubble-strewn floor of the Great Rift, and now on the third day they were a good way up the northern side. Lirael could see touches of the red dawn light high above, tantalising her with the potential to escape from the eternal twilight of the deep canyon.

'You still haven't, in the sense I think you're getting at,' said Nick with a very weary smile. 'But one day, I hope we will both be clean and not so tired it is almost impossible to stay awake even when on watch –'

'I haven't fallen asleep on watch,' protested Lirael.

'Neither have I,' said Nick. 'I said "almost impossible to stay awake". How is your hand?'

Lirael held up her golden hand and flexed her fingers. They moved slowly, and the usual glow was absent from the metal.

'It works,' she said. 'But slowly. I think we might reach the top of the northern side today.'

'Don't change the subject,' said Nick. 'Hold it out. I'll see if I can help.'

He took her hand in both of his and concentrated. He could feel both the Charter, distant and far away, and the raging, hot energy of Free Magic deep inside himself. It had grown stronger as the Charter faded, but he had not told Lirael that yet, nor was he going to, unless he felt he was losing control.

Nick drew on this energy, mentally connecting it with the Charter, drawing it closer. Marks began to drift into his mind, growing brighter and stronger. He didn't know what they were, but he welcomed them, and let them pass through him into Lirael's hand.

They stood together for several minutes with Nick clasping Lirael's golden hand. The glow soon returned to it, and she slowly flexed her fingers, but not enough to break his grip. Eventually, Nick let go.

'Done anything?' he asked.

Lirael moved her hand about. It was still somewhat sluggish, but considerably better than it had been.

'Yes,' she said, kissing him on the forehead. Her lips were slightly sunburned, and his forehead was dirty, but it was still nice. 'Let's go. Remember, if you start feeling short of breath, say so immediately. I don't want to suddenly find we are too deep into the airless place for me to do anything about it.'

Three hours of hard climbing later, they came out on the northern side of the Great Rift. There were no waterfalls here, no shrubs, no birds, no flying insects, no ants, no beetles, nothing alive. As far as they could see, there was a flat plain, the ground blackened in streaks as if by fire. But there were also flags, shredded rags that hung from nomad spears thrust with inhuman force into the rocky ground.

'Sorcerers have marked the way for us,' said Lirael. 'How much water do you have?'

'Two-thirds of a bottle,' replied Nick.

'A little over half,' said Lirael. 'Well, it will have to be enough until we can get back to that spring in the last cave but one. I guess it's time for me to look into Death, and see where that black thread leads.'

'What do I do?' asked Nick.

'Guard my body,' said Lirael. 'It will become covered with ice, by the way. Don't touch me unless we're being attacked, or some other danger threatens.'

'Why not?'

'It's dangerous for both of us,' said Lirael. 'It will distract me in Death, perhaps at some critical moment. And there is a chance you will also be drawn into Death, and the river would almost certainly take you under and away.'

'The river . . . I almost remember that,' said Nick. 'Where the Dog came to get me. It was very peaceful, I was floating –'

'No!' snapped Lirael. 'If, Charter help us, you do somehow end up in Death while still living, do not relax; do not float.

Fight against it. Fight the current. Force yourself back into Life.'

'I will,' said Nick softly. 'You too, okay?'

'Yes,' said Lirael. 'Me too.'

Lirael drew Raminah, noticing that the Charter marks on the blade were dull and did not move, save for a very few near the cross-guard. But the marks on Saraneth were as lively as ever. She looked at them, and thought perhaps it was because the bells were also a mixture of both magics. But she had no time to dwell on this. As Touchstone had drilled into her, they had a job to do, and the sooner it was done the better.

Lirael went into Death even more cautiously than she had the last time with Sabriel. She stopped almost at once, setting her feet against the current, and looked about, every sense taut, absorbing the slightest sensation. But there was nothing, just the soft rush of the current and the distant sound of the river crashing through the First Gate.

Lirael sheathed bell and sword, got out the box with the bone charm, and opened it. As before, two threads came up out of the water. One to the left, one to the right. Lirael followed the left-hand thread. It went barely six paces before going back out into Life, confirming the closeness of the sarcophagus.

The Abhorsen-in-Waiting looked around again, checking for any signs of lurking Dead. Then she put her head against the border, which was something to be sensed rather than a visible boundary, and closed her eyes. A moment later, she saw into Life. It wasn't quite the same as seeing with her eyes, more like imagining a picture in her head. But there was the path through the blackened wasteland, the flags on the spears marking the way, and there was the black thread. It followed the path for the first three flags, then veered sharply off to the left towards a slight rise ... no ... it was a very low mound. There, it went into the earth.

Lirael opened her eyes and immediately looked around. She had felt something, some twinge of her sense of Death. Was something creeping up on her? Or was she just tired and apprehensive? Quickly she put the box with the charm away, and drew her sword and a bell again, almost without thinking. As so often, the bell was Kibeth. Though she held it by the clapper, it seemed to sound faintly, with the echo of a distant, haunting bark.

The river swung around Lirael's knees, changing direction twice, and her left foot moved a fraction. Almost instantly she felt the ground under her heel disappearing, the river eating away where she had lifted herself up on her toes. Grimacing, Lirael plunged her foot hard down, and then slowly began to wade back to where she'd entered, to rejoin her body.

Nick let out a great sigh of relief as Lirael came back into Life. She had been gone so little time there wasn't much ice, only a few flakes falling from her face and left hand.

'Can we drink that?' asked Nick, pointing to where the ice melted on the ground. It was hotter here on this side of the Rift, much hotter. The sun seemed brighter, and was even a different colour, the yellow tinged with blue.

'I wouldn't,' said Lirael. 'Well, not unless we absolutely have to. I found where the sarcophagus is, or at least I think I have. Three flags in, and to the left. A low mound. We'll have to dig it out. With our plates, I guess. Or mugs.'

They had tin plates in their packs, but not much to put on them any more. Lirael had hardly eaten as an owl, just a few small animals snatched up here and there on the steppe, but they had also brought rations for only seven days. Just enough to get to the Rift and back again. Presuming Lirael could make another owl Charter skin.

'Onwards,' said Lirael. 'Remember, any shortness of breath, we step back.'

At the second flag, both of them stepped back, suddenly gasping, and with a glance, mutually agreed to retreat as swiftly as possible, staggering several paces in a near panic until their breath came more easily.

They had reached the point where the air disappeared.

There was no obvious sign of a change in the atmosphere, no mark on the ground, no difference in the light. Even the flag looked the same as the others, if a tattered rag could be said to have similarities to another tattered rag.

'I didn't like that,' whispered Nick. 'The choking, just nothing coming in, no matter what . . .'

'I will make us a globe of air,' said Lirael. 'It's much like making a Charter skin. A very well-known spell, for pearl-fishers and the like.'

She reached for the Charter, and nothing happened. Nick saw her eyes change, the panic rising there. Lirael gulped and looked at her hand. She tried to make a fist, but her fingers were frozen in place.

'It's gone,' whispered Lirael. 'The Charter! It's completely gone!'

chapter thirty-six

the battle begins

Greenwash Bridge,
the Old Kingdom/beyond the Great Rift

The first assault came exactly as foretold by Arielle, on the night of the full moon. Fog rose on the northern shore, not on the river, a fog summoned and thickened by many sorcerers. As it drifted towards the North Castle, horns sounded the alarm, which was repeated mid-river, in the South Castle, and in the newly fortified camp hastily built near the river's edge to hold the small army Touchstone had gathered to repel the invasion.

'So it begins,' said Sameth, as he joined his parents at the top of the tower in the mid-river bastion. It was taller by three dozen paces than anything in either the North or South Castles, and so offered the best view, though apart from its height it was otherwise considerably smaller than the keeps of the two castles.

'Yes, but how exactly?' asked Touchstone. 'The fog is sorcerous, without a doubt. But it is crossing well to the west of the north fort . . .'

'They may have lost control of it,' said Sabriel. 'It is drifting towards the river.'

'Against the wind,' said Ferin, startling Sam. She hadn't been behind him a moment before and he didn't think anyone should be that quiet on crutches.

'Yes,' agreed Sabriel, looking up at the flag that billowed out above their heads. 'So it is intentional. They haven't lost control. But why spread it over the river to the west?'

She raised her hand, fingers spread wide, and whistled five separate notes. With each whistle, Charter marks flew from her mouth to cluster on each finger. After the fifth note, Sabriel closed her hand, bringing all the marks together in one glowing ball, which she threw high in the air, whistling again, the five notes joined in an eerie tune.

The ball hurtled across the river and disappeared into the great bank of fog that was slowly drifting across the water.

Nothing happened. Sam heard Ferin let out a deep breath she had obviously been holding in expectation.

'Wha—' Ferin began to say when there was a sudden explosion of light. Five spears of lightning shot horizontally out of the fog bank like spokes of a massive, burning wheel, cloud wreathed around them. Within seconds, the fog was torn apart, and what lay beneath it was exposed to the light of the great red-tinged moon.

A line of spirit-walkers was entering the water half a league upstream of the bridge. Huge things of crudely shaped stone, each inhabited and animated by a Free Magic creature, they were immensely strong and almost impossible to harm with ordinary weapons. There were more than two score of them visible, and perhaps more already under the water.

'Why?' asked Touchstone. 'We can deal with spirit-walkers, particularly one by one as they come out the other side. A line abreast would make more sense. And big as they are, they're still going to get washed downstream a ways, and split up . . .'

'No,' said Sameth. He was looking through a telescope he had made himself, one magically augmented to increase available light. 'They're holding a chain of dark metal that will keep them together. But I do not think they are crossing to fight.'

He swung the telescope slowly along the northern bank. Without it, the others could see movement there, but not in enough detail to work out what was going on.

'Horse nomads,' said Sam, his voice suddenly very slow and deeper than usual. 'Thousands of them, I'd say, going back as far as I can see. They look as if they're preparing for a charge.'

'Across the river?' asked Touchstone.

'The spirit-walkers,' said Sabriel suddenly. 'The chain. It's all preparation for a spell. Freezing the water, perhaps. Or holding it back. They *will* charge across.'

'How do we stop them?' asked Ferin. 'We go out of the castles? They are too far away to shoot, even with your long-bows.'

'They can bypass the bridge, the castles and the camp, go on to kill and pillage wherever they want,' said Touchstone grimly. 'We don't have the mounted strength to pursue, or stop them. We'll have to try to hold them on the riverbank.'

'But there's *ten thousand* of them, maybe more,' protested Sam. He could see rank after rank of mounted nomads lining up on the northern bank, a vast column stretching back and back until the individual horses and warriors were indistinguishable, merging together so it was like looking at a forest or a feature of the landscape. It was all very orderly. He could almost believe it was some kind of illusion, though he knew it was not. 'We can't stop them!'

'We have to try,' said Touchstone. He looked through his own telescope for half a minute, then turned to the two aides who stood behind and snapped out orders. 'Send a messenger to the camp, everyone to move out *now* to take up defensive positions on the riverbank, the Guard to hold the centre where the charge will come. I will be there shortly to arrange the exact deployment. Another messenger to the North Castle – two-thirds of the garrison are to *run* south to join us at the riverbank. We'll take two-thirds from this bastion as well; tell Captain Kindred to pick them but to move immediately.'

'We have to break the spell!' said Sam, as soldiers ran down the steps behind with Touchstone's orders.

'There will be hundreds of Free Magic creatures *within* the chain; it must be the work of months or perhaps years,' said Sabriel grimly. 'It could not be unmade in hours, or even days.'

She took Sam's telescope and studied the monsters

lumbering into the water, and then the cavalry waiting in their patient lines.

'At least the spirit-walkers will have to stay on the riverbed. I can see no wood-weirds or sand-swimmers among that host on horseback,' said Sabriel. 'Sensibly, perhaps, for most horses are wary of such creatures, and they might disrupt the great charge they obviously plan. But it means they will likely be used against the bridge.'

She handed the telescope back to Sam, embraced him quickly, and turned to Touchstone.

'I will fight on the riverbank with you, my love.'

'You stay,' said Touchstone to Sam.

'But, Father –'

'I order you to take command here,' snapped Touchstone. 'Expect wood-weirds and the ilk. Hold out as long as you can. Lirael may still succeed. If Chlorr falls, this host will tear itself apart.'

He clapped Sam on the shoulder and he and Sabriel were gone, clattering down the stairs. Touchstone was already shouting orders for various officers to attend him.

'Hold out here?' asked Ferin. 'We should also go to the riverbank. That is where the battle will be!'

'With the North Castle stripped of troops, and only one-third of the garrison here, you will likely get plenty of fighting even if you stay right here with me,' said Sam.

'Ah,' said Ferin. 'That is different. You want me to fight at your side? I accept.'

* * *

'Hold my hands,' said Nick. 'Think of the Charter. Breathe slowly. Stay calm. You're the one who normally says that to me, by the way.'

'Yes,' said Lirael shakily. She took his hands and bent her head. At first there was nothing, and she felt the fear rise within her. Being cut off from the Charter was almost like not existing herself, as if . . . She fought off these feelings and tried to concentrate.

'It's there,' said Nick. 'I can sense it. Far away. But drawing closer.'

A single Charter mark blossomed in Lirael's mind. One small mark, an everyday mark, nothing in itself, one used for joining other marks together. But Lirael welcomed it joyfully, and then another followed, and another, and then there was a trickle of marks, all ones she knew, and more and more came, until the full flood returned and she felt the ocean of marks, the multitude, more than could possibly be known crash down upon her and flow through every part of her being.

Lirael opened her eyes, mouthed 'Thank you,' at Nick, and began to make her globe of air.

It was still more difficult than usual, but fortunately it was a spell she knew well, and one often used so that the marks themselves seemed to want to fall into place, the correct ones easy to find and take from the ceaseless flow of the Charter. When the spell was finished, Lirael raised her arms and let it spread around them, a glowing ball of light a dozen paces in diameter, with both her and Nick in the middle.

'Can you reach out and touch it?' asked Lirael anxiously.

Nick did so. As his hand touched the globe, the marks there grew brighter.

'I think you'll have to keep hold of the globe,' said Lirael. 'Otherwise it will just disappear when we cross that threshold of airlessness. Where the Charter vanishes entirely. You will have to sustain it.'

Nick looked across at the second flag, and then two or three hundred paces beyond that, to the third flag.

'If it fails, there's no way we can hold our breath long enough to make it back,' he said.

'No,' agreed Lirael. 'Just as there is no way the others can hold back the massed might of all the clans unless we can finish off Chlorr.'

'Well then,' said Nick lightly. 'I will be sure to keep it going.'

He raised his other hand so it also touched the globe, and wound his fingers around and through the glowing marks.

'Let's find out if it works,' said Lirael. She walked forward, and the globe moved with her, Nick stumbling along with his arms outstretched above his head.

'I look ridiculous,' he said. 'Though on the bright side, if there is a sorcerer out there they'll think I'm surrendering.'

'I don't think anyone is out there,' said Lirael. 'It is just the two of us, the only living things for leagues around. And the very first Chlorr, who has been in a sarcophagus for hundreds and hundreds of years, neither alive nor dead, but something in between.'

They walked on past the second flag. Nick found himself

taking a deep breath, but noticed Lirael didn't. He let the breath go as they continued on, and hoped she didn't notice. But of course she did.

'It works,' she said. 'Keep hold.'

Neither spoke again, as if talking might use more air, but they walked swiftly until they reached the third flag, and Lirael pointed to the little rise of ground some thirty paces away.

'It's under there,' she said. 'I'll dig. You need to hold the globe. I don't think it'll be far underneath.'

'No,' agreed Nick, scuffing with his foot. 'I reckon that's just wind-blown dirt that's piled up. At least I hope so. If it's hard-packed, we'd need a shovel and a pick.'

'And more air,' said Lirael. 'I just remembered the spell is for one person to have two hours of breathable air. But for two people, it will be half that. One single hour.'

'What's it been already?' asked Nick. 'Ten minutes? I'll . . . uh . . . breathe shallowly.'

'A little more than ten minutes, I think,' said Lirael, frowning. She stopped on top of the mound and knelt down. Nick crouched too, as the globe moved with her.

'Won't need to get out a plate,' said Lirael with satisfaction. She used the side of her golden hand to sweep back the loose soil, revealing a flat, worked stone beneath. A few minutes later, both of them moving backwards, she had cleared enough to reveal it to be a stone slab, the lid of a sarcophagus.

Strange, twisted symbols were carved into the stone. Not Charter marks, though they shivered and moved about. Nick averted his eyes from them. They made him feel sick but were also weirdly fascinating, and he had to resist the urge to touch them.

'Perversions of Charter marks,' said Lirael briefly. 'Free Magic. Spells to keep the sarcophagus secure and slay enemies. But too old and faded to have any effect now. Though I am glad I used my golden hand to sweep away the dirt.'

'So am I,' said Nick.

'The lid isn't very thick,' said Lirael, feeling with her golden hand. A few white sparks jetted out under her fingers, but no more, and after a moment the carved Free Magic symbols were still, all power spent. 'I think I can slide it off. Be careful to stay with me.'

She bent down low and pushed against the stone lid. At first it didn't move, but then it suddenly slid free, moving right across. Lirael slid with it, and so did the globe of air, Nick almost tripping over Lirael and into the sarcophagus as he tried to keep up and keep hold.

It was a fairly shallow coffin. Lirael looked into it, left hand on her sword hilt. Though it would be an awkward, same-side draw, at least she could be sure her hand would work.

Nick looked too.

'She's already dead,' he said, gazing down at the desiccated corpse in the sarcophagus. It was little more than a skeleton, with a few pieces of deeply yellowed skin here and there, and the rags of a funeral robe. 'How can you kill a bunch of bones?'

'Her spirit is still attached to it,' said Lirael heavily. 'Or rather, some fragment of her spirit. A small part that Chlorr didn't move to the new body.'

'So what . . . what do you need to do?' asked Nick.

'Go into Death,' said Lirael. 'And send the spirit on.'

'How long will that take?' asked Nick anxiously. 'Only . . . you know. The air . . .'

'Not long,' said Lirael. 'I'd best be quick. As before, try not to touch me.'

She hesitated, then closed her right hand into a fist that left space to hold a bell if her golden fingers did not work in Death. But she did not take out a bell, instead drawing Raminah as awkwardly as expected with her left hand.

'I'll miss you,' said Nick. He leaned in and kissed her. A soft, gentle kiss. Both of them had very cracked lips. 'Hurry back.'

'I will,' said Lirael.

She went into Death.

chapter thirty-seven

the river turns back

Greenwash Bridge,
the Old Kingdom/in Death

The full moon was so bright it was almost like daytime, so bright Sam could have read a book. The sky was completely clear, a multitude of stars making it brighter still.

Several silent, staring soldiers from the Bridge Company and the Trained Band of Orchyre who formed what was left of the mid-river garrison came up to the top of the tower to watch as the last three or four spirit-walkers waded in, carrying their chain of dark metal, to disappear under the swift waters of the river. But soon Sameth ordered everyone but the sentries and himself back down, to stand ready in case the nomads somehow managed to bypass the North Castle and get onto the bridge proper. Ferin, naturally, refused to go.

Sam kept looking out, occasionally using his telescope, which he had to constantly take back from Ferin. He saw his parents enter the camp, and there was suddenly a lot of movement there, with different formations coming down from the palisade walls to form up for the short march to the riverbank half a league to the west. Troops were marching out of the South Castle too, moving fast. The faint sound of all this hubbub could just be heard over the roar of the river, which was punctuated every now and then by the boom of a large piece of ice hitting the cutwaters of the piers or the rock of the bastion.

'The spell on the river begins,' said Ferin. 'Look at the northern side.'

Sam looked. The river shone with light, the reflection so huge in the water it was almost as if the moon had sunk there, dragging the stars down with it. At any other time, it would be extraordinarily beautiful. The river . . .

'It's stopped moving!' cried Sam. He stared at one particular spot, willing the break of white foam there to move. But it stayed where it was, and then, even more to Sam's horror, it started swirling backwards.

'The current is reversing?' asked Sam. 'But what will that do?'

'No,' said Ferin, who had much greater first-hand experience of this river. 'It is going back, true, but only a little way, and circling. It is as if a wall is rising where the spirit-walkers went in, a wall we cannot see. The water will not freeze, it will be held back, and then the Fazi, the Dnath, the Hrus, the Broal . . . all the horse-lovers, all the clans save my own, they will charge across the riverbed.'

Ferin was right, Sam could see. The river was swirling back from some invisible barrier, and it was growing shallower in front. A magical dam was rising all across the Greenwash.

'There must be something we can do,' he said desperately. 'When the river is dry, we will be able to attack the spirit-walkers. If we can get down there and break some of them, break the chain –'

'We would drown when the river comes back,' said Ferin. She looked along the river. 'Perhaps we will drown anyway. Surely, no spell can hold such a river forever. Once their army is across, where will all the held-back water go?'

Sam looked at the rising water, and then down below. Forty paces from the normal spring flood level to the deck of the bridge, a dozen paces up to the base of the rock where the tower was built, and the tower itself was eighty paces high and very solid. But water was extraordinarily powerful, and if all the spring flood of the Greenwash was backed up high and then let go . . .

He looked to the left and right. Both the North and South Castles were a good hundred paces beyond the riverbank, and were built on rocky outcrops, lifting them higher than the mid-river bastion, and their keeps rose higher and were massive. They might survive, but he was suddenly sure the tower where he stood would not.

'You think we have to get out anyway? North or south?'

'North,' said Ferin. 'Closer to the enemy.'

'Until they charge across,' said Sam.

'The horse warriors will charge,' said Ferin. 'But where are all their sorcerers and their keepers? And the Witch With No

Face? We cannot kill *her*, but we can kill sorcerers and keepers. Let's go and find some.'

'I don't know,' said Sam. 'Father told me to hold here, but if the river is released upon us once they get across . . .'

He looked at the river again. It was rising fast behind that unseen wall of magic, a strange and terrifying sight, muddy water climbing into the air, roiling backwards, spray flying as it met the barrier. The water was at least fifty paces higher than the normal waterline already, and in front the river was draining away, already low enough for him to see it had sunk fifteen paces or more below the western cutwaters of the bridge, which had been almost totally submerged only minutes before.

The thumping of many boots on the bridge decking below distracted him for a moment. Troops from the North Castle moving across, running as instructed. With the river already quieter, Sam could hear the bellowed commands, the shouts and catcalls, the clatter of arms and armour.

They were going to almost certain death, Sam knew. The small army on the southern bank, with Sabriel and Touchstone, and the Guard and the Rangers of the Clayr, could never hold against so many mounted warriors. Even the greatest Charter Mage could be killed by a lance through the throat, or an arrow in the eye.

And he and Ferin and his small garrison would certainly drown when Chlorr released the river again, as she was bound to do once the bulk of her troops were across. Drown without having done anything useful at all.

Sam felt fear rising inside him, rising as fast as the river climbed high in the air upstream. But it was not a fear of drowning, or of being killed. It was the fear of doing the wrong thing.

He could send to Touchstone for orders, but at the rate the river was falling in front of the dam, the nomads would be charging across the dry bed very soon. New orders would never come back in time.

Better to die fighting than to simply drown.

But better to fight and not die, if it could be done.

'We'll go to the North Castle,' said Sam. 'And then we'll see.'

But he spoke to empty air. Ferin was already hurtling down the steps, her crutches clattering like a drumbeat.

Lirael found the spirit without difficulty, almost as soon as she entered Death. Here, she appeared not as a dry and ancient corpse but a bright shape of spirit flesh, in the form of a young woman, only a few years older than Lirael herself. The spirit was suspended just below the surface of the river and her long black hair trailed about her shoulders, moving with the current of the river. She was dressed in what her physical body had been laid to rest in, a plain white robe, similar to the ones worn by the Clayr.

Her face was cruelly scarred. There was a misshapen, jagged X on her forehead where Lirael guessed there had once been a Charter mark, and raised welts on her cheeks. She would have been pretty once, or perhaps handsome would be a better word, for she had a strong, determined face. The scars were not good to look upon, but even so for a moment Lirael wondered why this woman had hidden behind a mask of bronze. A mask made by the Abhorsens for dealing with Free Magic things . . .

But there was no time for curiosity about such details, not when Lirael knew she must quickly return to Life, and she and Nick retreat from the airless plain. She braced herself against the current, raised Raminah high, and brought the sword down straight into the scarred woman's chest.

But the blade met no resistance in the spirit flesh, and Lirael almost lost her balance. She recovered, balancing on the balls of her feet, and then when she was sure the river could not take her, withdrew the sword.

There was no sign of any wound on the woman below her in the water. Raminah had done nothing. This fragment of spirit was too insubstantial for any weapons to work upon it, Lirael supposed. Even a Charter-spelled blade, for now they were in Death the Charter marks burned with new brilliance on Raminah, and Lirael's golden hand worked once again. Lirael could spare that no thought either, that the Charter should be here in Death, when it was not outside in Life.

She had more pressing problems. Lirael stared down at the suspended figure and tried to work out what to do. This relict of the original Chlorr *had* to be made to go beyond the Ninth Gate.

But how to do it?

Lirael ran her hand over her bells, wondering which to use.

Ranna she dismissed immediately. The woman was in the deepest possible sleep already. Mosrael needed slightly longer consideration, but that bell, too, she could not use. The Waker would send the woman out into Life, and Lirael further into Death. That was no use.

Kibeth. Her favourite bell, because Kibeth was the Disreputable Dog, and the Dog was Kibeth. But could Kibeth make such a suspended, inactive spirit walk? She did not think so.

Dyrim? Speaker was no use either. This was no silenced creature that needed a voice, nor one to be stilled.

Belgaer . . . the Thinker. To restore the patterns of a living person, to give them back what they once were, return independent thought . . . what would Belgaer do for this remnant spirit, something deliberately separated from the greater whole, to be planted in the river of Death for all eternity?

Saraneth, the deepest, lowest bell. Saraneth the Strong, used to bind the Dead to the ringer's will. But again, what could Saraneth do against this suspended spirit?

Then there was Astarael. Lirael's fingers hovered above the handle of his bell, but did not touch it. Astarael the Sorrowful, whose melancholy cry would cast all who heard her deep into Death. Everyone, including the ringer. Astarael would work, but she was well nicknamed Weeper. A bell of last resort.

Lirael thought for a few moments longer, then sheathed Raminah and drew Belgaer left-handed, keeping a tight grip on the clapper. Belgaer was very slippery, and could erase a mind – her mind – as easily as it might restore the sleeping woman's.

Belgaer sounded very loud in Death. A bright, clear note that Lirael felt through the bones of her head, clear into her brain. She swung it exactly as described in *The Book of the Dead*, silenced it immediately afterwards, and returned it to the bandolier.

Below her, the scarred woman's eyes opened. There was fear there, quickly overcome, and a moment later she burst from the water, coughing and spluttering, and grabbed at Lirael, who quickly stepped back. The river roared and coursed around the woman's legs, but somehow she held firm, still reaching out to Lirael.

'Go,' said the Abhorsen-in-Waiting. She drew Kibeth and rang it, and the woman spun around in answer to the bell's rising, exuberant call. She took two steps . . . three . . . but then stopped and turned around.

'I would if I could,' she said, her voice husky and weak. 'I think. But I can't. She . . . I . . . have made sure of that.'

She lifted one foot out of the river, and Lirael saw her ankle was bound with a thick black rope that led back to the point where she had been submerged. Not some slim thread designed to alert a necromancer to change, but a spell-rope of great power, used to fix the spirit in place.

'By "she" and "I", you mean Chlorr, don't you?' said Lirael. 'You are Chlorr.'

'I am the part of her that would not become what she became, when I found Free Magic again and had to make my choice,' said the woman quietly. 'Tell me: you are obviously an Abhorsen, but why do you also wear the blazon of the Clayr?'

'I am of both lineages,' said Lirael. She walked carefully over to where the binding cable was secured, setting her feet hard against the current, to inspect the strands of darkness. This was Free Magic of a high order. It could be undone with the bells, but first she had to find out how it had been made. Lirael cursed under her breath and knelt down, making sure she had a strong stance while also keeping an eye on the woman. She seemed unarmed and innocuous, but even a spirit fragment of Chlorr had to be dangerous.

Time passed differently in Death, but Lirael grudged every passing minute. She and Nick had to go soon, back to the second flag, back to where they could once again fill their lungs.

'Are you the Abhorsen yourself?' asked the woman.

'Abhorsen-in-Waiting,' said Lirael. She found another thread under the water, a trip wire, running off along the border of Life and Death. It was thrumming as if someone plucked at it far away, the vibrations travelling a great distance.

So now Chlorr knew that the anchor which kept her from the final Death had come adrift, for that black thread could lead nowhere else.

'Who is the Abhorsen now? Is it still Belatiel?'

'I know Belatiel only as a name on a list of past Abhorsens from long, long ago,' said Lirael. She felt the cable, trying to sense how it had been made, which bell had fixed it in place. It could be unmade by the same bell, but Lirael needed to know something else as well.

'What is your name, by the way? Who were you before you became Chlorr of the Mask?'

'Belatiel an Abhorsen from long, long ago?'

The woman frowned and gazed out on the river, as if she could see something which Lirael could not.

'It seems only yesterday I . . . we . . . were exiled, and for years I resisted temptation, did not seek to find new powers. But then, by pure chance or so I must suppose, I found the bottle . . .'

'What is your name?' asked Lirael.

'Azagrasir was within,' whispered the woman. 'For a long time I did not open it, thinking myself strong. But I was not. I undid the stopper, and Azagrasir came forth. We fought, and though I compelled it to serve me, I was badly wounded and like to die. There was a woman, a young woman of the Dnath, who served me. Azagrasir told me, told us I . . . we could take her body, to live on. I refused; despite everything else I would not do that. Yes, it is true I could not resist the lure of Free Magic . . . but I would not steal another's body. Yet I must have done. I see we did. Though I am also here . . .'

'Tell me your name,' repeated Lirael. Names had power, particularly here in Death.

'My parents were goldsmiths in Belisaere. My mother the most famous of them all. Jaciel. But *her* father was the Abhorsen, and the King our cousin,' said the woman. She was still staring out across the river, seeing something else. 'I am the grand-daughter of the Abhorsen.'

'Tell me your name!' snapped Lirael. She looked nervously in the same direction as the scarred woman, wondering what she looked at. Lirael could see nothing unusual, just the featureless river, the melancholy grey light. 'I need to know your name!'

'She comes,' said the woman. 'Or I do. It is confusing. I am remembering things that have not yet happened. Or had not happened when I was put here. I . . . she . . . has used so many bodies, so many young women . . .'

Tears fell like bright crystals, following the scars along her cheeks, only to instantly darken as they hit the river, to break and swirl away as if they were in fact drops of blood.

'And now she has no body at all?' whispered the woman. 'She is a creature of Death? That is what I have become?'

Lirael drew Saraneth and was about to ring it, to command an answer to her question, when the woman looked directly at her, and their gaze met.

'My name is Clariel,' she said very clearly. 'Abhorsen, please help me die the final death. We must hurry, before she comes.'

chapter thirty-eight

wasted fish upon the riverbed

In Death/Greenwash Bridge, the Old Kingdom

'She comes?' asked Lirael. 'Chlorr?'

'Her, and many Dead servants,' said Clariel, almost dreamily. 'She leaves a great battle, being fought by a mighty river . . . it is the Greenwash, I think, though strangely dry . . . I am . . . she is furious, enraged that I am awake, that I know myself again. It has come when she is most busy, the battle needing her direction . . . but now she must come here . . . to snap me up, make us whole again . . . No . . . no . . . You must help me go before she comes! I am the lesser part; I will not be able to resist should she draw close.'

'I'm trying,' said Lirael through gritted teeth. She had put Saraneth away and knelt back down into the icy water to lift a coil of the dark cable. But she still could not determine how the spell-rope had been made. Several bells had been used in its weaving, and she simply did not know how to unravel it. 'Who comes with Chlorr? How many exactly?'

'Dozens,' said Clariel. 'Shadow Hands. I am afraid of you, I mean she is, but not as much as if it were Sabriel.'

'How do you know about Sabriel –' Lirael started to say. Then a horrible thought crossed her mind. 'You can see what Chlorr sees, you know her thoughts. Can she do the same with you?'

'Yes,' said Clariel. 'Of course. We are one. Though I am slow, there is so much in my head, her head, so many things done. Terrible things . . . I am what she was; she is what I became. Hurry, there is little time. I do not know Death as she does. She comes swiftly and thinks she will soon slay you and take me back. Hurry!'

Lirael stood up, ignoring the river's sudden grab at her knees. She thought of Nick, out there in the airless plain, and felt a terrible pang in her heart. Was it already too late? Had she spent too long in Death? Would he turn and run back when her body crumpled, the ice cracked, and she lay dead at his feet?

She hoped he would, but feared he would not.

'This is what it is, to be an Abhorsen,' she said sadly, and drew Astarael.

The Greenwash rose sixty paces above the usual waterline, a churning rampart of muddy water from bank to bank. Everywhere downstream of the magic wall made by the spirit-walkers and their black iron chain was now a broad expanse of drying rock and mud, dotted everywhere with the silvery shapes of thousands of dying fish, and here and there the tumbled wrecks of long-lost boats, everything from sunken rafts used in the construction of the bridge to the narrow war boats of the clans, destroyed in attacks of long ago.

Sam and Ferin were in the North Castle now, on the wall. Both had bows in their hands, quivers leaning against the wall, arrows ready, waiting for the next attack. They had not needed to go further in search of sorcerers and keepers, for they were here aplenty. Dozens of wood-weirds had charged the walls only minutes after Sam had led his garrison into the castle, running from the south tower that joined the bridge straight to the battlements in answer to frantic blasts of the alarm horns.

But the wood-weirds came not to try to scale the high walls but to hurl great tubs of stone into the moat, under a storm of Charter-spelled arrows that left only four or five able to retire. The rest stood out there, no longer wood-weirds, now just burning stumps.

The second wave had been much harder to shoot at, for it was composed of forty sand-swimmers, huge undulating mounds of sand and grit that shimmered over the ground and were hard to differentiate from the earth around them. But again, they did not try to slither up the walls but instead poured themselves into the moat, filling the gaps between the tubs of stone. There, they were destroyed by more Charter-spelled arrows and spells cast by Sam and several Charter Mages from the Bridge Company.

But their work was done. The inhabiting Free Magic creatures had been banished or bound; the sand-swimmers became the raw sand and stone of their making, vast quantities of solid material, filling the moat for a stretch of two hundred paces, so the next assault could come right up to the walls. Sam could see this third wave preparing in the distance, four or five hundred warriors on foot. Out of bowshot, but well within sight, under the brilliant moon.

'I feared this,' said Ferin, and tore at her hair, releasing the queue she normally wore tightly coiled around her head.

'What?' asked Sam. They were very much outnumbered by the line of enemy forming up, but they did not look particularly formidable. They had no scaling ladders or any other siege equipment, and the walls above the moat were fifty paces high. Nor was there the glint of silver chain to show the presence of keepers and their charges, and the few wood-weirds who had survived the first assault had disappeared altogether.

'You will see,' said Ferin. 'Look, they reverse their coats, so we might see who we face, and gain honour from the knowledge.'

There was a flash of white in that line of warriors, and then another. It took Sam a moment to realise what he was looking at. They were turning their coats inside out, to show the white fur of the *athask*, great cat of the northwestern mountains.

'Your people,' said Sam.

'Yes . . . and no,' said Ferin. 'I am the Offering, the one they would give up so the clan may live. The best and the least.'

'Go to the northern wall, or the west,' said Sam. 'There will be other clans to fight there.'

'No,' said Ferin. 'You will need me here. They will be on the walls soon enough, and there are too few defenders.'

'But they have no ladders, no ram for the gate . . .'

'The Athask shoot ropes, and the Athask climb,' said Ferin, with considerable pride, alloyed with sadness. 'We must not let them get close. And perhaps . . . perhaps there is still a chance Lirael will slay the Witch With No Face, and we will live after all – you, me and the Athask.'

Sam began to say something, but it was lost in the sudden, ground-shaking sound of hundreds of nomad horn-blasts, mixed with the cheer from ten thousand nomad throats, and most of all the deep thunderous shudder of ten thousand horses breaking into a trot and then a canter and then, as they reached the flat, rocky bottom of the river, the full-out gallop of their charge.

'It is too late,' said Sam.

He reached down for an arrow, but his hand froze as his fingers met soft fur, and he looked down at two small almond-shaped eyes, bright emeralds in the moonshadow of the battlements.

'What's too late?' asked Mogget.

'Hold on to my hand,' said Lirael. 'Hold very tight!'

She thrust her golden hand at Clariel, who gripped it with both her own.

Lirael swung Astarael up, let go of the clapper, and caught

the bell by the handle as it fell, letting it swing behind her and up again in one great arc. As it moved, the bell sang one pure note, a sound that cut through Lirael everywhere, as if she were pierced all over by a thousand hair-fine needles.

Lirael screamed, her scream joining Astarael's call, and in that moment the river of Death rose up around her with sudden, tremendous force. She was picked up and thrown forward, tumbling and choking, thrust through the water-falls of the First Gate, no spells needed to open the way beyond Astarael's imperious, mournful cry; and then through the Second Precinct in one shocking, drowning swoop, Clariel smashing against her, though her spirit form was so slight Lirael barely felt the knocks, and she tried to drop Astarael but the bell was stuck fast to her hand and it kept on ringing, ringing with the one terrible single note of doom.

Onwards they went, straight down the whirlpool of the Second Gate, gasping for air, then bumping and sliding as the waters froze and the whirlpool became a spiral path, and they were dumped out into the Third Precinct, but only for a few seconds, the wave there catching them as Lirael staggered to her feet and once again tried to still the bell. But her hand, her hand of normal flesh, would not obey, and before she knew it she was underwater again, rushing through the mists of the Third Gate, surrounded by yammering, panicked, desperate Dead who had been picked up by the wave or caught by Astarael, the Dead washing one way and Lirael and Clariel another; and then they were in the Fourth Precinct, and Lirael exerted every scrap of will she possessed and made her hand move, and somehow she got the bell back into its pouch on her bandolier, and it was still.

The current was much stronger here than it had been closer to Life. Lirael slipped several paces before she could get her feet set, and lean the opposite way from the river's pull.

'Let go,' she said to Clariel. There was still a chance, after all, a chance she could get back to Life, get back to Nick before he died, choking for want of air. Astarael had not flung her as far as she had feared. 'The river will take you.'

'Thank you,' said Clariel. She bent her head, let go of Lirael's golden hand, and fell back into the river.

But the current did not take her. She floated there on her back, a puzzled look slowly gathering on her scarred face, while Lirael looked on in horror. Then Clariel slowly lifted one foot out of the water.

The dark spell-rope was still there. She could not go on unless it was broken, unmade, and Lirael did not know how this could be done.

Lirael shut her eyes, just for a moment; then she slowly took Astarael from the bandolier once more. Pins and needles shot through her fingers as she did so, and she could feel the bell shivering under her hand. Astarael was keen to sound again, to take them further.

Lirael knew she had no choice. She would have to go with Clariel to the Ninth Precinct, to stand with her beneath the unforgiving stars of the Ninth Gate. There was no spell-rope strong enough to hold against the Ninth Gate's call to a final death.

She swung the bell up and released the clapper.

'Mogget!' exclaimed Sam. He bent down and tried to embrace the little white cat, who avoided the move by zipping between Sam's legs. 'What are you doing here?'

'I smelled the fish,' said Mogget. 'Thousands of good salmon gone to waste. I smelled the Free Magic too, and I was curious.'

'Will you help us?' asked Sam swiftly. 'I know we cannot compel you. I ask as a . . . a friend.'

'What . . . who is that?' hissed Ferin.

'I am Mogget,' said the cat. 'Nice coat. I trust you fought fair for it?'

'Knife against claws, as is the custom,' said Ferin, very slowly. She kept staring at Mogget, then slowly hopped her crutches sideways to lower herself on one knee and incline her head, greatly surprising Sam. She hadn't done that for Touchstone. 'Are you . . . are you the *athask*? The great one?'

'Maybe,' said Mogget. 'I can't remember.'

'Mogget, can you break Chlorr's dam? Mother, Father, they're fighting on the other side, but if we could drown most of the cavalry –'

'No,' said Mogget blandly. 'None of my business. As I said, I was merely curious.'

'I knew you couldn't be the *athask*,' said Ferin, grumpily getting back up on her crutches and settling herself against the merlon so she could ready her bow again. 'Too small and too —'

Mogget blazed brighter than a star, and there was suddenly a huge white cat upon the wall, one three times the size of a nomad horse. He put his head back and yowled with tremendous energy outwards to the moon and the advancing nomads under it, a caterwaul that reeked of Free Magic, white sparks spraying out for tens of paces, accompanied by great gouts of white smoke and an almost overwhelming stench of hot metal. Then he lowered his face to yowl more softly at Ferin, who covered her face with one arm, fell off her crutches, and would have gone backwards off the wall to certain death if Sam hadn't flung himself forward and caught her.

'If you won't help, then go!' shouted Sam, holding Ferin with one hand as he clutched at an iron staple in the wall, his heart hammering with panic. 'I'm never going to catch a fish for you again! Or get you sardines from Ancelstierre!'

'You don't have to be like that,' said Mogget, shrinking down to his normal size. His green eyes twinkled. 'I have helped *you*. In a small way, I admit. But surely it's better than nothing. The rest is up to you lot, though I do hope you can make Chlorr regret interfering with one of my favourite rivers *and the fish in it.*'

With that, he leaped over the wall and was gone. The cat shouted something as he jumped, about sardine tins always rusting and the fish tasting terrible, but Sam paid no attention to that. He was too busy hauling Ferin in. As she fell across an embrasure, Sam let her go, wincing as he felt a muscle in his left arm stretch almost to tearing point. He massaged it, already thinking about a healing spell he would have to use, and quickly, so he could once again take up his bow . . .

Ferin made a noise, something between a choking laugh and a gasp of amazement.

Sam forgot his arm, and looked out over her head at the line of Athask warriors. They were not charging forward, but were instead in the process of reversing their coats once again, and those who had already done so were slipping away, in the opposite direction from the castle.

'So that was the *athask*, then?' asked Ferin in the smallest voice Sam had ever heard come from her, one filled with wonderment. 'He has given us his protection, and the clan have seen.'

'Maybe he is . . .' said Sam. He eyed the retreating mountaineers with relief, tempered by the knowledge they were only a small part of Chlorr's great host. 'I'll tell you about Mogget later. He's tricky. I wish he would have done more . . . it's all up to Lirael and Nick now. There's . . . there's no way Dad and Mother can hold the southern bank. Not against so many.'

'Then let us shoot some more, and make them fewer,' said Ferin. 'And hope Lirael can do what must be done. What else can *we* do?'

'Nothing,' said Sam grimly, and picked up his bow.

chapter thirty-nine

a time to die

Beyond the Great Rift/in Death

Nick looked worriedly at Lirael's ice-encased form once again, and continued counting. As soon as she had gone into Death he had done a rough calculation of the amount of air within the globe, and though he wasn't sure of the exact amount two humans would use, he figured what Lirael had said about the spell was probably right. One hour for two people, and they had used fifteen minutes even before Lirael went into Death. That's how long it would take to get back to where they could breathe.

'Nine hundred and eleven hippopotami,' said Nick. His arms hurt, but he kept them up, kept holding the globe. 'Nine hundred and twelve hippopotami.'

When he got to a thousand, he thought, he could drop the 'hippopotamus.' The numbers would be long enough said to be a full second. But when he got to a thousand seconds, they would have been stationery out here just over half an hour. There would be only fifteen minutes left for them to get back.

'Come on, come on,' he whispered. 'Come back to me,

Lirael. Come back. Damn. That must be four seconds . . .
nine hundred and twenty hippopotami . . . nine hundred
and twenty-one hoppopittami . . . damn again, I should
have used potato . . . okay . . . nine hundred and twenty-
three hippopotato, I mean nine hundred and twenty-four
potatoes . . .'

Something moved on Lirael, on her ribs, low on the left.
Ice cracked over the smallest pocket of her bandolier. Nick
stopped counting and stared at it, wondering what it meant
and what he should do. He counted the pockets while he
tried to remember the names of the bells. Lirael had talked
about them a little. So had Sam, but Nick couldn't remember,
and the pocket seemed to be the eighth from the top . . . he
counted them again, got eight again . . . but that couldn't be
right. There were only seven bells.

A long, pointy, tan-coloured ear suddenly stuck out of the
pocket, followed by the curve of a head, and another pointy
ear.

Nick drew his sword while keeping his left hand firmly
on the globe.

The complete long-snouted head of a dog burst out of
the pocket, and about two-thirds of a leg ending in a large
paw.

'Put that sword away and help me out!' barked the
Disreputable Dog. 'Hurry! No, don't let go of the globe.'

Nick dropped his sword, gaped for only a second, which
was far less time than he felt like gaping, and reached across
to pull on the Dog's foreleg. As he touched it, he felt the

sudden surge of both Charter Magic and Free Magic flow into his body.

The Dog came out all in a rush. She was smaller than Nick remembered from when she had sent him back into Life, but she was still the same pointy-eared, lolling-tongued, black-backed, mostly tan-coloured mongrel. She shook herself violently for several seconds, drops of icy water spraying all over Nick.

'Listen,' said the Dog quickly. 'You will need to put more of yourself into the globe and breathe less.'

'Breathe less! And what do you mean put more of myself?' asked Nick. 'What's happening?'

He could feel himself trembling from fear, fear for Lirael.

'Lirael has had to ring Astarael,' snapped the Dog. 'Lie down with your hands out to keep contact with the globe. You must feel the Charter within you, let it flow through your hands, give it to the globe. Shut your eyes and breathe shallowly. And stop that stupid counting.'

'Can you help her?' asked Nick, fighting the panic he suddenly felt, the urge to not breathe shallowly but to gulp air as fast as he could.

'No,' said the Dog sadly. 'But you can, if she makes it back.'

She went on point, nose forward, leg up – and then was gone, an intensely cold breeze rushing over Nick from where she had been. In her place, the little soapstone statuette balanced on two legs for a moment, and then fell over.

Nick took one last deep breath and edged forward, bringing his arms down, making sure he was still keeping hold of the side of the globe of air. Then he knelt, and lay down on his side so he could still see Lirael, though she was now entirely encased in ice. His arms felt like lumps of dead meat he had been holding them up so long, and he laughed dully at how stupid he'd been. It was much easier to touch the globe while lying down.

He felt the marks under his fingers, shut his eyes, and concentrated on the Charter that moved within him, swirling and shifting around the inner fire of Free Magic, willing both to rise, to move through him and into the magic that sustained his and Lirael's life.

Through the Fourth Gate, tumbling madly, rushed through the Fifth Precinct by a current so swift Lirael barely glimpsed the Dark Path above, and then she and Clariel were flung upside down and lifted up, swept high by the reverse waterfall of the Fifth Gate, spat out again in the shallow waters of the Sixth Precinct, where Lirael and Sabriel had talked of Chlorr so few scant weeks ago, but still Astarael sounded and Lirael's throat was raw from screaming and so she did nothing but croak and whimper as the Sixth Gate opened beneath their feet and they fell from the river upon dry ground, or something that supported them and was not the river, a circle some ten paces around, and it sank with them, the water rising all around, and again Lirael did not try to still the bell, but kept it ringing.

Deeper and deeper the small circle fell, the river around them but not crashing in, until they came to a stop and the water fell away on all sides, frothing and roaring, though Lirael hardly heard it, for she could hear almost nothing but Astarael's single note, the sound of a dying scream.

The river took them up again, the current lifting them, sending them like two tiny, bobbing corks to the endless line of fire that burned ahead, flames dancing on the water. This fire arched up as they approached, in answer to Astarael's call, as all the gates so answered, opening the way.

The Eighth Precinct was normally a place of great danger, where patches of fire burned upon the water, without apparent pattern or cause. But none would burn where Astarael rang, and the river took them on, rushing them, twisting and turning, Clariel holding tight to Lirael's golden hand.

The Eighth Gate was darkness, darkness complete and the absence of all the senses. No sight, no sound, no sense of touch or smell. Lirael wept as Astarael fell silent for those few seconds as they passed, or she thought she wept, for she could feel no tears.

The Ninth Precinct. Astarael was silent now, at last. Lirael slowly and clumsily returned the bell to the bandolier with her left hand. She kept her head down as she did so, knowing not to look up. The river was shallow here, only up to her ankles, and there was no current. The water was even warm, and it did not feed feelings of inadequacy and hopelessness.

Even looking down, with her eyes scrunched as close as she dared, Lirael could see starlight reflected in the water.

'It is so beautiful,' whispered Clariel. 'Like night in the

Great Forest, only more so . . . the sky . . . the stars. I should have come here so long ago. I thank you, Lirael.'

'But I do not,' snarled a voice from behind, a voice that crackled with Free Magic.

Lirael flung herself sideways as a flaming blade came down, smashing through the water, exploding the reflected stars. She drew Raminah, the blade bright with Charter marks, and just managed to parry a savage cut, gouts of white sparks flying as the two magics met and fought.

Her attacker was Chlorr of the Mask. Alone, for her Shadow Hands were left far behind, unable to move so swiftly in Death. She was a hulking shape of darkness and fire, wielding a blade of flame twice the length of Raminah. But Chlorr was strangely hunched over, as if already wounded, and she kept her head firmly down, the fires that burned there in the suggestion of the mask she had once worn dripping molten bronze-coloured drops which sizzled in the water and sent up small fountains of steam and choking smoke.

Lirael backed up, parrying another strike. She had to hold out for only a few minutes, she knew, before Chlorr would be unable to resist the compulsion to look up, to look up to the stars of the Ninth Gate. Lirael could feel the unbearable attraction too, almost as if someone were holding her, gently but so very firmly, tilting her head back . . . Lirael grimaced as she found she was doing exactly that, and jerked her eyes back down.

But in that instant, she caught a glimpse of a night sky above, a sky of perfect black velvet, so thick with stars they were one unimaginably vast and luminous cloud, sending down a light softer but as bright as a summer morning's sun out in the living world.

Many Dead rose towards that sea of stars above. Dead everywhere, but they were no threat. They came through the Eighth Gate and waded for a little way, or hardly at all, but soon enough all were caught by the stars above, and were lifted up, to go beyond to the final death from which there was no return.

Chlorr attacked again and Lirael parried, gasping at the strength of the blow. Raminah would have been torn from her grasp, but she brought her right hand up, her golden hand. The Charter marks on it shone brighter than ever, making it look as if it were molten gold. Chlorr winced back from that light too, as she did from the stars above.

Lirael wielded her sword two-handed. She parried Chlorr's blows, and stepped back again and again, always hoping that in the next moment Chlorr would look up. But the creature didn't, and with each blow Lirael felt herself weaken. She almost stumbled and narrowly avoided the next savage cut.

Then she did stumble, falling backwards into the river. She looked up and saw not stars, but the great dark bulk of Chlorr, the terrible sword rising for the final blow. Lirael tried to lift Raminah to parry, though she knew it was hopeless.

It was all for nothing. Lirael had brought Clariel to the brink of the Ninth Gate, but she had failed. Chlorr was too strong.

But the fiery blade did not come down. A small, scarred

woman, her arms outstretched, stepped in front of her greater self, standing between the huge creature of shadow and Lirael.

'Come,' said Clariel.

Chlorr slowly lowered her sword, and the red flames that licked along the blade went out. It was a reluctant movement, as if the Greater Dead answered to some unseen force, like a hunting dog called by a whistle, taken from its kill.

But the sword did not stay down. Chlorr made a noise, a dry clattering chuckle. She lifted the sword again and swung it back, clearly intending to sweep away the annoying remnant of her past, the tiny fragment of lost humanity who had so long served to keep her from the final death.

But in swinging back, Chlorr looked up, and was caught by the stars.

In that same moment Clariel stepped forward and closed her arms around the shadow-stuff of Chlorr, resting her head against the fires that burned and flickered over the creature's chest. Clariel's eyes were open, clear-sighted, knowing what she did.

'This path, I choose,' whispered Clariel. She spoke very low, but Lirael heard her clearly. Her voice was strangely like a bell.

Chlorr's sword fell, and was lost in the river. She seemed suddenly smaller, diminished and lost.

Greater Dead and remnant spirit rose to the sky together. Starlight wreathed them both, quenching the fires, stripping back the shadows, smoothing the scars away. Shadow and fire joined with shining spirit to become one again. A young woman who until the very end chose neither wisely nor well, and who had *existed* for centuries, but had died long ago.

Lirael found herself looking up, watching Clariel ascend, though she had not meant to do so. She wondered who she had been, this daughter of goldsmiths, and how she had become a sorcerer, a necromancer, and then one of the Greater Dead. Perhaps there would be something about her in the Library, Lirael thought. She would look it up.

Or not, for the Ninth Gate called.

It was time to rest. Lirael had done what was needed, for the second time. She felt the waters stir around her feet as the river let go and she began to rise.

'For everyone and everything, there is a time to die,' whispered Lirael. She knew too much time must have passed out in Life; there could be no way back for her and Nick. But, she suddenly thought, there might be enough air remaining for last farewells, and then they could die together, though she so much would have liked for them both to live.

'The third time, you will have me, but not before!' called Lirael, and forced her gaze down. A moment later she splashed back in the river, spray flying everywhere, though she sprang immediately from the water. She was suddenly consumed by the idea of seeing Nick again, to kiss him one last time, to go together into Death, to not go alone.

She had lived so long alone, and found new love too late. Now she was determined to wring even just a few more seconds from what she had so unexpectedly been given.

Lirael strode towards the Eighth Gate, the words of opening rising in her mind, and *hurry, hurry, hurry* beating a rhythm in her head. No dangers of Death, no Dead must be allowed to delay her; she would be swifter than she had ever been, the river's current helpless –

But the first word of opening fell silent in her mouth as she saw a familiar figure by the wall of darkness. A tan shape with sticking-up ears clearly outlined against the Gate, patiently waiting for her mistress, as she had waited by doors and gates and passages so many, many times before.

'Dog! Oh Dog!' wept Lirael, running forward to hug the dog around the neck, lifting her partly off the ground, so she had to rise on her haunches and balance her forepaws on Lirael's shoulders.

'Now, now,' said the Dog, gently licking Lirael's ear. 'I have come to run with you back to Life. We must hurry. Your young man sustains the globe of air, but he really *doesn't* know what he's doing.'

chapter forty

the return of lirael

Beyond the Great Rift

Ice cracked. Nick's eyes flashed open, but he managed to turn his gasp into a choke, so he did not draw in a breath. He struggled to his feet, now more careful than ever to keep his hands out and touching the globe. It had grown very warm inside, and the air was stale, but there *was* still air, and Nick somehow knew the spell was not yet close to failure; he could instinctively feel the strength of the marks.

More ice cracked, and Lirael came laughing to wrap her arms around him, though he could only respond by burying his face in her neck.

'Very nice,' croaked Nick. 'But we have to hurry back.'

'Yes,' said Lirael. She bent and picked up his sword, quickly sliding it home in the scabbard at his side, and then bent again to take up the little dog statuette. That she kept tight in her hand as she grabbed Nick's arm and they began to walk back towards the next flag. At first slowly, and then a little more swiftly, as Lirael sniffed at the air and found it more stagnant and far less refreshing than she'd hoped.

They did not speak until they staggered past the second flag and on a dozen paces to be sure. Before Lirael could dismiss the spell, or Nick let go, the globe fell apart around them, Charter marks dropping like dead moths to disappear into the stony ground.

Nick took a deep, shuddering breath, and filled his lungs. He whooped and grabbed Lirael and they went to kiss and banged their heads together and tried again, and then turned together to walk side by side towards the edge of the Rift. Nick held Lirael's golden hand, and Charter marks drifted slowly out of his skin and across her own. More and more marks flowed across, and slowly the gold began to glow again, and Lirael flexed her fingers and smiled.

'It's a long way back,' she said softly.

Nick shrugged and held her hand tighter.

'Not so far as we have come already,' he said.

'Yes,' said Lirael.

'Why were you laughing?' asked Nick. 'When you returned from Death?'

'Something the Dog said, something funny, but also it just made me happy,' replied Lirael.

'What did she say?' asked Nick. 'I mean, if you don't mind me asking?'

'I don't mind,' said Lirael. 'I thought I would never see her again, you know. She said my time with her had passed. But then, she came to me in Death . . .'

'And to me,' said Nick. 'She told me what to do.'

'And coming back, we talked, and she said . . . she said . . .'

Lirael started laughing again, the laughter that comes after a great fear is gone, a terrible enemy vanquished, and there is hope once more.

'She said she would come to our wedding,' said Lirael, half choked with laughter. 'She would dance at our wedding! Can you imagine, the Dog dancing! But it means I will see her again!'

'I like the sound of *our wedding*,' said Nick, straight-faced. 'Where would we have it? Your aunt Kirrith's place? That'd be *very* nice.'

Lirael laughed again, and they hugged as they walked, almost making themselves fall over. Nick started to laugh too, and giggling like small children, they began to run hand in hand towards the Great Rift and the start of the journey home.

epilogue

If the appearance of their tribal fetish and Mogget's expression of displeasure to the Athask was the first turning point in the Battle of the Greenwash Bridge, the absence of Chlorr was the second. She had gathered all the war leaders of the clans together on the riverbank, to keep them close and under her direction. Her sudden vanishing, and of many of the Dead she had with her, combined with the lack of any kind of second in command, caused the war leaders to immediately disagree on what everyone should be doing.

The disagreements quickly became arguments, and then the arguments duels, and the fighting of the leaders swiftly spread to the sorcerers and their keepers, and then to the lesser commanders, and from there to ordinary clan folk. Within a short time, almost all the nomads not actively fighting the Old Kingdom forces were fighting one another, and very soon after that, most of them realised that with everyone gathered at the bridge, there was nobody defending their homelands.

Or their neighbours' homelands. Whoever got back first would have the opportunity to settle every old feud with ease, and create the circumstances for dozens of new ones.

But though Chlorr was absent, she was not yet dead, and the chain-spell continued to hold back the river, and there were still many thousands of horse nomads fighting on the southern bank, even if the rear ranks were turning about to fight their former allies of five minutes before.

Sam and Ferin were among the first to see the change, and it was Ferin who pointed out where the Moon Horse warriors were trying to turn their horses back; and that the Ghost Horse clan were starting to ride away westwards along the northern bank; and the Yrus were no longer pushing new lines of warriors into the melee on the southern bank, where the Old Kingdom forces still held on, though they had been forced back several hundred paces from the river, and were surrounded on three sides.

Charter Magic spells flashed and sparked in that fierce combat, but so also did long whips of Free Magic fire, and the Old Kingdom army was still greatly outnumbered. Sam's heart was very heavy as he watched from the outer wall of the North Castle. Not through his telescope, because he did not want to see too well, did not want to see the end that must be coming, did not want to know if Sabriel and Touchstone had already fallen.

'I guess Lirael and Nick have failed,' he said heavily to Ferin. 'It will be an outright slaughter soon.'

Ferin watched by his side, and she was using the telescope.

She was quiet now they were largely out of the battle, at least for now. Much of her bravado was an act, Sam realised, to raise both her own spirits and those of the people around her. It worked very well.

'The chain on the riverbed,' said Ferin quite conversationally. 'The red fire on it . . .'

'What?' asked Sam. He tried to snatch the telescope back, but Ferin held it tight.

'It's going out.'

As the Free Magic fires in the chain died, so the spell holding back the river ebbed. Water began to trickle down from on high, hundreds of rivulets sliding through the air as if slopping over the side of a vast glass bathtub. Half a minute later the rivulets joined to become a solid sheet of water, a waterfall suddenly smashing down from eighty paces above the dry riverbed.

Sam stopped trying to grab the telescope and grabbed Ferin's crutches instead, slapping them under her arms.

'Get to the keep!' he shouted, waving at the others on the wall. 'Get to the keep! The river's coming back!'

A few seconds later, the invisible wall that had been slowly crumbling gave way entirely, and the vast mass of water that had been held back all came crashing down at once.

The wave was three times as high as the bridge, which disappeared under it with a titanic crack that was heard fifty leagues away. Water spurted even higher as the wave parted around the mid-river bastion, and spread sideways. These only slightly lesser side waves smashed against the outer walls of both North and South Castles, overtopping them to flood the outer baileys. The temporary camp on the southern side was swept away in an instant.

So too were most of the nomads still fighting, and a great many Old Kingdom soldiers. There would be mourning in Navis, and Sindle, and most of all in Belisaere, for almost the entire Trained Band of the Guild of Vintners was closest to the river, and they were all drowned or swept away.

Sabriel and Touchstone survived, though both were wounded. They rested on their swords for a moment, and looked at each other. They had survived many battles, some even more dire than this. Both knew there would be more battles, and one day, perhaps one or the other would not survive.

'The bastion tower stands,' said Sabriel, with relief. 'Sam should be all right. And the Athask girl, Ferin.'

They exchanged a private look, one of parental amusement at the trouble Sam might be finding himself in in the near future.

'And Lirael?' asked Touchstone. 'She has succeeded, but . . .'

'I would have felt her die,' said Sabriel. An Abhorsen always knew when another died. 'There was a moment . . . but no, I am sure she lives. I do so hope Nick survived, for she needs . . . she *deserves* some happiness, if anyone ever did.'

They had to stop talking then, as officers clamoured for attention, and the work of dealing with the wounded from both sides and clearing away damage began. The few nomads who had survived the great wave tried to fight on, but they did not fight hard, and soon succumbed to Charter spells of sleep and restraint, for they would not surrender if they could still hold a weapon.

Halfway up the keep of the northern river fort, in a room knee-deep in river water, Sam was retrieving Ferin's floating crutches. She sat up next to an archer's window slit that was still dripping water, on a kind of mound made up of empty arrow crates and the thick mats that could be put out to protect the wall from the stones cast by siege engines. She was holding up her leg and looking at her stump.

'I don't want a golden foot,' said Ferin. 'No good for night work. Black is good.'

'You'll be wearing a boot or a shoe on it, I presume,' said Sam, catching a crutch that was about to disappear with the rapidly receding water through one of the drain holes in the wall. 'So what does it matter?'

'Why would I wear a boot?' asked Ferin. 'If I have a magic foot I want everyone to see it!'

'I thought you wanted everyone *not* to see it,' said Sam in some exasperation. The crutch was stuck in the drain. He was very tired, and still somewhat in shock from the battle, though greatly relieved to have seen Sabriel and Touchstone through his telescope, directing the mopping up on the other side of the river. With the bridge gone, he would not be joining them soon. Perhaps in the morning, when the Paperwings would fly again . . .

'Leave that. Come and sit by me,' said Ferin, letting her leg drop back down. 'Rest a moment. I will tell you of some Athask customs.'

Sam sat down heavily next to her, and slumped, only to suddenly straighten into complete rigidity as she slid across next to him so their legs touched and, with great reserve and gravitas, she slowly put her tongue in his ear.

'What . . . what did you do that for?' he asked nervously.

'It is our custom, after battle,' said Ferin, her dark eyes bright with mischief. 'The beginning of a custom, anyway. There is more; I will show you. We have lived, and now we must be joyful.'

Sam looked sideways at her, his expression dubious at first, but then slowly his face brightened.

'Sometimes I'm a bit slow,' he said. 'I mean, apart from making things.'

'Yes, you are,' said Ferin. 'But it is of no matter. I am not.'

acknowledgements

I have many people to thank, as always. My agents: Jill Grinberg in New York; Fiona Inglis in Sydney; Antony Harwood in London. My publishers: Katherine Tegen and her team at Katherine Tegen Books/HarperCollins; Eva Mills and her people at Allen & Unwin; Emma Matthewson and crew at Hot Key. All the booksellers who have helped get the Old Kingdom books and my other works into the hands of readers; and of course to all the readers. If not for you buying books, I would almost certainly still write, but it would be a much slower matter, having to fit in with earning a living in some other way. I am very fortunate to be able to work at doing something I love. I hope I can continue!

No writing would have been done at all without the support and encouragement of my family: my wife, Anna; my sons, Thomas and Edward; my parents, Henry and Katharine; my brothers, Simon and Jonathan, and their families.

Thank you all.

HOT KEY BOOKS

Thank you for choosing a Hot Key book.

If you want to know more about our authors and what we publish, you can find us online.

You can start at our website

www.hotkeybooks.com

And you can also find us on:

We hope to see you soon!